THE ASCENSION

By

MICHAEL G. CORNELIUS

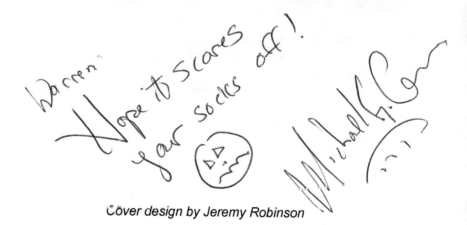

Cover design by Jeremy Robinson

BREAKNECK BOOKS
PUBLISHING COMPANY

Published by Breakneck Books (USA)
www.breakneckbooks.com

First printing, April 2007

Printed in the United States of America.

Visit Michael Cornelius on the World Wide Web at:
www.michaelgcornelius.com

for Joe

Acknowledgements

I'd like to offer up a big thanks to Jeremy Robinson and all the crew at Breakneck Books; Anastasia Brodeur; Bob Dickson and Lori Kranz for their wonderful listening skills; Joseph Garcia, for everything; and Dr. Halligan, who taught me more about the Dead Sea Scrolls than I ever thought I'd need. And lastly, thanks to Aunt Donna and Uncle Rick for my first "big break." Where would I be without you?

THE FIRST SUNDAY

TWELVE silent figures congregate softly around an unlit fire. Swathed in black robes, they sit perfectly still, flinching neither muscle nor sinew, the only sound piercing the inky darkness the slow and occasional hiss of silent, ancient breath. They huddle together, not for warmth, nor companionship, but in patient supplication, waiting, as they have for centuries, ever forbearing, ever vigilant, ever hopeful.

Tonight, their wait will not be in vain.

The gentle rustle of the tent flap announces his presence. With reverent steps the man enters into their midst. They know him. They know him of old. He left them once, long ago. Patiently they have awaited his return.

And now he has come.

In his hands he carries a blade, a curved, ancient weapon. It is heavy with the lives of untold legions, their crimson screams and eviscerated innards rusting the metal of the knife. He throws the blade into their midst. It lands with a dull sound onto the dusty earth at their feet. The figures stir. They can still smell the death that clings to its curve. Twelve empty faces turn at once and peer into the eyes of the man who has come.

It can only mean one thing.

"Kill them. Kill them all."

Monday

BISHOP Gregory Okeke was late. Very late. So kissing his little sister one last time and waving good-bye to her family, he rushed into his black Lexus sedan. It had been a good day. They had gone to a humble traveling circus, the Bishop's niece and nephew screaming on all the rides and marveling at the few animals the decrepit sideshow still maintained. He didn't see the kids very often, so the Bishop allowed himself to be persuaded into staying on, first for dinner, then for coffee, then to read the kids a bedtime story. Now, still stuffed to the gills with Loretta's infamous baby back ribs and collard greens, and flushed with the warmth of an excellent Chianti, the Bishop turned over his ignition and started up the car. It was almost midnight; he was supposed to have been back to the diocese no later than nine.

The Bishop sighed in contentment as he gently steered the car out of Loretta's neatly appointed driveway. He had needed this Memorial Day away. When he was first offered the post of bishop, everything had seemed wonderful. Pennsylvania was where he had grown up. He had spent his childhood as an altar boy at the small St. Gildas' parish in tiny Lower Saucon, right across the border from New Jersey. Okeke hated leaving his growing congregation in L.A., not to mention the far more hospitable climate, but the move would allow him to be closer to home, to his sister and old friends. Being offered such an important post at a relatively young age proved hard to resist—by accepting the position, Okeke became the youngest bishop in the entire United States. It was his chance to make a real impact, to reach out to the community, to help grow the diocese and its congregations. It was a real opportunity.

But that was before he realized the nightmare he had inherited. Bishop O'Malley, the previous leader of the diocese, had not only allowed two priests accused of harming children into his church, he had given them each congregations of their own. To let those monsters back out into the public…to allow them to have contact with children…Okeke seethed when he thought of it. How could any man do that, let alone a man of God? And even though it had all happened twenty years ago, it was only now, after the hue and cry of what had happened in Boston, and Chicago, and Phoenix, and North Carolina, and so on and so forth all around the country, that the victims had come forward here. O'Malley had retired in disgrace, and Okeke, unaware of what was going on, had inherited several damaging lawsuits and a congregation bitterly distrustful of church authority.

Eventually the lawsuits were settled, though of course the real harm—those poor boys and girls—could never be healed through financial reparations. The money was only cold comfort for what they had endured. Okeke felt that the victims had rights to every penny, and then some. The church—*his* church—had lost its way.

It was a cool night for late May, though the weather was expected to warm by tomorrow. The new moon made the night seem even colder than it was. Okeke knew Pennsylvania well, but he had only been in Chambersburg a few times, mostly on holiday visits to Loretta's house, the only family he had left. The drive back to Harrisburg would take at least an hour, and until he hit the highway the roads were dark and unfamiliar. Still, Okeke found it hard to focus on driving.

His mind reeled back to his flock's troubles. The lawsuits may have been settled, but the real task still lay before him. The congregation needing healing. It needed to regain its trust in the church. But how to do that? Okeke wasn't quite sure, but he did know one thing—he was the man to begin the healing process.

His parents had come to Pennsylvania from West Africa, settling into the small, rural community outside of Allentown after escaping a brutal civil war back home. They were one of the few black families in town, and Okeke remembered everyday the taunts and insults while waiting for the bus to school. Even in high school, even after ten years in the town, Okeke did not fit in. Growing up, he had felt torn between two worlds, the very traditional way of life his parents cultivated at home, and the slow but steady encroachment of 1970's America, where, even in a small Pennsylvania coal town, free thinking and free love seemed more than possible. It was in the church where Okeke found his two worlds met, in the good will and community fellowship he felt every time mass was celebrated, and in the mysterious sacraments of God, in the transubstantiation of the Host. Even now, even as Bishop, Okeke was still awed every time he performed the sacred act, every time he lofted up the body and blood of his Lord Jesus Christ. It was there, amongst everyday miracles and good, kindly people, that Okeke found a home. He became good friends with Father Macnamara, a doddering but witty and educated man. When he was a child, Father Macnamara would regale Okeke with tales from the Bible or lives of the saints. When he grew older, Father Macnamara encouraged Okeke to enter the priesthood himself. The good Father had died almost fifteen years ago, but Okeke was proud that he had lived long enough to see Okeke take his orders. The torch had been passed.

Okeke's mind snapped back to driving as a yellow sign entered his limited field of vision. DETOUR. An arrow pointed to the left, to a small, unpaved back road. Muttering softly to himself, Okeke turned the car left. He hoped this road would lead to the interstate.

There is so much work to do, he thought. So much damage has been done. So much destruction. But he was energetic and eternally hopeful. The wounds must be healed. The church could be made whole again. The people never lost faith in Christ; it was only Christ's keepers here on earth who had failed them. But as long as they had faith, Okeke thought, as long as they believed, he could reach them. He must reach them. It was his duty and his privilege. He must succeed.

WHAM!

A sudden crashing, thumping sound and the lurching of the car as it drove over a large, solid object snapped Okeke back to reality. Panicked, he slammed on the brakes, threw the car in park, and froze. He had hit something. He had hit something hard. It had been dark, and his mind had been wandering. Okeke could see nothing in the dim red glow his tail lights proffered, and listening intently, he only heard the hum of the car. What had he hit? He vaguely recalled seeing a shape the instant before the car hit it. The shape had been dark, and it was dark outside, terribly dark, but Okeke thought, or he remembered, or he believed, that it had been a man. That it looked like a man, like a human being. Okeke wondered if his mind was playing tricks on him in his panic. What would a man be doing on this road in total darkness on a night like this?

Okeke gripped the steering wheel hard, his knuckles turning white with exertion, as his frantic mind raced over his options. He could run, leave the scene and never look back. He didn't know what he hit—it could easily have been an animal or a tree limb knocked down by a storm. He didn't know for sure; he didn't *know* anything. So he should find out. Make sure it was an animal or a tree. He could easily check. Just take a quick look. It was the right thing to do. If it was a man, and he was hurt…he would need help. An ambulance. Okeke knew some basic first aid. Mouth to mouth. He could help.

But…but what if it had been a man. What if he had hit a man, or even a child? A boy, playing in the rain, a boy hurt like all those other boys had been hurt. It was an accident, just an accident, but everyone would know, everyone would know what he had done because it would be all over the news, a huge scandal. Okeke would be ruined, forced to resign. The Bishop paused. He had hit the object hard. Really hard. It must be dead. Right? It had gone under his wheels. He had driven over it. Whatever it is, whatever it *was*, it must be dead. He had run it over! There was nothing he could do. This man—if it were indeed a man—could not be saved, not by him, not by anyone. Why ruin two lives?

No! his mind shouted. You must help him. It was a man. I don't know that! I don't know anything at all. I will be believed. It was dark. Very dark. They have to believe me! It was an accident. I must be believed! It was an accident!

None of that will matter.

Okeke's hand hovered over his shift. Stay or go? He had to make a decision. But he couldn't decide. His hand touched the shift. Without thinking, he moved to take it out of park.

In the corner of his eye, in his rearview mirror, Okeke saw something. Motion. It was indistinct at first, but as it rose, Okeke clearly saw what it was. It was a man. And he was alive. He was alive! Okeke's joy quickly turned to puzzlement. The man was swathed in a long black robe and cowl that hid his face, his hands, everything. Okeke's eyes were glued to his mirror. He watched as the man slowly rose, and then, with a sudden motion, the man was instantly erect.

There was only darkness where his face should have been, and this darkness stared down hatefully at the Bishop. Okeke knew fear.

Something was wrong. Something was terribly wrong.

The dark shape continued staring at the bishop through the mirror, as if peering right into his eyes, right into his soul. Okeke panicked. No man could be unhurt after being hit by a moving car, not like that. Something was terribly, terribly wrong. For an anxious moment the two stayed locked as they were, the dark man staring right into Okeke, the Bishop unable to take his panicked eyes off the figure in his rearview mirror. Okeke's heart raced; frantic gasping whimpers came out of his mouth. Something was terribly, horribly, grotesquely wrong.

The dark figure took a step forward.

The figure's motion shocked Okeke into action. His eyes left the mirror and peered into the road ahead. His hand once again hovered over the shift. He needed to go, to drive. He needed to go. Now.

It took an instant for his eyes to adjust to the brightness of his headlights, but in that instant Okeke saw not one dark figure, but several, all in front of his car, linked together, forming a semi-circle around him, blocking his path. Okeke stifled a scream. The black spaces where their faces should be seemed to absorb the light from his car. Okeke panicked. Frantically, his mind fumbled for a plan, for what to do. He looked in the rearview again. He saw no figure back there. A terrible sense of dread overtook his body.

He looked at the figures in front of him. They had not moved. They were the size of men. They must be men, only men, Okeke tried to rationalize, but they seemed to him an impenetrable wall. Then, Okeke knew. He knew. Somehow, in the midst of his panic and fear, he knew.

He knew he was going to die.

The dark figure he had hit was no longer behind him. *Hail Mary, full of grace, the Lord is with thee*, Okeke prayed. It was on his side, slowly approaching the driver's door. *Blessed art thou amongst women, and blessed is the fruit of thy womb Jesus.* The dark man raised his right fist. Only now did Okeke see flesh, gray, cold flesh. *Holy Mary, Mother of God...*the fist pounded the glass once, and a small crack appeared ... *pray for us sinners...* a second time, pound ...*now* ... again, pound ... *now* ... again, pound ... *and at the hour...*once more and the glass shattered, showering Okeke with slivery bits of broken window... *at the* *hour of...* the hand grabbed Okeke's collar. Okeke gasped and screamed. Another one of the figures moved forward...his right hand held a large, sickle-shaped blade...*at the hour of...*the hand was slowly raised...*at the hour of my death...*

Amen.

TUESDAY

DETECTIVE Caldwell "Cal" Evans was nervous. He had parked his car outside the crime scene ten minutes ago, but he was still sitting in it, the steady blast of the air conditioning keeping back the anxious sweat that threatened to creep down his forehead. He tapped his fingers on the steering wheel with the steady *tat tat tat* of a man about to do something he didn't want to, or hadn't done, in a long, long time. "Fuck," he muttered to himself, turning off the car's ignition for the third time.

Cal wasn't used to being nervous, and he didn't like how it felt.

"Goddamnit!" he said, slamming his hands on the wheels. "Goddamn you Dan, you asshole!" Cal took a deep breath—one, then two, then three—and tried to settle himself. *Fuck this,* he thought. With a sudden lurch he yanked open the car door, stepped out, and squinted into the bright morning sunlight. He put sunglasses on over his eyes and dug around in his pocket for some identification. With a grunt, he strode towards the all-too-familiar yellow "Do Not Cross" police tape.

He was still nervous. But he was also mightily pissed.

Cal Evans was a tall man, well over six feet. He was a former football jock who found as he crept closer and closer to forty and further and further from thirty that his athletic frame was slowly starting to sag, thanks in no small part to a steady diet of cheeseburgers, bacon, ketchup and mustard, with just the tiniest hint of lettuce to appease his body's need for vitamins and minerals. Still, he carried his weight well, and with a thick shock of blond hair—most of it still there—and icy blue eyes, he cut a handsome figure. He was also, however, a formidable-looking man when he needed to be, and right now, he needed it in spades.

The officer working the crime scene perimeter recognized Cal before he even flashed his ID. She waved him on through with a small gulp and an even smaller smile. He'd said only two words to her: "Where's Dan?" She had pointed with a casual nod of her head and Cal had strolled off angrily in the same direction. The smile grew bigger. Cal's look could only mean one thing.

"Dan! Dan!" Sheriff Dan Moore turned to face the voice that called him. He'd been expecting this. "What the fuck, Dan? What the fuck?"

Dan held up his hands in front of Cal. "Calm down, Cal," he said patiently. "Let me explain."

"Explain? What's there to explain? We had a deal. We had—an arrangement. Two months was all I asked. Two months was what I needed. I went to you Dan, as a co-worker—hell, man, as a friend. Two months. And it's been—" Cal consulted his watch to make his point more effective—"not even five weeks and you call me in on some shit like this?"

Dan calmly stared Cal in the eye. "You done?"

"No! No, I'm not done! I'm not even supposed to be here, Dan. Fuck, you know that!"

"I do, Cal, I really do."

"Then why Dan? Why call me in on this?"

Dan took his opportunity. He pointed a stern finger at Cal. "Because I need you, Detective Evans. This thing here is bigger than both of us."

Cal shook his head and lowered his voice. "That's easy for you to say, Dan. Do you know I had to sign out to get here? I literally had to check myself out. It was fucking humiliating, Dan."

"Yeah, I know, Cal, I know, but I need my best man on this, really, I do."

"Dan, I'm not your best man anymore. I'm no good to you at all like this. Just let me go back. Or go home."

"I wish I could buddy, I really do, but I can't, I need you here."

"Yeah, well, fuck you!" Cal suddenly shouted. All eyes at the crime scene turned to face Cal. They'd seen him like this before. "You know something, Dan, I don't need this fucking job, I don't need this fucking town, I don't need any of it, and most of all I don't need some pencil-dicked, small town *politician* running my ass into the ground simply because it's a fucking election year! I'll just quit this fucking job and screw you all! How do you like that?"

"Fine!" Dan bellowed back. Cal was surprised. Dan almost never yelled—it was one of the things that made him a good sheriff. "You can quit, for all I fucking care. You've quit on everything else in your life, and Lord knows I don't need all the fucking headaches you cause me. Hell, after the shit you pulled I should've fired you myself. But not today, you hear me? You are *not* quitting today. Tomorrow, next Wednesday, when you solve this case, yes, quit. Do us all a favor and quit. But right now I need you, goddamnit. I need my best man on this case, you hear me? And like it or not, you are it."

Cal took a deep breath. Dan saw that getting angry had been the right approach. "I'm sorry, Dan," Cal said quietly. "It's just—it's been so hard, without—"

Dan clapped a meaty hand on Cal's shoulder. "I know, I know. And when this is over you can go back—take a vacation—quit if you really like. But this is bigger than both of us."

"You got Ramirez…give it to Ramirez."

"Ramirez is a rookie, barely been a detective for six months. He's never done a homicide before. He's in way over his head. It's been all I can do to keep him from contaminating the crime scene. You should know how lousy he is," Dan added with the hint of a smile. "You trained him."

"Nice," Cal said, feeling a bit less nervous and a whole lot less pissed off.

"Look, Cal, I know this isn't easy for you, but this is big, you hear me? Bigger than both our problems. I need you on this. Other-wise…otherwise I'll have to call in the Feds." Dan was lying, but he knew how much this would piss Cal off. "If you can't handle it, buddy, if you honest to goodness can't handle it, let me know, and I'll put the call into FBI headquarters myself."

Talking about the Feds always stirred Cal. "Dan, you know I worked with those assholes for ten years when I pounded a beat in D.C."

"I know."

"We don't need them here in Chambersburg, Dan."

"We don't?"

"No," Cal said with more confidence than he felt. "You got me."

"Good." Dan smiled, clapped Cal on the shoulder again. "Get in there and show the rookie how it's done." He started to walk off.

"Dan?" Cal called. Dan stopped. "Why's this one so special anyway?"

"You don't know?" Cal shook his head. Dan looked incredulous. "That's the Bishop in that car, Cal."

"Bishop of who?"

"Jesus Christ," Dan said. "Sobering up hasn't smartened you up, that's for sure. The Bishop of fucking Harrisburg, Pennsylvania. Big time holy man. This one's gonna bring national coverage. All the networks have already called in. The media is gonna be all over us. The fucking Vatican themselves are gonna be all over us." Dan paused. "So now you understand why I need you on this?"

"Yeah," Cal said, feeling more nervous than ever. "I won't let you down," he added, not believing it.

Dan reached out to shake his hand. "It's good to have you back, Cal."

"SO what's the story?" Cal said to the medical examiner. She had just finished examining the body for the second time, being as thorough as possible. "Got a preliminary report for me?" Cal thought it best to talk to her before he surveyed the scene. *Take it easy*, he said to himself.

The ME stood erect to give Cal her report. "Death was likely caused by a large stab wound to the heart. Shredded most of the muscle there and the aorta as well."

"Likely," Cal said, picking up on her language. "What's so fucking 'likely' about a shredded heart?"

The ME shrugged. "Three of the wounds could have been the fatal blow. One to the neck, the one to the heart, and one to the main artery in the thigh. I'll know more when they bring him to the lab. Whoever did this really did a number on him."

"What kind of number?" Cal asked. "How many wounds are we talking about here?"

"Twelve, that I can find," she said. "There may be more. He's a real mess. Strong bastard, whoever it was who did this."

"Twelve wounds?" Cal swallowed in surprise. "Shit. Someone was really pissed off. What about the weapon?"

"Big blade. Curved. Like a sickle, only smaller. Never seen anything like it before. Really shredded him up. Shouldn't be hard to match if you can find it."

"I take it's not lying next to him." The ME shrugged and shook her head. "Time of death?"

"I'd put it between eleven and one, but I can't say that for sure until I get him to the morgue."

Cal nodded. "Thanks."

"No sweat. I'll get you my full report as soon as I got it. You want to survey the scene before I cart him off?"

"Is it bad?"

The ME nodded, almost nonchalantly. Nothing bothered her. "A few of the newer guys lost their breakfast. Over there," she said, pointing, "just so you don't step in it."

Cal felt his mouth go dry. First day back on the job after leaving the clinic three weeks early and now this. "Thanks," he said. "Just gimme a minute, okay?"

"No problem." The ME saw the sheriff waving her over and started towards him. "Cal?" she said, turning around to look him in the eye. "It's good to have you back."

"Thanks," Cal mumbled. He heard the sound of crunching grass as the ME walked off behind him.

Cal took a minute to survey the scene. The car, a shiny black sedan, was parked against a tree, half-obscured by some thick green bushes. He checked the ground. No skid marks, no tracks at all. It had been dry for days, so no footprints, no soft ground, nothing to work from. He looked around some more. The ME was talking to Dan. A few cops were busy keeping the media out of the way and off to one side. Only a few of the local reporters had made it, but Cal knew the Harrisburg television crews wouldn't be far off. A group of tech guys, some local, some from the state police, dusted the car for prints, while a few others surveyed the ground around it for anything out of the ordinary. From his angle, Cal couldn't see into the car, but he could catch a glimpse of the canvas being used to cover up the victim. And there, inspecting the opposite side of the car, was Ramirez.

Cal called one of the tech guys over, a short, bald-headed man named Dixon. "What have you got?" he asked. Cal could feel butterflies pounding in his stomach. He was glad he'd skipped breakfast that morning. This way there was nothing to puke up. Still, he knew the best way to calm down was to stick to the routine. He'd get back into the swing of things soon. He hoped.

The technician paused for a moment and scratched his bald head. "Preliminarily speaking, we've got nothing. No footmarks. A few interesting soil samples maybe. They don't look right for this area. A few blood spatters here—" he pointed only a few feet away from where the two men stood talking "—indicates that the Bishop was probably attacked here, in his car, and then the perp moved him over there to hide him. It's a pretty effective cover, at least at night. Some morning commuters saw the car. One of them got curious and checked it out. She's the one who called it in."

"That's just what you need to see first thing on a Tuesday morning. Right?" Cal weakly joked. Dixon only stared at Cal, ignoring his lame attempt at humor. Cal sighed. "How long before you guys are done?"

Dixon shrugged. "Less than an hour. We're doing a larger perimeter search now, but I doubt we'll find something."

"Keep me posted." With a nod the smaller man walked off.

Cal took two steps towards the car and froze. It was shit like this that got him drinking so much in the first place. *Not just this shit…*he thought as he ordered his feet to move towards the car. *It's okay. You've seen all this before. Just keep walking.*

Cal finally halted about five feet from the driver's side door. He closed his eyes and bent down. He could already smell the rusty, acrid scent of spilled blood. Cal forced his eyes open. He could see the man-shaped form under the canvas. He reached into his pocket and pulled out a glove. He had seen this type of thing before. *It'll be okay. Just pull back the canvas. It's nothing you haven't seen before.*

Cal was wrong.

Holes. Cal's first impression as he saw the body was holes—gaping, mawing holes that covered the chest, belly, and neck. The knife had been twisted in the victim, turned this way and that in a violent and gruesome manner. Strong bastard indeed. A thin sheet of blood covered everything—the victim, the entire front seat, the windshield and steering wheel. Cal put one hand to his mouth. He could feel the bile rising in him. He fought it. *Down, down.* He put the canvas back.

Stepping away from the car, he inhaled deeply, one breath, two, great gasps of the warm morning air. "Jesus Christ," he mumbled. "Show some respect," a voice said behind him. Ramirez.

Cal turned and saw Ramirez facing him. He glared at Cal, clearly unhappy that his senior detective had been called onto the scene. "He was a man of the cloth, after all. One should show respect by not taking the Lord's name in vain in front of him."

"Save it for Sunday school, Ramirez," Cal said. He could feel his disgust at seeing the body being replaced by aggravation. And some fun—needling Ramirez was always good sport. "This is not a catechism."

"No; no, this is a tragedy," Ramirez said gravely.

"All death is a tragedy, Ramirez; this one is no different than the rest." Ramirez opened his mouth to protest, but Cal raised his hand for silence. "Tell me what you see."

This was their standard method of teaching. Cal would ask Ramirez for his opinion of the scene, and then tell him why he was wrong. Ramirez hated it. Cal did not.

Ramirez sighed. "No obvious sign indicating the Bishop was forced off the road. He must have known his attackers. Except…"

"Except what?"

"Here." Ramirez walked around to the front of the car. Cal followed. He saw a large dent in the front of the hood. "It seems like the Bishop hit something," Ramirez added.

Cal snorted. "That's obvious. What did the tech say?"

"No paint marks or any sign that he hit another car. No, they figure a large animal of some kind, like a deer, except there's no blood, no hairs, and no body. And the dent seems wrong for a deer. More likely the animal was bipedal—that's walking on two legs."

"I know what it means—I went to college, same as you."

"Sorry. Anyway, could have been a bear. Could be he didn't hurt the animal that badly. He could have hit it and it wandered off."

"Hardly wounded, and a dent that size? I doubt it." Cal also doubted that a bear had made that dent.

Ramirez shrugged. "Could be some object put in the middle of the road to slow the Bishop down, or stop him altogether. No evidence supporting that, though it could be the case."

"That's a lot of 'could be's', even for you, Ramirez."

Ramirez kept talking. "Of course, we don't know when or where the dent was made. *Could be* it happened earlier," he said, emphasizing the "could be" with a particular sneer. "Could have been months ago for all we know."

Cal considered this idea. "Could be, though I somehow doubt the diocese of Harrisburg wants their top man driving around in a beat-up Lexus."

Ramirez shrugged. "They do take a vow of poverty, after all."

Cal changed the subject. "How'd the car get here?"

Ramirez surveyed the ground. "No skid marks—it wasn't an accident that he ended up there. He either drove it in there himself, or..." He left that sentence unfinished, since he couldn't think of what else may have happened. He continued. "Of course, the million dollar question is why? What was the Bishop doing here, on this road, in the first place?"

Cal turned to Ramirez. "Start at the very beginning, Detective. The first question really is, why was the Bishop in Chambersburg at all?"

Ramirez checked his notebook. "Visiting his sister. One Loretta Fayne. She and her husband have a house over in that new development—Canterbury Trails. Up by the college. Went there to spend Memorial Day with them and their kids. The diocese confirmed all this. According to them, he was supposed to be back by nine."

"Nine?" Cal furrowed his brow. "The ME says he died no sooner than eleven. What time did he leave the sister's?"

Ramirez shook his head. "We're trying to track her down now."

Cal sighed. "Wait a minute—did you say Canterbury Trails? You leave there, take a right, connect up to route 997 and you got a straight shot to the interstate. Why'd he take this road?"

Ramirez shrugged. "Pretty desolate spot. No businesses, no bars letting their customers out at two. Closest house is a farm house about two miles that way—" Ramirez pointed east "—and that's so far off the road you can't really see it anyway. Certainly they didn't see anything interesting. We already checked."

Cal surveyed the scene again. "So our Bishop got off the main drive, took this lonely stretch of road, and ended up getting twelve stab wounds for his trouble. The question is why? Did you see the body?" he added, suddenly rounding on Ramirez.

Ramirez looked a little green under the gills at the thought of the body. "Yeah," he said.

"What'd you think?"

Ramirez considered carefully. "Some religious wacko? Set a trap for the Bishop? Upset about—who knows? The molestation crap?"

"Well, this is one priest who won't be bothering any little kids any time soon."

"Jesus, Cal," Ramirez said in disgust.

"But you're wrong about one thing," Cal added. "This wasn't some wacko hacking away at the good Bishop for some Catholic revenge. Look at the body, Ramirez. This was personal."

"Meaning?"

"Meaning the Bishop knew his attacker. He came here to meet someone. Probably for sex—a girlfriend, a boyfriend. Drug dealer? That many knife wounds means only one thing—someone was really pissed off at the Bishop. And you don't get that mad at someone you don't know."

Ramirez eyed Cal. The tension that had been simmering between them seemed ready to explode. "Why'd you come back?" he suddenly said. "We don't need you."

"Your boss seems to feel differently," Cal said evenly.

"Yeah, well, after the crap you pulled, he shouldn't even be your boss anymore."

Cal fought the urge to sock Ramirez right in the mouth. "That's over now, Ramirez."

"Is it?" Ramirez got his face right into Cal's. Their eyes locked. "It's because of you that guy got off. Got off and got to go home to his lovely wife, whom he then proceeded to pound into a fucking coma. She lost her spleen, she lost her fucking *micha*, man. They had to cut it out of her. Now she can't even have any kids, ever. It was lucky she woke up at all. And why did he get away? Cause you didn't show up for a court date."

"Shut up, Ramirez," Cal muttered. He wanted to cover his ears, to block out Ramirez's words, but it didn't matter; he'd said the same thing to himself a hundred times already.

"And why didn't you show up? I'll tell you why. You were wasted. You missed a ten A.M. court date because you were too busy getting your fix."

Cal could feel himself getting angrier and angrier. "That's in the past, Ramirez. I went to rehab. I'm clean now."

"Once a drunk, always a drunk, that's what I say." Cal grabbed Ramirez by the collar and cocked his fist back. Ramirez hesitated for a second, than gave him a small grin. "Do it," he said. "Don't worry, we can blame it on the booze."

Cal seethed, but he slowly let go of Ramirez's lapels. The other cop straightened them out with a quick snap. "We're partners now," Cal said. "Whether you like it or not. I know I don't. But I'm still your superior officer. Remember that."

"Yes, 'sir'," Ramirez said sarcastically. "But just remember, 'partner,' I've got my eye on you."

That's it, Cal thought. None of this was worth it. One quick shot to the gut and another quick uppercut would teach Ramirez a little respect. But before Cal could act, a shout from one of the techs drew both their attentions.

"Detectives!" The tech was shouting and waving at them about a hundred yards down the road. "Come here!"

Cal and Ramirez hotfooted it down the road. As they approached they could see something in the grass. It was a series of lines and figures, triangles, circles, and slashes. It might have been a message, written in some language that Cal did not recognize. But he did recognize what the message was written in.

It was written in the Bishop's blood.

"Jesus," Ramirez said. Cal was tempted to make a smart remark, but he felt so unnerved by the sight he let it pass. Ramirez turned to Cal. "Now what?"

Cal turned away from the blood writing. "It's personal, remember? We talk to the people who knew him."

LORETTA Fayne was five years younger than her brother. Graceful and tall, her high-cheeked ebony features belied only the smallest hint of her foreign birth. Her beautiful dark eyes, red from crying, would not meet the detectives' gaze as she asked them to sit.

"Ma'am, first of all, we'd like to say how sorry we are for your loss," Ramirez began. Cal had to hand it to the little putz. He did have a knack for talking to the victim's families. "We know this is a trying time for you, but please understand, we have to ask you some questions."

Mrs. Fayne nodded softly. She was a science teacher, and had the graceful bearing of a natural educator. "I do not know what I can tell you," she said quietly, "but I will do anything I can to help."

"Your brother was visiting you yesterday, correct?" She nodded. "What time did he leave?"

"Eleven. I remember the news had just started."

"The diocese said he planned to be back there by nine."

Mrs. Fayne smiled faintly. "He was late getting off, Detective. We spent the whole day together. The kids had Memorial Day off from school. My brother was very good at keeping a schedule, but he decided just this once to stay late. He didn't think it would cause any harm." At the thought of this she looked ready to cry. "Who would do something like this?" she asked piteously.

Ramirez coughed. "That's what we're trying to find out, ma'am. How was your brother yesterday? Was he nervous, anxious about something? Did he act unusually at all?"

Mrs. Fayne shook her head vigorously. "No, no, he was quite himself, Detective. He had a wonderful time playing with the children. We all stayed up late because of it. It was a lovely day."

"He didn't mention any plans about meeting someone, either here or in Harrisburg?"

"Oh, no. He didn't know anyone else here, not really. And who would he meet in Harrisburg at such a late hour?"

"Mrs. Fayne, we found some damage to his car. Was it damaged when he left here?"

"Oh, no, Detective, it was fine."

"Are you sure? The damage was on the front…a dent in the hood…"

"No, no, I'm sure it was okay."

The time had come to ask the more difficult questions, but Ramirez was hesitating. Cal could sense his reticence. He became ready to take over the interrogation. "Mrs. Fayne," Ramirez continued carefully. "You must understand, at a time like this, with such a brutal crime, we look first to the associates of the deceased, to the people he knew. You understand?" Mrs. Fayne nodded. "Then, to your knowledge, did your brother have unsavory associations that might give us a place to begin our search for suspects?"

Mrs. Fayne looked confused. "I—I don't understand."

"Did your brother have a girlfriend, a boyfriend?" Cal blurted out.

"Detective!" Mrs. Fayne said shocked, turning her full gaze onto Cal for the first time.

"Did he have anything to do with this child abuse stuff we've been hearing about? Of course, it could be something different. Drug problems…gambling debts?"

"Detective!" Mrs. Fayne said again, with a little more force. "I resent your implication. My brother was a respectable man. He was kind, and decent, and…he was a fine man and a fine member of the cloth. How dare you accuse him of…of…" she faltered, remembering Cal's line of questioning.

"Mrs. Fayne, I understand this is difficult for you. But if you hide something from us it will only help those who killed your brother. We need to know the truth."

Mrs. Fayne stood firmly and walked to her door. She opened it resolutely and pointed to her sidewalk. "My brother was a good man," she said with fire in her voice. "That *is* the truth, whether you choose to believe me or not. Are we done here?"

"Mrs. Fayne—"

"Are we done here?" It was not meant as a question.

Once the door had closed behind them, Ramirez rounded on Cal. "It's nice to see that sobering up hasn't made you any less of an asshole," he said.

"Fuck you, Ramirez," Cal replied as they walked towards the car. "You'll never be a good detective if you can't ask the tough questions."

Ramirez paused before the passenger side door. "And did you get any useful answers?" he asked before getting in the car.

THE two spent the day canvassing the neighborhoods the Bishop may have passed en route to getting killed. No one had seen a thing. Several phone leads about suspicious cars lead nowhere. Detectives in Harrisburg questioned all of the Bishop's colleagues. Everyone said the same thing about him: the man was a prince.

"We must be missing something," Ramirez said. The two were back at the station house. It was getting late.

"And what's that, exactly?" Cal replied.

"I don't know," Ramirez said, more than a little irritated. "We've come up with nothing, so we must be missing something."

Cal snorted. "You sound like a bad cop movie, Ramirez. We've come up with nothing because so far there's been nothing to find."

"So what are you saying? That we're not going to solve this one?"

"Boy, you give up easy, don't you? I'm not saying that at all. You just expect, though, that this is like those mysteries you read about in books, that the solution has already been neatly laid out and we just have to arrange all the clues in the right order. Well, this isn't a detective book and we're not the Hardy boys. This is real life. And in real life, cop work takes time. It takes patience. We're still waiting for the lab results. We've still got witnesses to talk to."

"Like who?"

"Like the Bishop's associates. The people up in Harrisburg. The sister hardly ever saw him. She isn't going to know what he's really up to."

"You still think that's the angle it could be? Some dark secret in the Bishop's life?"

Cal shrugged. "That's what it usually is."

Ramirez shook his head. "I don't think so. Besides, the Harrisburg PD already interviewed those suspects. They all said the same thing."

"Rule number one of good cop work, Ramirez. Never let someone else do your job. Tomorrow morning I'm headed up to Harrisburg myself to interview those suspects."

"And what am I supposed to do?"

"You're coming with me, bright boy. Take some notes. You might even learn something."

"And if that's a bust?"

"If that's a bust, then we'll deal with it. Rome wasn't built in a day."

Ramirez looked uneasy. "I think you're wrong. I think there's more to this than meets the eye."

Cal shrugged. "Maybe there is. Maybe the lab techs will come up with something good. Should have a report by tomorrow afternoon."

"What about this?" Ramirez asked. He passed over to Cal a black and white snapshot of the strange markings they found at the scene of the crime. Cal shivered when he saw them, remembering the red stain that had seeped into the ground. He inhaled sharply.

"That," he said, "is a problem. Could be something; could be nothing."

"It's not nothing, Cal."

Silently, Cal agreed. Still, he thought, his version of events seemed most likely. "Look, Ramirez, I thought we agreed on this. For whatever reason, the Bishop pulls off the side of the road to meet up with someone. The meeting goes bad. Our perp pulls out the knife and does a number on the good Bishop. End of story."

"But the writing? The blood?"

Cal looked at the strange marks again. "Go home," he said.

"What?"

"Go home. Go home, Ramirez, go home to your family. Get some sleep. See you first thing in the morning."

"Cal—"

"Go." Ramirez finally nodded. He stood up and slowly walked out of the station house, a little angry, and more than a little worried.

So was Cal.

BROTHER Rich Brantridge longingly waved good-bye to the last of his prayer group as they headed off to their cars. With a soft smile he locked the meeting hall doors behind him. It had been a good prayer meeting. There had been a large turnout. That was no surprise, considering the horror of that morning. Tragedy always brought faith to people. Why, after the terrorist attacks on New York, the hall had been filled for months. At moments like this, everyone turned to God.

The genial man ambled back towards the center of the hall, picking up a stray Bible on his way. It had been a good group. Prayer meetings always left Brother Brantridge feeling warm, feeling hopeful. Even in a time of crisis. Everyone came together, as a community, to seek counsel, to speak to the Lord. A society of friends, yes, the name did say it all. There was always such an outpouring of heart-filled expression, love for their fellow man…well, except, of course, for Mrs. Oglander. Mrs. Oglander and her incessant need for prayers. Mrs. Oglander was too busy asking everyone to pray for her to take out time to pray for somebody else. Pray for her glaucoma. Pray that her grand-niece passes her driver's exam. Pray that Mrs. Oglander passes gas! Brother Brantridge chuckled at that last thought. She was an old biddy, always the first to arrive and the last to go, though she never helped to set up or put any thing away. A harmless old woman, but always demanding to be the center of attention.

It was a dark night, and the stillness of the hall grew as Brother Brantridge shut off the lights. The only light that streamed in was the dim glow off a small corner streetlamp. The pastor winced as he leaned down to pick up one last Bible. His back was sore again. Course he probably needed to lose some weight to help with that, but that was difficult to do. Not with Mrs. Nielson's shoo-fly pie and Mrs. Murray's walnut fudge brownies. Next week, he would try to stick to one dessert.

A sharp noise from outside suddenly caught the pastor's attention. It sounded like—like a gasp, a startled sound. Brother Brantridge paused. He heard only silence. He began to walk towards the entrance to his small living quarters on one side of the hall.

Bam bam bam

The sudden and urgent pounding on the door sent a shock through the Quaker leader's system. He held his breath for a minute, and then smiled. Likely someone forgot something. It was just—the suddenness, the violence of the knock that startled him.

He shuffled back to the door. *Bam! Bam! Bam!* "Coming!" he called. "Who is it?" There was no response. Turning the key slowly, Brother Brantridge cautiously peered out the door. "Why, Mrs. Oglander!" he said, opening the door wider. "Did you forget something?"

Mrs. Oglander made no movement, or no sound, save for a small, raspy gasp. "Mrs. Oglander…are you alright?" With a sudden pitch the woman fell forward into the prayer leader's arms. She was a large woman, and Brother Brantridge could barely hold her. He saw, on her neck, two deep puncture wounds. Blood trickled swiftly from them, staining her flower-covered blouse. "What in God's name?" It was only then that he noticed them.

Men—a group, three, four…maybe eight or more. They were dressed all in black, in deep robes that hid their faces, their arms and flesh…everything except their right hand. Brother Brantridge could see the cold gray flesh of their right hands, mainly because he could also see their knives—sharp, curved blades pointed right at him.

Brother Brantridge dropped Mrs. Oglander. She slumped dead to the floor. He took a step back, two, but suddenly they were upon him, swarming over him as if locusts. "Oh, God," he said, a whisper. Two of them grabbed him, a wrist in each right hand. They pinned him to the ground. He struggled as furiously as he could. Their grip was cold iron, but he managed to wrest one hand free. He grabbed for his attacker, clutching onto the sleeve of the left arm of his assailant. Only…only it wasn't an arm he felt in there. Not a human arm. It was strong, and coiled, and undulating, not like an arm, not a human arm anyway…

Before the prayer leader could finish his thought they were all upon him, pinning him down while one of them plunged his knife into the pastor's chest, again and again, the grinding sound of bone and metal echoing throughout the prayer hall. With a loud and final gasp Brother Brantridge died when they plunged the knife directly into his heart, his eyes wide open, his face desperately turning towards a picture of his Lord and savior.

He died as he turned towards God.

WEDNESDAY

"THAT was a royal waste of time," Ramirez complained as they headed back towards the car. "We talked to seven witnesses, and they all said the same thing. The man was a fucking saint, Cal, a fucking saint."

It was a little after noon. The sun burned straight up in the sky. Cal slipped on a pair of shades before sliding behind the wheel of the car. He checked himself out in the rearview mirror. The shades gave his round face more angles. Besides, they looked cool. Very Hollywood.

"Are you even listening to me?" Ramirez was saying. "This pretty much blows your theory out of the water, Cal."

"Why do you say that?"

"No secrets, no skeletons in the closet. We tossed his place and found nothing—do drugs, no pornos, nothing."

Cal snorted. "A guy like that doesn't get to his position in life by openly advertising his problems. And we only gave the place a quick search. He's smart. He's going to hide his dirty little secret well. But don't worry, rookie. We'll find it."

"I'm not a rookie. I've been a cop for nine years. And Cal, I'm serious—I think we're barking up the wrong tree here."

"It's motive, Ramirez. It's all about the motive. If we find that, we find our killer. Hey, look!" Cal interrupted. Ramirez whirled in his seat. "What?" he asked excitedly. He didn't see anything. "There!" Cal pointed. "Roman's Burgers! I'd forgotten about this place!" Cal made a quick right turn and pulled in the parking lot of the burger joint.

"Lunch?" Ramirez asked. "Shouldn't we be heading back?"

"Why?" Cal said, stepping out of the car and slamming the door with a flourish. "We need to eat, don't we? Keep our strength up. Besides, the lab results won't be in until late this afternoon. If anything else came up, you've got your cell on, right?"

"Yeah, let me just check—shit!"

"What?"

"Battery's dead. I must have forgot to plug it in last night."

Cal shrugged as he opened to restaurant door. The overpowering smell of burning beef and sizzling bacon assaulted his olfactory sense. He loved it. "Bunnie!" he shouted to a round, fortyish woman behind the corner. "Caldwell Evans!" she shouted back. "If it isn't my handsome policeman boyfriend!"

"I thought I was your boyfriend, Bunnie!" some wag called out from another table.

"You're my mechanic boyfriend, Bill. You're good for when my car breaks down!" she guffawed. "A girl needs a mechanic boyfriend to fix her broken car, a policeman boyfriend to fix her tickets when she drives too fast in her car, and a doctor boyfriend—to buy her the car in the first place." It was a joke they had all heard before, but the joint still laughed before everyone turned their attention back to their lunches. Bunnie walked over to Cal. "Gimme some sugar," she said, planting two wet sloppy kisses on each of his cheeks. "Goddamn you, where you been?"

"Here, there, and everywhere" Cal said evenly, grinning. "Hey Bunnie, how about two of the usual for me and my junior partner here."

Bunnie smiled. "Two of Bunnie's special bacon cheese with the works, coming right up!" she said, bustling back behind the counter.

Ramirez made a face. "I'm trying to cut back," he said.

"Relax, Ramirez, you can work it off at home later, cleaning out the gutters or changing diapers."

"Cal, did you hear what I said about the phone?"

"Ramirez, for Christ's sake, will you fucking take it down a notch? Yes, I heard, the phone's dead. So what? Anything that's that important can wait. Geez. If you keep it up at this pace, you're gonna have an ulcer before you're thirty-five."

Bunnie brought over two Cokes and straws. "So what brings you two handsome men into my little shop?" she said.

Cal looked jokingly severe. "Official police business, Bunnie," he replied mockingly. "Very hush-hush."

"Ooooh, is it about that Bishop being murdered down in your neck of the woods? I saw that on TV. Sounded awful." If Bunnie had said "sounded amazing," her tone of voice would have made more sense. "Of course, I'm a Baptist, so what do I care?" she added, slapping Ramirez's shoulder with a laugh. Ramirez grimaced. "Oh, I'm just teasing, sugar. Who's your partner, Cal? He's so handsome, but he needs to smile more."

"That's just what I was telling him, Bunnie. Maybe you should leave him your number. I bet you could put a smile on his face."

Bunnie squealed in delight. "Cal Evans, you are a charmer! Yes, you always have been!" With a chuckle she turned away from the table and moved on to other customers.

Ramirez was eyeing Cal critically. "If I didn't know better, Cal, I'd say you are enjoying this."

"Bunnie's a nice lady; she just likes to flirt."

"Not just Bunnie. This whole thing. Back on the beat, solving a big case...this Bishop being murdered is the best thing that's happened to you in a long while."

"Don't be ridiculous, Ramirez. I'm just doing my job like everyone else," Cal said. But it was a lie, and they both knew it. Truth be told, Cal *was* having fun. The adrenaline of working on a big case, chasing leads, interviewing suspects...it had been a long time since Cal had felt this good. He couldn't remember the last time he felt this way. *Before the divorce for sure*, he thought to himself. *Before moving to that little town, before rehab...before Dani...*Cal pushed that unpleasant thought out of his head. This was a good moment, sober and clear. Enjoy it.

Their burgers arrived, piled high with American cheese, bacon, relish, onions, lettuce, hot peppers, tomatoes, ketchup, mustard, mayo, and "...olives?" Ramirez asked dubiously.

Cal picked up his precarious sandwich and took a big bite. "Try it," he said, his mouth full. "Eat up. Enjoy it while it lasts."

THEY got back to Chambersburg a little after 2:00. When they walked into the station, they sensed a change. The place was abuzz with activity. Phones rang off the hook; every uniform was busy talking to someone, taking calls, examining paperwork. The sheriff was hunched over a desk, furiously writing something. Next to him stood a tall, statuesque woman. She caught Cal's eye right away. About thirty, thirty-two. Curly red hair—dyed, but expertly done. Well-built. Proportional and curvy in all the right places. A fancy writer might have considered her patrician or Rubenesque; Cal just thought she had tits till next Tuesday and an ass you could serve Thanksgiving dinner off of. He was definitely hooked.

The redhead noticed them first, and tapped the sheriff on his shoulder. He whirled around, took one look at Cal and Ramirez, and exploded. "Where the fuck have you two been?" he yelled, storming over to them. "I've been fucking calling you all morning. Why didn't you goddamn pick up the phone?"

Cal shrugged. "No juice," he replied. "Dan, what's going on?"

The red-headed woman spoke up. "There's been another murder," she said icily.

"What?" Cal quizzed. "What—I mean…"

"Another preacher was killed last night," Dan explained. "Quaker prayer group leader, right in the meeting hall after the group had met. Cleaning woman found him this morning. Call came in over an hour ago. Same MO, and from what the ME just told us, same murder weapon."

"But, I don't understand, I mean…" Cal sputtered and stopped. It didn't make sense! None of it made sense.

"Cal, we've got some fucking psycho preacher-hater on the loose," Dan said. "And you're off God-knows-where doing God-knows-what!"

"Dan, I told you, we went to Harrisburg, to canvas the people who knew the Bishop…you saw it, Dan, the murder scene, the motive, a personal crime!"

"You were wrong, Cal," Dan said. "And now I've got two dead preachers on my hands. Shit, this whole thing has become a real clusterfuck," Dan said, running his hands through his rapidly-thinning hair.

Cal sank heavily into the desk chair beside him. His mind was reeling. "But, Dan, it can't be some stranger killing. It can't. Why would the Bishop have gone where he did if it wasn't to meet up with someone he knew?"

The sheriff nodded at the woman. "Tell him," he said.

The redheaded woman cleared her throat. "A witness I spoke with who was westbound on 997 at the approximate time of death remembered seeing the back end of a highway sign. However, the state department of transportation has no documentation of any highway sign in that vicinity. We can conclude, then, that it was that sign that directed the Bishop off the main road and onto the side one."

"A detour sign, Cal," Dan said gravely. "A fucking detour sign!"

Cal's head was spinning like a top. He thought he was going to faint. "What witness...who?" he stammered. He looked up at the redhead. "Who are you?"

"Agent Rabinowitz, Bureau of Alcohol, Tobacco, and Firearms."

"ATF! Dan, Dan...you called in the feds? You promised, Dan!"

"It wasn't me, Cal."

Agent Rabinowitz cleared her throat. "Actually, the governor called me in this morning. I came as a favor to him. I'm a bureau specialist in theological crime and cult activity."

"She's been brought down in a strictly advisory capacity. She only got here hour ago," Dan said. He crouched down to look Cal in the eye. "Cal, are you still with me here? I need you. We need you. Are you okay?"

Cal nodded. He only half-heard. There was another, more persistent voice in his head: *I need a drink.*

Ramirez spoke up. "Agent Rabinowitz, I'm Detective Ramirez. Hidalgo Ramirez," he said with a flush. They shook hands. "This is my partner, Cal Evans. Obviously this news about a new death has thrown us for a loop. But we're glad to have you on board."

"Thanks, Detective," Rabinowitz replied.

"Have you been to the scene yet?" Ramirez asked.

"We were just on our way," said the sheriff. "Jump in your car and meet us there. It's the little church on Miller Ave. You know it? Good."

"Cal?" Ramirez said after the sheriff and Agent Rabinowitz had left. "Cal, we gotta go. Cal? Are you okay?"

"Fine," Cal said flatly. He handed Ramirez the keys. "Here. You drive."

THE small interior of the church's prayer room was coated in blood. Agent Rabinowitz surveyed the room coolly. "Was the other scene this bloody?" she asked.

"Yeah," the sheriff answered, distracted. He signaled to Dixon, who was the closest tech to him. "Report," Dan said.

Dixon shook his head. "Almost identical to the last scene. Nothing much to go on, preliminarily speaking. Same weird message on the wall, though."

Agent Rabinowitz was staring at the message as he spoke. "You found one of these at the last scene?" she asked. The sheriff nodded. "That information wasn't in the newspaper."

"We held it back," Sheriff Moore said. "In case anyone decided to come forward and claim responsibility when they really didn't do it."

Rabinowitz nodded. It was common police procedure. "Have you deciphered it yet?"

The sheriff shook his head. "We've sent pictures of it to some code guys at the FBI, but so far, no word."

"I don't think it's a code," she said, crouching down to get a good look at the bloody scrawls on the wall. "It's a message. Whoever did this wants us to read it. I just think it's in some foreign language."

"It's no foreign language I've ever seen," the sheriff said.

Rabinowitz squinted as she stared at the script. "Somehow, it looks familiar to me."

"Do you think...could it be Arabic? Could this all be some weird terrorist plot?"

Rabinowitz shook her head. "Doubtful. It's not Arabic. There are some minor similarities, but it's definitely not Arabic. I just can't shake the feeling I've seen it somewhere before." She straightened up. "Is there a college or university in this town?"

"Yeah. There's a little private college right on the north side. Milton College. Not even five miles from here."

Rabinowitz smoothed out a wrinkle in her skirt. "Send a copy of both messages to their languages department. They've probably had a lot of exposure to different languages. One of their faculty just might recognize it. Knowing what language it is might point us in a particular direction until the FBI can figure out what it actually says." She gave the sheriff a wry smile. "I've found that the FBI rarely works fast enough to satisfy me, especially on something like this." Rabinowitz turned around and looked at the faces in the room. "Your detectives haven't made it here yet," she said.

"I don't know what's keeping them," Sheriff Moore seethed.

Rabinowitz shrugged. She moved over to a corner of the room largely undisturbed by the investigation. A large sheet covered some old debris. "Have your officers checked out this side of the room yet?" she asked. The sheriff paused. "No, we're still focused on the victim and the immediate crime scene," he said. Rabinowitz nodded. She pulled a glove out of her pocket and slipped it on. Delicately, she reached down and slid the sheet off the debris, looking down to see what it hid.

Mrs. Oglander's dead eyes looked right back at her.

CAL and Ramirez were sitting out in the parking lot. Ramirez couldn't tell if Cal was having some sort of breakdown or what, and frankly, he didn't care. "So you fucked up," Ramirez said, more than a little pissed off. "Get over it."

"It's not—" Cal halted, staring off into space. "It's just…" He trailed off.

"You fucked up," Ramirez repeated himself. "You made a mistake. Better cops than you have made mistakes."

"How would you know, Ramirez? You'll never make a good cop." Even insults couldn't make Cal feel any better.

Ramirez wrenched open the car door and got out. "You know what makes a good cop, Cal?" he said, leaning through the open space. "A good cop gets his ass out there and lays it all on the line. A good cop keeps plugging away. A good cop doesn't give up. And you know who I learned that from?" Ramirez paused. "So, yeah, you were wrong. But you could have easily been right. And yes, someone else died on our watch. *Our* watch, Cal. And I know this: if you don't get off your ass and stop feeling sorry for yourself, someone else is gonna die, too." With these last words Ramirez slammed the door and started walking towards the church.

"It's not that," Cal began, but Ramirez was long gone. Cal sighed. It wasn't that he'd been wrong in his theory of the crime; shit, that happens to every good cop. The problem was Cal couldn't figure out *what* his problem was. When he heard about the second murder, something in his head just seemed to snap, and, despite every effort to block it out, that little voice kept whispering over and over in his head: *God I could go for a drink.*

"ARE you all right, Agent Rabinowitz?" The sheriff was at her side. Rabinowitz took a deep breath. She'd let out a little scream when she saw the body, and now was embarrassed that she had done so. "Just a little startled, that's all. I wasn't expecting to find anyone under there."

"Was she stabbed, too?" Dan signaled the ME to head over to them.

Rabinowitz quickly studied the corpse. "No, I don't see any wounds…cause of death isn't immediately evident—hold on." Rabinowitz noted something on the victim's throat. She leaned over for a closer look. "What is it?" the sheriff asked. Rabinowitz straightened up. "Puncture wounds," she said. The sheriff peered over her shoulder. The ME had joined them, too. "What do you think?" he asked her, indicating the puncture.

The ME did a quick exam. "Not enough blood loss to have exsanguinated. We'll have to get her to the lab." The ME gave a grim smile. "Looks like we got a vampire on the loose."

"What's going on?" Ramirez asked, coming up to them. Cal was behind him, still looking green. "I thought there was only one victim at the scene."

"There was," Dan replied. "Agent Rabinowitz just found another. What took you two so long to get here?"

"Got lost," Ramirez replied evenly. "Guess I didn't know quite where it was after all."

Dan eyed them both for a minute. "Get to work," he finally said. "All of you. We'll meet back at the station house in an hour and compare notes."

AN hour later Dan, Cal, Ramirez, and Agent Rabinowitz sat huddled around Dan's messy desk in the cramped sheriff's office. "What do we got, people?" Dan said. "And make it good."

"Still waiting on the lab reports from the first victim," Ramirez said. "Should get them any minute now."

"Fine. When we're done here, go to the lab, sit on them until those reports come. Then call us." Ramirez nodded. "Agent?"

Rabinowitz cleared her throat. "It's difficult to draw any theory off the case so far, except of course to say that clearly someone has a problem with religious leaders. I'd recommend that the sheriff's office call every minister, priest, pastor, and rabbi within fifty miles. Tell them to stick to groups, stay at home."

Dan shook his head. "Already on that. Anything you can tell us by way of a profile?"

Rabinowitz hesitated. "I'm not a trained profilist," she said. "But, judging from what I've seen, we're dealing with a male, middle-aged or younger, white. Very strong. The way in which the Bishop died shows that he stalks his victims, though they likely don't notice it. The murders may be messy, but they're carefully planned, almost ritualistic. The murder weapon reinforces that idea. He's been very bold, but cautious. The fact that he didn't slice up the woman found at today's scene suggests that he's angry towards religious leaders only, perhaps male religious leaders specifically. Could be a victim of abuse. All the attention it's been getting has maybe stirred up some painful memories. He likely has a prior record. Assaults, violent fights. Check for someone in the area recently paroled."

"In a town like this, that won't take too long. Cal, why don't you do that? Cal?" Dan looked at his friend. He was staring at the ground. His eyes looked empty. "Cal!" Dan said a bit more forcefully.

Cal haltingly stood up. "I—I'm sorry. Dan, I—sorry. I have to go."

Rabinowitz was startled. "What's his problem?"

Dan sighed. "He's been going through a rough patch," he said.

Ramirez snorted. "He's a drunk," he replied.

CAL drove home as quickly as he could. When he got there he raced through the door and began frantically searching. He tore through his kitchen cabinets, opening them roughly and slamming them shut. Nothing. He pulled bottle after bottle out of his refrigerator—Coke, water, spoiled milk, ketchup and mustard. Empty. He checked the cabinet in the living room, behind the sofa. Bare. He ran upstairs to check his sock drawer and nightstand.

He knew they were all empty. He knew there was no booze in the house. He'd emptied it out before going into rehab, and did a good job of it, too. But somehow, Cal found comfort in the pattern of searching, of coming home from a shitty day and looking for something—anything—to make it all go away. Of course he wouldn't find anything. There was nothing left to find.

Or so he thought.

At the back of his sock drawer Cal felt something small but solid, rolled up into an old red sock. He unraveled the sock, turned it upside down. A small bottle fell out. It hit the floor hard and rolled under the dresser. Cal instantly dropped to his hands and knees and frantically began reaching for it. It had nestled itself against the back wall. Cal couldn't quite reach it.

Frustrated, he stood up. With a grunt he grabbed the corner of the dresser and gave it a heave. A bottle of cologne fell of the top and smashed to the floor. Cal didn't care. He wanted that little bottle of booze.

He got it.

Captain Morgan's Rum. *With natural pineapple flavors*, the label read. He remembered this. A souvenir from a Caribbean trip he'd taken after the divorce came through. *After Dani had…*the trip was supposed to help Cal get away from it all, but he'd spent the entire four days drunk as fuck. The little bottle he'd picked up on the air ride home.

Cal sat on his bed and stared at the tiny parrot on the label. He could already taste the rum. It was only one drink; only one gulp. He read the label. Only 1.69 fucking ounces! That wasn't much. He'd hardly taste it. But he'd feel it. He'd feel the warmth, the bitter spicy flush as it traveled down his throat and into his gullet. And it would feel good. Hell, it would feel great.

Cal trembled. He'd been sober forty-three days. Did he really want to throw it all away?

He opened the bottle, brought it to his lips, and tilted back his head.

"THE message is the key to finding this guy," Rabinowitz was saying. "He wants to communicate to us. That means he wants us to communicate back. Deciphering the message should be our number one priority. My suspicion that is that it's a Middle or Far Eastern language. Could mean our perp is Asian or Middle Eastern."

Dan sighed. "Can I get you to work on that?" he asked. "We're stretched a little thin as it is." Rabinowitz nodded. "I'll personally follow follow up on it."

Ramirez was shaking his head. "Something about this doesn't make sense," he said. "Some violent parolee is going around hacking up priests with a ritual knife and leaving messages in a language no one can read." He sat down on the chair Cal had vacated and crossed his legs. "It just doesn't make sense."

Rabinowitz considered Ramirez's statements. "You may be right," she said. "But it's the best theory right now, with what we've got."

Dan stood and gestured towards the door. "Then go out and get me more."

THE sheriff's directions to the college were spot on. Rabinowitz pulled in through the ornate, wrought iron gates. The Milton College campus was verdant and sprawling, but late in the afternoon on a warm summer day, it was also dead as a doornail. Finally finding a stray student wandering around, Rabinowitz asked for directions to the languages department.

Languages was housed in a building called Warfield Hall, an old war-horse of a structure complete with crumbling parapets and cracked antique tile. It seemed the perfect home for musty academics. Rabinowitz found the secretary's office with little problem. A young-ish woman with hair halfway to heaven sat behind the desk reading what appeared to be a Harlequin romance novel. "Hi, Robyn," Rabinowitz said, reading the nameplate at the front of the desk. "I'm hoping you can help me. I'm looking to speak with someone in your department who may be a specialist in Far or Middle Eastern languages."

Robyn only gave Rabinowitz a bemused glance. "Huh?" she said in a bit of a stupor.

Rabinowitz handed the secretary a photograph of the message scrawled on the church wall. "I need someone who can identify what language this is," she said.

Robyn studied the scrawl carefully in her perfectly manicured hands. "What is that, red paint?" she asked. Rabinowitz nodded. "Something like that," she said, pulling the picture away from the secretary's Lee press-on nails. "Can you help me or not?"

Robyn gave Rabinowitz a cross look, as if this line of questioning was hardly worth interrupting her valuable romance reading. "Try Professor Miller. Her office is on the first floor, all the way to the end of the hall. She taught a class today and may still be in."

"Is she an expert in Middle Eastern languages?"

The same look, only amplified. "First floor, all the way to the end of the hall."

"I'VE got your report," Dixon said, handing Ramirez a thin file.

"It's about time," Ramirez said. "Did you get anything?"

Dixon shook his head. "No fingerprints on the car that we couldn't already identify, no blood types other than the victim's own which means no DNA. We found some strands of black material in the damage to the front of the car, though."

"Meaning what? That the Bishop actually hit a person?"

Dixon shrugged. "Could be. But I doubt it. If he had hit someone hard enough to make that kind of impact, I doubt that person would be walking around anymore. Maybe it was an obstacle in the road, covered with black cloth to make it less visible."

Ramirez nodded. "Something to make the Bishop stop the car."

Dixon continued. "If you find the material, we can match it up, but it looks like a pretty standard cotton. It won't help you track anyone down."

Ramirez sighed. This was getting frustrating. "Was there anything useful there?"

Dixon paused. "We did have one unusual finding."

"What's that?"

"Soil sample. One of the guys found some soil at the scene that didn't look like it matched the surroundings. We brought in a sample and ran an analysis."

"And?"

"Most of it was a simple clay composite with a little hay thrown in—you could find that in a million places around here. Then we got a hit. We found something in that soil you don't usually see everyday in Pennsylvania—excrement from an *elephas maximus*." Ramirez's face registered blank. "Or, to put it bluntly, elephant shit."

"Elephant shit?" Ramirez asked incredulously. "Are you sure?"

Dixon nodded. "Ran the test twice to be sure."

"Elephant shit," Ramirez said thoughtfully.

"Asiatic elephant, to be precise. Most common kind you find in zoos around here. What does that mean? Our psycho is some kind of zookeeper?"

"Maybe," Ramirez said. "Maybe not. Have you told any of this to the sheriff yet?"

Dixon shook his head. "I was told to report to you and Detective Evans. Besides, the sheriff's out chasing down some parolee right now."

Ramirez nodded. Each of the reports was duplicated; one copy went on file to the investigating officer, the other was kept in the tech department itself. Ramirez took one copy of the soil sample. "File these," Ramirez pointed at the rest of the reports, "but give this soil test to the sheriff the second he walks in the door," he added, heading out that way himself.

"Wait, where are you headed?" Dixon called after him.

"Out." Ramirez paused and looked Dixon square in the eye. "I've only got a few hours to catch this guy before he kills someone else. I'm not about to let that happen."

Dixon swallowed hard. Ramirez was serious. "Should I call Detective Evans, or that lady ATF agent?"

Ramirez shook his head. "I'll call them from the car. You just sit tight and wait for the sheriff. Remember—get it to him the second he walks in the door. Don't file it—hand it to him personally. Oh, and good work, Dixon. You may have just opened up this case for us." With a flourish Ramirez walked out of the station house and trotted out to his car.

Dixon smiled to himself. He wondered when they caught the guy if he'd be interviewed for national TV. He'd especially like to be interviewed by that Katie Couric. She was kinda cute. If only they could somehow arrange that...

RABINOWITZ found the door to the last office at the end of the hall slightly ajar. She pushed it further open and stepped into the tiny office. It was the most cluttered closet she had ever seen. Three of the four walls were covered completely in bookshelves, and each of those shelves was overflowing with thick, dog-eared tomes. In addition, books and papers were piled in precarious stacks all over the floor, sometimes three, four feet high. There was no place to sit except at the desk, though the desk itself was a nightmarish realm of loose papers, a collection of carved wooden animals, and a computer that looked old enough to vote. In short, Professor Miller was clearly a pig—an intellectual pig, but a pig nonetheless.

"Hello?" Rabinowitz called out in a soft voice. She didn't see anyone in the office, but it was possible that a body might be tucked away behind a row of books.

Sure enough, a head popped out from behind the desk, looking very surprised to see the agent. The head belonged to a youngish man, perhaps twenty-five, with messy ash-brown hair, thick glasses that sat slightly askew on his round face, and a distinct glob of mayonnaise on his left cheek. "Hi," he said, his mouth full of sandwich. He held up a finger while chewing as rapidly as possible. "Come on in," he said, mouth still full, waving Rabinowitz further into the office.

Since there was no place to sit, Rabinowitz stood in front of the desk awkwardly while the young man frantically finished chewing. Finally swallowing, he took a generous swig of Pepsi, and with a small yet satisfied burp asked, "Can I help you?"

"I'm looking for Professor Miller," Rabinowitz answered. "Do you know where I can find her?"

"Home," the man replied matter-of-factly. "Class is over, and she's gone for the day."

"Is there any way I can reach her?" Rabinowitz asked.

The young man looked hesitant. "She doesn't like to be disturbed while home," he said. "She's busy working on a new translation of *The Odyssey*. It's been her life's work. See, she believes that the women in *The Odyssey* have, historically speaking, gotten kind of a raw deal. I kind of think Professor Miller actually believes that the poem wasn't written by Homer, but by Homer's wife or mistress or something like that. She's kind of tight-lipped on that particular detail." Rabinowitz found it difficult to concentrate on the young man's words; she was too distracted by the mayonnaise, which was now doing a slow but merry jig down the side of his face. She delicately pointed to her own cheek, to make him aware of it, but oblivious to her motions, the young man just continued lecturing. "There was this interesting theory that went around for about six or seven years in the seventies that said that the epic was written by Naussika, who's actually a character in the book. I'm not sure what evidence there is for that, though Professor Miller would know. She published a little about that, though she never really came down on one side or the other. Anyway, my point is—" Rabinowitz thought it would never come "— that she gets really pissed when I interrupt her for anything other than a dire emergency."

"You have mayonnaise on your face," Rabinowitz blurted out, unable to ignore the big white blob any longer.

"Oh, thanks," the young man said nonchalantly. He looked around the desk for a napkin to wipe it off with. Finding none, he eventually used his sleeve. "Maybe I can help you out," he said.

"Are you one of her students?" Rabinowitz asked.

"One of her grad students. Actually, I'm her only grad student. Milton has a small program and most students don't survive working with Professor Miller. She's a genius and a really respected scholar in the field but she's a total bitch who eats grad students for breakfast. Don't tell her I said that, by the way. But we get along, don't ask me why, and man, the education is really worth it. I'm working on my doctorate in Greek, and she's definitely one of the best to study with. I've actually just started my dissertation—part of this mess is mine— and, it's really interesting. I'm going to argue that Euripides' famous play *Medea*—you know, the one where the mother kills her own kids to get back at her ex-husband—was actually the first piece of feminist rhetoric. I guess you could say I've been influenced by Professor Miller. Not that I think Euripides overtly advocates child homicide.

Of course, I'm not so sure he doesn't either. You know the Greeks. Oh, my name's Abe, by the way." The young man held out his hand. Agent Rabinowitz shook it and took advantage of his momentary silence.

"I need to identify what language this is, and, possibly, get what it says translated," she said, holding out the clearest photograph of the blood-scribed message on the meeting hall wall to Abe.

Abe took it and studied it intently. "It's hard to make out," he said. "What is this written in? Everything's jumbled together. It doesn't make any sense."

Rabinowitz checked her watch. It was getting later and later. "It is vitally important that we identify if not translate this as soon as possible."

Abe looked at Rabinowitz with great curiosity. "Why?" he asked.

Rabinowitz sighed. "It's part of an on-going investigation," she said.

"What kind of investigation? Are you a cop?"

"I'm an ATF agent, and it's part of a homicide investigation." The words "ATF agent" seemed to hardly stir the young man. It was no surprise; Alcohol, Tobacco, and Firearms rarely got the respect the other "acronym agencies" got, inside or outside of Washington. Still, Abe again directed his gaze at the message. "Please, can you identify it?" Rabinowitz asked. The only answer was silence. Several moments passed. "Look, if you don't know it, maybe Professor Miller—"

"It's Aramaic," the young man suddenly said.

Rabinowitz paused. "Aramaic?" she queried. "Are you sure?"

Abe nodded. "It's not your garden variety Aramaic and it's definitely a big mess, but yeah, there's no doubt, it's Aramaic."

"But, Aramaic, isn't that an ancient language? Not used anymore? As old as the Bible?"

"It's more than that," Abe said. "Aramaic *is* the Bible. The first drafts of the Bible that we have are written in this stuff. This is the very language that Jesus Christ spoke." The young man paused. "What does a message written in Aramaic have to do with a homicide?" he asked.

Rabinowitz wished she had an answer for him.

Ramirez followed the Conochocheague Creek as it paralleled Westhook Drive. He was west of town, where houses were few and far between. Only a few decrepit, run-down farms interrupted the thickly forested landscape.

He'd tried to call Cal but had forgotten his phone was dead. He planned on stopping but there was nowhere to stop. It was getting dark. Whoever was doing all this would be out hunting soon. Ramirez gritted his teeth. He was not about to let that happen.

Elephant shit. There was no zoo in town, and therefore no zookeepers. The closest elephant was probably at the National Zoo in Washington, D.C., and no D.C. zookeeper was going to drive to Chambersburg to kill a preacher. Nope, that elephant angle seemed like a dead end.

Except Ramirez had a kid. And, according to his wife Minnie's idea of good parenting, every weekend meant a trip somewhere with his son. Fishing, the ballpark, the art museum—and last weekend, the circus had been in town.

It was a small touring show, one that still had carnival games and a midway. There'd also been the usual clowns, jugglers, and acrobats. They even had a freak show. Raul had been scared of the clowns, and both he and Minnie refused to see the freaks, so Ramirez went in alone. Lurid signs showed grotesque images of lizard and snake men, rotund bearded women, Siamese twins, and various other freaks and geeks. Ramirez felt a little thrill as he entered the long, dark tent, hoping to catch a glimpse of something truly bizarre. But the lizard man was just some weird guy who had forked his tongue with a pair of kitchen shears, the bearded woman was just a chunky housewife in need of some electrolysis, and the Siamese "twins" were just an old two-headed frog in a jar of formaldehyde. Worst of all, the snake man exhibit, the finale and *piéce de resistance* of the freak show, was closed, with nothing more than a small sign apologizing for Ramirez's "inconvenience."

Ramirez hadn't felt inconvenienced; he'd felt ripped off, three bucks down the drain that he'd never see again. Only now, it was paying dividends. Because, between the freak show tent and the merry-go-round, the circus had elephant rides. It had only been one old, sorry-looking elephant doing all the work, but one was enough for Ramirez.

On some level, it made perfect sense. Carnival workers were transient; they often had criminal records. It would be easy to join the carnival, move from town to town, kill a few holy men, and then move on. No suspicious activity; no roots to tie you down. No one to be the wiser. It was the perfect cover.

By now Ramirez had made it to the fairgrounds about twelve miles outside of town. The place was deserted. Popcorn still littered the ground, its stale buttery smell permeating the air. Cans and bottles overflowed the few bins that had been left out to collect them. He saw papers fluttering by in a small, unfelt breeze, but other than that, nothing remained of the circus. Everyone was gone.

Then, out of the corner of his eye, Ramirez saw an old man shuffling along, poking at the papers with a stick and putting them into a garbage bag. "Excuse me," he said, flashing the old man his badge. The old man barely blinked. "When did the circus pull out?"

"Right after they was done, late in the evening," the old man replied. "Monday night. Once it's all done and over with they just pack up and go, leave nothing behind but a mess. That's what I gets to do. Clean up their mess."

"Do you know where their next stop was?" Ramirez asked.

The old man shrugged. "Somewhere south, in Virginia, I think. I don't know."

Damn, Ramirez thought. *It would be almost two hours to Virginia. If they left Monday evening, they probably weren't around at midnight.*

"Did anyone leave the circus, stay behind after it was all over?"

The old man looked peeved. "Now why would they do that, sonny?" he asked.

"And you're sure no one's been here since they left?"

"How can I be sure of something like that?" the old man replied, testier than ever. "I don't live here, son. I don't police what people do here at all. That's *your* job."

Ramirez swore under his breath. He thought he'd been on the right track, but if the circus had left town before the first murder had occurred...

"And you're *sure* none of the circus folk aren't still around?"

"Well, I didn't say that..."

"You just told me they weren't!"

"No, I didn't. Now don't go gettin' all excited, son," the old man replied. Ramirez realized the old man was enjoying this interrogation more than he should, but felt it best to humor him. For now. "You asked me if any of 'em stayed behind once the circus was over. I asked you *why* any of 'em would do something like that. I never said they didn't actually do it."

Ramirez was becoming frustrated. "Well? Did they?"

"Uh-huh. From what I heard, some of those freaks they have there in that show came to town and then, right before the last day of the show, just up and left the circus flat as you please, without none a word to nobody. The management was pissed off about that, let me tell you."

"Why did they leave like that?"

"I don't know, sonny," the old man said. "I'm only tellin' ya what I heard."

"Sorry," Ramirez said, though he didn't know why he was apologizing.

"They was uppity performers anyway, never wanting to go on, that's what one of the Midway folk was sayin'. She said they was real distant-like, kept pretty much to themselves all the time. Anyway, I heard that they sent one of the hands down to talk to 'em. I heard they was living in one of them circus tents down in Eden Hollow, 'bout a half-mile down the creek thatta way. I heard that the guy was told to either bring them back or get the tent back. And I heard he come back with nothin' at all and shakin' like a leaf. After that, the circus folk done decided to just up and leave them alone."

"Half a mile?" Ramirez asked, pointing in the same direction. "This way?"

"Yup. There's an old Presbyterian church out that way, all run down now. There's a little footpath behind that church. Used to be a good spot for campers, or young lovers, down by the creek."

"Used to be. Why isn't it anymore?"

"Snakes." The old man's beady eyes smiled as he said the word. Ramirez shuddered involuntarily. "Rattlesnakes to be precise about it. One of those government programs, designed to keep animals from gettin' all killed off. What's that word—*extinct*. From goin' all extinct now. I don't know what's so val'ble about a rattler, anyway, but ever since they become protected the population has just boomed down that way. Some kids got bit—ohh, 'bout five, six years ago—and people generally avoid it ever since. But not those freaks. They prolly lovin' it down there." He chuckled

"Why do you say that?" Ramirez asked.

The old man was still chuckling. "Cuz those folks is snakes, too."

"CAN you translate the message?" Rabinowitz was saying.

Abe quickly shook his head. "Hunh-uh. I can only tell what it is by a few of the more distinct letters. With the right books, maybe I could. I'm not sure. But this isn't the Aramaic I'm used to. I can't really understand or translate it without a lot of help."

"Could Professor Miller?"

Abe took another bite of his sandwich. Rabinowitz kept looking at her watch while he chewed. *Hurry up, damnit!* she thought. "Yeah," he finally said, swallowing a last bit of turkey. "It might take a while to get the hang of the style, but I'm sure she could do it. What's this written in, anyway? Paint?"

Rabinowitz felt a sudden vibration in her pocket. Her cell phone was on silent ring. She fished it out and held up a finger to Abe, indicating that she needed to take this call. "Rabinowitz," she said curtly as she answered the phone.

"Moore here," Dan's voice spoke into her ear. "You get anything on that message yet?"

"I'm working on it. I'm at the college right now," Rabinowitz replied, catching a glimpse of Abe, who was still studying the message and now in danger of dropping a big glob of mayonnaise onto the photograph. She quickly rescued the picture and handed Abe a napkin from under a stack of papers on the desk before anything of use got covered in condiment. "Any news on your front?"

"Nothing. No recent violent parolees in the area, no reports of any like crimes coming through from anywhere. We've warned the local preachers to keep a low profile, but now we've got them so scared out of their wits that most of my crew is out chasing shadows or hunting down any funny noise they hear. I just left a call where a Baptist minister thought someone was hiding out in his backyard— turned out to be his own garbage can."

Rabinowitz nodded to herself. She had suspected something like this would happen, though she knew the Sheriff's office had no other recourse. "I'm thinking it might be time to bring in the full resources of my office," she said.

The sheriff sighed. "You're probably right, though it might be too late to help anyone out tonight." Rabinowitz could hear the tension in his voice. "Let's just hope everyone's locked up safe and snug in their beds by now."

"Any news from Ramirez or Evans?"

The sheriff sighed again. "Ramirez's phone is still out. He's off somewhere—no one knows where. I'll get back to the station house as soon as I can to check out those reports, see if I can pick up the same clue he did. Right now, I'm headed off to a rabbi's house on a report of a suspicious noise. Probably his cat's in heat."

Rabinowitz choked back a quick laugh. "What about Evans?"

"Cal?" The sheriff sounded angry. "Who the fuck knows where Cal is. Listen, finish up at the college and get back to the station house ASAP. I'm going to need you. Don't plan to be getting much sleep tonight."

"I won't, sheriff," she said, hanging up the phone. Rabinowitz turned to Abe. "Can you get it done? Tonight?"

Abe looked serious. "What's this all about?" he asked. "I mean, don't you people have linguists to do this sort of stuff for you?"

Rabinowitz was frustrated. She *could* wait for the FBI to report what it learned about the strange message, but she had no idea when they might be finished deciphering it, and sitting around doing nothing did not appeal to her. "You see that?" she said to Abe, pointing to the message. "That's not red paint, it's not red dye, it's not red finger nail polish. It's blood. A minister's blood. And here—" she pointed to the second picture "—this is a bishop's blood. People are dying, Abe, and you hold our best clue as to why in your hands. And unless you figure this thing out, someone else is likely to die tonight." She sighed. If that didn't motivate him, she didn't know what would.

Abe stood up resolutely. "I'll call you as soon as we have something," he said, clutching her card in his hand. He moved quickly about the room now, picking out a few different volumes from the overstuffed shelves in the wall.

"Thanks," Rabinowitz mumbled as she headed out the door.

"THEN I could feel it—sitting there, in my mouth. Tasted like shit, to be honest—like varnish. Still, I wanted it so much. I felt like—like if I swallowed it, everything would be better. All the shit would go away."

"But you know that's not true."

"Yeah. I know."

"So what did you do?"

Cal paused. "I spit it out," he said. "I went to my bathroom and spit it out. I spit it out and brushed my teeth, and sat on the edge of my bed, the phone in my hand, trying to think of any lie I could tell you, any lie I could tell myself, that would keep me from having to tell you about what I did."

"You didn't have to tell me," his sponsor said. "You could have simply *not* told me."

Cal thought about this. "I had to tell you, Frank," he said. "If I didn't…it would be the same thing as taking that drink."

The older man nodded. They were sitting in a dark little Italian restaurant. Cal took a furtive sip from his soda and fiddled with a crusty breadstick. "You're right, Cal," Frank said. "You did have to tell me. And I'm glad you did. And you know what I have to ask you."

"I know," Cal said. His voice dripped with dejection. "I don't know, Frank. I honestly don't know why I did it. It was just…for the first time in a long while things felt right, you know, like they used to? I was working the case, everything seemed to be falling into place…"

"And Dani?" Frank asked.

Cal was uneasy. "What about Dani?" he asked evasively.

"Where was she in all this?"

Cal sighed. *Dani.* "Nowhere, I guess," he said. "I guess for a little while there I just…I just forgot all about her."

"And wasn't that why your drinking got carried away in the first place? To forget all about her?" Cal nodded slowly. He felt a lump forming in his throat. "Listen, Cal, forgetting about Dani isn't dealing with her death at all. Just as drinking didn't help. Maybe…maybe it's time you talked to that counselor."

Cal nodded. He just wanted the pain to end. "Maybe so, Frank." He knew Frank was right. It just felt too sudden, too mechanical to deal with Dani's death like that. Cal felt the need to grieve on his own, though he couldn't explain why.

"Here," Frank said, handing Cal a small chip.

"What's this?" Cal said picking it up. With a small frown he recognized it. "A first day chip?"

Frank nodded. "You know the rules. You've got to start over." The older man reached across the table and took Cal's hand in a sign of support. "It's not a punishment, Cal. This isn't about failure. It's about moving forward, always moving forward." He let Cal's hand go. "I had a few starts and stops myself along the way," he said. "You're going to make it. You're going to be all right."

Cal nodded numbly. He wasn't so sure he was going to be all right.

REVEREND Eugenia McKee gently piloted her small, aging Volvo down the alley that ran behind her house. It was late. It was dark. She was nervous.

Her secretary, Mabel, who was really just a community volunteer who answered the phones and kept the books, had forwarded the message from the Sheriff's office earlier that afternoon. Eugenia, or Genie as her friends called her, was already at the Mid-Atlantic Methodist ministers' convention in Baltimore, scheduled to return that night. Mabel had urged Genie to stay on in Baltimore, but Genie knew no one there, and couldn't afford her eighty-nine dollar-a-day hotel room for one more night. Not on what the church paid her. Her talk on homosexuality and ordination within the church was scheduled for 4:00. Genie gambled that if she gave her speech, did a quick Q and A, jumped right into the car and drove like hell without stopping, she could make it back to Chambersburg just before sunset. It was late May, after all, and the sun was setting pretty late.

But Genie's talk had proved highly controversial, and the Q and A session quickly turned into a free-for-all shouting match. Genie kept trying to leave but was pressed further and further into theological debate. Her late start meant that she hit traffic, a lot of it, and idling on the highway caused her to have to stop for gas. By the time she pulled into the Chambersburg city limits, it was well after ten.

Genie paused at a stop sign before quickly accelerating. They'd got Bishop Okeke—a man she knew, and respected—in his car. She hardly felt safe driving then. Once she was home, with her kitchen door double-locked and the Louisville slugger used for Saturday softball games tucked firmly beside her bed, well, then she'd feel safe. But now, here, in the dark behind her house, Genie felt very vulnerable as she slowly pulled her car into the small lot.

It wasn't a house, actually, but an apartment, the top half of an old Victorian. When Genie had rented this place, she had appreciated the ample parking available behind the house's garage. Now she shuddered at it. She had to park her car behind the garage—the garage itself was too full of lawnmowers, ladders, and other such paraphernalia to actually fit a car in it. She would then have to walk around the garage building, through the gate that opened up to the back yard, and then up the brick path to the back porch stairs that opened into her kitchen. A little over thirty yards in all.

It had never seemed like a long walk before.

Genie paused, sitting in her car, her headlights on high beam, listening. She could hear nothing. She could see nothing. In fact, it was almost *too* quiet. Leaving her lights on, she turned her car off and listened again. It was so still Genie could hear her own heart pounding, as loud as firecrackers, *pop pop, pop pop, pop pop.* She took a deep breath. Thirty feet around the garage. Quickly through the gate. Twenty yards to the door. Her back door key was at the ready.

The space where Genie parked would be thrown into darkness the second she turned her lights off. But once she rounded the garage, the motion-sensing eye of the garage light would see her and flood the backyard with light. The light from her downstairs neighbor, Mr. Shaw, also lit up her back porch. Mr. Shaw was always in his bedroom watching television at this time of night. If anyone was waiting anywhere, Genie could see them and run back to her car. It was a good plan, a smart plan.

But Genie couldn't work up the nerve to execute it.

This is ridiculous, she thought to herself. No one is out there. There are hundreds—well, dozens of clergy in this community. Genie had a small congregation in a small church downtown. She didn't live in the church. She hadn't been in the neighborhood that long. No one really knew who she was. No one knew she was a minister.

I hope not.

Stop scaring yourself! she screamed in her head. Be quick and be smart. Okay? Okay. Ready. Set.

Go.

Genie turned off her lights, dashed out of her car, and quickly slammed the door shut. It bounced back open. The seat belt. Damn! Swiftly she moved the seat belt out of the way and slammed the door shut. She rounded the corner of the garage and ran smack into something. She went down hard on her hands and knees, gravel etching itself into her palms. Mr. Shaw's garbage can—the old coot never remembered to put it back after garbage day. Genie stood up, kicked the can out into the alley, and raced up the side of the garage.

The light did not come on.

Genie hesitated. She took one step closer towards the light and waved her hand in front of it. Nothing. It was busted. Great. Mr. Shaw's window was also dark. He must already be asleep. What a night to go to bed early!

Now what do I do?

Genie listened. She heard a small rustling sound—softly, and to her left. Probably a rabbit. Her yard was full of them. Maybe she should go back to her car. Her hands trembled. She desperately held back a frightened whimper. Why the fuck wasn't the light working? Genie wanted to scream but she remained silent. She took a deep breath—one, then two. She forced herself to calm down.

She heard a noise.

Whirling, Genie turned and saw—nothing, nothing at all, just a few branches fluttering in the gentle evening breeze. Everything was still. Too still. Her breathing grew more and more shallow. She felt frozen. She didn't know what to do.

Run.

Pell-mell Genie dashed through the gate. It clapped open with a loud slam and shut just as hard. Genie ran up the brick sidewalk as fast as she could. The brick was crumbly and old and Genie turned her ankle about halfway, but she managed to keep her balance and kept on running. She could hear them now, hear someone behind her, running towards her, lots of footsteps running, galloping, loud clapping sounds like hoof beats. She hit the steps and took them two at a time. Halfway up she missed a step and fell down hard on one knee. Her purse flew off the steps but she didn't care. She was crying. She was scared. She scrambled up the rest of the way on her hands and knees. She reached the door. She could hear them behind her. Her keys—where was the right key! Her hands shook fiercely. She inserted the key in the lock. It sometimes stuck—there! Genie thrust the door open and raced inside. She slammed it shut. Grabbing the lock, she turned the little knob, and quickly threw the deadbolt, too. Putting her back to the door, Genie gasped, sobbed, sank to her knees. She was home. She was okay.

She was safe.

Regaining her composure, Genie stood up in her darkened kitchen. She opened her kitchen window curtain a slit and peered outside. There was no one there. The yard was as empty as it had been before. Genie smiled, lightly laughing at herself. It had all been in her head. There was no one there. She had scared herself half to death over nothing.

With a small but very relieved sigh, and still looking through the widow, she reached over and flicked on her kitchen light. Bright yellow light flooded the room. Genie smiled, laughed at herself again, and turned around. There had been no one there.

Because they were already here.

The dark figures were upon her before she could scream; their knives were cutting into her before she could make a sound; blood gushed out of her before she could even form a coherent thought.

Genie was dead before she could hit the floor.

RABINOWITZ had been back at the station for an hour before the Sheriff finally pulled up. "Anything?" she asked quietly. He shook his head. "Any word from Cal or Ramirez?" he asked her. Now it was her turn to shake her head.

Dan swore. "Goddamnit, where are those two! We're running out of time."

Rabinowitz looked up at the clock. Even though it was only a little after eleven, she had a feeling it was already too late.

IN his office, Dixon had waited for the Sheriff to return. And waited. And waited. Finally, he'd set his head down on his desk. It had been a long couple of days. He was so tired. Surely just a moment's rest wouldn't hurt. He could take a little nap. Maybe even dream about him and Katie Couric...

THE ME saw Dixon sleeping on his desk, snoring softly, drooling oh-so-gently onto some type of report. Wonder if I should wake him, she thought? Nah, let the poor bastard have his rest, she concluded as she headed back down the hall. She felt like she could use some sleep herself.

"THOSE reports tell us anything?" the Sheriff was asking Rabinowitz.

"Nothing on the Okeke case. Nothing so far on the Brantridge case, either."

The ME walked up to them. "Just finished working up your Mrs. Oglander," she said.

"And?" the sheriff prodded. "What was the cause of death? Exsanguination?"

The ME shook her head. "Snake bite," she replied matter-of-factly.

The Sheriff looked at Rabinowitz. They were both puzzled. "Snake bite?" he said.

Before Rabinowitz could reply, there was a commotion at the front door. A short, official-looking Asian man with rapidly thinning hair and a brusque gait herded a small cadre of similar-looking men and women into the station house. "Who's in charge around here?" asked the leader. One of the officers pointed at Dan. "Sheriff Moore?" the lead man queried. Dan nodded in confirmation. "Agent Nguyen, FBI," the man said. "Care to explain to me how you and your department have managed to make a complete clusterfuck of this situation?"

"DETECTIVE Evans, Cal, are you there? It's Agent Rabinowitz…I'm calling from the station house. Things have gotten really out of hand here. The FBI has arrived and is in the process of completely running the Sheriff down. Ramirez is missing; no one has seen nor heard from him in hours. The rest of us seem to be officially off the case. Are you there? Can you hear me? Ramirez is missing. I'm not exactly sure what you can do about it, but from what people seem to be saying around here, you're the one they need right now. Can you hear me? Detective Evans? Hello?"

ABE tried calling the number on the card, but it automatically forwarded to voicemail. He hesitated at leaving a message. Professor Miller was still working on the translation, and had initially found it more baffling than Abe had anticipated, but a few of the initial findings might prove useful. Abe wasn't sure whether or not to leave a message. He felt that, if it was really so important, he should talk a person in charge. He didn't want to let Agent Rabinowitz down. Searching quickly for the professor's phone book, he found the number for the Chambersburg police department and dialed it. "Hello?" a man's voice answered.

"Hi," Abe said unsurely. "Can I speak with Agent Rabinowitz, please?"

"Not here," the man on the phone said.

"It's important," Abe added.

"Why don't you try her cell phone, huh? We need to keep this line clear."

"I've already tried her cell. I didn't get through. See, it's about the message, the one with left at the murders—"

"How do you know about that?" the voice over the phone interrupted angrily.

Abe swallowed hard. "Agent Rabinowitz asked me to help translate it. You see, I identified it as being Aramaic and I said that Professor Miller—she's my mentor—maybe I'd better start at the beginning. See, I'm from Milton College…"

"Listen, I'm not sure what arrangement you had with Agent Rabinowitz, but that message has already been translated by the FBI."

"It has?" Abe asked incredulously.

"Yes. Now, while we appreciate your calling…"

"But, but…"

"We've got a lot on our hands at the moment, and like I said…"

"But, excuse me, sir…"

"We'd like to keep this line clear."

Abe stared at the dead receiver in his hands. He didn't know what to do.

Finally, he hung up the phone.

CAL was in the shower, the steaming water pouring down over him, blocking out the sound of the incessantly ringing phone. His skin had wrinkled with the constant pounding of the hot, lush water, but he didn't care. He was so tired that his body ached with exhaustion. Physical exhaustion, mental exhaustion. And so he cried. He stood there, in the shower, crying, for Dani, for himself, for the life—the lives—that had somehow gotten so lost.

When he got out of the shower, his eyes blurry from water and tears, he crashed, tumbled into bed, falling asleep almost immediately.

He failed to notice the desperately blinking light on his answering machine.

RAMIREZ had been waiting for his hours. He did his best to stretch his back; it was beginning to cramp.

He was nestled against an old tree stump that effectively hid him from the ground of Eden Hollow. If anyone was using this place, they'd be there, on the flat area next to the creek. He's seen the signs of human presence—an old campfire, still a little warm to the touch. But there was no sign of the tent the old man mentioned. The rotted, falling-down church the old man had described was there, but looked like no one had been in it in decades. Still, Ramirez set out to wait—and ended up waiting half the night.

He should have left hours ago. He had no back up, no infrared scope, nothing to really see by except the very dim light of a waxing crescent moon. Still, anyone moving around down there would be silhouetted against the water. And Ramirez was afraid that the moment he left, something would happen—something he hoped to prevent happening.

Ramirez cursed his aching knee. He wanted desperately to get up and walk around. He wondered where they were. Were these snake men even the guys they were looking for? Had they gone out to kill again? Or was the old man just some kook? Ramirez hoped not, but somehow, by this time, he felt uneasy about it. It was late, too late.

One way or the other, he thought, whether he was on the right track or not, someone else must have already died.

Suddenly, Ramirez saw someone—at least, he thought he did, some bit of motion against the water. There it was again! There was someone down there—no, wait, a least two people, three, five! Ramirez grew excited. He hoped they would light a fire, give him something to see by, but they did no such thing. He couldn't make out any features, articles of clothing, nothing—they all seemed to be shapeless, without form. Perhaps they were wearing some kind of cloak and hood. Ramirez thought perhaps it might be best to creep forward and try to get a closer look.

Then he thought the better of that plan. There were simply too many of them. He couldn't keep them all covered with just one gun. He'd parked his car about three hundred yards down the road. He'd make his way back there, head out with no lights, and hotfoot it back to the station, bringing back some extra men, guns, dogs, and lights. Then he could properly interrogate them, see what was going on. Hopefully, this would end it all right here, tonight.

Quietly, without a sound, he backed away from his position.

He felt something—on his neck—something that coiled around him. It felt rough and smooth, scaly and tender and terrifying. Ramirez held back a scream as he whirled around. He saw a man, a figure, draped head to toe in black. It appeared that it was the man's arm that was around his neck, but Ramirez could tell by the way that it moved that this was no arm.

Ramirez panicked, and his mind went on autopilot. *Gun.* But before he could reach for his gun, two other men dressed all in black appeared, grabbing his arms and pinning them at his sides. The man on top of him—it felt like a man, all of him save that arm, his left arm—grabbed his gun and flung it into the brush. Ramirez struggled, wondering what they planned to do with him. He could see no knives or weapons of any kind. But he knew he was going to die.

With a great shove Ramirez managed to wrest free his right hand. He used it to grab at the cowl of the man on top of him. He pulled it back. He pulled it back and saw the face of his attacker. He looked him right in the eyes.

At the same instant Ramirez felt two sharp pricks on his neck. His eyes swam; dizziness flushed his body. He was drowning, losing himself, dying. And as he died he looked up, looked up and saw nothing, saw only darkness, inky darkness, two luminescent, inky pools of darkness looking back down at him.

THURSDAY

"RAMIREZ is dead."

"What?" Cal was standing at his front door, a robe wrapped around his body. He'd still been in bed when he heard the incessant pounding on his door.

"Ramirez is dead," Rabinowitz repeated. Her face was an icy mask, barely hiding the contempt she was feeling at the moment.

"But…how?" Cal staggered a few feet back into his home. Rabinowitz walked past him and closed the front door. Cal owned a small row house at the end of a quiet, dead end road. It was a newly built home. The inside was rather bland but inoffensive, and not nearly as messy as Rabinowitz had expected it would be.

Cal staggered over to an easy chair and sat heavily down on its leather exterior. He looked like crap. "Have you been drinking?" Rabinowitz asked suddenly, startling him with her question.

"No, I…what? Why are you asking me that? That's none of your business," Cal replied defensively.

Rabinowitz shrugged. She selected a simple stuffed chair for herself and sat down on it. "It was a logical conclusion. After your disappearance act yesterday, everyone jumped to the same conclusion."

"Yeah? Well, everyone's wrong," Cal said testily, suddenly standing up from his chair. Rabinowitz's icy glare made him both angry and nervous. He began to putter around the room, cleaning up stray pieces of newspaper from several days prior. "Who have you been talking to? Ramirez?"

"I told you. Ramirez is dead," Rabinowitz said quietly.

"Oh. Right." Cal hadn't processed the news quite yet. Ramirez. "How—how did he die?"

Rabinowitz pursed her lips. "Snake bite."

"Snake bite?" Cal asked incredulously. Rabinowitz nodded. Cal stared into her soft brown eyes. "That doesn't make any sense," Cal said.

"I know," Rabinowitz replied.

"An accident?" Cal asked. "Was it some kind of freak thing?"

Rabinowitz paused. "He was found in his car this morning by a couple of your officers down off Westhook Drive. He had two bite marks on his neck. The ME hasn't actually confirmed yet, but…"

"Was the car a wreck? Did he go off the road driving for help? Where the hell did he find a poisonous snake around here anyway?"

"Cal, they found him in the backseat of the car."

"What?" Cal sat back down in his chair, but now his eyes bore into Rabinowitz's. "Are you saying this…this was a homicide?"

Rabinowitz nodded. "It looks that way."

Cal was taken aback. "That doesn't make any sense. Why would you kill someone with a snake? *How* would you kill someone with a snake? This isn't a fucking Sherlock Holmes story."

"A poisonous snake can be a deadly weapon. Cleopatra died from a snake bite, so the legend says."

"Cleopatra killed herself. You just don't hold a guy down and have a snake bite him. It doesn't make any sense. I mean—" Cal stopped. Ramirez. Ramirez was dead?

Rabinowitz reached out her hand. She took Cal's clammy fingers into her grip. "Detective Evans, I'm sorry about your partner."

Cal was still trying to wrap his mind around the news. "I was always hard on him, you know, always on his case, but—I didn't mean it, you know, I was just…" Cal trailed off. "This—this doesn't make any sense," he said.

Rabinowitz dropped Cal's hand. "None of it makes sense. But, Detective, he wasn't the only one. Remember Mrs. Oglander—the Quaker woman we found at the scene of yesterday's attack?"

Cal nodded, understanding. "Snake bite?" Rabinowitz nodded. "Does Dan have any—does he have any idea who did it?"

Rabinowitz shook her head. "He's not in charge of the case anymore. The FBI came in last night and took over jurisdiction. The lead agent is a guy named Nguyen."

Cal sighed. The Feds. "Well, maybe that's for the best. We weren't getting anywhere fast." His hands were shaking. Ramirez was dead. Dead. "Did—did they find another body from last night?"

"No, at least, not yet. No one's reported anything, and the FBI is attempting to contact all the people the sheriff's office warned last night, just to make sure. They've decided to go public with the whole case. They think it's the best way to warn everyone in the local area. There's some fear that the guy might move off, start killing people somewhere else. They think they might have made it too hot for him here."

"No," Cal muttered, more to himself than to Rabinowitz. "No, he's not going to move off. He's not done yet."

"What do you mean?" Rabinowitz leaned in towards Cal, peering at him, staring directly in the eyes. "What do you mean, Detective Evans?"

Cal started. He hadn't realized he had spoken aloud. "I'm sorry," he said. "I—I haven't offered you any coffee. Would you like some?"

Rabinowitz took a deep breath. "That would be nice," she said. Cal stood up and padded off to the kitchen. Rabinowitz stood, too, surveying the room more carefully. It was pretty bare. Two chairs, one small sofa, and a man-sized television dominated the décor. "Do you take cream or sugar, Agent—you know, I'm sorry, but with everything that's been going on, I don't remember your name," Cal called out from the kitchen. "It's Rabinowitz," she called back. "Actually, it's Velvet."

"Velvet?" Cal popped his head in from the kitchen. Rabinowitz could see he was suppressing a small laugh.

"Yeah," Rabinowitz said with a small smile. "That's my name, Velvet. It's a little—unusual, I know."

"No, it's not that bad," Cal said. He did his best to give Rabinowitz a weak smile. "What, was your mom really into fabrics? Or old Elvis paintings?" Despite herself, Rabinowitz gave off a little laugh. "Could be worse. She could have called you felt."

"Very funny," Rabinowitz replied, managing a large grin.

"Seriously, though, how did you get named Velvet?"

"My mother was a really big fan of the book, you know, *The Velveteen—*"

"—*Rabbit*," Cal said, interrupting her. "I get it. It's nice, actually."

"No, it's not."

"No, really. It's different, but—it's nice." Rabinowitz smiled. She could see that Cal had a certain charm when he wanted to. "Call me Cal," he was saying.

"For Calvin?" Rabinowitz asked.

"Actually, for Caldwell."

"Caldwell? And you laugh at Velvet?"

"Hey, be careful now. Caldwell happens to be my mother's maiden name. Well, that's what I tell people anyway."

"But that's not the truth?" Rabinowitz asked with a quizzical smile.

Cal's small grin grew into a wide smirk. "Naah. Truth is, Caldwell was the last name of my mom's boyfriend before she met my dad. See, this other guy was my mother's first choice, but he seemed shy about commitment, so my mother started dating my father, and, lo and behold, he proposed first. My mother totally settled when she married my father, so she named me after her one true love, to remind herself that there were better men out there."

Rabinowitz nearly choked from holding back her chuckles. "I almost believe that story," she smiled.

"Anyway, *Velvet*, cream or sugar?"

"Skim milk, if you have it, thanks, *Caldwell*," Rabinowitz replied.

Cal gave her one last dopey grin. "Coming right up." He scampered back into the kitchen.

Rabinowitz continued her small survey of the living room, stopping to peruse a small bookshelf. She found mostly books on true-crime and golf. Funny, she mused. She wondered if Cal actually did golf. He didn't seem the type. Too high-strung. Then again, she thought, remembering the conversation they had just had, maybe there is more to this guy than meets the eye. She crouched to take a look at the books on the lowest shelf. A small photo frame caught her eye. The picture itself had pitched forward, so Rabinowitz picked it up. It was the image of a small, infant girl, probably no more than two months old, sleepy-eyed with a small pink bow stretched around her nearly bald head. Rabinowitz smiled.

"I don't have skim milk; I only have Cremora," Cal was saying as he walked back into the living room carrying two steaming cups of coffee. "And it's decaf. I hope you don't mind, but I really don't need—where did you get that?" Rabinowitz had stood up to take her mug of coffee. The picture was still in her hand.

"I'm sorry," she stammered. Cal snatched the picture out of Rabinowitz's hand. "Is that your daughter?" she asked quietly. She instantly regretted the question when she saw Cal's entire body stiffen.

"What do you know about it?" he said gruffly, staring solemnly at the picture in his hand.

Rabinowitz took a deep breath. "A lot, actually. You were a beat cop in D.C. for ten years before passing the detective's exam. Captain Rygert at the 62nd Precinct said you were one of the brightest detectives he'd ever seen. Had a natural instinct for the job. Solved a dozen important cases, got a conviction on every one. You even found the D.C. child strangler. No one had any leads at all and then bam!—you caught him. You were a hero; you were the top. Then something happened. It all got you. You started drinking more. Fights with your wife. That sort of thing." Rabinowitz could see by Cal's dejected shoulders that her information was spot on. "And then…" Rabinowitz paused. She wasn't sure if she should deliver the final blow.

"Go on," Cal said, waving his hand at her in an angry yet dejected gesture. "Don't stop now. You're on a roll."

Rabinowitz continued. Her voice had grown soft and quiet. "Then your daughter died," she said softly. Instantly she regretted saying it. Though it had happened over two years ago, from the look of pain that crossed Cal's face, the wound was obviously still quite raw. She felt it best to end her speech as quickly as possible. "Eventually, your marriage fell apart, and you moved here, running away from it all."

"And then I royally fucked up a case by being drunk on the job, got pushed into rehab for my trouble, and now here I am, sitting in a bathrobe in the middle of the morning, having my life read back to me by some chick I hardly know," Cal said loudly, barely controlling the emotion quavering in his voice. "Bravo. Well done, Agent Rabinowitz. The ATF must be so proud. I had no idea their agents were so resourceful. After all, your department royally fucked up that whole Waco thing. But you, you must have really done your homework."

Cal collapsed onto the couch. He was angry and hurt, but he couldn't look Rabinowitz in the eyes, so he looked at his feet instead. "I made a few calls," Rabinowitz demurred quietly.

Cal barked a short, painful laugh. "I bet. I see a few old colleagues from D.C. can't keep their mouths shut. But you know, you got one thing wrong. I didn't come here to 'run away.' I came to start over. There's a difference."

"Not really." Rabinowitz sat on the couch next to Cal. She wanted to reach out and touch him, assure him somehow, but felt too timid to do so. "You couldn't face your problems back in D.C.—couldn't face the idea of waking up as your old self in your old place, with your same old painful life. So you left it, hoping that by changing scenery, you'd change everything else. But it doesn't work that way."

"Oh, God, what are you now, my shrink? Did you major in psychology in college?"

Rabinowitz squared her shoulders. "As a matter of fact, I did," she said. "Double major in psychology and women's studies at Smith."

"Oh, great," Cal said. "A feminist shrink. Now you're going to tell me why none of my relationships work out, either, right?"

"Because you're an arrogant self-loathing jerk who would prefer to objectify women rather than get to know them. It's less dangerous that way. In fact, I'm sure that when you first saw me, your immediate thought ran something along the lines of, 'Damn, what a fine ass that chick has.'"

Cal stared at Rabinowitz, his mouth agape. He never expected her to say something like that. "Actually, when I first saw you, I thought more about your tits than your ass," he replied, wondering if it was the right thing to say.

"Oh," Rabinowitz said, taking the comment in stride. She nodded her assent. "They're good, too," she said.

Cal continued staring at the woman in front of him. "Who are you?" he asked. "Why are you even telling me this?"

Rabinowitz looked Cal directly in the eye. "I'm an ATF agent staring into the face of what is possibly the biggest murder spree this country has seen in years, and every fiber in my being is telling me that the FBI is about to royally fuck this investigation up, and that if someone doesn't do something now, a lot more people are going to die before it's all over. And I'm telling you this because every single person I've spoken to about you all tell me the same thing—that you're a damn good cop, and that if anyone can see through this shit and figure out what the fuck is going on, it's probably you." Rabinowitz took Cal's hands in hers. "Look, I know you've been through some tough shit lately. But we're cops. When we're on the job we put all that aside. Protect and serve, remember? We're here to keep shit like this from happening in this world. If I didn't need you, I wouldn't be here. But I do need you. You know this area; you know the people. But even more than that, you know how to solve a case others can't. It's still in there. I have to believe that. I have to believe what everyone keeps telling me. Otherwise..."

Cal cocked his head to look at her. "Otherwise what?"

Rabinowitz bore her eyes into him. "Otherwise we're all fucked."

DIXON woke up stiff as a board, his neck so painfully bent that he thought it might break if he moved it too much. What time was it? he wondered. His windowless office gave him no clue. He looked at his watch.

Shit.

Dixon bounded out of his office, desperately trying to reappoint his comb-over while cleaning out the creases in his shirt. Ramirez was going to kill him. He couldn't understand why nobody woke him up.

He dashed into the main station house room. The place was crawling with suits. Dixon knew what that meant—Feds. He asked the nearest suit to point out the person in charge and soon found himself standing in front of Agent Nguyen. "Yes?" the agent snapped. "Who are you?"

Before Dixon could reply, one of the other suits laughed and said, "He's the sleeping beauty from the lab." A few of the other agents laughed along with him.

Dixon ignored his flushing cheeks and showed the soil analysis to Nguyen. "What is this?" the FBI man asked. In halting breaths, Dixon explained the significance of the report.

"Yes, yes, we've already seen this, a copy was filed with the other tech reports," Nguyen said. "We wondered where the other copy had gone, but as a rule we automatically double check all reports against their tech copies. These hick station houses have a way of being unorganized. Yes, it was interesting, elephant droppings, and we're working that angle now. Yech—what did you do, spill water all over this paper?"

Dixon did his best to ignore the comment, but found himself not liking the agent in charge a whole lot. "Yes, but you don't understand. Detective Ramirez said this report was particularly important. He said it could break the case wide open."

"Did he?" Agent Nguyen's eyes narrowed as he stared at Dixon intently. "Did he say why?"

"N-no," Dixon stammered. The agent's stare unnerved him.

"And you have no idea why he thought so?" Dixon shook his head. "Very well, then, that doesn't do us much good, does it?" Nguyen snatched the paper from Dixon and stalked off behind him.

"But-but wait!" Dixon called over his shoulder. "Can't we just call Detective Ramirez and ask him why it's so important?"

Nguyen stopped and turned to face Dixon. Those same narrow eyes bore into Dixon again. "Detective Ramirez is dead," he hissed. "I guess you hadn't heard. Now, if you will excuse me…"

Dixon couldn't think of anything except "Fuck you" to say to Agent Nguyen as he walked off, so he said nothing at all. Ramirez was dead. A second later, a horrible thought hit Dixon; what if it was somehow his fault?

CAL took a deep breath. "You think the FBI is fucking the investigation up?" Rabinowitz nodded. "How?"

Rabinowitz stood up and paced the floor. "I can't say anything specifically. It's just this vague feeling I have. Somehow, I think we've all been wrong on this from the get-go."

Cal sighed. "Okay, okay, let's do this. Let's start at the beginning." It was an old police gambit, to talk the case over with your partner; it was a training tool he'd used with Ramirez a lot. *Ramirez. Shit. Try not to think about it.* Cal squared himself. "Okay, what do we got. We got a dead bishop in his car on Monday night. Pulled off on the side of the road."

"Lured there," Rabinowitz said, picking up the thread. "By the highway sign. So if he's lured there, then he wasn't planning on meeting anyone, which probably means he didn't know who killed him."

"*If* the highway sign theory is true, you're probably right," Cal said.

"Of course," Rabinowitz added, "with what we now know, the Bishop almost definitely didn't know his killer."

Cal nodded. "True, true," he said. "Okay, the Bishop is stabbed, what—twelve times? Okay, stabbing is personal, it's up-close, it's bloody, it's dirty work."

"It's violent, aggressive, visceral," Rabinowitz chimed in. "The manner of death suggests rage. But that kind of rage against someone you don't know?"

"The Bishop stood for something. It was symbolic rage," Cal said.

"Symbolic rage, good one," Rabinowitz approved. "You almost sound like a psych major."

Cal smiled. "Let's not get too cocky," he said. "So the Bishop represents...what?"

Rabinowitz took over. "Religious authority. The killer may have been a victim of abuse, maybe he is mad at the church over...I don't know...divorce? Annulment?"

"Most people would kill to get an annulment, not because they got one."

"You don't have to tell me," she said. "Not an annulment, of course."

"You too?"

Rabinowitz shook her head. "Not me personally. My parents. Lovely people, but the most fucked up marriage you ever saw. I've been trying to convince them to get a divorce since I was twelve."

"Twelve?" Cal asked incredulously. "That either makes you one well-adjusted twelve-year-old, or one really screwed up thirty-year-old."

"Or both," Rabinowitz said with a wicked smile. "Anyway..."

"Yeah, you're right. We're way off-topic. Maybe we should move on. Okay. Victim number two. Quaker prayer leader. Also stabbed. In the same manner, the same number of times, the same weapon."

"But a very different creature," Rabinowitz said. "Ideologically, Catholics and Quakers disagree on a lot of things. In fact, except on the most basic stuff, they don't agree at all."

"So it hardly seems reasonable that a psychopath who hates Catholic priests would then go after a Quaker prayer leader?"

Rabinowitz nodded. "Exactly. Why not go after other priests? There are plenty around. Or someone whose ideology is as conserva-tive as a Catholic's? A traditional Anglican, Methodist, Baptist...or even someone more fundamental. But our killer doesn't do that. He goes after someone completely different. The only thing the two victims have in common is, well, Jesus."

Cal took up the train of thought. "So our killer doesn't care which holy men he kills, just as long as it's an actual holy man."

"So it seems," Rabinowitz added. "So, are we saying that we have a guy angry at…God? Striking out at God's envoys here on earth?"

Cal considered this idea. "Could be," he mused. "Could explain those two deaths. But then we have—"

"—Mrs. Oglander," Rabinowitz jumped in. "Who is *not* stabbed. Who is not disfigured or mutilated in any way. No, instead, she's bitten by a snake. Just like—" Rabinowitz broke off.

"Ramirez," Cal added quietly. They both were silent for a second. "So why kill someone with a snake? What does that mean? Do we know for sure it was an actual snake? Could it be someone just wanted it to look like a snake?"

Rabinowitz shook her head. "No, the ME was quite certain it was a snake bite, though she hasn't identified which kind. They're doing a trace on the poison now. She said it was nothing she'd seen before. Nothing indigenous to these parts, she was sure about that." Rabinowitz trailed off. Silence hung in the room. Rabinowitz took a sip of her coffee. It was getting cold, and was entirely too weak for her taste. She would have preferred a mocha latté for her breakfast, but her quick search for a coffee shop this morning had proven quite futile.

"Okay," Cal said, obviously thinking something through. "Okay, so, if we assume that Ramirez was…onto something, then it makes sense to…but, I mean, the question still remains, *why* kill Mrs. Oglander in the first place. And why a snake?"

"Evidence seems to show that Mrs. Oglander was killed outside the prayer hall—a few drops of blood outside a tan Ford. Who knows? Maybe she saw something. Wrong place at the wrong time. As for the snake…" Rabinowitz couldn't answer that question.

"Okay," Cal was saying, "you save the knife for the preachers. They're holy, maybe the knife is holy, maybe the whole thing is sacred. You know, like the Aztecs, how they used to rip the beating hearts out of sacrifice victims? You know, they would just rip open the chest and tear out the heart while it was still pumping and throw the body down their pyramid steps or whatever it was?"

Rabinowitz grimaced. "Ick. Okay, I get your point."

"Sorry. You don't look the squeamish type," Cal said.

"I'm not. But I'm working on one hour of sleep and, no offense, this coffee sucks. So neither is doing much for my constitution."

Cal barked a short laugh. "Yeah, Leah never liked my coffee either," he said.

"Leah?" Rabinowitz asked curiously. "Was she your wife?"

"Yeah." Rabinowitz could tell by the change in Cal's tone that this was another sensitive topic. "Sorry," she said. "I didn't mean to...shall we get back to the Aztecs?"

Cal smiled gratefully for the change in subject. "My point was, maybe this is some kind of sacrifice. A religious experience for the killer."

Rabinowitz considered this idea. "Some sort of crusade. Yeah. I can see that."

"So he can't stab Mrs. Oglander or...anyone else, because it would make the knife un-holy. Is that a word? Un-holy?"

"That's a word."

"Right. Anyway, so, instead of a knife he uses a...snake."

"Not just any snake. An exotic, non-indigenous poisonous species."

"A pet?"

"An illegal pet, if it is one. You can't house a creature like that without a permit." Rabinowitz got a sudden idea. "We could check local animal permits, see if anyone is housing a dangerous species."

"Not a bad idea, though I'd bet this snake is hardly registered with the Kennel Club."

"Funny."

Cal shrugged. "Maybe it's not a pet at all. Maybe it's...a god."

"A god?'

"No, not a god...an idol. An object of worship. You know, like those snake-handling wacko religious nutjobs you see on TV."

"Is that a technical description?"

Cal smirked. "And what do you know about it?"

Rabinowitz returned his smirk. "Snake handlers. Also known as the Church of God with Signs Following. An offshoot of the Pentecostal movement, founded, it is believed, by one George Wert Hensley, circa 1908, in Cleveland."

Cal was amazed. "Ohio?"

"Tennessee, actually. Cleveland is a small town in the Tennessee hills. Now look what you did. You made me lose my flow."

Cal smiled. "My apologies, professor. You were doing admirably. Pray continue."

"Thank you. As I was saying, as legend has it, Hensley was preaching at a small church in Cleveland, *Tennessee,* when a group of local men poured a box full of rattlers out in front of him."

"Why would they do that?"

Rabinowitz shrugged. "Maybe they felt the sermon was going on way too long. Who knows? Anyway, according to the story, Hensley bent over, picked up one of the snakes, and continued preaching with it the entire time. Boom! His legend was born, and so was a new Christian sect.

"The idea picked up some tempo but was never very popular. Like most fundamental and Pentecostal religions, snake handlers adhere to a very strict and literal interpretation of the Bible. One of their favorites is Mark 16:17-18: 'They shall take up serpents and it shall not harm them.' This, and other scripture, gives them the belief that only those truly sanctified by God can handle snakes. Am I impressing you so far with my knowledge of obscure Appalachian religions?"

"Hell, I was impressed when you showed up here this morning. Seeing me in my robe is a true test of anyone's courage."

Rabinowitz laughed. "Anyway, snake handling was outlawed by Tennessee in 1947. A few too many people getting bit and dying. It's outlawed now in all the states where it's practiced, but that hasn't completely killed it. Currently, my office estimates that there are about 2,000 practitioners of snake handling left in the Appalachian mountain range and other rural areas of the southeast."

Cal clapped. "Most impressive. Don't tell me you also majored in theology at Wellesley?"

"Smith. And no, I minored in it. But I am a theological crime and cult specialist for the ATF, remember?"

"Remember? I didn't even know they had such things. Does this mean that snake handlers are considered a cult?"

"Yes, and no. The religion itself is classified as a cult by my office, but the churches are largely autonomous, so we don't watch them too closely. As a group, they're quite diffuse. They don't really communicate or interact with each other all that much, which makes them, generally speaking, much less potentially dangerous than larger, more organized cult religions."

"Really? Do we have a lot of those in the United States?"

Rabinowitz looked pensive. "You'd be surprised. Shocked is more like it. Of course, everyone knows it's usually a very small step from extreme religious fundamentalist to armed militia. Most don't take that step, but we try to keep an eye on the ones that have the potential to do so."

"And your office is the one watching them"

Rabinowitz gave Cal a demure smile. "Mine and others. You'd be surprised by the various groups your government considers to be potentially dangerous cults."

"Really? Like who?"

"Moonies, for example."

Cal scoffed. "That's hardly a surprise."

Rabinowitz considered. "Mormons?"

"Really?" Cal asked. The agent nodded in assertion. "I had no idea. Wow, the entire state of Utah must be like some potential giant powder keg to you guys. And they seemed so nice, what with the Jell-o and all. Oh! And what about the Osmonds? Are you telling me they're dangerous, too?"

Rabinowitz nodded gravely. "We have them under constant surveillance." She burst into a fit of giggles. So did Cal. "Come on," he said. "You've been pulling my leg for a while now."

"Maybe." Rabinowitz sat back down on the couch, next to Cal. "The point is, cults are out there. And they are always a potential threat."

"But the snake handling...I mean, come on, isn't it fake? Aren't those snakes de-fanged or something?"

"It's possible. They may also be milked to reduce their venom, or fed right before handling to make them more docile. But the truth is, most anthropologists who've studied this religion—and to be honest about this that's not a large number—have never concluded that the snakes are as a rule tampered with in any way."

"Really?" Cal asked. "So it's all legit?" Rabinowitz nodded. "So how do they not get bit?"

"They do," Rabinowitz declared. "All the time. And since most members of Pentecostal faiths don't believe in medical science, they tend to die when they get bit. That's why the religion was banned in the first place. Still, some preachers have shown a remarkable ability to handle the snakes without getting bit."

"Yeah, well so did that poor Australian guy who ran around on TV in those way-too-tight shorts saying 'Crikey' or some shit like that all the time," Cal mused lightly. Rabinowitz laughed. "You know who I mean?" Cal asked. She nodded. Cal continued. "So, what about this?" he asked, getting back to the crime. "Could these murders be the result of some snake-handling cult?"

"I don't think so," Rabinowitz said slowly. "First of all, we have no proof that any snake handlers even operate anywhere around here. Of course, they could move. But why Chambersburg? The nature of the crime seems to suggest a more local killer. Plus, snake handlers believe that handling the snake is a sign of their covenant with God. If it was some snake-handling minister gone off the deep end, then one would imagine that the snake itself would be the ritualized murder weapon. But it's the secondary choice. It just doesn't add up. Oh! There's something I forgot to tell you."

"What?"

"The Aramaic."

"The Ara-who?"

"Aramaic. An ancient language. The language of Christ, actually."

"How is that relevant to anything?"

"The message, the one found at both crime scenes. It was written in Aramaic."

"Really? How do we know? What did it say?"

"I took a photograph of the messages over to the college yesterday. A grad student over there identified it for me. He was supposed to working on a translation of it with a Professor Miller, but I never heard back from him. Anyway, early this morning, when the FBI took over, I passed along what I knew and they had it translated."

Cal leaned forward, interested. "What did it say?"

Rabinowitz looked puzzled. "That's just it; it didn't say anything at all. The FBI guy said it was just a bunch of gobbledygook, a hodgepodge of various Aramaic words."

Cal furrowed his brow. "That doesn't make any sense. Why go to all that trouble to write out some message in blood and have it mean nothing?"

"The FBI believes that the Aramaic is in and unto itself the message," she said. "That our killer wasn't trying to write anything specific, but that his use of Aramaic was another attack on the church itself, or something like that. I think at this moment Nguyen—he's the agent in charge—has dismissed the message as being anything useful."

Cal shook his head emphatically. "That doesn't make sense," he began. "Why write a lengthy message if that's the case? One or two words would suffice. And where did he learn the words anyway? Why go through the trouble of teaching it to yourself and then not saying anything with it?"

Rabinowitz agreed. "I can say this; some of the symbols used in the message you could find doing an Internet search. I know; I looked. But I couldn't find a good number of them, well over half."

Cal followed that up. "That's exactly my point. Whoever wrote that message took his time in doing it. Why say nothing with it?" There was a long pause. "Velvet," he said. "Did you say earlier that Mrs. Oglander was killed in the parking lot?"

Rabinowitz consulted her memory. "Yeah. Well, she was attacked there. A few small spots of blood, consistent with the wound, were found by her car."

"Were there any drag marks on her shoes?"

"No," Rabinowitz began. "The parking lot was pavement. There really wouldn't be visible marks."

"I know, I know," Cal said. "Not on the parking lot, but on her shoes. If you dragged her to the church, her shoes would be all scuffed up."

Rabinowitz could begin to see Cal's point. "I see, I see," she said. "No, none of the reports mentioned finding anything like that."

"So whoever it was carried her into the church. Wasn't she a rather large woman?"

Rabinowitz nodded. "At least 250 pounds, probably more."

"That's a lot of weight for one man to carry."

"Yeah, but she probably didn't die right away. Even the most potent venom takes time to work. She might have made it there under her own power."

"But that's just it; that's it exactly! Think about it. We have an attack in the parking lot with a snake. The guy has to control the snake and the victim and still find time to kill the preacher. And Ramirez. I mean, if he got bit by something, wouldn't he still have time to draw his gun? Ramirez was a healthy guy. And even if the venom did kill instantly, how did Mrs. Oglander get into the church?"

Rabinowitz leaned in closely. "Cal, what are you getting at?"

Cal's voice was excited. "Velvet, it's the only thing that makes sense. It was all this talk about cults that brought it to my mind. Contain the snake, restrain the victim, kill the preacher. Carry Mrs. O. into the church. Velvet, don't you see? This isn't just one guy doing this."

Rabinowitz's eyes opened wide. "Cal," she said slowly, "I think you're right."

Cal nodded solemnly. "We don't just have one psycho on our hands," he said. "We've got a whole bunch of them."

DAN carefully parallel parked the patrol car between two other cars on the busy street. It took him about six attempts, but he finally got the patrol car in the spot. Fortunately, the other drivers all waited patiently, with no honking, cussing, or middle-finger gesticulating to frustrate him. It was nice to know some people still respected the police around here.

Dan sighed. Truth is, he was feeling mighty frustrated. The FBI had come in and run roughshod all over his investigation. He had never worked with the FBI before. He had heard stories about small-town sheriffs having to work with the Feds, and in each of those stories the Feds came off like a bunch of big-city jerkwads, trusting none of the local officials to do their jobs while privately wondering if the station house would have indoor plumbing or if they shit into a hole in the ground. Dan grunted. He'd always heard those stories and figured they were just his colleagues blowing off steam. Now he knew they were more truth than fiction.

Dan sighed as he ambled up a crumbly old sidewalk. He knew his office didn't have adequate resources to cover this case; he accepted that. But to be put out to pasture on a case like this…this was a time when everyone should work together. But the FBI has their methods, and they don't need anyone "interfering". Interfering! As if Dan could "interfere" with work going on in his own station house. He swore quietly as he rang the doorbell in front of him. Who the hell did Nguyen think he was anyway? Dan hated how he walked around the station house pretending his farts smelled like Chanel Number 5. Just because it seemed like no one died last night, Nguyen thought he was making progress. Dan took a deep breath and rang the bell again. Making progress? More like treading water. He knew the FBI was no further along than his own office had been.

Dan furrowed his brow in concentration. This morning had been the worst he'd ever spent on the job. To lose one of his own…he'd been the one to tell Ramirez's wife. That was his job. But somehow, in a small town like Chambersburg, he never thought he's ever actually have to do it, to tell one of those women he saw every summer at the barbecue and every December at the Christmas party that her husband wasn't coming home…and then to be pulled from the case by FB-fucking-I…Dan rang the doorbell again and started pounding on the door. "Hello?" he called. "Chambersburg PD! HELLO!" He was out answering a routine call. Neighbor complaint. The dispatch operator had said that the guy calling sounded old. Dan sighed. Probably just some retired coot complaining about the neighbors having a party and not inviting him. He hadn't answered one of these calls since he was a patrol cop fifteen years ago, but this way, he kept busy. And right now that was damned important to him. "Hello!" he shouted, pounding the door again. "Anybody home?"

Finally Dan could hear a shuffled walk and a muffled yell in reply. The door opened, and he was right—an old codger stood before him, eighty if he was a day, completely bald and covered in wrinkles. "Mr. Shaw?" Dan asked. "I'm from the Chambersburg PD. I heard you called in a complaint about your neighbor?"

The old man stared at Dan for a minute. "I'm sorry I took so long answering the door," he said. "I was taking a wizz."

"Right," Dan said, waiting for him to go on. Unfortunately, Mr. Shaw went on about taking a leak. "I knew as soon as I went to the bathroom you'd come. That's how it always happens. One time, I was waiting for the cable guy—you know how they make you wait—and I had to go real bad, not a wizz you know, but a number two, but I didn't want to miss him cuz then I wouldn't get to watch my shows, and, anyway, long story short, I got so bunched up I didn't number two for four days."

"Mr. Shaw—"

"I don't think that's very healthy, do you? Anyway, I figured you would wait, since it was only a wizz, and I came out as fast as I could, didn't even take time to wash my hands, to tell you the truth of it..."

"Mr. Shaw, I'm here about your neighbor."

"Oh, she's nice young woman, always takes her garbage out on time, keeps the porch nice and neat."

"You'd like to make a complaint against her?"

The old man stared at Dan blankly. "No, no, why do you say that?"

"Mr. Shaw, if you don't wish to raise a charge, then why did you call the police?"

"I found her purse."

Dan waited again for Mr. Shaw to finish his statement. Apparently, that was it. "Well, that's nice of you, Mr. Shaw, but if you're sure it's hers, you can just return it on your own. We trust you to handle that. I'm sure she'll be grateful you found it for her."

"I tried. She didn't answer when I rang the bell this morning."

I know what that's like, Dan thought. "Perhaps she's out of town."

"Her car is in the lot. Besides, a woman don't go nowhere without her purse."

"Perhaps she's still asleep. Maybe she doesn't know it's missing yet."

"It was in the yard," Mr. Shaw said.

"In the yard?" Dan asked. "What do you mean?"

"Just what I said. I found it this morning in the yard. All tipped out and open like it was flung there. Thought that was a little strange." Something about the description of the purse made Dan feel uneasy. An alarm bell started ringing in his head. "Anyway," Mr. Shaw continued, "I figured with what's been going on and all, I should report it to the police."

"Mr. Shaw," Dan asked slowly, almost dreading the response, "what does your neighbor do for a living?"

"She's a minister," Mr. Shaw said. "Methodist. At that small church down on Sycamore. That's why I called you. Now do you see?"

"Yeah," Dan said, the feeling of slow dread coursing through his body. "I see, Mr. Shaw. I see."

"SO what are we talking about here?" Cal was saying. "A large group like the Manson family?"

"No, something smaller," Rabinowitz said. "Two, maybe three. A pair or trio of symbolic brothers, one dominant, leading the others in everything."

"This completely changes the investigation," Cal said. "The psychology we've assumed from the start is all wrong."

"But it's a good jumping-off place," Rabinowitz replied. "Why, now we can—" She was interrupted by the ringing of her phone. A second later, Cal's own telephone exploded in noise. They looked at each other for a moment, and then, as their phones exploded again, each picked up during the second ring.

"Hello?" they said, almost simultaneously.

There was a long pause on the other end. "Are you both there?" an angry voice yelled out. It was Dan.

"We're both here," Cal said.

"Velvet, did you find Cal? Is he okay?"

"He's fine, Dan," Rabinowitz said.

"Really?"

"Yeah, Dan, honestly. We're both been doing some thinking about the case, too. We may have a new theory that'll help open it up."

"Save it for now. Tell me when you get here."

"Get where?" Rabinowitz asked.

"I'm at 129 Winterbourne Ave. Upstairs apartment. You two need to get your butts here now."

"Has there been another murder?" Cal asked. Dan didn't answer. He didn't need to. They already knew.

"Just get here," Dan said again before hanging up.

BY the time Cal and Rabinowitz arrived at the scene, more than a dozen FBI agents were swarming all over the small apartment. And with them were several news crews.

"Dan, the media?" Cal asked incredulously. Dan shrugged. "It wasn't my idea," he said.

"It was mine," a voice said from behind them. Cal turned and saw a short FBI agent staring at him, with a small but salient smirk on his face.

"Detective Evans, Agent Nguyen," Dan said by way of introduction.

"We've already met," Nguyen said smugly. "On the White-Chappel case in D.C. That was some good work you did."

"Yeah, thanks," Cal said unevenly. "What's with the news crews? Haven't been on television enough lately in D.C.?"

Agent Nguyen's smile grew wider. "Always ready with a quip, Cal. You haven't changed a bit." Nguyen took two steps towards the house, then turned to respond to Cal's earlier remark. "But to answer your question, the media is here because it serves as the most effective warning to other possible victims out there. By the end of the day this will be the top story on every news network in the country, local and national. It's important that the public be warned on all aspects of the case. I've already given them a briefing, informing them that the FBI has now taken over jurisdiction and keeping them apprised of all our progress. I've scheduled another press conference for noon. Stick around to watch, if you like." And with that same smug smile Nguyen walked back into the crime scene as several reporters followed him.

"I wasn't aware you two were acquainted," Dan remarked to Cal.

"Old friends," Cal replied sarcastically. "Dan, have you been inside? What's the scene like?"

Dan sighed. "Like all the others," he said. "Blood everywhere. That woman was gutted practically from head to toe." Dan paused. "You two said you have something?"

Rabinowitz's phone rang. "Excuse me," she said to Dan and Cal, who were busy conferring on their new theory of the crime. She took a few steps away from them, plugged her other ear with her finger, and opened up her phone. "Rabinowitz," she said evenly. She listened. "I'm sorry, can you speak up?" Between the media bustling and moving about and noise on the scene, it was difficult to hear. "Are you sure?" she said again after listening for a few minutes. "Okay, okay. Where? We'll be right there."

She walked over to Dan and Cal. "Hey," she said to Cal. "We gotta go."

Cal surveyed the scene before him. "We should stay here, try to help out—"

Rabinowitz grabbed Cal by the arm. "We gotta go. Now."

MINUTES before, Professor Beatrice Miller was seated comfortably in her stuffed wingback chair, her back erect, her eyes glued to the television screen. This was a new experience for her; rarely did she watch television, and when she did, she was never really all that interested in it.

She could hear her graduate student out in the kitchen, making a pot of coffee. Even from another room, Professor Miller could hear the lethargy in his steps and actions.

They'd been up all night working on the translation. Even after Abe had found out that the FBI had already completed translating the text, Professor Miller still found herself intellectually curious about the text. It was, after all, a delicious riddle—a message in an ancient language left at the scene of a bloody murder. It sounded like something straight out of a detective novel.

They had finally finished the translation an hour ago. When they read it, they were surprised at what they found. It was—chilling, to say the least. Professor Miller shrugged. Clearly a very disturbed person was perpetuating these crimes.

The television was now reporting on the very same information Professor Miller and Abe had uncovered. The FBI man was speaking. "We've discovered that the message the killer has left behind on the walls is written in ancient Aramaic, but, unfortunately, the message is nothing more than a hodgepodge of various Aramaic words. It doesn't tell us anything." As he spoke, the news channel showed a photograph of the message—the very photograph Professor Miller was now clutching in her hand. The news channel flashed away from the FBI agent for a moment. "Now joining us is Dr. Achmed Gomes, a specialist in Arabic and Biblical languages from Georgetown University. Welcome, Dr. Gomes. Can you tell our viewers something about Aramaic?"

While her colleague gave a brief morning lecture to the news audience, Professor Miller became lost in her thoughts. Doesn't tell us anything? How absurd! The man was wrong—very, very wrong.

"Abe!" she called out. "Abe!" again, more insistent.

She heard the hard padding of tired footsteps. "Yes?" he said sleepily.

"Call your friend, the FBI agent, call her at once!"

"She's an ATF agent, Professor Miller, and we called her last night, remember? She never called me back. She's probably really busy right now."

"I know that," Professor Miller said curtly. "But they just had it on the news. And it's wrong. It's all horribly wrong. We must talk to them. Tell them the truth. They need to know what it says." Abe stared at her, still tired and a bit stupefied. "What are you waiting for?" Professor Miller was saying. "Call her. Now!"

RABINOWITZ followed Abe's directions to an old, rambling brick house tucked in the back lot of a small cul-de-sac on a tree-lined street. Parking behind a red Nissan SUV in the driveway, she and Cal bounded out of her car and up the front steps of the house.

The door opened before they could knock. A concerned-looking older woman gave them both furtive glances. "Agent Rabinowitz?" she asked uncertainly, glancing between Rabinowitz and Cal. "Yes, ma'am," Rabinowitz answered, reaching out her hand. "That's me." The older woman took Rabinowitz's hand and shook it softly. "I'm Beatrice Miller," she said. "Velvet Rabinowitz," the comely agent replied. She nodded in Cal's direction. "This is my partner, Detective Evans of the Chambersburg Police Department." Cal winced when Rabinowitz called him her "partner." It sounded weird to hear that from someone other than Ramirez. Still, he managed a grim smile as he shook Professor Miller's hand. "Thanks for contacting us, ma'am," he said. "We understand you have some information that you think might be helpful to us."

"Oh yes, I do, I do, come in, please, come in," Professor Miller said as she opened her front door wide and, with a sweep of her arm, welcomed the two police officers into her home. "Welcome."

After seeing her office firsthand, Rabinowitz had expected that the home would also be in the same state of messy disarray. But to her surprise it was neat as a pin, almost spartan, simple Shaker furniture occasionally interrupted by an unusual artifact that was somehow no doubt representative of this woman's life work. Rabinowitz gave Professor Miller an appraising glance. She was a tall woman, and had probably been quite handsome in her day, though she was now fast approaching sixty. She had a marvelous bun of steel-gray hair, thick, lined glasses, and red-rimmed eyes indicating a lack of sleep. Rabinowitz would have half-expected her to be wrapped in an old shawl that covered a frilly white blouse and a long woolen skirt. Instead, the professor wore a polyester pantsuit in white and aqua blue that screamed 1972. Rabinowitz grimaced, just a bit. The outfit definitely didn't match her idea of what a classicist should wear. It was also not enhanced by the simple silver cross Professor Miller wore around her neck; rather, those clothes cried for big plastic beads and numerous clanging bracelets.

"Please, have a seat," Professor Miller was saying, indicating a stuffed sofa near the entrance of the home. Cal and Rabinowitz sat, while the Professor herself chose a simple wooden-backed chair facing them. "Would you care for some tea?" she asked the two detectives decorously, and before they could nod their assent, Professor Miller craned her head and bellowed loudly, "Abe! They're here! Bring the tea!" Smiling excitedly, the Professor then turned her blue eyes back onto the two detectives.

Rabinowitz coughed discreetly. "Professor Miller, I don't mean to be in a rush, but your student said on the phone that you had some information that could help us. I'm assuming that this relates to the message I left with him yesterday?"

Professor Miller nodded vigorously, her cheeks flushed red with excitement. "Oh, yes, at least I think so, I really do, if what I've heard on the television is quite accurate anyway. You see—" Professor Miller stopped as Abe came into the room just then, bearing a tray loaded with cups of tea, cream, and a plate of snicker doodle cookies. He placed the tray on the coffee table in front of her. "Oh, good," she said, passing out the tea. "Cream, Detective?"

Cal could not help but feel that this whole scene was a little ridiculous. Taking his cup of tea gingerly, he wondered if this old woman really had anything useful to tell them. After all, cops always got a lot of crank calls during any big case, and this woman looked and seemed as though she had a few too many bats in her belfry to be some ancient languages expert. "No, thanks," Cal said, placing the cup in front of him. He hated tea, but helped himself to two of the cookies. Oh, well, Cal thought. If nothing else, I'll get a quick breakfast out of the deal.

Professor Miller finished passing out the tea. She settled back in her chair with a small "oomph" and surveyed the group sitting around here. Like any good teacher, Professor Miller loved an audience. "Now, before we begin, perhaps we should have introductions all around, hmm? Abe, I believe you know Agent Rabinowitz."

The young man nodded. "Yeah, we've met. Did you get my message last night?"

Rabinowitz shook her head. "No, I didn't. Did you leave it on my cell phone?"

"No," Abe said. "I was worried that maybe you were re-charging your phone or something, so I called the police station directly and left the message there. The man I spoke with said he'd give it to you."

"Well, he didn't," Rabinowitz said, giving Cal a meaningful glance.

Cal frowned. "Another brilliant play by the FB-fucking-I," he muttered. Realizing what he just said, Cal quickly apologized. "I'm sorry, Professor Miller. I'm not used to having to mind my language so much."

"Don't worry about it, Detective," Professor Miller archly replied. "I don't mind a good expletive now and again myself." The professor turned to her graduate student. "Abe, this is Detective Evans."

"Cal," Cal said, extending his hand. The pudgy graduate student stood up to meet Cal's hand. He had a surprisingly strong grip. "Abe Ruth," he said in reply. "Abe Ruth?" Cal said with a small laugh before he could help himself. "Are you serious?" The young student flushed and nodded. "Let me guess, your dad was a big baseball fan, right?" Abe shook his head. "Actually, it was my mom," he said, sitting back down.

Cal shook his head, still chuckling slightly. "Abe Ruth, Velvet Rabinowitz. I can just imagine both your mothers sitting somewhere together, picking out baby names, each one trying to out-weird the other."

"You're one to talk, Caldwell," Rabinowitz replied, more-than-gently punching Cal on his shoulder. Abe shrugged and shook his head. "It's an odd name, for sure. I think my mom was disappointed I never played baseball at all, either. Not even Little League."

"People, please," Professor Miller cut in, sounding slightly exasperated. "There is a serious matter at hand here."

"We're sorry, ma'am," Rabinowitz said, delicately nibbling on a cookie. "We mean no disrespect. When I got Abe's phone call this morning, we both came over as quickly as we could to hear what you have to say."

"Yes, and I appreciate that."

"But I feel I should tell you," Rabinowitz continued before Professor Miller could go on, "that the FBI had a specialist already translate the Aramaic found at the crime scenes. He determined that the message was just a bunch of nonsense."

"Yes, I know," Professor Miller said. "They reported that on the news. After I saw that, I had Abe call you immediately."

"Well, then, I don't understand what we can do for you, ma'am," Cal said. "If the message is completely meaningless…"

"But it's not meaningless. Not at all. It has a very significant meaning."

Cal furrowed his brow in thought. "Are you suggesting that the Aramaic is some kind of code…that maybe we should have a cryptographer examine it?"

Professor Miller shook her head vigorously. "I'm not saying that. I'm not saying that at all."

Rabinowitz leaned forward. "I'm confused then, Professor Miller. What light can you shed on the Aramaic message that the FBI expert could not?"

Professor Miller's eyes shone in triumph. "I can start by telling you this—that message is not in Aramaic. Not at all. And I am willing to wager that that is far more significant that you can even imagine."

WITH a bit of a cocksure gait, Agent Nguyen strolled before a throng of frenzied reporters, each one with a hand and microphone desperately thrust into the air, a dozen questions being posed a second. Dan watched him in silence from the back of the room, his face a mask of impassive stone that barely concealed his contempt for the scene he was witnessing. Nguyen took a moment to survey the reporters before him, and then raised his hands for silence. "The FBI is naturally very concerned over the activities of the man you've all dubbed the 'Clergy Killer.'" Dan winced. Still it was better than the names being tossed around the office—the Reverend Ripper, the Minister Mangler, the Father Fillet-er. "Please be assured we are taking every precaution necessary. As a matter of fact," Nguyen added, "I've pulled FBI and other Federal agents off of duty shifts from West Virginia, Maryland, Washington, D.C., and Virginia to ensure that every local clergyman and woman will have his or her own personal guard tonight. We will do everything we can to ensure the safety of the good religious leaders of Chambersburg." Dan knew that while Nguyen sounded calm and officious, he was really throwing down a challenge to the killer. He knew that Nguyen hoped the killer would try to breach one of the FBI's defenses and expose himself. Of course, if Cal and Agent Rabinowitz were correct, and there was a group of two or three men committing these crimes…Dan sighed. He hoped those Federal agents knew what they were getting into.

"**WHAT** do you mean it's not Aramaic?" Rabinowitz said, keenly interested. "Abe identified it as Aramaic, and the FBI expert confirmed and translated it.

"I know, but he's wrong," Abe said, his face a bit flushed. "So was I. It *looks* like Aramaic. It shares a lot of the same properties. In fact, they're probably closely related languages. One of them is an elevated offshoot of the other. You see—"

"I, too, thought it was standard first-century Aramaic at first," Professor Miller said, leaning back against the hard wooden back of her chair. "But maybe we'd better start at the beginning. Tell me, Detectives, what do you know about the Dead Sea Scrolls?"

"The Dead Sea Scrolls?" Cal was surprised. "I've heard of them, of course, but I don't know anything about them." He turned to Rabinowitz. "Velvet," he said to her, "this sounds like something that would be right up your alley."

She gave Cal a small, slightly pained smile. "I'm more of an expert on contemporary religious activity," she said, adding, "but I'll tell you what I know. The Dead Sea Scrolls are a series of religious texts, found in the Israeli desert some fifty years ago—in caves near the Dead Sea, obviously. Mostly various versions of the Bible—the earliest versions that have ever been discovered, from what I understand. Obviously they're a very important archaeological find, but other than that, I'm not sure what I can add."

"You've started us off well, Agent Rabinowitz," Professor Miller purred. "But let me fill in the necessary blanks. The Dead Sea Scrolls are the name given to a large finding of complete scrolls and scrolls fragments that were first discovered by native Bedouin peoples in 1948 at a small abandoned Jewish outpost called Qumran. The site had been known to scholars for centuries, but was largely ignored because it seemed insignificant—that is, until the scrolls were discovered there. The climate and area around the Dead Sea are as perfect for preserving manuscripts as the climate in Egypt is for preserving mummies. The find was truly the most astonishing to date in Biblical archaeology."

"That's all very well and good, Professor," Cal interrupted. "But how does this relate to the case we've got going on today?"

"Bear with me, Detective, and I'll get to that as quickly as I can. Believe me when I say that this information will all become relevant soon enough. After the initial discovery was made a team of archaeologists was selected to work on translating, preserving, and researching the history of the scrolls. Here is a brief version of what they uncovered.

"The scrolls were mostly written between the first century BC and the first century AD. The Qumran settlement was populated at that time by a group called the Essenes. The Essenes were Jewish fundamentalists, believing in a strict and superior interpretation of Talmudic law. They gained a reputation for being stern and strict Biblical interpreters—more zealous than the Zealots, if you will."

Cal was lost. "So...you're saying that they were a bunch of religious fruitcakes?" he queried.

Professor Miller pondered this. "It's a crude way of putting it," she said. "Religious fundamentalism was certainly more admired in their day, though I daresay many of the individuals around them found their activities a bit extreme. Oh, they weren't violent people— far from it, as a matter of fact. Pliny the Elder mentions their peaceful ways, as does Josephus, the famous Jewish historian. Think of them as a type of cult—a peaceful cult, but a group as fanatic as any cult today."

Cult. At that word, Cal's ears pricked right up.

"As I was saying, the Essences inhabited Qumran. It was mostly a deserted area, so they were largely left alone by the various authorities of their day to do their own thing in relative peace and quiet. We don't know as much about them as we should, but they did leave behind the Dead Sea Scrolls. Some of the texts were versions of Old Testament books or other popular religious texts, and some included proscriptions for daily life at the Qumran settlement. All of it was most illuminating, though nothing discovered was as revolutionary as some might have hoped for.

"What is of particular interest is that the texts came in a multitude of languages—Hebrew, Aramaic, and even Greek texts were found. This suggests a very educated population, or at least an educated caste within the community's small populace. Quite likely their Council of Elders, the group of twelve men who governed the community, were mostly responsible for this. This group was lead, by the way, by the Essenes' Teacher of Righteousness. He would have been their religious as well as political leader, very well educated, a man of peace and learning. In fact, some of the texts tell of the crucifixion of one Teacher of Righteousness by the wicked priest-king Alexander Janneus in 88 BC, an act the Essenes decried but did little about."

"A crucifixion?" Cal asked. "Like Jesus?"

Professor Miller cocked her head and gave Cal an approving glance. "There have been some parallels drawn between the Essenian Teacher of Righteousness and the New Testament's portrayal of Jesus Christ," she said. "Some people have even suggested that Christ was an Essene himself, that at one time he held the post of Teacher of Righteousness. Still, there's no real evidence of that, and crucifixion was not an uncommon method of capital punishment in Roman times." She paused to take a sip of her tea. Cal took the chance to grab two more cookies. Rabinowitz gave him a slightly disapproving glance. Professor Miller ignored them and continued. "Where was I? Oh yes, I mention all of this—the languages the texts were in— because in 1952 an extraordinary discovery was made. Two of them, actually. In a cave north of the settlement archaeologists found a grouping of fragments that at first seemed to be non-Biblical texts written in Aramaic. When translated, however, they made no sense. It was just a bunch of nonsensical gibberish. So a group of linguists tackled the problem anew. They eventually discovered that the text written on these parchment fragments was not Aramaic at all, but a distinct language derived from the Aramaic tongue. Aramaic was its originating language, but this was a distinct social dialect of the mother tongue."

"Okay, hold up," Cal said. "You lost me somewhere around social dialect. What are we talking about exactly here?"

"Look at it this way," Abe said excitedly. He fished around in a small desk behind him and pulled out a pad of paper and a stray pencil. "Imagine your name written in all capital letters. C-A-L E-V-A-N-S. Imagine that this is your name written in Aramaic. Okay?"

"Okay," Cal said slowly. Rabinowitz nodded that she understood as well.

"Now let's write your name in all lowercase letters. c-a-l e-v-a-n-s. You see how some of the symbols—the 'c', the 'v', and the 's'— remain the same in both versions? Even if someone had never seen any lowercase letters before, they would recognize the phonetic value of the 'c', 'v', and 's'. Right?"

"Right," Rabinowitz said. Cal could hear the interest in her voice.

"Thus, some of the letters would be recognizable. However, just as many of them would not. The capital 'A', for example, has a distinct look from the lowercase 'a'. And so on. Thus at a cursory glance one might recognize a few of the letters and say, 'This is an Aramaic text.' That's what I did when I saw that message on that church wall. But the truth is, it's not at all."

"Social dialects are created to foster a type of communication that keeps out certain castes of people," Professor Miller said, picking up the lecture. "In the case of the documents found in the north cave in 1952, it was eventually decided that, at some point in their history, the Essenian Council of Elders must have decided to create a social dialect based on the common language of Aramaic so that they might communicate amongst themselves without the rest of the community comprehending what they are saying. It's not that uncommon, really. Most societies have one form of social dialect or another. Regardless, this language was dubbed High Essenian by the linguists studying it. To any outsider, the words all looked Aramaic, but made no sense. But to someone who had knowledge of the language, a coherent message could be deciphered from the text."

"So you're telling us," Rabinowitz said, catching on, "that the message we found at the crime scene is High Essenian."

"Exactly," Professor Miller said with a triumphant smile.

"How exactly does that help us?" Cal asked. "I mean, what makes one old language all that different from another?"

"Ahh, but this is an exceedingly rare 'old language,' as you call it. It's known to only a select few scholars in the world. That's why that FBI expert misunderstood the message so completely. The only reason I understood it was because my own mentor, Elijah Grund, was one of the project leaders on the 1952 dig."

"How many people are we talking about here?" Cal asked.

Professor Miller shrugged. "Twenty, twenty-five, at most," she replied.

"But couldn't our killer have just lifted this message straight from the texts you just told us about?" Rabinowitz asked.

Professor Miller shook her head. "Those texts have never been published, Detective. They are only known to a small select group in the academic community. The High Essenian texts have never been released to the public at large. Many scholars don't even know they exist."

"So you're telling us that that message was written by one of a few select experts in the field?" Cal asked incredulously. "That our killer is some sort of religious archaeology expert? Because, quite frankly, that seems a bit farfetched to me."

"I'm not saying anything like that, Detective," Professor Miller responded. "I can only tell you what the message is. Figuring out how it got there is your area of expertise."

"But you can translate it?" Rabinowitz said. "You know what it says?"

Professor Miller nodded anxiously "Oh yes, I do indeed. We both do."

"Well?" Cal asked after an interminable pause. "What does it say?"

Professor Miller took a moment and glanced unwarily around the room. Then, in a low voice, she intoned the bloody message's meaning: "Leave the Christ alone; he does not belong to you."

"NGUYEN! Nguyen!" Dan called out across the station house. The press conference had lasted over an hour. Dan was only now getting a chance to talk to FBI agent about Cal and Rabinowitz's theory.

"Look, Agent, we need to talk. My detectives have found out some stuff that might help you out."

Nguyen eyeballed Dan warily. "I have to brief my district commander now," he said. "We can meet in an hour." He started walking away.

"An hour may be too late!" Dan called out. He saw Nguyen stop, take a deep breath, and turn around.

"Very well," the FBI man finally said. "But this had better be good."

THE bloody words' message had stunned the room into a cold silence. Even Abe, who had read the message several times, felt an eerie dread course through his body upon hearing the words aloud. "Jesus Christ," Cal said, suddenly realizing the irony of his outburst. "I mean, damn, 'Leave the Christ alone'—that just leaves you cold, you know?"

"Yeah, I do," Rabinowitz said. "I mean, I'm Jewish and it even freaks *me* out."

"But what does it mean?" Cal asked, furrowing his brow in thought. Rabinowitz shrugged; she was still too stunned to form a truly coherent thought. Cal rounded on Professor Miller. "Professor, does it mean anything to you?"

The Professor slowly shook her head. "I'm afraid not," she said. "It's pretty awful, whatever it means."

Cal paused for a moment. "Professor, does this make sense? I mean the connection between that message and the Essenes at all?"

"No, truly, I can't think of one."

"What happened to them? To the Essenes, I mean."

"Oh, well, that's an interesting question, actually." Professor Miller stopped to take another sip of her tea. She grimaced a bit. "It's gone cold," she said. "Anyway, where was I? Oh, the Essenes. Yes, it's an interesting story. According to Pliny, sometime around 66 AD the Jewish peoples living under Roman subjugation revolted; the Essenes weren't a part of this at first, but they must have eventually joined up, because the Romans laid siege to Qumran around 70 AD. You have to understand; Qumran was built on a rocky plateau and with a few recent modifications had been turned into an excellent fortress. Eventually, though, the Romans won out, and the Essenes were slaughtered to a man."

"That's strange," Rabinowitz said. "If they were so peace loving, why would they take up arms so suddenly?"

Professor Miller shrugged. "It's one of the many mysteries that surrounds the Essenes and the Dead Sea Scrolls," she said. "One can only surmise that, like many other Jews at the time, they got caught up in the fervor of Jewish independence."

"What about Gaius Constans?" Abe shot in with an eager look at his mentor. "What about his version of the Essenian downfall?"

"Gaius who?" Cal asked. "Who's that?"

"Gaius Constans," Abe answered. "An early second-century historian based out of Constantinople. He's the only one who provides any details of the Roman siege of Qumran."

"It's a bunch of utter nonsense," Professor Miller added. "Gaius Constans was no historian; he collected old wives' tales and fantastic legends. He's good for a few chuckles, but was possibly the worse historian in recorded history."

"But what does he say about the Essenes?" Rabinowitz asked out of curiosity.

Professor Miller sighed. "Oh, that they had become pagan idol-worshippers or some such nonsense. That they had turned away from Judaism altogether. Utter rubbish. I will say that there is some evidence that the Essences included a form of idol worship in their daily prayers, but this is hardly unheard of in early Judaism, and certainly nothing like what Gaius Constans writes about. And the other things Constans says are absurd. That the Essenes believed they could bring about the coming of the Messiah. Or that they were immortal beings. Or that they were killing innocent passers-by for sport! Really, it's nothing but anti-Semitic sensationalism."

"I don't know," Cal said evenly. "Don't Christians believe they're immortal too?"

"The soul, yes," Professor Miller said with a smile. "Thanks of course to Christ's sacrifice on the cross. But this is not the type of immortality Gaius Constans writes about. He insinuates that the Essenes could not be pierced by sword or arrow—and then has them being cut down by the Romans on the very next page. Really, what he writes is more appropriate for the old legends, Gilgamesh and Enkidu and the like."

"Getting back to the matter of the High Essenian language," Rabinowitz said. "Professor, can you provide us with a list of anyone in, say, the northeastern United States who may be proficient enough to write that message?"

"Of course," Professor Miller said. She took Abe's notepad in her hand and, tearing off a clean sheet, began to compose her list. "I'm afraid, though, that it will be a very short list. And I certainly don't know everyone who may be proficient in the matter. As you may know, my area of expertise is Greek. I only know of the High Essenian through my old mentor, as I said. And I certainly can't imagine any of these individuals being involved in such heinous crimes as these are."

"Anything will be a help," Rabinowitz said. "We need to start somewhere. Perhaps there's someone else we can talk to to create a more comprehensive list. Perhaps your old mentor—what did you say his name was?"

"Grund. Elijah Grund. I'm afraid he won't be of much help you, though." Professor Miller leaned towards Rabinowitz and lowered her voice conspiratorially. "He has Alzheimer's. It's so sad. He was probably the smartest man I have ever known. Jewish history scholar. Absolutely brilliant. An absolute expert on so many ancient Biblical languages. I'd heard he was a Holocaust survivor, but he never talked about it. He does live around here, though, in a nursing home in Quincy. I'll get you his address. He has his good days, though they are few and far between. I try to get out and see him when I can. Here you go," she said, handing Rabinowitz her list. Rabinowitz saw about a half dozen names in a shaky but somehow elegant scrawl. "Those are the people I can think of that are located in the northeast, as you request. If you like, I'll compile a more comprehensive list using some indexes around the house here and e-mail that to you later."

"That would be great," Rabinowitz said. She took a card out of her pocket. "My e-mail is listed here, as is my cell phone, should you need to reach us. We can't thank you enough, Professor Miller. You've given us a very interesting lead."

"I only hope it helps," she said. The group stood up and Professor Miller walked her guests to the door. "I have a question," Cal popped in all of a sudden. "Professor Miller, you said that they uncovered two dramatic finds in that cave in 1952. One was the High Essenian documents. What was the other?"

Professor Miller gave Cal an indulgent smile. "It's funny you should mention that," she said, "because, when it was uncovered, it really was quite a sensation. What they found were two scrolls, wholly complete, fashioned entirely out of thin sheets of copper."

"Copper?" Cal asked incredulously. Professor Miller smiled, her eyes twinkling with the joy of an educator reaching one of her pupils. "Why was it made of copper? What was written on it?"

"A treasure map," Professor Miller announced dramatically.

Cal stopped cold. "Really? An honest-to-goodness treasure map?"

Professor Miller nodded. "Yes, well, at least, the map was real enough. It gave a listing of various caches of coins and other items of worth and directions to find them. Of course it turned out to be completely useless. In the end, the whole matter was regarded as some form of Essenian hoax."

"A hoax?" Cal asked. His eyebrows shot up. "That doesn't make any sense. Why go through all that trouble for some weird joke, especially when it's hidden away in a cave like that?"

Professor Miller shrugged. "Who can say? There are so many mysteries from ancient times. That's what makes their study so fascinating—and so important."

Cal nodded thoughtfully. "Well, thanks again, Professor, and Abe—for everything."

"Thank you Detectives," Professor Miller said. Then, quietly, she added, "You know, I've always been a Catholic, always been a believer. I knew Bishop Okeke personally, and I believe he was a good man. I don't know who is behind this—if the man is ill or what—but I hope and pray to God that you catch him."

Cal gave Rabinowitz a look before turning back to Professor Miller. "So do I," he said. "So do I."

"WHAT do you expect me to do?" Nguyen was saying. He ran a flustered hand through his thinning dark hair. "What can we do that we aren't already doing?"

"I know this isn't much to go on," Dan replied, "but it does give us a whole new direction to look in—"

"Look," Nguyen interrupted tersely, "if everything goes according to plan, we'll catch this guy tonight. End of story."

"I know all about your plan," Dan said, "and it's pretty fucking crazy if you ask me."

"Well, I didn't," Nguyen replied.

"You can't just draw this guy out. It's not just one guy. It's a fucking committee, Nguyen. *They're* not going to fall for it."

"It's only a theory that this is the work of some weird group or cult, Sheriff. An unsubstantiated theory at that. I doubt we have another Manson family on our hands. And even if we did, my plan still holds firm. Draw them out. They've attacked three nights in a row. You know serial killers don't alter their patterns. This guy is in a groove. He'll attack again tonight—and we'll be ready for him."

"That's what I keep telling you," Dan said. "It's not just some guy—it's a group of them. Your men won't be expecting it, even if it does all go down as you think it will."

Nguyen's eyes flashed with anger. "My men are the best trained agents in this country," he said. "And they're backed up by teams from all over the district and the state police."

"Don't forget the local police department," Dan added dryly.

Nguyen eyed Dan warily. "And the local PD," he said. "They're prepared for whatever is out there."

"You're playing with people's lives here, Agent."

Nguyen stuck an angry finger in Dan's face. "I know what I'm doing, Sheriff." His voice was no more than a terse whisper. "You'd be well advised not to question that."

Dan sighed. He was getting nowhere. "Look, maybe Cal can explain it to you better than I can—" Dan's thought was interrupted by a knock at the door. Cal popped his head in. "Mind if I interrupt?" he asked, squeezing into the room. Nguyen rolled his eyes. "Great timing," Dan said. "I was just trying to explain to Agent Nguyen the basis of your multiple perp theory. For the third time."

"Forget that for the moment," Cal said. "I've got some new information you're not gonna believe." As quickly as possible he told Dan and Agent Nguyen all about Professor Miller's interpretation of the message and what she had relayed to them about the Essenes.

"'Leave the Christ alone,'" Dan repeated, muttering to himself. "Jesus Christ, what does that mean?"

"This is all very—" Agent Nguyen was searching for the right word "—remarkable, but do you have anything to back it up?"

"What do you mean?" Cal asked.

"Our expert says one thing, yours says another."

"Listen, Nguyen, you should talk with her. She knows what she's talking about."

"Still," Nguyen considered, "none of it changes our primary objective or our course of action for tonight."

"The hell it doesn't!" Cal exploded. "We've got some modern-day cult acting like some weird, ancient group of killers and you're still acting like we're dealing with your average, run-of-the-mill psychopath out here!"

"No," Dan interjected, cutting off Cal's tirade, "Agent Nguyen is right."

"What?!" Cal said. "Dan, you cannot be serious."

"Listen to me, Cal," Dan replied evenly. "Right now, our primary responsibility has to be to protect the clergy in this town as best we can. This person—these people—aren't above breaking and entering or killing innocent by-standers to get what they want. Securing the townsfolk has to be our number-one duty."

"But Dan—"

"I don't like it anymore than you, Cal. But that's the call the FBI has made. We've got to support them in that."

"I'm glad to hear you say that," Agent Nguyen chimed in. "Because I've assigned you and your officers duty posts tonight."

"It doesn't mean I agree with it," Dan said to Nguyen. "Or that between now and then we won't work on advancing Cal's theory."

"You can do what you want," Nguyen said. "I'd advise you to get some sleep, though, gentlemen." He was at the door and opened it to leave. "We're all going to be in for a very long night."

"What an asshole," Cal said after the door had closed behind Nguyen. "We should be out looking for the perps. Not wasting time playing security guard."

"You know it and I know it," Dan said. "And we got a few hours before sunset, so what are we going to do about it?"

Cal sighed. "The Professor gave us the names of all the experts in the country who could ready or identify High Essenian. Rabinowitz is tracking them down now."

"You don't really think some old stuffy archaeologist-type is involved in any of this, do you?" Dan asked incredulously.

Cal sighed. "Who knows? Maybe indirectly. Maybe one of them wrote this phrase out for someone else. Could have said it was for a novel or something." Cal gave Dan a pointed look. "It's a lead, Dan," he said. "We haven't had too many of those in this case."

"Yeah, I suppose," Dan sighed, sitting hard in a small wooden chair. "Let's just hope it comes to something. And soon."

PROFESSOR Beatrice Miller's last class of the day was an introductory course in World Mythology. The class consisted mostly of freshmen, and Professor Miller always enjoyed teaching them, introducing them to legends and stories that most of them knew only in passing or from corny television shows like *Xena, Warrior Princess.* Professor Miller sighed. She had never seen this *Xena* show, but still, every semester one student always raised a hand and asked, sometimes rather sharply, "When are we getting to Xena?"

At the moment, though, the class was deep into Egyptian mythology. Today's lesson had included the pharaoh contests between Set, the dark god of thunder and war, and Horus, the falcon-headed son of the previous Pharaoh, Osiris. Professor Miller had always enjoyed spinning the various yarns of their spirited contests and the devious ways that Horus' mother, the goddess Isis, would devise to help her son cheat his way to victory. Professor Miller chuckled at the thought of the goddess' ingenuity. In one contest, for example, the two gods were to construct boats made of rocks and race them down the Nile. Of course, rocks don't float, and the great war god's boat sinking was always a funny image in the Professor's mind. Even funnier must have been the look on his face when Set realized his competitor's boat was made of reeds and only design to look like rocks. It was a familiar tale, though few of today's students had ever heard of it. Still, even the few who thought they knew the whole tale had usually missed out a few of juicier details—such as the contest wherein Set and Horus were locked in a dark room overnight, engaged in combat until one emerged victorious by implanting his seed in the other. Professor Miller relished that part of the tale for all its carnal details, and enjoyed the look on her students' faces when they realized the ancient Egyptians were far more wanton than they had ever imagined.

Professor Miller balanced a stack of books in one hand while she opened her office door with her key. No, wrong key...she could never quite get the door to open easily. It usually jammed when turning the key left, and sure enough, today it did so. The precariously tipping books careened to the floor and Professor Miller bent gingerly to pick them up. Scooping them up in her hands, she paused for a moment to stretch her back. Ohh, she was getting too old for all this, she thought. Getting too old for everything. She pushed on her knees to help her rise from the floor, and with a soft "oomph" she finally made it up.

She hadn't seen the man standing behind her.

"Goodness!" she swore, dropping her books again. The man—boy, really, a student—hastily crouched down to retrieve them. Professor Miller envied the ease in which he swooped down and rose again. "I'm sorry, Professor," the boy said, slightly flushing a bit. "I didn't mean to scare you. I just wanted to talk to you is all, for a minute."

"Yes, yes, of course," the Professor said, her heart still pumping a bit too loudly in her ears. She gathered the books from the young man—what was his name? She couldn't quite remember. After so many years of teaching, all the students had started to look alike to her. He sat in the back room on the left side. If only she could remember his name.

"Come in," she said, pushing her way into her office and hastily clearing a spot for him on one corner of an office chair. She placed the books on a disastrously careening stack of similar books and sat in her own chair behind her desk. "Now what can I do for you, err, umm—what can I do for you?"

Then the floods came, the myriad excuses for a missing paper. Ahh, yes, Professor Miller remembered. One of the students had not handed in the last assignment. It must have been this young man. Perhaps that was why she couldn't remember his name.

The student went on and on about a dying grandmother or something like that. Truth be told, Professor Miller had heard it all in thirty years of teaching, and wasn't interested in hearing it again. She cleared her voice and waited for a moment to break in on the young man's speech. "Now, look, I'm very sorry for your, umm, difficulties, but as my syllabus clearly states, all late papers are docked one letter grade per day late. No ifs, ands, or buts." This started another tirade, another speech laced with more emotion, pleading, and even the minor hint of a threat. "I'm sorry, but you'll just have to get it in as soon as you can," she said as evenly as possible. "Now if you will excuse me, I've got an appointment I'm going to be late for." This last bit was a lie, but it was as good excuse as any to get the young man out of her office.

Professor Miller spent the next hours chasing down references for Detective Evans and Agent Rabinowitz. Something tugged at her mind, as if…as if there was something she thought she should have mentioned but did not. That nagging thought burned in her for well over an hour as she pored over old tomes, checking and re-checking to see if there was anything she has inadvertently left out of her story.

Finally, exhausted and spent, Professor Miller took a moment to look at her watch. It was almost eight o'clock, still barely light out because of the long days of late spring, but well past dinner time. Professor Miller took a few moments to answer one last e-mail before closing down her computer and packing up her things. She paused before one of her cramped bookshelves and selected a few volumes that contained more information about current scholarship in High Essenian. These should help me in compiling my list of scholars for those detectives, she thought.

Suddenly Professor Miller snapped her fingers, and with an exultant "Ah-ha!" desperately searched her desk for a pencil. She had finally remembered what she had been trying to recall all day. Finding a pen, she wrote herself a quick word of remembrance on a small pad next to her computer. Throwing the pen back into the fray, she moved to rip off the paper.

The phone rang.

The noise startled Professor Miller into inactivity for a moment or two. Then, slightly hesitant, she picked up the phone. "He-hello?" she spoke. "Beatrice Miller here." There was no response on the other end. "Hello? Is anyone there?" Still silence. After another minute's wait, Professor Miller placed the phone back into its cradle. She stared at it, waiting, as if daring it to ring again.

It remained silent.

Now it was late. Quickly gathering her materials together, Professor Miller ambled out her office door, letting it swing shut and lock behind her.

The note of remembrance was left behind, forgotten.

With two canvas bags stuffed to the gills, Professor Miller slowly made her way towards her car. She had parked under a wide red maple at the far end of the expansive college lot, a great place to keep the car shaded from the afternoon sun, though now, as the sun went down, it was a lot less hot outside. By this time, during the summer, the entire lot was deserted; all the staff and students had already gone home. Professor Miller was eager to get home herself; she was exhausted from last night's research, but the two heavy bags slowed her progress quite a bit. *And my sore knee doesn't help much, either,* she thought gloomily. Professor Miller sighed. One of things she'd loved most about studying ancient cultures and languages was going on digs. She remembered her first one, as an assistant to Professor Grund at a small Roman outpost in northern Africa. It had been a desolate spot, with nothing to do but sift sand and dirt all day in the off chance of finding an important relic. Though nothing of note had been uncovered on that dig, they had learned a lot about daily life at the outpost, and seeing two thousand years of history peeled away before her own eyes hooked her on digs for life. She went on one every three of four years after that, whenever the college could afford to send her, or during summers, sometimes paying out of her own pocket. Her last dig had been on one of the Greek isles, where they discovered the first ruins of an olive press found off the mainland. Oh, in the grand scheme of things it may seem like small potatoes, but to Professor Miller, nothing in the world had ever seemed more significant or revelatory than that simple olive press.

Now, though, Professor Miller needed reconstructive surgery on her knee. With a sore hip and a bad back, she was simply too damn old to dig anymore. She sighed. Teaching she loved, but the daily drudgery of grading papers and student excuses wore her out so quickly. With the possibility of digs always looming on the horizon, none of the rest of it mattered. But now, with no digs in her future, Professor Miller was seriously considering retiring. She could settle down and finally finish her translation of *The Odyssey*. Finish her career with something significant to stamp her name to. Still, getting old was a terrible thing. She thought of poor Professor Grund, his mind a shell of what it once was, not even recognizing the people who came to see him anymore. Professor Miller shuddered. She hoped that would never happen to her.

Still a good fifty feet from her car, she heaved another sigh. *Why do I park over here?* she thought. But the air conditioning on her little Honda was broken—had been for years—and Professor Miller always told herself that the walk really was good for her. Of course, it didn't feel quite that way now. Finally, though, she parked her aching bones in front of the driver's side door.

She dropped her bags with an unceremonial *whump* and rooted around in her purse for her keys. Finding them, she looked for the key to the door. The sun had just set, and the dim glow of twilight did not aid in her search. Suddenly, a loud *click* startled her. It was just the parking lot lights coming on. Still uneasy, Professor Miller took a cautious moment to peer around the parking lot. Now flooded with light, she could see that she was the only person in it. Well, it was no surprise she was on edge. Not with everything that had been going on lately. And that message...she shuddered as she finally moved to slide her key in the door.

It grabbed her ankle from beneath the car. Professor Miller gave a soft startled cry. Her grasping hands were flung up in the air and her keys went flying. Panicked, Professor Miller looked down and saw something wrapped around her ankle. Whatever it was acted like a hand, but it wasn't a hand. It was covered with a swath of dark cloth. Underneath the material she could see movement, undulating scales and coils. Realizing what it was that had her, Professor Miller screamed again, this time in earnest, as she saw a hand—a real, human hand this time, though its flesh was gray and dead—reach out from under her vehicle, a large, curved blade in its hand. She acted on instinct, using her purse to smack the hand away from her, but it had no affect. She felt the knife tear through her Achilles tendon with a ragged, violent thrust. Now gasping in pain, Professor Miller felt her other ankle freed. She spun, tried to walk, and fell hard onto the concrete parkway. She glanced over her shoulder quickly, trying to catch a glimpse of what was behind her, but the space under her car was too dark, and she saw nothing. Turning, gasping, she looked ahead and tried to stand. Groaning in agony, she fell again and felt cold flesh trying to grab her other ankle. She screamed again. Her frantic eyes saw—there, near her, her keys, glinting in the artificial glow of the parking lot lights. She reached out her left hand—she could almost reach them—she tried to kick with her injured foot but her kicks were feeble and useless. She stretched, she almost had them, just another inch—she had them. She had them! But it had her. She wrapped her fingers around the keys just as the other hand wrapped around her ankle. With a firm grip and unnatural strength, the hand pulled Professor Miller completely under the car. A short scream was followed by a muffled whimper and then a wet, tearing sound, followed by stony silence, and then, finally, almost imperceptibly, the gentle, lulling sound of blood discreetly flowing from a savaged neck.

FRIDAY

"**AND** while this is still preliminary information, of course, I'm happy to report that as far as the FBI is concerned, the so-called 'Clergy Killer' did not strike last night. It appears that efforts to protect the clergy of Chambersburg were a complete success. I'd also like to add that no reports of any clergy members being hurt in any way have come in from within at least a one hundred mile radius of the town. To me, this is encouraging news. Clearly, we are on the right track."

"Agent Nguyen, Agent Nguyen, are you any closer to identifying the killer?"

"I'm sorry, I'm not at liberty to reveal any specifics about the case, except to say that we are pursuing numerous leads with the utmost diligence."

"Agent Nguyen, over here, what about the reports that this is some kind of terrorist attack?"

"The FBI in conjunction with the U.S. Department of State has concluded that, at this time, there is no evidence to support that these attacks are in any way related to terrorism or are supported by any foreign power, group, or individual."

"Agent Nguyen, what about the CNN report that these attacks are the result of some individual or individuals who have suffered abuse by priests in the past? Care to comment on that?"

"Ladies and gentlemen, please, let us do our job as best we can, and we'll do our best to keep your informed of our progress. Let me just reiterate that any persons out there with any information about these attacks should not hesitate to call the FBI at the 1-800 information hotline we've set up for the case. That's all for now. Thank you and—"

Lindsay Cole shut off her radio as she pulled into the large college parking lot. She quickly checked her watch. She was running a bit late for class, which would explain why the lot was already full. Damn! She hated it when she was late, though truth be told, she was late for every early morning class she ever had. Why did they schedule classes for eight in the morning anyway?

She cruised the lot looking for a place to park. She was glad no one had died last night. Oh, Lindsay wasn't religious herself, but in all her nineteen years, she'd never heard of anything as horrible as these clergy killings. She couldn't remember anybody being murdered in Chambersburg at all before this. Some people—her little stepbrother included—thought all this blood and gore was pretty exciting, but Lindsay thought it was disgusting. She hoped they caught the guy soon. Frankly, it all made her a little nervous. She knew the guy was only killing preachers and stuff, at least for now, but she was a pretty girl, and you never know what a sicko like that might do next.

Lindsay turned into another row of the lot and slowly made her way down it. Goddamn it, she thought, why don't they ever make these lots bigger? Even during summer sessions they were full up in the morning. She pushed a stray strand of blond hair out of her eyes as she checked her watch again. Damn. She was *really* going to be late.

Finally Lindsay saw a spot next to a blue Honda in the corner of the lot. She pulled in quickly, gathered her books and her purse, and stepped hurriedly out of the car. Her white sneaker immediately stuck to something all over the pavement. Gross, she thought, as it took some effort to free her foot. A dark, rust-colored liquid was smeared all over her sneaker. What is that? Lindsay thought. Oil? Whatever it was, it was coming from the Honda. Lindsay knew she was really late, but since there was a lot of the liquid, she thought she'd take a quick peek anyway. Just to make sure everything was okay.

Lindsay screamed.

THE television was on in the station house. Dan rolled his eyes when Nguyen mentioned the toll free number. "Great," he muttered, "now every nut in the state is going to be calling up with helpful hints." Rabinowitz gave him a rueful smile. She knew that most of the calls coming in would be useless, but on the off chance that one of the calls might prove to be a genuine lead, the number may prove helpful.

The mood around the station house was certainly different than yesterday. It was upbeat, energized—almost triumphant, Rabinowitz thought. The FBI people all took turns patting themselves on the back for a job well done. They busily answered phones, traded reports, made coffee. They looked well rested, energized and enthused, even if most of them had only gotten a few hours sleep. Rabinowitz sighed. It was no use being too excited. Yes, it was good that no one had died last night, but until these people were caught, she knew she would not get a good night's sleep.

Nguyen strolled in from his press conference just then. "Well," he said to the room at large and to Dan in particular, "looks like the FBI did its job last night after all."

"Looks like," Dan said noncommittally.

"No hard feelings, Sheriff," Agent Nguyen continued smugly. "I know you would have done the same thing, if you'd only had the resources. And the manpower. And the finances to pull it off."

Dan fumed quietly, but kept his comments to himself. Nguyen turned to Rabinowitz. "Where's your new partner in crime?" he asked her.

"He's busy at the moment," Rabinowitz replied evenly.

Nguyen smiled. "Probably getting a bit of sleep after a long night. I daresay we could all use forty winks. I know I've got to be up, but there's no point in all of you staying here. Why don't you go join Detective Evans and get some rest?"

Rabinowitz's smile never faded. But she knew she couldn't join Cal, even if she'd wanted to.

CAL stood before the group. He'd been here only a few days ago, maybe less, but now, with everything that had happened, that's still happening…it seemed a lifetime ago.

"Hi," he said. "My name's Cal."

"Hi, Cal," the group replied in chorus.

Cal grimaced. Something about this early morning meeting…the people here seemed more cheerful than the ones who attended the meetings held at night. Cheerful and annoying. "My name's Cal," he repeated, "and I'm a drunk, err, a recovering alcoholic, and a few days ago I had a drink. I didn't want to have a drink, but…I did it anyway." He gulped again. Cal had to share for five minutes, his sponsor said. He had to talk about his feelings, about his life and why he had that drink. For five whole, damn minutes. Cal looked at his watch.

Four minutes, forty-five seconds to go.

"WE'RE fine," Dan was saying to Nguyen. "My question is, what does the vaunted FBI do now?"

"What do you mean?" Nguyen asked.

Dan folded his arms across his chest. "Maybe nobody died last night, but we're no closer to finding the actual killers. Forensics has turned up nothing, and there've been no witnesses to any of the crimes. We've got nothing to go on from here."

"This isn't the murder of some random big-city liquor store clerk," Nguyen hissed angrily at Dan. "This is huge mass of killings in a very small town. I've got dozens of agents working on every aspect of this case. Something will come up—and soon. And until then, I think I've proven I can keep this area safe."

"Agent Nguyen?" a voice called out. All three of them turned to see who was speaking. The voice belonged to a young FBI agent clutching a phone to his chest. "Agent Nguyen, I've got a 911 dispatcher on the phone here."

"And?" Nguyen said when the man stopped talking.

"They found a body, sir."

"CAL, is that you? I can barely make you out."

"Yeah, it's me, Velvet. Is everything okay?"

"How was the meeting?"

"Pretty much as I expected. Did they find anyone? I haven't heard anything."

"Did you talk? Did you get up and speak?"

"It's called 'sharing.' And who are you for asking, my mother? Velvet, what's going on? Why aren't you answering my questions? They found someone, didn't they?"

Rabinowitz's voice was quiet. "I don't know, Cal."

"What do you mean you don't know?"

"All the known preachers in this area are accounted for."

"Somehow that doesn't make me feel better when you say it like that, Velvet."

"They found a body. Woman. No identification, purse and wallet missing. Throat slit. Pushed under her car. Doesn't match the MO of our killers at all. Could be a mugging gone bad."

"There hasn't been a homicide mugging in Chambersburg since— hell, I don't think there's even been a homicide mugging in Chambersburg. Where'd they find the body, Velvet?" Her answer was garbled by the transmission. "What? I can't hear you?" Cal looked around. He was driving through a pretty woodsy area. "Goddamn fucking technology," he said. "Velvet? Hello? Where did they find the body? Can you hear me?"

In a barely audible voice, Cal heard her reply. "The college," she said. Somehow, the strain in her voice and the sound of those words made Cal's blood ran cold.

VELVET, Dan and the FBI were already there when Cal arrived at the scene. He moved as quickly as he could towards the police line, cutting through a horde of interested students and passers-by, flashing his badge the whole way. "Move aside, move aside," he said angrily. He saw Rabinowitz near the front of the group. "Cal!" she said. Cal didn't stop when he heard her. He kept walking. He had to see the body. He had to *know*.

"Cal!" Rabinowitz said again, grabbing his wrist. He pushed against her, but Dan wrapped an arm around his chest. "Damn it, Velvet, no," he said. He looked her right in the eyes and saw her barely perceptible nod. "Fuck!" he said, too loud. "Fuck, fuck, fuck!" Cal stopped trying to move forward and looked around for something to pound his fist in. He couldn't find anything, so he settled for smacking his own open palm. "Fuck, Velvet, how did they know, how did they know!"

"Maybe they didn't, Cal, maybe this is something different," she said softly. But he could tell she didn't mean it.

"What's going on?" Cal looked up to see Agent Nguyen walking towards them. Cal gritted his teeth. Maybe he could sink his fist into Nguyen's face. "What's all this commotion about? Evans? Did you know this woman?"

"No," Cal replied instinctively. "I mean, yes. Not really. Not like you mean."

"She was helping us on the case," Rabinowitz interjected. "She was our expert witness in High Essenian."

"Oh." A puzzled look crossed Nguyen's face. He turned to Rabinowitz. "You didn't tell me you knew the victim," he said accusingly. Rabinowitz gave him a stony glare. "I was waiting for you to finish your primary investigation before letting you know," she said. Nguyen looked at Rabinowitz as if she were lying. She continued. "You'll be happy to know I've already contacted someone about coming to the station and identifying the body."

"Who?" Nguyen's eyes narrowed sharply. "A relative?"

Rabinowitz shook her head. "She has no living family, no one close," she said. "This is a co-worker, the person who knew her best." Nguyen seemed satisfied at this and stalked off.

"Abe?" Cal asked softly, under his breath so Nguyen could not hear. "You called him?"

Rabinowitz nodded. "That was why I didn't tell Nguyen right away. I wanted the chance to call Abe myself. I feel like we owe him that since…well, since I got them both involved in this mess in the first place."

"Velvet…Velvet, hey, come on, this isn't your fault."

"But how did they know about it, Cal? How can people keep dying like this without us being able to do anything about it?"

Cal wanted to reach out and put his arm around her, to comfort her, but somehow felt it would be inappropriate. "I don't know," he said slowly. "None of this makes any sense to me at all."

"You two want to fill me in on what you're talking about?" Dan said as an aside to them. They both shook their heads. "It's nothing," Rabinowitz said, obviously not meaning it.

Dan was about to press them further when a small voice interrupted them. "Agent Rabinowitz?" it said. It was Abe. Rabinowitz and Cal shared a glance. They knew this day was about to get much, much worse.

THEY were in Professor Miller's office. Abe was crying. Cal had suggested going somewhere quiet after Abe had identified Professor Miller's body. Abe had a key, and Rabinowitz had gone upstairs to visit the helpful Robyn and secure Abe a cup of coffee. She was pressing it into his hand now.

"I just can't believe it," Abe said. "How did this happen?"

Cal shrugged his shoulders slowly. Seeing the poor guy like this, he felt like crying a little himself. A memory tugged at his mind...*Dani...in her crib...so still*...Rabinowitz was rubbing a consolatory arm over Abe's back, up and down, up and down. "We're not sure yet," she replied softly, answering Abe's question.

The young man sniffled softly, grabbed for a tissue, and loudly blew his nose. "Was it—was it the guy whose been doing all this?"

"We don't know that either yet," Rabinowitz replied.

"Abe," Cal said, "is there someone we can call for you?"

Abe shook his head. He took a sip of his coffee. "No, I—I'm okay, thanks," he said bravely.

"Okay, then," Cal said. He moved towards the door. Rabinowitz stood up, too. "We're sorry, but you understand, we have to go, we have a job to do. Will you be okay here?"

Abe paused, then nodded. "I guess," he said solemnly. Rabinowitz gave him a gently maternal glance, and one quick hug before they turned to go. "What about her books?" Abe asked.

Cal and Rabinowitz exchanged a puzzled look. "What about what books?" Cal asked.

"Her books. We were still working on stuff—looking up that stuff you guys wanted us to, on the High Essenian scholars and everything. About that message that was left at the crime scenes and what it means. After her class last night, she was going to bring home some more books for us. A whole bunch."

Rabinowitz was confused. "They didn't find any books," she said slowly. "Are they still here?" She wasn't sure how anyone could tell if something was missing from the office or not.

Abe shook his head though. "No, they're not here. And they're not in her car. I looked when they—when they showed me her."

"Maybe they're at home?" Cal said. Abe shook his head again. "She—she never made it home," Abe replied. Cal cursed himself for his thoughtless reply. "I thought you guys might have them for some reason," Abe continued.

"We don't have them," Rabinowitz said slowly. "Abe, did Professor Miller tell you specifically what she was researching?"

Abe lowered his face. "No, she didn't. She called me at home. Told me she was looking up some stuff. I offered to help her, but she told me—she told me to get some sleep, said she could call me later. I was so exhausted I slept right on through morning. She—she never called."

Rabinowitz shifted her weight from one foot to the other. "Abe, is there any way to find out what she was working on?"

The young man thought for a few moments. "Maybe. If I do an inventory of her office, I can find what's missing. Maybe knowing what books aren't here can give me some idea of what she was looking into." He paused and looked at them both. "You have to understand, though. I mean, I'm just her student. She knew so much more than I did. Even if I know what books are missing I won't know exactly why she wanted them."

"We understand that, Abe," Rabinowitz reassured him. "Just do the best you can."

"Besides, you were the one who told us about that guy—what was his name—Gayus something?" Cal added, trying to be helpful.

"Gaius Constans," Abe replied glumly. A funny look crossed his face. "Actually, that's what I was reading last night. *The History of Gaius Constans*. I went back and re-read his version of the Roman siege of Qumran. Professor Miller was right. It was a total crock. I can't believe I ever brought it up in the first place."

"You were just trying to be helpful," Cal said. "It was all interesting."

Abe was half-crying, half-laughing. "It's a bunch of nonsense, like she said. The Essenes as killers. They were a religious group. Peaceful. Can you imagine a bunch of zealot Jews turning into snake worshippers?"

Both Cal and Rabinowitz's ears immediately perked up at the word "snakes." No connection between the "Clergy Killer" and snakes had yet been made. This was the one fact the FBI was holding back—no one knew, except the police, that snakes were involved at all.

"Snakes?" Rabinowitz said, a tinge of hope etching her voice.

"What about snakes?" Cal said, as attentive as Rabinowitz.

Abe seemed confused by their sudden interest. "What—what do you mean?" he asked, a bit dazed.

Rabinowitz crouched towards the floor so that she could look Abe straight in his eyes. "Listen Abe, this is important. I think we need to know exactly what this Gaius Constans says about the Essenes. Every detail you can remember. Don't leave anything out."

"Oh—okay," Abe stammered, a little unsure of himself. "Um, well, up to a point, Gaius doesn't differ in his account of the Essenes from Pliny or Josephus or any other classical historian. He's a bit more colorful but he tells pretty much the same story. Then sometime in the early part of the first century—at least that's what we think his dating is—Gaius talks about a new Teacher of Righteousness arriving at Qumran. That has to be wrong because the Teacher of Righteousness was someone elected from within the community, not without. But supposedly this Teacher of Righteousness taught them the secret of everlasting life, of immortality. But only the Council of Elders learned this information. Then there's some sort of internal power struggle because a new Teacher is named, and this is supposedly the last Teacher of Righteousness—which again has to be wrong, since it's about forty years or so until the Romans show up, and these men were pretty old when they achieved this post. The guy would be practically ancient by Roman standards to have lived forty years after achieving that post. I suppose it's possible—people live to be one hundred all the time nowadays, and with good diet and some lucky genes, I suppose an ancient man could live to be quite old—still, it seems that—"

"Abe," Rabinowitz said, interrupting him. "Get on with the story, please."

"Oh, okay, sorry. Anyway, Gaius says that this new Teacher of Righteousness really changes things, shakes things up. They reject the old traditions—that's Judaism—in favor of what Gaius calls a new religion, but what appears to be some sort of amalgam of an animagus religion, an animal-worshipping religion."

"And the animal they worshipped was snakes?"

"Yes, that's right. Actually, Gaius' exact words were that they 'became' snakes, but obviously people don't become snakes. That's probably just a manuscript corruption, or Gaius' idea of a colorful description. Anyway, the Essenes were always isolated, but under the new Teacher of Righteousness they become isolationist to the extreme. They even went out and started killing people, especially from other religious sects."

"Other Jews, you mean?"

"Actually, the only people Gaius mentions by name are the Nazarenes."

"Who were they?"

"Nazarene is one of the earliest names for Christians, especially by someone writing outside the faith. Gaius was likely describing some early Christian sect whose name has been lost to time. Remember that Christianity was still very new and very radical, so some early Christian communities likely wanted to hide out and isolate themselves as well. Gaius says the Essenes slaughtered them all, but that's probably his anti-Semitism and his anti-Christian bias coming in. Gaius was a Roman citizen of a somewhat noble birth, so he likely practiced emperor-worship, the official Roman religion of the time."

"Then what happened?"

"Well, it seems the Essenes were causing such a problem that the Romans came in and dealt with them as best they could—they destroyed their settlement, stole all their goods, and massacred the entire community. According to Gaius this happened around fifty AD, about twenty years before the Jewish revolt, which would make this a totally separate incursion into the territory altogether for the Romans. But then Gaius says that the Essenes are immortal and can never die, and that they still wander the desert looking for their home. Seems like he got his Old Testament Moses legend mixed up in there somehow."

"Abe," Rabinowitz asked slowly, "did Gaius give a source for his history?"

"Oh, yeah," Abe said. "Gaius had a source for everything. It's one of his hallmarks—he always says stuff like, 'I got this story from this ancient text,' or 'I heard this story from this survivor of the siege.' In this case he says he has the story from the ancestor of a Roman soldier who was actually at the siege of Qumran—but most of this is just made-up. He tries to add to the credibility of the history by making up sources. Historians did that through the Middle Ages. It was a very common practice."

"But it could be true?" Rabinowitz said. "Symbolically, anyway, the Essenes could have become snake-worshippers?"

Abe shrugged his shoulders. "I doubt it, but anything is possible."

"So maybe someone's trying to revive the old religion," Rabinowitz said to Cal.

"Could be," Cal replied. "Someone else got a hold of Gaius and decided that they liked his ideas."

"What are you talking about?" Abe interjected.

"Abe," Cal said, ignoring his question, "does Gaius say specifically *how* the Essenes killed the Nazarenes and those other groups?"

"Yeah," Abe said slowly.

"It wasn't by using snakes, was it?" Rabinowitz added.

"How did you know that?' Abe asked incredulously.

"For real?" Cal echoed. "That's what he says?"

"Not exactly. Actually, Gaius says that the Essenes 'put their enemies to the snake.' Archaeologists differ on what that means. Although the Essenes didn't kill their enemies' religious leaders in the same manner."

"No," Rabinowitz said slowly, "I bet they just carved them up like a Thanksgiving turkey." A short silence filled the room. "Well?" Rabinowitz said, looking to Abe for confirmation of her theory.

"Yeah," Abe said. "Like a ritual sacrifice."

"Holy shit," Cal said. "A ritual sacrifice. I can't believe it. All this time, we've been running around looking at forensics and trying to find witnesses to the crimes to get some answers."

"Yeah, and really we should have been taking a trip to the public library," Rabinowitz finished. She turned to Abe. "Does anyone still practice the Essenian religion today?"

"There is no distinct Essenian religion," Abe said. "Gaius Constans made it all up. It never existed."

"Yeah, well it does now," Cal said. He started to pace the floor, full of nervous energy. Now that they had a handle on this, he wanted to get out there, find these guys, shut them down.

"What are you talking about?" Abe asked. Cal did not respond. Abe repeated his question to Rabinowitz. "What is he talking about?"

Rabinowitz answered carefully. "Abe, we think someone is trying to revive the Essenian religion. Or approximate its existence somehow."

"Why would anyone do that?" Abe asked.

"That's the million dollar question," Cal replied.

"Is there anything else you've left out about the Essenes?" Rabinowitz asked. "Think, Abe! Even the smallest detail could be of the utmost importance."

Abe thought for before shaking his head. "No, I can't think of anything. But I'm not an expert on this."

"Yeah." Cal said slowly. "Maybe we should talk to that other guy—Professor Miller's mentor. What was his name?"

"Grund. Elijah Grund. But he has Alzheimer's, remember?" Rabinowitz replied.

"I know. But when my grandmother had Alzheimer's it was mainly because she couldn't remember the people and things around her. But ask her for the ingredients to any of the hundred recipes she was famous for and she could name them all no problem. Besides, didn't Professor Miller say he has good and bad days?"

Rabinowitz gave Cal a wry smile. "Let's hope he's having a good day." She turned to Abe. "Abe, can you get us an address on him?" For answer, Abe began to paw through a stack of papers on the professor's desk. A moment later he came out with a small address book. "Here it is," he said, copying the address down on a piece of paper.

"Thanks," Rabinowitz said. She looked back at Cal. "What's our next step, Detective?"

Now that they had a solid lead, Cal was feeling familiar energy coursing through him again. "First thing, we go back to the station house and report in. Maybe the FBI has an expert or two they can get on this who won't fuck it up this time. See if forensics turned anything up on the last crime scene." At this indirect mention of Professor Miller's death, a pained look crossed Abe's face, but Cal didn't see it. "Since we know more what we're looking for, we can start checking out various places a group like that might be hiding out— abandoned homes, old warehouses, stuff like that. Chambersburg isn't that big—we can probably cover that entire list today if we search efficiently."

"Sounds like a good job for the FBI to help out with," Rabinowitz added, "if, of course, Nguyen will listen to us now."

"Oh, he will," Cal said confidently. "With what we've got? He has to."

"Okay, then what?"

"Well, while the FBI checks out any place this group might be hiding, we'll go talk to Elijah Grund. See if he can give us any other useful information."

Rabinowitz smiled at Cal. "Sounds like a plan, Detective," she said.

"Damn, Velvet," Cal replied enthusiastically, "I really feel it. Like today we're going to break this case wide open."

"I hope you're right," Rabinowitz replied smoothly. "Abe—" she added, then stopped, unsure how to proceed. In their enthusiasm over the case she'd momentarily forgotten about the young man who'd just lost his mentor. "Abe, Detective Evans and I can't thank you and Professor Miller enough. What you've done—your contributions may have really opened this case wide up."

"I hope so," Abe replied glumly.

"Do you think—could you keep checking on stuff? Try to find out what Professor Miller was working on last night?"

"Of course, Detective. And if I do find something, I'll call Agent Rabinowitz's cell phone right away."

"Thanks." Cal and Rabinowitz stood to leave.

"Umm, Detective Evans, Agent Rabinowitz?"

"Yes, Abe?"

"How did they know about her?"

Cal was perplexed. "What do you mean?"

"She never went on TV or anything. She only met with you that one time. And yet—I mean—they got to her, didn't they?"

Rabinowitz and Cal exchanged uneasy glances. "Yeah, they did," Rabinowitz said softly.

"So, I mean, I was wondering, how did they know about her—involvement?"

Cal shook his head slowly. "We don't know that yet, Abe."

"Do you think—I mean, is it possible—am I next?"

Cal was dumbstruck. He hadn't even considered that possibility, and the fact that he hadn't really bothered him. One look at Rabinowitz told Cal that she felt exactly as he did.

"You know, you might be right," Cal said. "Maybe we should escort you somewhere safe."

"No!" Abe replied, a bit too sudden. He explained. "This is where Professor Miller was working last night. Any answers as to what she was working on would be found here. I want to stick around—I want to help." He paused. "I want to help nail the motherfuckers who did this to her. I don't want her—death to be in vain."

"Fine," Cal said. "But I'm going to radio a member of the Chambersburg PD to come over and watch you. They're going to stick to you 24/7, so get used to it. In the meantime, call campus security and have them send a guy over. Okay?"

Cal could tell Abe was relieved at the idea. "Okay."

"Good." The two police officers turned to go. Cal turned back. "Just be careful, okay?" he said to Abe.

Abe stared at the concerned detective for a moment. "Okay."

BACK in the car, Cal felt his exuberant mood slipping. He slapped his hand against the steering wheel. "Damn it, Velvet, how *did* they know?" he roared in frustration. "Christ, feels like every time we come up with something in this case something else comes along and fucks it all up."

"Two steps forward, two steps back," Rabinowitz observed. She tried to sound as wry as possible, but Cal could tell that she was worried about Abe as much as he was. She sighed. "So what do we do now, chief?" she said, trying to keep the mood upbeat.

Cal considered their options. "I think our best bet is to stick to the plan. Head back to the station house, initiate a building-by-building search of all abandoned domiciles, and talk to Elijah Grund. Let's just hope—" he broke off.

"Let's just hope what?" Rabinowitz prompted.

Cal stared blankly at the road ahead of him. "Nothing," he said blandly.

BISHOP James "Jimmy" Atherton looked at his watch. Again. Only 1:05. He sighed, nervous. Was this shift ever going to end?

The customer before him was saying something. "What was that, Mrs. Hardy?" he asked again.

The elderly woman standing on the other side of his orange-red counter glowered at the bishop. "My change," she said again testily.

"Oh, sorry," he replied absent-mindedly, handing her a few bills and coins. With a noticeable "hmph" she left the small pharmacy, the door swinging slowly shut behind her.

Now Jimmy was alone. And scared. True, it was mid-day; the sun was burning bright in the late spring sky. And it was certainly busy outside; passers-by walked past on their way to get groceries at the Giant Supermarket store, or alcohol at Happy Times Liquor. Jimmy frowned, distracted; he disapproved of that store, but his own shop had been here first, and he was damned if he was going to move. Not that he'd ever use the word "damned" to describe how he felt, of course.

Jimmy was a member of the Church of Jesus Christ and Latter Day Saints—Mormon, though he always referred to it as LDS. A devout and lifetime member of the church, Jimmy was used to the anti-LDS bigotry he often faced: the sniggers from classmates at his school, the constant questions from his non-LDS peers, the Jell-o jokes from his college mates at pharmacy school. Jimmy tolerated them all, always spoke back with a smile, but inside, he hated every last second of it. He hated their ignorant questions and their stupid jokes. They weren't really interested in becoming LDS, in accepting the truth of God's spirit into their hearts. At best, they were curious, treating Jimmy like he was a freak, and at worst, mean-spirited, acting as if LDS were some weird doomsday cult. Jimmy snorted. Anyone who wasn't LDS could never understand, and if they didn't accept God into their hearts, well, then they never would.

Usually, though, this was the biggest problem Jimmy faced. Other than that, life was pretty good. He and Roberta had been married twenty years. They had two sons: Aaron was sixteen and Josiah twelve. He'd owned this shop for eleven years. They made a good living, tithing regularly but still with plenty left over to visit Roberta's parents in Provo every year at Christmas. And last year, of course, Jimmy received the honest honor he could have imagined when he was called to be Bishop of his ward. It was a sign of respect, and a sign that he was living the right kind of life. He had accepted with a heart full of gratitude and honor. He knew it was a lot of extra responsibility. He'd have to balance the time between his work, his family, and his duty to the church. But what could be more worth it?

Only now…only now, with everything that was going on, with the killings…Jimmy was wishing he'd thought twice about answering that call. Of course the church was still his primary responsibility, but now someone out there was targeting good Christian men, killing them in the most horrible of ways. Jimmy knew that these other religions were not the one true faith of God, but these men were good Christians and deserved to die better than they did. Oh, and that woman too—that felt strange to Jimmy, a woman church leader. Oh well, these liberal religions these days.

A sudden yet delicate *"clink"* startled Jimmy from his thoughts. It was nothing; just a customer. Jimmy scrutinized the young man carefully. Tall, strongly built, early twenties. Not white—possibly Italian, possibly Hispanic. He couldn't tell. Jimmy ran a small shop; mostly prescription drugs and a few toiletry products, toothpaste, mouthwash, shampoo. He knew most of his customers because they were members of the church; LDS always supported other LDS in their businesses. Just another example of the community at work. But Jimmy got a lot of run-off business from the grocery store, so a stranger in the shop was not uncommon. Still, guys like this made him uneasy. A lot of pharmacies are robbed, not for their cash on hand, which was never very much, but for the drugs themselves. They made an enticing target to drug dealers. A young, possibly Hispanic male…that was always a potentially dangerous customer, Jimmy thought warily.

The young man, however, did nothing more than select an anti-plaque rinse, bring it to the counter, purchase it with a friendly smile, and leave as quickly as he had come.

And Jimmy was alone again.

He looked at his watch. 1:10. His counter assistant Shelly was at lunch, and wouldn't be back for another twenty minutes. Jimmy sighed. He hated this apprehension, this silent waiting. He'd asked the police for protection. Yes, they came last night and guarded his home and family, and they'd done a fine job of it. But then he asked one of the officers watching his home to come with him to work. "To the rectory?" the officer asked. Jimmy had to explain to him that he had a regular, nine-to-five job. The officer seemed confused, but he called in the request. Ultimately, the answer came back: no. The officer told him that the force was stretched too thin as it was, that they needed to sleep to prepare for tonight's watch. He had told Jimmy that no one had been killed the night before (thank God for that!) and that no attacks had happened during the day. He advised Jimmy to keep with other people, avoid dark areas, avoid being alone or taking any unnecessary risks. Jimmy felt like telling the man that he did that every day regardless, and that what he needed now was protection, not useless advice. But he thanked the officer for his trouble and came in to open the shop.

Jimmy sighed. Usually he closed the shop, so that he might help his wife get the children off to school in the morning. Shelly would open it, and Jimmy would work until closing time. More prescriptions were filled during the dinner hour than in the early morning anyway. Jimmy frowned. So much had already been disrupted by these killings. The church felt it wise to cancel its Wednesday night service. And now Jimmy had to open the shop today, so that he might be home well before dark.

He looked at his watch again. 1:15. Shelly would be back in fifteen minutes. That would make him feel better. He would be off at 4:00, home by 4:15. The officers would arrive promptly at 6:00. So until then, well...Jimmy always had the Lord to keep him company.

"THAT'S some wild story you got," Agent Nguyen told Cal and Rabinowitz, barely hiding an amused smirk. He glanced over at Dan. "You sure do have some imaginative folks on your team," he said.

"Get your head out of your ass, Nguyen," Rabinowitz spoke up crossly. Cal looked at Rabinowitz in surprise. He already liked her, but now he found himself liking her even more. Nguyen, however, was eyeing Rabinowitz rather angrily at the moment. "Listen to what we have to say. It's the only thing that makes sense."

"It hardly makes sense," Nguyen retorted. "The revival of some ancient cult that never really existed? You think that's what's behind all this?"

"It's the only answer that fits the crime. You know that," Cal said impatiently.

"No, I don't know that," Nguyen replied. "I grant you some of the aspects come together. But you're talking about something known to only a few experts around the world. You're trying to get me to buy that some crazy cultist living in Podunk, Pennsylvania reads up on—what was this guy's name again?"

"Gaius Constans," Rabinowitz glumly replied.

"Yeah, okay. So this guy decides that some obscure cult Gaius Constans mentions in passing sounds like a great idea, and then creates said cult by convincing a bunch of hicks to become Jewish extremist isolationists who kill pastors for what—ritual sacrifice?" Nguyen crossed his arms over his chest and barked out a short laugh. "I mean, come on, you don't expect me to buy all this shit you're selling, do you?"

"If I can interject something," Dan spoke up before Cal or Rabinowitz could jump in. "Agent Nguyen's wholly uninformed and ridiculously idiotic opinion of this town and its inhabitants aside—" Nguyen threw Dan a dirty look "—I have to agree with him that your theory does sound a bit farfetched."

"What?!" Cal exploded. "Dan, come on, you know me."

"Yeah, I do Cal," Dan said quietly. "But I also know you've got no evidence to support your theory."

"Bullshit," Cal interjected, but even before he said it, he knew Dan was right.

"However," Dan continued, "I do think Cal and Velvet are right when they talk about this crime being the work of multiple parties. And the idea that it's cult-related is not so farfetched. Do you agree, Agent Nguyen?"

Nguyen's dark eyes flashed for a moment. "Agreed."

"Then what about the search?" Cal asked.

Dan nodded. "It's a good idea," he said. "We can check out abandoned buildings and look for any signs of cult activity or any indication that someone or *someones* has been staying there."

Nguyen was eying them both. "Okay. But you're assuming this 'cult' is meeting somewhere abandoned. Most cults meet in occupied domiciles—homes of members of the cult, seemingly legitimate churches or businesses. Very few destructive cults meet anywhere as risky as an abandoned building. Still, it's a start."

"Maybe we need to do more," Cal said. "Maybe we need to go public with what we know. If there is a cult active around here, someone's bound to have seen something."

"No," Dan said quietly.

"But, Dan—"

"Cal, no. You go on TV and tell this town there's some mad cult running around and we will have mass hysteria on our hands. It's bad enough now as it is. We can't spend all our time chasing down false leads about kooky neighbors or some weird fire that turns out to be a guy burning his garbage. We don't have any hard evidence of cult activity, so let's keep this under wraps and avoid a general panic, okay?"

"Besides," Nguyen added snidely, "I'm sure we don't want to give any of the good Christian folk of this town an excuse to string up any of their not-so-Christian neighbors, right? Hell, if I were Jewish or Muslim, I'd be afraid to leave my house as it is."

"Shut up, Nguyen," Dan said.

Rabinowitz had been silent this whole time, but now she spoke up. "Professor Miller," she said. "She was the one who first broached the subject of Gaius Constans. Now she's dead. That has to link the Essene theory to these crimes."

"Yes. Yes!" Cal said excitedly. "It does. You're right, Velvet. It has to!"

Nguyen shook his head vigorously. "No, it does not. We don't even have any evidence that the killing of the Miller woman is even related to these crimes."

Cal threw his hands up in exasperation. "All her materials related to her research for this case were stolen," he said. "What more evidence do you need?"

"Her purse was stolen, too," Nguyen replied. "And may I point out that no other victim had anything stolen from his or her body?"

Cal was about to reply but a sudden commotion from one corner of the station house distracted the squabbling group. Several FBI agents had been watching the television news, and now one of them was turning the volume on the small office set up. Another was waving his colleagues over. "Listen to this!" he was saying.

"And to repeat: Channel 8 has learned that Beatrice Miller, last night's potential victim of the Chambersburg Clergy Killer, in fact started out her life as a nun in the Sisters of Perpetual Mercy Convent in Summer Hill, New York. It would seem, then, that another religious figure has been cut down by the mysterious and terrifying Clergy Killer. We will keep you updated as this story continues developing. For Channel 8 Action News, I'm Yolanda—"

"Turn that damn thing off!" Nguyen roared, frustrated. "Jesus Christ," he said in answer to Cal's, Dan's, and Rabinowitz's questioning eyes. "Fine. Yes, they're connected. Well? What are you waiting for? Sheriff, we're going to need a list of every goddamned abandon building in town. We're going to start a search—and we're going to find those fuckers. Today."

ABE was engrossed. At least he was trying to be. He was sitting in a wheeled desk chair, perusing the bookshelf in front of him, gently rolling back and forth as he jotted down book title after book title. Keeping busy. It was the best way not to think about Professor Miller. Best way not think about her body being found under her car. Best way not think about the grey pallor of her skin and the blank, lifeless stare in her eyes. Best way not think about the gaping red gash that crowned her neck from ear to ear.

When he first saw her, Abe thought it was some sort of scarf, carelessly tied around her neck as a weird fashion statement. Professor Miller had been known for oddball choices in clothing. But then he saw the jagged edge of the gash and the dried, rust color of de-oxygenated blood. Seeing it made him want to vomit; he nearly did, but there had been nothing in his stomach except for a diet milkshake, the regretful morning-after drink of a worried night's binging on Oreos and Fruit Loops. Thank heavens for that, anyway.

He'd been trying to lose himself in work ever since, pushing himself on with the urgency of the mission. He had started by cataloguing the books still remaining in the office, hoping it would jog his memory of the ones which were no longer there. Abe sighed. It was hopeless. Professor Miller had no method to her madness. Sure, she knew which books she had and where they were. But she never put anything back when she was done with it. She'd just toss it to the side and pick up another text. It would take Abe hours to even figure out what books were actually in the office. Then there were the books she might have at home. There had to be a better way.

Abe was so engrossed that he didn't hear the footsteps in the hall.

"Mr. Ruth?" a voice said at the same time that Abe heard a gentle knock on the door. Despite the softness of the knock, Abe nearly jumped out of his skin.

He quickly looked up. A police officer was standing in the door. "Y-Yes," he replied, recovering.

"Hi. I'm Officer Davison. Vance Davison. Detective Evans sent me. I'm posted to watch you. Just in case of…well, you know…so…I guess I'll just be out here."

Abe gave the officer small smile and a thankful nod as he turned and walked back out the door. He watched him go. He had to give a small laugh. It was almost funny to have a cop outside guarding him. Like Abe was someone important. Seemed like something out of a movie. "Oh, who are you kidding?" Abe mumbled to himself. "You haven't seen a movie in months. You spend all your spare time on line…that's it!" Abe shouted, interrupting his own train of thought. He rolled the chair over to Professor Miller's computer. Quickly he turned it on. With a gentle "ping" the machine whirred to life. "Come on, come on," he said impatiently as the computer loaded. He couldn't believe he hadn't thought of this before. The Internet browser! Abe could check out the history on the computer's browser to see which sites Professor Miller had been to recently. He knew the professor used the Internet as much as anyone else might—it always had more up to date information than her musty books could provide. It was an invaluable tool, even to classical scholars.

"Come on," he urged again, frustrated at the seemingly snail-like pace of the machine. He began to clear space on the desk around the keyboard. Scrap paper…spotting Professor's Miller's phone pad, Abe picked it up. There was some writing on the top piece of paper in Professor Miller's familiar scrawl. "C scr, sheath." The words didn't make any sense to Abe. With a small sigh he ripped the page off, crumpled up the paper, and tossed it in the trash.

HAVING never set foot in one before, Cal found the Country Pastures nursing home much nicer than he had expected. After all the crap he'd heard about old folks' homes, Cal had half-thought they'd find dozens upon dozens of old bodies piled on top of the other, covered in their own feces and dribbling strained prunes down their faces. Instead, the lobby of the facility resembled that of a hotel—and a damn nicer hotel than Cal could afford on his salary.

Cal and Rabinowitz walked over to a stout but smiling woman sitting at a large front desk. They flashed their badges. A mild look of concern crossed the woman's face. Her nametag read "Shirley." "We'd like to see Professor Grund," Rabinowitz said.

Shirley's only response was a blank expression. She seemed to be still dazed by the badges. "I'm sorry, who?" she said, shuffling some papers in front of her.

"Professor Grund," Rabinowitz repeated. Shirley still looked confused. A nearby nurse spoke up. "E.J.," she said to Shirley. "They want to see E.J."

"Oh. Why didn't you say so?" Now that she knew what the two police officers wanted, Shirley's voice and expression were pure sugar and honey. "Now isn't that nice? No one ever comes to visit him. Well, not much, anyway. Course that's true of so many of our residents here." She clucked sympathetically. Rabinowitz rolled her eyes. She preferred the quiet, dumbstruck Shirley. "Course I'm not sure why the police would want to talk with him; I don't think he's robbed any banks lately." Shirley was the only one laughing at her lame joke. "Now let me see, it's just after 2:00, so I guess E. J. would have just got back from OT. That's occupational therapy. Hold on a moment while I check up on him. You can wait for him over there, in the reception room." And with some considerable effort Shirley got up from her desk and waddled off.

"Why do you call him E.J.?" Rabinowitz asked the nurse.

"Well, we give nicknames to just about everyone who comes in here. It's a thing we do." With that she walked off.

Rabinowitz gave the nurse a contemptful stare. "Can you believe this?" she said to Cal as they found seats in the reception room. "How we treat the elderly in this country is so undignified. You know, in most European nations the family takes care of their elderly. And in Japan they revere the elderly. Here, we just lock you up in some home tucked out of sight where people like Shirley go around all day calling you 'E.J.', not even knowing your real name. It makes me sick."

Cal gave Rabinowitz an amused smile. "I've never seen this side of you, Velvet," he said, half-joking. "I kind of like it, but you're going to make me forget all about the demure ATF agent who first crossed my path."

Rabinowitz rolled her eyes at Cal. "Are you trying to tell me this place doesn't turn your stomach?" she said.

"Actually," Cal replied, "I think it's pretty great. Nice décor, three square meals a day, nurses fluffing your pillows…if it wasn't for the old people smell, I might move in next week."

Rabinowitz finally gave Cal a genuine smile. "Well, I suppose in a few years you will qualify for social security," she glibly struck back.

"Ouch," Cal said, laughing. "Making jokes about my age—that's just cold, Velvet. Tell you what—let's call a truce, shall we, before you start making cracks about my waistline."

"You look fine," Velvet said dismissively. "I'm the one who needs to lose five pounds."

Cal's jaw went to the floor. "You're kidding, right?" he said. "Forgive my stab at sexual harassment, but hey, you look great. Hot, in fact."

Rabinowitz laughed. "Okay, I promise, no more age jokes."

They saw Shirley advancing on them just then, pushing an old man in a wheelchair. The man in the chair looked one hundred if he was a day. His face was lined with wrinkles. Thick Coke-bottle glasses magnified his eyes to ten times their original size, though Cal figured the old guy still couldn't see worth a shit. Cal also noted that he had more hair coming out of his ears than covering his head, though the liver spots on his pate were more than enough to break up the expanse of shiny, wrinkly skin. He wore a burgundy cardigan sweater, and a flannel blanket covered his legs. He was, in short, very much the picture of a very old man.

"Here you go, E.J., these are the nice people who want to see you," Shirley was saying as she parked his wheelchair in front of them and set the brake. She turned to Cal. "When you're done, just let me know and I'll wheel him back to his room. It's the one in the corner back there in case he needs anything. You can just bust on in if you like; he has that whole big room to himself." She leaned conspiratorially towards the two detectives. "He's got money," she whispered, rubbing her thumb and forefinger crassly together before shuffling back to her desk. Rabinowitz rolled her eyes while Cal barely suppressed a laugh.

"Professor Grund?" Rabinowitz said gently. The old man's head was nodding towards the floor. Cal couldn't tell whether he was asleep, about ready to fall asleep, or just plain dead. "Professor

Grund?" she said again, a little louder. "My name is Velvet Rabinowitz. This is Cal Evans. We're with the police department over in
Chambersburg. We'd like to ask you some questions. Sir? Is that
okay?" Again, Cal noticed no discernible reaction from the old man
in front of them. His stillness was seriously creeping Cal out. Rabinowitz tried again. "Sir? Professor Grund, can you hear me?"

"Of course I can," he said suddenly in a surprisingly loud and
strong voice. He strained to lift his head to see the two officers. "I'm
not deaf, you know."

"And do you know who we are?" Rabinowitz said evenly.

"Of course I do," he replied. "You're Johnston's kids. What're
your names—Kip, yeah, Kip and Allison. Kip. What a stupid name.
Figures a moron like Johnston would come up with something like
that."

"No, Professor Grund, my name is Velvet Rabinowitz. Velvet.
This is my partner Cal Evans. We're with the police department." But
nothing seemed to be registering with the old man. Cal decided to
give it a try himself. "Sir, can you tell me anything about the Essenes.
The Essenes? Do you remember, sir?"

"Course I do, Kip," Professor Grund grunted. "I remember the
Essenes. Used to live next door to them, back in the 70's. Bob and
Rosemary. What a bunch of stupid hippies. And their dog was always
taking a shit in my yard."

Cal turned to Rabinowitz. "This is getting us nowhere," he said.

Professor Grund was still raving on about his former neighbors.
"What was that damn dog's name? Snuggles. What a stupid name for
a dog. Little thing. Yapping all the time. I ran it down one day. With
my car."

Rabinowitz agreed with Cal. "I guess he is having a bad day," she
said.

"On purpose," Professor Grund added with a note of triumph,
finishing his story.

"Professor Grund, listen to me," Cal said loudly. "The Essenes,
the religious group, the cult...do you remember anything about
them, sir? You used to be an expert on them. Can you tell me anything about them at all?" The old man was silent, almost eerily still.
Cal sighed. "This is—" he started to say to Rabinowitz when the old
man's hand shot out and grabbed Cal by the lapel. He was surprisingly strong for his age. Cal leaned in as the professor pulled on him,

bringing his ear closer and closer to the old man's mouth. The professor's breath came in short, ragged bursts, phlegmy and wet, but Cal forgot all about it as he listened to the professor speak.

"Leave the Christ alone," the old man intoned. "He does not belong to you."

FBI Agents Corey Richards and Diane Murney were tired, dirty, and a little bored. Ever since they'd started this case sleep had become something of a luxury, but after searching two abandoned houses and one empty ketchup factory, they both needed a shower much more than a nap.

"Do you buy this whole cult idea?" Corey asked Diane as they searched yet another abandoned house, a small, decrepit duplex on Edler Avenue. The house was stifling hot, full of debris, and stank like the dead dog they had found in the basement. Gun in hand, Corey moved slowly up the stairs, hugging the filthy wall as he did so. He sorely hoped they wouldn't see any mice; the yelp he let out when they saw the rats in the ketchup factory was enough fodder for Murney to question his manhood for weeks to come.

"I don't know," she replied. "It's pretty hard to swallow. Wacky cults seems more like a California thing than an East Coast thing to me."

"Those are suicidal cults," Richards replied. "Murdering cults is more Texas."

"Those are chainsaw cults," Murney responded glibly, "and that's only in the movies."

Approaching the top of the steps, the two grew silent. They tensed their arms, holding their guns firmly out before them. Richards signaled Murney with his eyes; she took point. "FBI!" she shouted, bursting into the master bedroom at the top of the stairs.

Empty.

Richards put his gun back in its holster, unsure whether to be grateful or frustrated. "How many more places do we have left to check?" he said. He looked at his watch; it was close to 4:00.

"Two," Murney replied, checking a small piece of paper tucked in her pocket. "An old farmhouse, and an abandoned church. Both north of the city. Might be a bit of a drive."

"Right." Richards grabbed the radio attached to this belt and prepared to sign in. "This is Team Delta, reporting in. The Edler Avenue domicile is clear, repeat, the Edler Avenue domicile is clear. Over."

"Roger that," the dispatch operator's voice crackled over the tinny radio speaker. "Proceed onto the next search. Over."

"Have any of the other teams reported finding anything? Over."

"Negative, Team Delta. Over and out."

Richards sighed. Looked like another wild goose chase to him. And night would be here before long. "A bit of a drive?" he said to Murney. "Think we might pass a soft-serve joint on the way?"

Murney gave her partner a small frown, then grinned. "I hope they have frozen yogurt," she said as the two headed down the stairs and into the fresh air of the day.

"**ARE** you sure that's what he said?" Rabinowitz asked Cal.

Shirley had just wheeled Professor Grund back to his room. Cal and Rabinowitz stood outside the nursing home. Rabinowitz had been briefly enjoying the warmth of the day after the coolness of the strong air conditioning in the home when Cal had told her what the Professor had said.

"Yes, Velvet, for the third time, yes! I practically pissed my pants when he said it, so I'm sure that's what he said!"

"Okay, okay," Rabinowitz replied, holding up her hands in a mock gesture of surrender.

Cal sighed. "I'm sorry. I'm just so fucking frustrated. Here I was thinking we were getting nowhere with the old man and then he pops out with the same phrase we've found at each of the murder scenes. And then he goes completely silent and falls asleep on us. What the fuck does it all mean?"

"I don't know," Rabinowitz said. "Maybe...maybe he was just remembering something he'd read once. Something associated with the Essenes. We were prodding him an awful lot. Maybe his brain just associated what we were saying with some phrase he'd read somewhere before."

"But where?" Cal asked. "Professor Miller had never heard of it. Abe can't find anything about it. How does an obscure phrase known only to a wheelchair bound loony tune end up all over our crime scenes?"

"Maybe he put it there," Rabinowitz said slowly.

Cal threw her a cock-eyed glance. "Be serious," he said. "The old gork hasn't been out of his chair in years. He's not strong enough to walk out of this home, let alone stab a bunch of people to death."

"That's not what I meant," Rabinowitz said. "Just listen up for a second. Let's say you've become fascinated with this obscure religious cult. Where do you go to find out more information about them? The Internet? Your local library? You research your crazy-ass heart out because somehow you know you're going to bring this cult back, hell, you're going to surpass the original. And then you find out that the world's foremost authority on this group lives in some old folks' home. What do you do then?"

Understanding dawned on Cal's face. "You pay him a visit," he said.

"That's right," Rabinowitz continued. "And maybe he's having a good day. Maybe he can tell you things you didn't know. Maybe he can tell you about their language. Maybe he can even translate something for you into an obscure language no one else can read."

Velvet furrowed her brow. "Cal, maybe this is why all the killings are happening here. In Chambersburg. Because of Professor Grund. These guys came here to see him and decided to stay."

"You really think so?" Cal asked.

Rabinowitz shrugged. "There's only one way to find out," she said. With a defiant gait she strode back into the home. After a brief pause, Cal followed.

Shirley was still at the desk. "Shirley," Rabinowitz said, "I'd like to know who else has been in to visit Professor Grund—err, E.J.—in, say, the past six months."

"Oh, dear," Shirley said, looking a little uncomfortable at the authoritative gaze Rabinowitz was throwing her. "Well, you see, officer, I'm not really sure. We don't have a sign-in policy or anything like that."

Rabinowitz lowered her face to look Shirley directly in the eye. "Try to remember," she growled.

"Oh, yes, oh, well, let's see, well there is that one nice lady who comes about once a week or so, I think she lives in Chambersburg, used to be his student I believe. She's awful nice, but dresses so funny, you know? Very out of date. Oh umm, let me see…I really honestly cannot think of anyone else. He doesn't have any family you know. Never married. I've often wondered if he wasn't a…well, you know." Shirley giggled a bit. Rabinowitz looked as though she wanted to practice some police brutality on the woman. "One of those men. But to be honest, officer, I can't think of anyone else who has ever visited E.J. But let me ask around, just to make sure." Picking up the phone, Shirley quickly punched in some numbers and made a few calls, confirming that, as far as anyone knew, Professor Miller had been the only person to ever visit Professor Grund in the home.

"You're sure no one else has ever been in to see him?" Rabinowitz asked.

"Quite sure. You know, just that one woman. Well, and the doctor of course. And that priest."

At the word "priest" Rabinowitz's ears pricked up. "Priest? What priest?"

Shirley looked confused for a moment. "Oh, well, let me see, it was about—what? Six months ago I think. Maybe a little longer. A very handsome man. Rather young. And Italian. I do love a handsome, Italian man," Shirley smiled warmly to herself, enjoying whatever lurid imaginations about Italian men that were currently running through her head. She caught herself a moment later and resumed talking. "Well, it's quite common, you know, for the residents to want to see a spiritual leader. Though of course E.J. never asked for him, at least not to me, and I'm the person who coordinates such visits. He just showed up out of the blue, asking for a Professor Grund, just like you. Oh! I should have remembered that E. J. was a professor. Oh, well. You can't remember everything, can you?"

"Can you remember this priest's name?" Cal urged.

"Let me think…he did tell me—I remember it was a city somewhere…Father Rome? No…Father Florence? Oh that's just ridiculous…ah, yes! Father Padua! I remember because my son was reading *Romeo and Juliet* in school at the same time. And that book is set in Padua. So I'm sure that's right."

"Had you ever seen him before? Or since?" Cal pressed.

Shirley shook her head. "Can't say that I have. And I know every minister, priest, and clergyman for miles around." She shrugged her shoulders. "Still, maybe he was an old friend or something. Only he didn't act like he knew E. J. And he wasn't very old. Strange."

"Did anything happen during the visit?" Rabinowitz asked. "Anything out of the ordinary? Was Professor Grund overly excited, or did he talk about anything they spoke about?"

"Nope. Nothing unusual about it at all. Although he has deteriorated so much since then. It's like making your peace with God just takes all the wind out of your sails. Well, that's the way of the world. But sometimes they linger on so. That's not for me. Quick. That's how I'd like to go—before I ever knew it was happening."

Cal thought of all the bloodied bodies he'd seen the last few days, their throats gashed wide open, their intestines turned inside out, their eyes still blankly screaming in unimaginable dread. He grimaced. "Be careful what you wish for, Shirley," he said. "You just might get it."

JIMMY Atherton looked at his watch. 3:30. Another half hour and he could head home. The whole family would eat a quick early dinner, then go upstairs and watch TV on the king-size bed in his bedroom. One by one, they'd all nod off eventually. All except Jimmy. Once the kids were asleep, once Roberta was asleep, Jimmy planned to go into his bedroom closet, unlock his strongbox, and sit up all night with his .38 in his lap. He knew the cops would be outside, but he wasn't planning on taking any chances.

ABE paused to stretch his aching hands. He'd been banging away on Professor Miller's antiquated computer for just under two hours, but it had turned out to be a goldmine. He ran his fingers through his thick, messy, straw-colored hair, thinking furiously. *The Dead Sea Scrolls*, he thought. *She had been looking at information about them. That makes sense. The Essenes wrote them after all.*

But one thing Abe uncovered did not make sense. Professor Miller had performed numerous searches looking specifically for information on the Copper Scroll. *She always thought it was just some silly hoax, a bunch of crap*, Abe thought. *Why was she so interested in it now?* It didn't make any sense, and yet there was no doubt about it; something about the Copper Scroll had really interested her.

He had pulled up an on-line facsimile version of the scroll and studied it intently. It was as he always remembered—a series of directions to various buried treasures. It wasn't even written in High Essenian; it was just simple ancient Hebrew. Abe thought back on everything he had just read about the scroll itself. Nothing stood out as new, significant, or out of the ordinary. Nothing to indicate why Professor Miller was so interested in it. And yet, Abe felt there was something he was forgetting, something important…if he could only remember. He mulled the problem over in his brain. The Copper Scroll. The Copper Scroll. He began to doodle the name over and over again, hoping it might jog his memory. The Copper Scroll. The Copper Scr—

With a sudden burst of inspiration and an even more sudden flash of movement, Abe dived straight towards Professor Miller's trash can.

RICHARDS greedily took another big slurp of his chocolate cone, being careful not to drop any of it in his lap or careen off the road as he drove north on Route 11. They'd been lucky to find a little ice cream joint right off the main drag; the place was hopping, and as he dug into his cone again, Richards appreciated the smooth texture and rich flavor. "This is good," he said to Murney, his mouth half-full of ice cream.

Murney sighed. Her small dish of vanilla frozen yogurt wasn't nearly as appealing as Richards' towering chocolate cone. "Don't talk with your mouth full," she replied sulkily, trying to enjoy another spoonful of her dessert.

Richards smiled, took another big lick, and kept driving. They were headed for the farmhouse. Thinking back on the assignment at hand made him a bit uneasy. With a slight chill he realized that, if they found what they were looking for, this might be his last ice cream cone. Ever.

"LOOK at this description. I think Shirley used the word 'handsome' twelve times in describing this guy."

"Do you think he's our man?" Cal asked as they drove back to Chambersburg. "Is this the guy we're looking for?"

"I don't know," Rabinowitz replied. "An evil pseudo-priest cult-leader killing other clergy? It almost seems like a cliché."

"Not much of a description, either. 'Late 30's. Short, dark hair. Flashing dark eyes. Graying at the temples.' Sounds like a romance novel to me. What is it with you women and clergymen anyway?"

"It's the *Thorn Birds* syndrome," Rabinowitz glibly replied. "A guy goes without sex for forty years, you figure he's got to have a lot of passion built up inside him."

"Sounds like you speak from experience," Cal joked, gently teasing her.

"Not me," Rabinowitz laughed. "I've got no rabbis in my closet."

They both smiled at this, then fell silent. Finally Rabinowitz spoke. "Think this is our guy?" she repeated. Cal didn't respond. He didn't have to. They both knew, even if it was, it wasn't much to go on.

Cal checked his watch. It was almost 4:00. They hadn't heard from Dan at all. In this case they both knew that no news was bad news. Really bad.

Cal looked at the position of the sun, sinking slowly in the sky. They still had four hours until sundown. But he knew it was getting late. Almost too late.

ABE finally found the balled up piece of paper and studied the Professor's scrawls, this time with more intent. "C scr sheath." It had made no sense before. He hadn't paid any attention to it.

Now it made sense.

RICHARDS and Murney arrived at the farmhouse. With a gentle *crack* he swallowed the rest of his cone and the two prepared to go inside. The place was isolated. The outside was a ramshackle gray, the paint having all peeled off years ago. The front steps were cracked and splintered, protruding out at odd angles. A rusty nail stuck up from the top step, almost taunting Richards to step on it.

Richards took out his gun, waving Murney to the other side of the steps. She took out her gun as well. They stood before the creaky battered door. Richards took a deep breath—one, then two.

They burst inside.

4:00. Jimmy was done. With little more than a quick "good-bye" to Shelly, he collected his keys and headed straight out for his truck.

The parking lot was only a quarter-full of cars, most of them in front of the supermarket. The lot immediately in front of Jimmy's pharmacy was largely deserted, but the milling customers loading groceries into their cars and the stock clerk gathering stray grocery carts comforted Jimmy.

He had parked as close to the store as possible, right next to the handicap parking spot, so it only took him a few steps to get to his truck. His key was already at hand, and he deftly inserted it into the car's lock.

"Bishop Atherton?" a small voice squeaked behind him. Even though the voice was gentle and meek, Jimmy hadn't known anyone was there, and to hear his name called made him jump clear out of his skin.

He quickly turned. Standing before him was a young woman he knew. Her name was Lisa Point, she was sixteen, and she was a member of his ward, although he had not seen her around in some time. Her parents had said that she was living with and tending to an elderly grandmother, but now, with the girl standing before him, Jimmy could see that they'd been lying to cover up the truth.

The girl was pregnant.

Jimmy sighed. Instantly a flood of emotions coursed through him—anger and shame at the girl's condition; anxiety and nervousness over pausing in the parking lot like this; disappointment in this great country that it had led another young girl astray from the teachings of God.

But those emotions were quickly replaced by the horror of one specific memory: this girl and his own son laughing together, close, friendly.

"Lisa," Jimmy said, his voice tight and tense, "who did this to you, girl?" The girl looked ready to cry; numbly, she shook her head, as if refusing to answer. Jimmy grabbed her by her shoulders, more roughly than he intended, desperate to know the answer. "Who did this? Who is the father of your unnatural child? You must answer me!"

When she spoke, her voice was barely a whisper. "Aaron," she murmured in reply.

"Are you sure?" Jimmy spoke. His voice tinged with anger and rage. His own son! "Are you sure about that? Have you been whoring around, girl?"

"No, Bishop," she said plaintively. "It was just with Aaron, just those few times." There was something in the way she spoke—a delicateness in her tears—that convinced Jimmy she was telling the truth.

All other thoughts had been cast aside. "Why are you here? Where have you been all this time?"

The girl was openly weeping now. "My mama's been hiding me ever since she found out. I've been at my aunt's house in Greencastle. But a friend of my father's saw me when I went to the doctor for a check-up. He told. He told! My papa came and got me and threw me out, said I am not fit in the eyes of God nor man. Please, Bishop, you have to talk to him, you have to get him to let me come home, please! He will listen to you!"

"Does your father know that Aaron is this baby's daddy?" Jimmy asked.

"No," Lisa softly replied. "I haven't told anyone."

"Good girl," Jimmy said. "Good girl. We're going to keep it that way, you understand?" Lisa nodded. "Good. Okay now, hush child, stop your crying. I promise I will speak to your father. We will work something out. Maybe we can give up this baby for adoption to a childless Mormon couple who could raise it in God's intended way." Jimmy thought with a twinge that he was talking about his own grandson, but he cast that thought aside. Focus on your son, he said to himself. "You hear me? It's going to okay. I will take care of everything. I promise. Okay?"

"Okay." With a loud sniffle Lisa stopped crying. She looked up to face the Bishop for the first time, and gave him a weak but genuine smile.

Only the Bishop wasn't smiling back.

Instead, his eyes had grown wide, really wide, and his entire body tensed while his face turned redder by the second. He looked like he was choking, or like he was trying to say something, but the words wouldn't quite come out.

And then Lisa saw a knife stick straight out of Bishop Atherton's throat.

A spray of blood caught Lisa in the face and she screamed, but most of her cry was muffled by her surprise at what she saw. The knife slipped back out and the Bishop fell to the cement ground with a distinct *thud*. In his place stood a man draped in a black robe, and now Lisa screamed again, this time with a full throat. In all the time she had been crying she had not noticed the battered green van park next to the truck, or the two strange beings in dark robes leap out. Even now she didn't notice the other being behind her, but she felt him, felt one hand cover her mouth to stifle her screams while the other hand—no, not a hand, it wasn't a hand at all, but something else entirely, something cold and rough and scaly where a hand should be. She felt that thing at her neck, felt a prick and then pressure, and then the warmth of trickling blood. She felt herself falling, hitting the cold concrete with a solid thud. She was paralyzed now, couldn't move or scream or do anything but whimper softly, and watch, watch the man in front of her as he raised his knife, watch as he pointed it at her swollen belly. "Not my baby!" she wanted to cry, but she couldn't, couldn't do anything but feel the inky darkness of death rush over her as the knife pierced into the top of her round, firm belly and slickly, gushingly, slit its way past her belly button and bury itself deep into her cervix.

"HOLY shit!" Abe said to himself. It was all coming together. There it all was, right there on the screen. "Hey," Abe called out to the cop stationed outside the office. He picked up the phone and dialed. Rabinowitz's voicemail picked up immediately. "Hey!" he said a little louder. Officer Davison poked his head in. "What is it? Is something wrong?" he said.

"Nope. Something might finally be right," he said. "At least I hope so. You got a car outside?"

"Yeah. Why? You need a ride home?"

"We're not going home. Not to my house, anyway. We're going to the station house. And fast! If you have sirens, now would be the time to use them. Clear a path for us. I'll follow you in my SUV."

"But why?"

Abe gave the officer a lopsided grin. "Because I've got a helluva an interesting story to tell your bosses. And I hope they like it."

THE farmhouse was a total bust. All Richards and Murney found was a very active nest of honeybees. "Damn it," Murney said, pulling a stinger out of her forearm. She blew on the area. "That's not going to make it feel any better," Richards replied, barely suppressing a grin. He didn't have a scratch on him. "Shut up, Richards," Murney crossly replied. "Next time you can be a gentleman and check the basement first."

Richards was still grinning. They were proceeding north, with one last abandoned building to search. "How are we doing on time?" he asked.

Murney consulted her watch. "Running late. Shit. We need to check out this church quick, or we'll barely have time for a cup of coffee and a shower before we have to report for tonight's guard duty."

Richards yawned. "Great. Keep this up for another day or two and I'm going to start to look as bad as I feel."

Now it was Murney's turn to grin. "That must be pretty bad, because you look like shit now."

The crackle of the radio interrupted their banter before Richards could reply. "All search squads are to report immediately to their night guard watch. Repeat, all search squads are to report immediately to their night guard watch. Over."

Murney picked up the radio sender. "Delta Squad, orders confirmed, over and out." She looked at Richards. "Guess that shower will have to wait," she said as Richards turned the car around and headed back into town.

BY the time Cal and Rabinowitz made it back to the station house, the place was abuzz with activity.

"God, did you hear how they did it?" Cal overheard one FBI agent saying to another. "They slit her open to get at the baby. The baby actually had bite marks on it. They didn't even take it out of her. They just did it there. The ME says that the baby would have died from the mother's wound, but they didn't wait. They cut their way in and took care of it themselves."

The other FBI agent shook her head. "Disgusting," she said, wrinkling up her nose as they walked away.

Cal's mind was a whirlwind of activity. What were they talking about? What was going on here? Frantically, he searched for Dan. One of the agents told Cal that Dan was in a small room used for interrogations at the back of the house. When Cal and Rabinowitz got to the room, the door was closed, which was usually a sign not to disturb whatever was going on inside.

Not today.

Cal burst through the door without a second thought, Rabinowitz two steps behind him.

Dan was standing near the only furniture in the room, a small table with a stiff wooden chair. In the chair sat an aging Asian woman, into whose hand Dan was pressing a rather large cup of coffee.

"What happened?" Cal said, ignoring the woman. "What are they talking about out there?"

Dan sighed. "There's been another attack."

Both were incredulous. "In the middle of the day?" Rabinowitz asked.

"Yeah, I saw it!" the Asian woman interjected. She spoke with a mild accent and her voice quavered with adrenalin. "It was horrible!" She took a sip of the coffee and turned to Dan. "Blech. This is terrible. You got any good creamer? Like French Vanilla? But I only drink fat-free. I got to watch my figure."

The woman was as thin as a green bean, but Cal ignored the second part of her speech anyway. "You saw it?" he said. He turned to Dan. "There were witnesses?"

Dan nodded. "Almost a half dozen," he said. "Cal, Velvet, this was different than the other attacks. Out in the open. Brazen."

"Where did it take place?" Cal inquired.

"In the Giant parking lot," the woman said. "I saw it. I was coming out with my groceries. It was right there by the handicap parking spot. They did him in good. It was horrible," she repeated. "Awful. Disgusting."

"Who were the victims?" Cal asked quietly.

"Mormon bishop and a teenage girl he was talking to," Dan replied quietly.

"A pregnant girl," Cal added. Dan nodded. He didn't ask how Cal already knew that.

"Did they catch the guys?" Rabinowitz interjected. "Did they get a good look at them at least?" Slowly, almost imperceptibly, Dan shook his head.

"You've got to be kidding me!" Cal shouted angrily. "A daylight attack in a busy parking lot and nobody saw anything?"

"I saw it! I saw everything!" the woman said again, her voice demanding attention. She took another sip of the coffee. "Blech. This really is terrible. Got anything to Irish it up with?"

"Mrs. Fong," Dan said slowly. "Can you do me a favor and tell these two officers exactly what you saw?"

"Yeah, sure, no problem," she said. "I was in the grocery store, and was coming out. I only went in to buy a few things but you know how it goes, you see the moon pies and you think you have to have them, cause they make those nice displays with them which remind you how good they are. I just love that marshmallow filling you know? So I ended up getting a lot more groceries than I even needed, and it cost me sixty dollars, and I think that that's too much, but you know how groceries are getting these days? So expensive for everyone."

"Mrs. Fong," Dan interrupted tersely. "Could you get on to what you saw as you exited the store?"

"Yeah, I was just getting there. Anyway I come out and I see this man talking to this very pregnant girl in the parking lot and I think to myself, this man has got this girl in a bad way, you know? And shame on him because he is so much older than her, why he could be her father, but then I see these two things in robes come out of nowhere."

"Things?" Rabinowitz jumped on this. "What do you mean by *things*?"

"Well, they were covered head to toe, you know, in these big black robes, very scary and dramatic, so you couldn't tell if they were boys or girls or what. I don't know what you call it when you see a person but do not know if it is boy or girl. So, *things*."

"Okay, I'm sorry to interrupt, please proceed, ma'am."

"Anyway, well, it all happened so fast, like something from a movie, these two things just came on them like that—" at this, Mrs. Fong clapped her hands together in a loud retort, causing both Cal and Rabinowitz to start "—and then it was over. But they did it, you know, they took this knife and I saw them stick it right here—" she was pointing to the back of her neck "—and then he fell down. *SPLAT!* And that girl—she didn't know what was going on—they got her too."

"Did they stab the girl, Mrs. Fong?" Cal asked. "Did you see?"

The older woman shook her head vigorously. "No, they didn't do that, the other thing didn't have a knife at all, it just sorta touched her, like it was that Vulcan neck thing on TV, like Mr. Spock, and down she goes, and I thought to myself, 'Wow, they just did the Vulcan neck thing on her, just like Mr. Spock on TV, and it works, too!' but then they cut her open—ohh, that was awful. So much blood everywhere. All over the parking lot." She paused, then looked at Dan. "I'm never going to park in that spot again, even after they clean it up, I don't care."

Cal threw Dan a significant look. Dan knew the silent question he was asking. "Snake bite," he said in affirmation. "Shit!" Cal replied angrily. He slammed the table with his fist so hard that Mrs. Fong nearly jumped out of her seat. "Watch it!" she said. "You almost spilled my coffee!"

Cal ignored the disgruntled witness. "What the fuck is going on around here!"

"What about the message?" Rabinowitz asked. "They wouldn't have had time to write one and make a clean getaway."

"Prepared beforehand," Dan said quietly. "They found it on a piece of paper planted next to the bishop."

"What the *fuck* is going on around here!" Cal repeated again. Mrs. Fong's eyes had grown wide at the detective's language and demeanor. Dan turned to her. "Here, Mrs. Fong," he said, placing an arm on her back and guiding her up from the table. "Thanks so much for coming in to talk to us. If we have any further questions, we'll give you a call," he added as he directed the witness out the door, closing it behind her. He turned to Cal and Rabinowitz. "Did you get anything out of the old man?" he asked. Rabinowitz considered the question. "Maybe," she demurred. "Nothing substantial."

"Jesus Christ," Cal swore, "why can't we get a fucking handle on all this?"

A Chambersburg police sergeant popped his head in just then. "Agent Nguyen is looking for you, sir," he said to Dan. Dan sighed, and without a word to the other two, got up and followed the sergeant out of the room.

"None of this makes sense," Cal said. "We have a group of wackos who are possibly being led by some Italian guy in a Catholic priest's outfit who may be attempting to revive a two thousand year old cult which was Jewish before potentially turning pagan. It's a big ball of supposition, and frankly, Velvet, it's a big ball of shit."

"I know," she said quietly.

"People are dying left and right, being slaughtered in the middle of the fucking day. The whole town is on edge. People don't know whether to riot or flee for their fucking lives. And we're as helpless as ever. No forensics, no clues, no palpable theory of the crime, nothing to go on at all. We have all these cops working on the case, tons of tech guys sifting through tons of reports, and we've come up with a big pile of shit. Nothing but shit."

"Shit," Rabinowitz repeated softly. "Cal, you may have given me an idea here."

Cal shot Rabinowitz a look. "An idea based on shit?" he said. "I'm not sure I want to hear this."

"No, listen up," she said. "When Ramirez saw the report on the soil sample from the first attack, he thought that the elephant dung found in the soil was significant. He said so to that tech guy, Dixon. Remember?"

Cal nodded. "Yeah? So?"

"So? We never followed up on that."

"The FBI chased that lead down days ago, Velvet. They came up with nothing."

"But Ramirez came up with *something*," she said. "He had to have found something important, something threatening to this group, or else he wouldn't have been..." she let the rest of the sentence trail off. No need to say what they both knew happened. "Don't you get it? The FBI traced that lead, but they gave up because they found nothing. They thought it was insignificant. But it *must* be significant, Cal. Otherwise…"

"Otherwise Ramirez wouldn't have died tracking it down," he said. "You may be onto something, Velvet. But what if Ramirez just accidentally stumbled over something? What if he never intended to find what he did in the first place?"

"Yes, but if we can retrace his steps, maybe we can stumble across the same thing," Rabinowitz pressed.

"How do we retrace his steps?" Cal asked. Then, as if answering his own question, he stood up, and without another word swept out of the room and started winding his way to the back of the station house.

Rabinowitz followed. "Cal? Cal!" She quickened her pace to catch up to him. "Where are we going? Cal!" They walked through a door at the back of the house. Rabinowitz blinked as fading sunlight dazzled her eyes. She hustled to keep up with Cal as they raced towards a fenced-off area behind the police station. It was the vehicle impound lot.

There was no one manning the lot. The gated fence was locked with a thick chain and padlock. "God damn it," Cal said, shaking the lock in a rage. He looked around for a moment, then pulled his gun out of its holster. "Cal? Are you crazy?" Rabinowitz said, but for a reply Cal took careful aim at the lock and shot. *BLAM!* The shot was sure and the lock flew apart, the chain sliding with a heavy *thunk!* onto the paved parking lot. "Cal!" Rabinowitz repeated, grabbing him by the elbow. He shrugged her off and continued stalking his way through the lot. He finally stopped in front of a rather nondescript green Chevy. "What the fuck are you doing, Cal?" Rabinowitz shouted as he dug around in his pants pocket. Taking out a set of keys, he unlocked the driver's side door and leaned in. He began to systematically search the car, though Rabinowitz had no idea what he was looking for.

Using the automatic lock release, Rabinowitz unlocked all four car doors and walked around to the passenger side. She opened the door and leaned in, facing Cal as he continued frantically searching the vehicle. "Cal," she demanded, "whose car is this? Wouldn't it have already been searched before being impounded?" Cal's silence only frustrated her. "Jesus Christ, Cal," she finally said, "stop being an asshole and talk to me!" Silence. "No wonder your wife wanted a divorce." That got his attention. He swung his head up to look at her. Rabinowitz took advantage of the moment. "Now that you're actually looking at me, would you mind explaining what we're looking for?"

Cal paused. "I don't know," he finally replied.

"You don't know?" she said. "You discharge your gun on the lock of the impound lot, which will probably get your ass fired and who knows what the ATF will do to me, and you don't know what we're looking for? Whose car is this anyway?"

"Mine," Cal replied in a bit of a huff. "And Ramirez's."

"Oh." Understanding dawned over Rabinowitz's countenance. "This is the car they found him in?"

"Yeah."

"But, Cal," Rabinowitz said, "wouldn't they have gone over this car when they found it with a fine-tooth comb?"

"Yeah," Cal replied, "*they* did. But I didn't."

"But, Cal, listen—"

"No, you listen, Velvet. I'm a good cop. Or I used to be until this case came along. When I started investigating the Okeke case I followed up all our leads like a good cop. It was only after the second murder happened that I started chasing weird ideas about cults and snake handlers and all this weird shit. And all those ideas just took me away from doing what I do best—average, everyday, run of the mill cop stuff. I'm tired of all this bizarre, stranger-than-life cult crap. We're not going to find any solutions to these crimes in old books or in crackpot theories. We're going to find it in the evidence—including here, in this car."

Rabinowitz opened her mouth to argue with Cal, but then abruptly closed it. "Okay then," she said. "What are we looking for?"

Cal was reaching under the driver's side seat, pulling out scraps of paper, used wrappers, and other pieces of garbage. Rabinowitz did the same on the passenger's side. "Two guy cops used this car," Cal said. "And we're both slobs. I've got to hope Ramirez left something behind that night that might tip us off to where he was headed." He looked at the bits and pieces he'd pulled out so far. "This is mostly my shit," he said with a grunt, reaching under the seat to look for more.

"What's this?" Rabinowitz said, pulling out a fast-food bag. "Nice to see you guys are health-food junkies," she joked as she looked inside the bag. "Aww, look, there's even a wrapper in here from a Happy Meal toy. Who got to keep the toy, you or Ramirez?"

"Let me see that," Cal said. He rolled his eyes when he did. "That's Ramirez's kid's toy, thank you very much. He sometimes used the car to drive his family around when they needed to get somewhere."

Rabinowitz's eyebrows shot up. "That can't be regulation," she replied.

Cal shrugged. "Hey, the guy made crappy pay and had a wife, a kid, and a mortgage payment. So he borrowed the car for personal stuff. We all do it."

Rabinowitz raised her arms in a "don't-yell-at-me" gesture. "I'm not pointing any fingers," she said. "With the rent I have to pay in D.C., all my home office supplies come straight from work. And I've got about a year's supply of toilet paper, too, courtesy of the ATF," she added with a laugh.

Despite the situation, Cal had to laugh, too. "I don't know," he said. "Government toilet paper, might not be worth it." He noticed that Rabinowitz was looking at a small scrap of paper and frowning. "What is it?" he asked.

"I'm not sure," she replied. "It's a ticket stub. There's a date marked last weekend. 'Admit one' is written on the end. The only other parts I can read are 'Chamb-' and 'Fair-' and 'Slim's Ci-'. The rest has been torn off."

"Let me see." Rabinowitz passed Cal the ticket piece. "Well, the 'Chamb-' and the 'Fair-' are obviously the Chambersburg Fairgrounds. They're located about ten miles north of here. 'Slim's Ci-.' What could 'Ci' stand for?"

Rabinowitz furrowed her brow. "It shouldn't be too hard to figure out what was going on at the local fairgrounds a week ago. But how can that be relevant? Ramirez was obviously there last weekend, not last Tuesday."

"'Ci'—'Ci'—Circle? Circuit? Slim's Circuit?"

"Circus?" Rabinowitz suggested.

Cal's eyes shot wide open. "Holy shit," he said. "Circus! I remember now! I saw a few advertisements around town. There was a circus here last weekend. And, Velvet, where there are circuses, there are—"

"—elephants," she said, finishing his sentence for him. "You think Ramirez was heading out to the fairgrounds the night he died?"

"There's only way to find out," Cal said.

The two detectives quickly slammed the doors shut on the impounded car and made their way back to the station house. There, Abe waylaid them. "I've been looking all over for you!" he whined. "Where have you been?"

"Aren't you supposed to be home, under direct police protection?" Cal asked crossly.

"My police bodyguard has been with me every step of the way," he said, pointing at Officer Davison, who was busy chatting up a young female FBI agent at the moment. "Anyway, I think I figured out what Professor Miller was working on."

"Later," Cal said, pushing past Abe towards the front door. "Right now we're in a hurry."

"But it's important!" Abe pleaded.

Cal stopped for a moment to look the young graduate student right in the eyes. "Look, we all appreciate everything you've done around here, really we do, but now you've got to leave the police work to us. Go on home and lay low. Let us take care of this." With that, Cal swept Abe aside and headed for the front door of the station house, with Rabinowitz only two steps behind.

"But I know why they're doing it!" Abe called out to them.

Cal stopped, frozen in his tracks. He didn't have time for this. He really didn't. But maybe Abe did have something important. Maybe he could explain why all these killings were happening.

And part of Cal really wanted to know...

"Okay," he said. He grabbed Abe by the elbow and pushed him into Dan's office. Rabinowitz followed and closed the door behind them. "You've got two minutes," Cal said. "Talk."

"Well," Abe began, somewhat breathlessly, "I started out trying to do what you asked, to figure out what Professor Miller might have been working on. I tried cataloguing what books were in the office and which ones weren't to see if I could get some sense of what direction her research had been headed. Unfortunately the books were never in any real order, and it was too messy to—"

"Can we fast forward to the useful information?" Cal said impatiently.

"Right. Sorry. Anyway I got the idea to check her Internet browser history, on her computer, you know? To see if that could give me any clue. I wasn't sure if it would work or even if Professor Miller had been using the Internet—"

"Get there quicker," Cal growled.

"The Gold Scroll," Abe suddenly said. With that, he grew silent.

"And?" Cal said. "What about it? What is the Gold Scroll?"

"Do you remember the Copper Scroll?"

"Sure," Rabinowitz said. "That was that treasure map found in those caves in 1952. Right?"

"Exactly. Ever since the discovery of the two Copper Scrolls, scholars have been in a frenzy trying to figure out what they were doing there, because, on the face of it, the scrolls made no sense. Why would the Essenes, a people who placed no inherent value in money, hammer a treasure map out of copper? The fact that it was made like that suggests it was of great importance to the Essenes, but that flies in the face of everything we know about them—that, plus the fact that no treasure was ever found where the map indicated, suggested something else was going on with the scroll.

"As I was going through Professor Miller's computer I noticed she kept looking at various sites that talked about the Copper Scroll, and I couldn't make the connection. What was so important about it? At the same time I was doing that I found a note that Professor Miller had left behind—just a simple note to herself that she had probably forgotten about—that didn't make any sense to me. Then I realized the note wasn't referring to the Copper Scroll itself, but rather to the Copper Scroll Sheath. You see, at the same time that they found the Copper Scroll they found a small capsae, a box designed to hold a scroll or manuscript. The capsae was made of stretched, tanned hide and was inlaid with silver. Obviously, whatever was supposed to go into to it was of great importance, and the scholars who made the find assumed it was supposed to hold the Copper Scroll. Only, there was a problem with that theory."

"What was the problem?" Rabinowitz said. Both she and Cal were now deeply immersed into Abe's story.

"It didn't fit," Abe answered. "The Copper Scroll was simply too long to fit into the capsae. The archaeologists who made the find ultimately assumed the two pieces were unrelated. But then along came Geoffrey Aucter."

"Who's Geoffrey Aucter?" Cal asked.

"Geoffrey Aucter is—was—a British theologian and Dead Sea Scroll historian. He was more radical than the men who were placed in charge of the scroll research. Aucter believed that the scrolls would ultimately re-write the history of the early church itself. That, of course, never happened, but that didn't slow Aucter down for a minute. When the Copper Scroll Sheath was uncovered he developed a whole new theory about the Essenes.

"Aucter believed that the Copper Scrolls were complete fakes. He thought that two millennia ago someone stole whatever was supposed to go inside the sheath and replaced it with a treasure map that was essentially an ancient practical joke. Aucter theorized that what was really inside the sheath was a scroll made not out of copper, but out of gold."

"Why would he think that?' Rabinowitz asked.

"Aucter noted that the sheath was inlaid with silver. Archaeology has shown that capsae, boxes, sheaths, or anything designed to hold an object of value were also usually decorated with precious objects, but less precious than the object inside. Well, the only thing more precious than silver to Jewish or even Roman society at that time was gold. Aucter said that a Gold Scroll was the original item that belonged in the sheath, and that the Gold Scroll itself would have contained the most valuable secret of the Essene people."

"What would that be?" Cal queried.

"A list of the Teachers of Righteousness."

Cal was confused. "Why would that be such a big deal?"

Abe paused for dramatic effect. "Because Aucter theorized that one of the names on that Gold scroll list would be Jesus of Nazareth."

"What?" Cal asked incredulously. "You mean Christ was an Essene?"

"No, no. This is only a crackpot theory," Abe explained. "Aucter believed it, however. Using Gaius Constans, Aucter felt that the Essenian Teacher of Righteousness who came to the Essenes from outside their community was Jesus Christ, and that the Gold Scroll would prove this. Aucter thought the scroll was stolen so no one would uncover this fact, and that the Copper Scroll was put in its place so later generations wouldn't infer that anything was missing in the first place."

"Wow," Rabinowitz said softly. "But this is all nonsense, right?"

"Well, yes, it is, at least it sounds like it, doesn't it? Most of the evidence Aucter gives for his theory is circumstantial at best. However, in 1992 Aucter convinced the scroll authorities to allow the Copper Scroll Sheath to undergo a metallurgical exam to prove whether or not the Copper Scroll had ever been housed in the sheath. Well, the exam found no trace amounts of copper present in the sheath. But they did find trace amounts of gold."

"So Aucter was proven right," Cal said slowly.

"Not exactly," Abe said. "There could be a hundred reasons why microscopic traces of gold would be in the sheath. The craftsman who made it could have been a goldsmith, for example. But it did revive interest in Aucter's theory and the whole notion of Christ being an Essene was again circulated."

"Okay, this is all really interesting," Cal said sincerely. "But how do we go from some possibly fictitious and definitely missing two-thousand-year-old scroll to Chambersburg, Pennsylvania, today?"

"Don't you see?" Abe said. "If what Aucter says is true, then the Essenes were the first people to literally worship Jesus. They were the first real Christians." Abe paused for a moment to let that notion sink in. "Aucter also says that when Gaius Constans reports the Essenes attacking and killing the Nazarenes, they did so not because they were isolationist, but because they viewed other versions of Christianity as distinct and heretical from their own. That's why, according to Aucter, Constans makes no reference to any Jewish or Roman peoples being killed. Aucter believes Constans' reference means that the Essenes were only killing Christians—or literally, *other* Christians, because they weren't true Christians, because they didn't worship Jesus as the Essenes did. Remember what was written at the crime scenes?"

"Leave the Christ alone; he does not belong to you," Rabinowitz whispered.

"If what Aucter says is true, then a statement like that could come right out of an Essenian guide to being a good Christian."

Cal was stunned. "So what you're saying is, we're not dealing with an extreme anti-Christian cult at all, but rather…"

"You're dealing with a group of people who think that their version of Christianity is the first and only true version of it. And if history is repeating itself, they'll kill anyone who thinks otherwise."

"HOLY shit," Cal said softly. "It makes perfect sense now."

Five minutes has passed since Abe had dropped his bombshell on Cal and Rabinowitz. They both needed that much time to let it all sink in.

"But Aucter was a nut, you said so yourself..." Cal said to Abe, his words faltering at the end.

"He was, or, at least, he probably was," Abe agreed.

"But someone doesn't think so," Rabinowitz said.

"Someone like a handsome Italian priest?" Cal responded.

"What priest?" Abe interjected.

They both ignored him. "A priest to whom a cadre of fanatical followers has flocked, believing that their version of Christianity is the only way," Rabinowitz said. "They've gone from fervent devotion to zealous killings. Cal, this could be big—bigger than we ever thought."

"Velvet, a group of people like that—they've got to worship, don't they? They have to hold mass?"

"Of course."

"Then you know what this means."

Rabinowitz nodded. "We're looking for a church," she said.

"What church?" Abe asked. There was no response from either detective.

"Okay, but how does the circus tie in to all this?" Cal demanded.

"What circus?" Abe asked. He was ignored again.

"Only one way to find out," Rabinowitz repeated.

Cal quickly checked his watch. "We've got an hour of daylight left at least. That ought to be enough to get us out to the fairgrounds and get a good look around."

"Take me with you," Abe said.

That finally got Cal's attention. "No way," he replied. "It's far too dangerous."

"But these people killed my mentor!" he said.

"Yes," Cal replied, "and they may be after you next."

"But you don't understand!" Abe said. "These people practice a religion that's been dead for two thousand years. I have to see this!"

"No," Cal said definitely.

Abe did not give up. "But I can be a help to you. I grew up here. I know the area like the back of my hand."

"No!"

Rabinowitz tried a gentler approach. "Abe, we appreciate all you've done and your desire to see this through, but we can't guarantee your safety out there. You understand, don't you?" The graduate student paused, then finally nodded. "Good," Cal said. He stuck his head out the door. "Davison!" he barked. "Take this guy home!" He turned to Rabinowitz. "Let's go, Velvet," he said.

Abe watched the two of them leave as Officer Davison sidled up beside him. Davison looked annoyed that his conversation with the cutie FBI agent had been cut short. "Ready to go?" he said.

Abe considered for a moment. "Uhh, mind if I go to the bathroom first?" he said. The officer shook his head. "Right through there," he said, pointing at a frosted glass door.

"Thanks," Abe replied. "Uhh, this might take a while, okay, so if you want to keep talking to your lady friend, that would be cool."

Davison nodded with a little grin. "Thanks," he said, sauntering back across the room to pick up where he'd left off. Davison smiled. Agent Masters was quite the hot dish, and he'd been about ten minutes away from asking her out. Now if only that grad student's bowels would last that long.

Officer Davison was so involved in talking up the pretty young FBI agent, he failed to notice that the man he was supposed to be guarding never made it to the bathroom door. Instead, he furtively made his way to the back of the police station house and slipped quietly out the back.

THE fairgrounds were deserted; no event was scheduled there for this weekend. Cal and Rabinowitz only gave it a quick once over before returning to their car and attempting to trace Ramirez's last steps.

They drove the stretch of road between the fairgrounds and the place where Ramirez's body was found, but they found nothing more than a few ramshackle farmhouses and a whole lot of cows. Undeterred, they returned to the fairgrounds to start again.

"We know he was found west of here," Rabinowitz was saying, "but we found nothing on the most direct route between the fair-grounds and the place where the car was dumped."

"So let's try some indirect routes," Cal said. "It makes sense for the killers to move the car to a different road than the one they were on. But they had just killed a cop, so you have to imagine they wanted to dump the body as fast as possible." Calling Ramirez "the body" was painful, but Cal wasn't up to using his former partner's name in a sentence like that. Not quite yet.

"So you think that we're better off still checking out the area west of the fairgrounds?" Rabinowitz asked.

Cal nodded. "Go west, young man," he quipped, trying to sound lighter than he felt.

Rabinowitz understood what he was doing. "It's young woman, thank you very much," she said, playing along.

The first road heading west led directly to the interstate highway, and ultimately seemed an unlikely route for the killers to have taken. The second proved to be a quick dead end, but the third was a lonely, winding road cutting through the western woods on the outskirts of Chambersburg township.

"Look at that, Velvet," Cal said as they slowly approached a clear-ing in the woods. Nestled in the back of the clearing was an old church, long since abandoned to time and the elements. "If I was running a crazy cult, an old abandoned church like that just might be the place to go."

"Drive on past," Rabinowitz suggested. "We'll swing back on foot to check it out."

Cal parked the car about a hundred yards down the road. "I won-der if the FBI made it out here to check this place out," he said.

"Only one way to find out," Rabinowitz replied. She quickly pulled out her cell phone, punched in a few numbers, and talked rap-idly to the person on the other end. "No," she said to Cal when she had flipped her cell phone shut. "They never made it out here before this afternoon's attack occurred."

The two officers left their car and walked quickly towards the old church. Coming up to the clearing, they finally got a good look at it. It was a decrepit old building surrounded by weeping willows and myrtles that had wildly overgrown to cover any windows that might have looked inside. The church itself was small, a plain rectangular

building probably built sometime at the end of the nineteenth century. The steeple had collapsed on itself, and most of the white paint
had long ago peeled away. The front door was obliterated by debris,
the front steps having rotted away decades ago.

Cal slipped his gun out of its holster. Its heft and weight reassured
him, though nothing could settle the butterflies in his stomach. Out
of the corner of his eye he saw Rabinowitz holding her gun aloft as
well, her face grimly determined. Without a word he motioned to her
to move forward with him, creeping along the line of the myrtle to
stay out of sight as best they could while they circled around the back
of the church.

Once they had reached the back, Cal spotted something that
brought a small smile to his face. He motioned excitedly to Rabinowitz, but she had already seen it, too.

It was a green van.

Ecstatic but extremely nervous, Cal and Rabinowitz crept slowly
forward, guns at the ready. Cal slipped quietly around to the van's
passenger side while Rabinowitz went for the driver's door. As if on
cue they simultaneously wrenched the doors open, their guns pointing directly in front of them.

Nothing.

Silently as possible they crept to the back of the van. Rabinowitz
had her gun at the ready and nodded to Cal. He understood. Lower-
ing his own weapon, he put his hand on the handle of the door. He
looked at Rabinowitz. She nodded. After a silent count of one, two,
three…Cal wrenched the door open.

Empty.

The two officers visibly relaxed. Cal leaned in close to Rabinowitz.
"We should go back to the car," he said, "use the phone, call for
back-up." Rabinowitz nodded, knowing they didn't have sufficient
manpower or the right equipment to check out the church. The two
softly slipped their guns back in their holsters and turned around to
head back to the car.

A figure was standing in the road.

Where it had come from they could not say. They had not heard
or seen anyone moving behind them, but there he—it—was. It was
draped head to toe in black material, and in the rapidly dimming twilight the gauzy dark material made the figure appear hazy and inco-
herent. Cal felt a tingling surge of dread course throughout his body

at the sight of the figure, and for a moment, neither he nor Rabinowitz could move. Cal scanned the dark area where the figure's face would be, but he could make out no features, only a formless black shadow. He could see nothing save that same shapeless black cloth, fluttering carelessly in an unfelt breeze.

Cal's first instinct was to run, but the figure was blocking the path back to the car.

Cal's second instinct was to calm down. The figure may look creepy, but it was nothing more than a man, a human psycho, yes, but a human being. And there was only one of him, so...Cal quickly scanned the area around them. This was a group, a cult, but he saw no more figures, only the one in the road. Why the fuck doesn't it do something! Cal's mind screamed, unable to fathom why the figure in the road stood dead still, flinching neither bone nor muscle, moving neither to advance on them or to run away.

Then, seemingly without doing so, the figure moved. It reached its right hand behind its waist, and came back holding a long, rusted, curved blade. It didn't advance; it didn't attempt to move at all. It just stood there, holding the blade, menacing, threatening Cal with its inactivity.

Immediately Cal and Rabinowitz drew their weapons and trained them on the figure before them.

The gun made Cal feel strong, powerful, but not secure. He would have liked to see the figure flinch, or flee, but it moved not a muscle, remaining as still as before, the blank black area where its face must be still staring intently at the two officers. Cal decided to take the offensive. He stepped forward. Rabinowitz followed him. They closed to within fifteen feet of the figure. "Freeze!" Cal shouted. "Police! Drop the weapon!" Time seemed to stand still as Cal waited for the figure to respond. "Drop the weapon or I'll shoot!" Cal warned again. He wondered if the figure could hear the panic in his voice. His knees felt quavery, and his hands shook perceptibly as he trained the gun on the figure in black. Still, the figure did not move. Even at this distance Cal could not make out any features on it, but he could see its size, its height, and the flesh of its hand—gray, cold, seemingly inhuman. "Drop the weapon! Now!" Cal yelled again.

The figure did not heed the warning. Instead it raised its arm and took one step toward them.

BLAM! Cal fired one shot directly into the chest of the cloaked figure. In the first instant after the shot Cal recoiled with horror. There had been time. He could have shot the guy in the leg; it didn't have to come to this. He had reacted out of terror more than out of cop instinct. In the next instant, though, his horror intensified when he realized that the figure did not go down from the shot. Cal knew he had hit him. He couldn't have missed at this range, but the figure looked barely troubled by the bullet that had been blasted into his chest.

BLAM! This time it was Rabinowitz, a sure shot right in the heart. Cal could see fragments of the cloth blast open and shred apart as the bullet ripped through the thick material. *Go down!* Cal silently urged. But the figure barely paused.

BLAM! Both of them this time, both in the head, both shots sure and true. Years of experience backed up those two shots, and both were direct hits. This time the figure recoiled, its head flung far back, so far that the cowl of the figure's robe flew off the face and onto its back. But the figure itself did not fall, did not die, and, in seconds, it had righted itself once again, straightening up, knife still held high, still blocking the road, still advancing on Cal and Rabinowitz.

Only now they could see its face.

Its face looked human, mostly, but what drew Cal and Rabinowitz's gaze instantly were the eyes. They weren't normal eyes. They weren't human eyes. Instead, the figure had large obsidian orbs, solid black pools that stared unmercilessly at the two officers. The features around the eyes, too, were less than human; Cal could make out distinct ridges in the soft, ever dimming light, scaly ridges that covered the brow and curled insidiously underneath the eye itself. The nose and chin looked normal, but flattened, and the mouth seemed human, too, but when the figure opened its mouth, no sound came out but a hiss, a low and throaty sound, an angry, violent, evil sound.

Cal could see, in the figure's forehead, two blast holes, practically side by side; a small trickle of dark red blood oozed from the holes. But the figure itself barely seemed to feel anything, barely seemed to understand it had been shot.

Barely seemed to know it should be dead.

But it wasn't dead, was it? It was still blocking the road, still advancing on them, and in the tumbled, jumbled morass of his mind Cal suddenly knew that this thing was not human, that this thing could not be killed by them, and that this thing was going to kill them, kill this whole fucking town if it wanted, because nothing he did, nothing Rabinowitz did, nothing anyone could do was going to stop it.

Cal knew they were going to die.

He could see Rabinowitz tense up next to him, ready to spring, to fight, or perhaps to run, to make a mad dash for the car. Cal himself could do no such thing. He could only wait to die. His mind wandered, and he thought of his darkest moment, of Dani, Dani in her crib, Dani lying there, Dani dead. *Oh, Dani...I'll be with you soon, baby.*

Cal saw the truck a half second before it struck the figure. It was moving at top speed and rammed the figure with a violence Cal had never witnessed before. The dark figure never saw it coming. Unprepared, it flew thirty feet past the front of the truck, violently landing in a pile of gravel on the side of the road. For a second, twisted and deformed, a heap of what it once was, it almost looked human.

Then it began to stir.

The window of the truck opened; a voice screamed, frantically, "Get in!" Rabinowitz moved forward; Cal was rooted to the spot. He couldn't move. He was going to die. Rabinowitz reached back, grabbed Cal by his elbow. "Come on!" she said. The figure was pushing itself up. Cal shook himself from his nightmare; he allowed himself to be pulled into the vehicle. He heard the door slam behind him and the truck peel out a half a second later. Mentally, Cal checked himself over. He was breathing. He was alive. He was okay. He was going to be okay.

The guy driving the car raced recklessly down the road, driving pell-mell away from the church. They were going to be okay. Cal turned to see who his savior had been.

The driver of the truck looked Cal square in the eye. "What the fuck was that?" Abe asked.

SATURDAY

RABINOWITZ smoothed out her long black skirt, trying unsuccessfully to clear out the wrinkles it had picked up while rolled tightly in her suitcase. She moved her finger to ring the doorbell, then hesitated. She was nervous. She was nervous about what she might find. She was nervous about interrupting what might be happening on the other side of the door. And she was nervous that her somber black skirt and suit outfit and didn't-get-any-sleep-last-night hair wouldn't exactly inspire the man on the other side of the door to stop doing what she thought he might be doing.

"Great," Rabinowitz said to herself with a groan. She hadn't been expecting that last thought to pop into her head. She sighed, ran her fingers through her hair one last time, and rang the bell.

Silence was the only response.

Rabinowitz waited, then rang again, three times quickly in a row. She was hoping the ring sounded insistent and impatient, but figured it was probably more obnoxious than anything else.

Still no response.

Rabinowitz was frustrated, restless. She began to pace the small area of the front stoop. Was he even in there? Was he awake? Was he passed out? Was he dead? That last thought stirred her again, and she stepped forward, fist held high, ready to pound on the door, when she finally heard the bounding of steps coming down the stairs.

Cal opened the door abruptly. His face looked flushed and wet, as if freshly showered, and his hair was all neatly plastered in place. He gave her a swift, sad look, one that she returned in spades. He moved aside, and she stepped in.

The house looked exactly the same as it had—when was that? Wednesday? Only three days ago, and yet to Rabinowitz the memory of her previous trip here already felt as old and stale as the microwave breakfast biscuit she'd picked up this morning at the local 7-11. She gave Cal a long once over. He was still in the middle of dressing; his shirt was only half tucked into his pants, and a red striped tie hung casually around his neck, knotted but not tightened, waiting to be slipped into place. It almost looked to Rabinowitz like some type of gaudy hangman's noose, and she shivered at the thought.

"Morning," she said noncommittally. Cal nodded in reply. He turned and busied himself in the front closet, apparently looking for a pair of shoes to match the suit he was wearing. Rabinowitz paused, thought about what she should say, and tried again. "How are you feeling this morning?" she asked.

Cal glared at her. "I'm not drunk," he stonily replied. "I haven't had anything to drink except coffee—plain, black coffee."

"Run out of Cremora?" Rabinowitz lamely said, attempting to make a joke. She didn't feel like laughing right now and could tell by the dirty look Cal shot her that he didn't, either. "Okay, sorry," she replied. "How did you know?" she added.

"How did I know what you were thinking?" Cal replied pointedly. "It was written all over your face, Velvet. I could see it a mile away." He gave a short bark, almost a laugh. "Hell, I could tell by the way you rang my bell. I'm surprised you weren't pounding on the door."

Rabinowitz blanched, feeling guilty that she was a mere second away from doing exactly that. "Cal, I was just worried about you, that's all. After last night—no one could be blamed for having a drink after last night."

"Well, I didn't," he said, finally producing a pair of shoes that would go with the suit. "I didn't even want a drink. I'm not sure what I wanted, to be honest." He paused for a moment and then looked at her critically. "Not that it's any business of yours."

"Cal, I just—"

"It's not your business," Cal said again, more firmly this time. Rabinowitz opened her mouth to argue, then shut it abruptly.

The room was silent for a few moments. Rabinowitz had nothing left to say—nothing that she thought she *should* say, anyway. Cal was the one who finally spoke. "Where's Abe?" he said. "I thought you were going to stay with him."

"He's in the car," Rabinowitz replied. "I thought it best he not see—I thought it best if I came in here and collected you myself." She knew Cal wouldn't like the way that sounded, but at this point, Rabinowitz really didn't care.

Cal looked as if he was going to argue the point for a moment, but he finally decided to let it slide. "How is he?" Cal said. "How's he dealing with all this?"

"He's pretty freaked out," Rabinowitz replied. She paused. "So am I, Cal," she added quietly.

Cal nodded slowly. "That makes three of us, Velvet," he said.

"You know," Rabinowitz said, her voice quavering just a bit, "I've been running the same question in my head all night long, over and over. 'What are we going to do? What are we going to do?' No other thoughts, no other images, just that same question, over and over."

"Got any bright answers?" Cal asked. He was tucking in his shirt, sliding his hand inside his waistline and smoothing out any wrinkles that still might be present. Rabinowitz was shaking her head. "No," she said. "I hate to sound defeatist, but if four bullets didn't stop that thing…I mean, the two in the chest I can understand, the guy might've been wearing a vest, but the two in the head…that's not Kevlar, Cal, and don't try telling me it was. Not to mention getting hit by an SUV going sixty-five. Frankly, I can't think of any rational way to explain it." From the tone of her voice, though, Cal could tell Rabinowitz hoped he could.

Cal's response was quiet. "Neither can I."

"So what do we do?" Rabinowitz asked again, plaintively, though with a hint of fear in her voice.

Cal answered her question with a question. "Did you talk to Dan and Agent Nguyen this morning?"

Rabinowitz nodded. "I went in at 7:00 to report. I wanted to report what we found. I wanted to give Dan that glimmer of hope that we were on to something. But every time I opened my mouth to speak, I thought about what I was going to tell them." She stopped.

"And?" Cal prompted. He was looking in a mirror, fussing with his hair, but Rabinowitz could tell he felt as nervous as she did.

"And—and I realized that it sounded insane. 'Gee, Dan, we found your killers, but, unfortunately, bullets didn't stop them, even two to the head.' There would be no way they would believe me. I just sat there, thinking the words in my head, and hell, even *I* didn't believe me. But I did get something useful while there. A name. Elmer Coffin."

"Who's that?"

"He's the fairgrounds caretaker. Basically he's the go-to guy when any event is using the facility. It might be worth talking to him to follow up the elephant dung lead."

Cal paused, still examining his face in the mirror. "His last name's Coffin? Really?"

Rabinowitz nodded. "That's what I was told."

Cal shook his head and sighed. "This case just gets fucking weirder by the minute," he mumbled, more to himself than to Rabinowitz. The ATF agent grimaced, took a moment to examine her feet, and then looked up at Cal. He was fumbling with his tie, squaring the knot up against his Adam's apple. He turned to her as if for final inspection. She stood up, walked a step over to him. She was close to him. She could smell his cologne—faint, but masculine. Or was that just Cal himself? Rabinowitz felt like throwing herself into his arms. She wanted to be held. But instead she settled for straightening his tie. She took her time with it—she wanted to be this close to him. "Cal," she said again, softly, "what are we going to do?"

For a second their eyes locked. Rabinowitz thought, somehow, in the midst of all the tension and anxiety and fear that they might kiss, right now, right there in Cal's living room, and she wasn't one hundred percent sure what she thought about that. But, instead, she stood there, frozen, and so did Cal, and eventually he broke away, walked over to his couch, and pulled on the suit jacket that had been strewn across it. He slipped it on and buttoned it up, presenting himself to Rabinowitz one last time. "Very handsome," she said, and then, without another word, the two turned and walked out of the house and into the light of day, where Abe was waiting for them behind the wheel of his truck. They got in, and Abe wordlessly greeted Cal with a small nod before driving off.

Rabinowitz did note, and with very little comfort, that Cal had never answered her last question.

THE cemetery was lush and verdant, as most cemeteries are. The day had dawned warm and sunny. A bright American flag draped the coffin. The minister was speaking rapidly in Spanish. Cal didn't understand a word of what he was saying, so he found it easy to let his mind wander. He knew he should be thinking about the matter at hand, or at least be thinking about the case, but his mind kept wandering back to the very last time he was in a cemetery, to the last time he wore that suit, to the very last funeral he had attended. Cal sighed. He knew that here it would be impossible to think of anyone but her.

He remembered how she looked beforehand, before it happened. So small, and delicate, and yet amazingly serene, always soaking in what went on around her, calm and contemplative. She was going to be a smart one; Cal always knew that. He remembered the first time he held her hand, that little itty-bitty fist grabbing onto half of his pinky. He remembered her tiny fingernails, soft and translucent, so clean, so neat, as if…as if exploring her world wasn't drudgery, or work, but joy, simple, sheer joy. He remembered her gurgly laugh, her wide innocent eyes, and the few fuzzy strands of hair on her head.

The hardest thing about finding her was the blankness of her face, the absolute stillness of her expression. It was almost grotesque to see her like that, wholly inanimate and doll-like. It had taken Cal too long to realize what had really happened, so dazed was he in his own stupor. Too long…too late…

It was cold the day they buried her. Autumn. The falling leaves cascading across her plot on that cold, windy day seemed the most fitting tribute Cal could imagine; standing there, watching her small white coffin being slowly lowered into the earth, Cal remembered shivering through his coat, Leah crying hysterically next to him, Leah a mess as any mother would be. But Cal, Cal felt cold, just cold, inside and out, nothing more, nothing less, just plain cold.

"Hey," a voice said, interrupting his thoughts. Rabinowitz. Velvet. Cal turned to look at her. She looked so different than Leah—fuller, softer, more feminine. "Everyone's leaving," she was saying.

Cal quickly looked around. The casket had been lowered to the ground; the young widow and her son had begun the long procession back up the verdant hill towards the waiting limousine. Everyone was slowly streaming away, leaving behind only Cal and Rabinowitz, and Ramirez, of course.

Cal turned back to look at the place where his former partner now rested. "I was supposed to be watching her," he started. "Leah had left for a day's shopping. My birthday was coming up soon. It was my first day off in eleven days, and I was dead tired, but I was kind of looking forward to it. Just me and her, you know? Just the old man and his little princess, together."

"Cal," Rabinowitz began. She had been startled by Cal's speech, but now she spoke up. "Maybe this isn't the right place to…"

"We had a nice morning. Not doing anything. I watched TV. She rested on my belly. Just what dads and daughters do at that age. I fed her, put her down for a nap, made myself a sandwich. I remember—Leah had made a roast beef two nights before. That was a pretty rare occasion, and it was a good piece of meat. I made a sandwich—just the meat, and some mustard, on a big Kaiser roll. I said I'd have just one beer. Just one. The game was on. It was my day off."

"Cal—"

"One somehow became four which somehow became eight which became twelve. I don't know. I was so out of it. I dozed off for a while—passed out—whatever you want to call it. I came too and saw the time. The kid should have been up hours ago. I was surprised she wasn't crying, waiting to be changed. I knew she needed to be changed by now. God, that kid could shit! She was a sweet girl, and smart as a whip—regular rocket scientist—but she could shit up a storm. Filled up that diaper every time. So I knew she needed to be changed. I stumbled off to her room. Still pretty much out of it. I got the diaper table all set—fresh new diaper, powder, a rattle to play with. All set.

"It took me—it took me a while to figure out something was wrong. A few minutes at least. I was so tired, everything was in such a haze. I—I called the ambulance then, and the EMT's came, and they took her in. The doctor said it was SIDS. Said nothing could have been done. She said sometimes, sometimes it just happens like that, and they couldn't tell us why. Couldn't give us a damn reason why."

Rabinowitz was listening, intent and sympathetic. "That's true, Cal, there was nothing anyone could have done." She couldn't tell if Cal could hear her or not.

"But that's just it, isn't it?" he said. "What if she had cried out, or something, and I was too piss drunk to even notice? What if she needed her old man while I was fucking passed out on the couch? Nobody said anything—not even Leah, not then anyway. But they could smell it. They could smell me. They knew. And you know what I did? When we got back from the hospital, you know what I did? I went to the kitchen and poured myself a drink. A big, tall vodka on the rocks. Instead of comforting my wife or crying for my kid, I just had a fucking drink." Rabinowitz's eyes glistened as she heard Cal's confession. She stroked his arm softly, though she wasn't sure he could feel anything right now. His face was blank, and he had a faraway look in his eyes that Rabinowitz could only chalk up to being deep in the throes of memory. "And that's what I did for the next couple of years. I drank away the pain, I drank away my marriage, hell, I drank away my life. But it didn't work. When I stopped drinking, it was all still there, only more fucked up than ever."

"That kind of pain never goes away, Cal," Rabinowitz said soothingly. Cal blinked and looked at her. "So what do we do?" he whispered. She shrugged. "You just get back down to the business of living," she said. "Somehow, the rest of it will work itself out. That's what I believe."

Cal inhaled deeply, holding in the breath before letting it out in one long, slow release. "I've always been a cop, Velvet, I've always been out there saving people. And, then, when it mattered most, I...I didn't save her, Velvet."

"You couldn't have, Cal," she said. "No one could have saved her." She saw a solitary tear roll out of Cal's eye and across his cheek. Rabinowitz felt like crying herself, but she kept her emotions in check. "All you can do is love her, remember her, and live your life as best you can. That's all any of us can do, Cal."

Cal sighed again. "Jesus," he said with a short bark that resembled a laugh. "I've never told any of that to anyone."

"So why me?" Rabinowitz asked, surprising Cal with her question. "Why now?"

Cal considered her question. "I'm not sure," he finally said. "I guess, maybe, being here, after last night..." He trailed off, leaving his thought unfinished. He cleared his throat. "We should get going," he added. "We've got a lot to do."

The two began to walk back to the row of mourners. Cal could see Abe waiting for them respectfully. Dan was standing next to him.

"Cal," Rabinowitz was saying as they made for Abe's truck, "do we have any idea exactly what we're going to do yet?"

"Well," Cal said, "we're going to talk to that fairground guy, right?"

"Then what?"

Cal stopped and looked Rabinowitz squarely in the eyes. "Pray," he said, only half-jokingly.

Dan nodded to Cal when they finally made it up to the truck. "How are you holding up?" he asked quietly. "Fine," Cal said. He didn't even bother asking Dan the same question back. The sheriff looked as if he'd slept maybe seven hours in the last seven days, and now he'd just buried one of his men. "You got anything for me?" Dan asked. His question was directed at Cal, but he glanced at all three of them, his eyes throwing off a combination of wariness and hope. Cal thought it best to remain noncommittal for now. "Maybe," he said. "Soon as we have something concrete we'll let you know." Dan nodded. He leaned in real close on Cal. "Get the job done, if you can, Cal," he said softly. "Whatever shit comes out of it, I'll deal with that. But if you can get the job done, then do it, you hear me?" And without another word he stalked off, joining his wife briefly before heading back to the station.

Abe looked at both Cal and Rabinowitz. "Now what?" he said, his first words to Cal all day. "I mean, I haven't said anything yet to the Sheriff or the FBI or anyone, but shouldn't we be telling them something?"

Cal shook his head. "Not until we know what exactly to tell them," he said.

"But, I mean—we don't have to tell them *everything*, do we? Couldn't we just point them to the church with a whole lot of guns and stuff and they can just wipe out whatever that thing was?"

Cal shook his head again. "I'm not sending a bunch of cops into a shit hole like that without first knowing what we're dealing with. We got to find that out first."

"Well, how do we do that?" Abe asked.

Cal made a face. "We go see a man about a circus," he said.

"And then—" Abe faltered.

"And then what?"

"Then—we kill those things?"

Cal nodded once. "You better fucking believe it," he said.

ELMER Coffin's address took them to a small house at the very end
of Ryder Street, a short little trail in one of the poorer parts of town.
He lived in a ramshackle white clapboard house with a concrete yard
and a rusted out wrought iron fence. Cal stepped cautiously up the
rotted out stairs and knocked on the door. A sun-burnt old man with
beady eyes and a dirty trucker's cap answered the door. He held a
large wooden Louisville Slugger in his hands, most likely, Abe
thought, to be used as defense in a neighborhood like this. "Elmer
Coffin?" Cal asked. The old man gave them all a long stare down before putting down his bat. "You cops?" he finally said, his statement
more a challenge than a question. For answer Cal and Rabinowitz
flashed him their badges. Abe thought the old man would step aside
to let them in, but instead he almost casually leaned against the door-
frame, blocking their entry, as if challenging the two officers. Abe
gulped. Somehow, he didn't think this would end well.

If Cal and Rabinowitz were at all apprehensive about the old man,
they didn't show it. Instead, to Abe they looked really pissed off.
"You sound like you've been expecting us," Cal was saying. The old
man blinked his reptilian eyes at them, but kept silent. "Why would
you be expecting us?" Cal pressed.

The old man licked his dry lips before speaking. "I have my reasons," he said.

Rabinowitz spoke up now. "Maybe it has something to do with
what's been going on in town, huh? Maybe you saw something up at
the fairgrounds. Maybe you know something. Or maybe you're even
involved."

"That's a lot of maybe's there, missy. You got anything important
to actually say?"

"I do," Cal said. He grabbed the old man by his shirt collar. Twisting it, Cal pushed him up against the door, stepping forcefully into
the house. Rabinowitz was right behind, and Abe trailed the two of
them, stepping into the front entranceway of the house. It was as
dingy and ugly inside as it was outside. The furniture was shabby and
falling to pieces, though Abe did notice a brand-new twenty-one inch
Sony plasma television set and a large stack of *TV Guides* stacked
neatly on one corner of a dingy sofa.

Cal was still talking. "If you've got anything to tell us, old man, you'd better speak up. People are dying all around us, though somehow I doubt anyone would miss you."

Abe knew that if he had been in Elmer Coffin's shoes he'd be so scared he'd probably have pissed himself, but the old man didn't appear rattled at all. "Go ahead, sonny," he said. "I doubt you got the balls to do anything about it."

"Maybe not," Rabinowitz said coldly. Abe saw that she had her gun out of its holster and was pointing it very directly into the old man's crotch. Abe felt his knees go weak at the sight; he wasn't sure he could handle much more of this. "But if you don't start talking, it's your balls I'd be concerned about," she said.

The old man gave a short barking laugh while looking at Rabinowitz with pure scorn in his eyes. "Go ahead, missy. They don't work right anymore anyway. I doubt I'd really miss them much."

Abe could see the frustration etching the faces of both Cal and Rabinowitz. He wanted to help, but intimidating the old man wasn't getting them anywhere, and Abe wasn't sure he could actually intimidate anyone. "Why don't you all go on home," Elmer Coffin was saying. "I'm an old man. I don't fear death, and I certainly don't fear you. I know my rights as well as anyone, and I want you out of my house. Now."

Abe wasn't sure if Cal and Rabinowitz were going to give up or if they might actually hurt this guy, but he knew either solution wasn't going to get them anywhere fast. Suddenly he got an idea. He picked up the bat and swiftly made his way to the center of the room. "Uhh, Mr. Coffin?" he said, his voice more timid sounding than he'd hoped. "Maybe you should just cooperate and answer our questions, okay?"

The old man gave Abe a sneer. "What are you going to do about it, boy? Gonna bust my kneecap with my own bat?"

"Nope," Abe replied, slipping into his role as interrogator, "not your kneecap. I was thinking more of busting this." And hiding his shaking hands as much as possible, Abe gently tapped the screen of the plasma television with the end of the bat.

The old man's eyes grew wide at this. "Now see here, you step away from that, boy," he said, a small tinge of panic echoing in his voice. "I don't want you messing with that."

"I don't know," Abe said, his confidence soaring now that he could tell he had Mr. Coffin twisting in the wind. "If I don't hear some cooperation soon, my hand just might slip and whammo! Bye-bye plasma TV."

Cal and Rabinowitz both relaxed their grips on the old man, and Rabinowitz re-sheathed her pistol. They both knew Abe had Mr. Coffin's complete attention. "Hey, listen, I know my rights. You bust that TV and I'll get a new one out of the police department faster than you can shit yourself, boy. That you can guarantee."

"Actually," Abe said, smacking the bat in his palm as he walked menacingly in front of the television set, "I'm not with the police department. I'm just your average Joe Citizen. So if I bust your TV set, you're going to have to take me to small claims court to get your money back. And with two police officers as my witnesses saying I never touched your television, why, I can't imagine any judge in the county is going to give you a penny."

"But I saved up a year for that TV!" The old man was desperate now.

Cal cut in. "And if you want to keep enjoying it, you'd better start answering my questions," he said. "And you can start out by telling us why you've been such a dick since we knocked on your door."

The old man was defeated, and everyone in the room knew it. With a weary sigh he sat down heavily in a battered old chair. "Cause I know what you cops are like," he said, "when another cop gets killed. But I didn't have nothing to do with any of it, I swear."

"You mean Officer Ramirez?" Rabinowitz interjected. She could see that the mere mention of Ramirez had raised Cal's ire, and thought it best that she continued questioning Mr. Coffin. "What do you know about it?"

"I saw him," the old man said. "Right before he died, he was up at the fairgrounds, asking all sorts of questions about the circus that had just left. I told him to be careful. I warned him they was all up in there."

"Who?" Rabinowitz asked. "Be careful of who?"

"The snakes," the old man said. The tenor of his voice and the empty, lifeless look in his eye sent a shiver down Rabinowitz's spine. "I told him that place was crawling with snakes. I warned him as best I could. It ain't my fault he got himself bit."

"What place?" Cal demanded. He was doing his best to control his temper, and he fought the urge in his body to smack the old guy right across the chops. "Where did you send him?"

"Eden Hollow," the old man said.

Rabinowitz turned to Cal. "Where is that?" she asked.

Cal shook his head. "I don't know," he replied.

Abe spoke up. "I do," he said. "It's a clearing on the river. When I was in high school kids used to go there to do stuff. You know, smoke pot, or drink, or to get—amorous. Especially the getting amorous part. That's why it's called Eden Hollow. You know, the Garden of Love. I never went there myself—not that I couldn't have if I didn't want to, I mean I certainly could have gone there with someone if you know what I mean, it was just that—well, I mean—"

"Abe," Rabinowitz interrupted. "Not now."

"It's been abandoned for years," Abe continued helpfully. "Nobody goes there anymore."

"Why not?"

"Snakes," the old man hissed. The word sent a shiver down everyone's spine. "Rattlers. It's a breeding ground up there. Place is crawling with them. I warned him. I told that officer not go to. But he did anyway. He was foolish and yet I knew you all was gonna come after me. I know how you cops stick together."

"How do we get to Eden Hollow?" Cal asked, directing his question at Abe.

Abe shrugged. "I'm not exactly sure. Like I said, I never went there."

Cal turned to old man for an answer. The old man paused. "Don't go there," he said. "That place is cursed, I tell you. People go there and they don't come back."

"Where is it?" Cal pressed.

"Go out west of the town. Take the turn-off before the fairgrounds. There's an old church—it's back behind there a ways. There's an old trail. I don't know if you can still see it, but it's there."

"Jesus Christ," Cal whispered. The old church. Ramirez had found the old church. Ramirez had found—them.

For a moment, the trio was too stunned to say anything. But then Rabinowitz remembered one important question they had neglected to ask the old man.

"Why?" she asked. "Why did he want to go there?"

"To see *them*," the old man replied.

"Who?"

He gave Rabinowitz a look that cut straight to her soul before answering. "The snake men," he finally said. "He wanted to see the snake men."

AGENT Richards could barely suppress a yawn as he listened to the pastor go on and on and on. This church had no air conditioning, and it was stifling hot. That, combined with about two hours of sleep, made Richards sleepy as hell. He could barely keep his eyes open, and the droning pastor certainly didn't make things any easier.

"Now is the time for all good Christians to cling to their faith. We see the signs all around us. The Rapture will soon be upon us, of that there can be no doubt. Who amongst you will rise to the heavens, and who amongst you will be left behind, cast aside to suffer the torments of the Tribulation? Only those who have been saved will be saved, my children." And on and on. Richards spied Agent Murney, looking as tired as he did as she leaned against a wooden pillar. Making eye contact, Richards rolled his eyes at the pastor's words. Murney didn't bother trying to suppress her smile; she was just as amused by all this talk of the end of the world as he was.

They'd been hoping for a morning off, for at least six solid hours of sleep. But then the call came in about the Saturday service. Richards knew that Nguyen was urging every church in the area to cancel their Sunday masses—no point sticking the ministers out there for someone to take a potshot at. A few of them needed some extra convincing, but for the most part they only seemed too eager to stay hidden where they were or hightail it out of town as fast as they could. Richards thought that was great; the less people the FBI had to guard, the more they could all concentrate on nailing the guys behind the killings. But then came the call from this group. What were they called again? Richards wracked his exhausted mind. Seventh Day something or other. They didn't worship on Sunday. They worshipped on Saturday. And since they seemed all high on this end of the world shit, their pastor was in hog heaven right now, spewing and pontificating from his pulpit. There was no way they were going to cancel their service, so Murney and Richards and two other agents were assigned to guard the church while the faithful sat there, taking in every word the minister said. Richards snorted. He didn't see what it would hurt for them to miss a week of this stuff. He laughed to himself. In fact, they'd be better off at home. There was a much greater chance of being hurt here.

Still, to be honest, he wasn't too concerned. Two agents stood at the front doors. Murney was at the west entrance, Richards the east. It was a small building, easy to maintain. Anyone wanting in would have to come through one or more of the agents. And they were all armed and, after the last few days, ready to shoot at a moment's notice.

Richards further surveyed his surroundings. The building itself was small, with just one tiny little room off the main church where the pastor changed into his garb. It was all easily contained. The windows were relatively high up, and all of them were closed and locked, which explained why it was so damn hot in here.

Besides, there weren't that many people in here at all anyway. Along with the guy preaching in the pulpit, he saw one elderly couple, one older man who appeared to be a church deacon or something like that, and two young couples, one with three kids in tow, the other with a baby. Twelve people in all. Easy to move in case of an emergency. Richards smiled. *I guess the Clergy Killers have scared more than a few of the faithful away, huh?* Then again, he reasoned, most people liked any excuse to sleep in on a Sunday morning. Or Saturday.

Richards yawned again. He was as alert as possible. He had hoped they'd have some coffee when he got here—he remembered the Baptist mothers always had a great spread set out after church—but these people didn't believe in coffee. *How could you not believe in coffee?* Richards thought to himself. *It seemed so—un-American somehow.* Folding his arms across his chest, he struggled to keep his eyes open. *God, doesn't this guy ever shut up?* he thought. *He's like the fucking Energizer bunny of religion—he just keeps going and going and going...*

PASTOR Thomas Sears surveyed the pitiful group in front of him as he continued to preach. He knew some of the faithful would be too afraid to come. But he also knew that, in the worst of times, especially in a time such as this, the faithful needed the power of Christ more than ever. And to break one of his Commandments—on the Sabbath, no less—was a grievous sin indeed.

Pastor Sears had called them last night, called all his families one by one, spoke to them, talked to them about their fears, encouraged them to come. Why, the Federal Bureau of Investigation of the United States of America was guaranteeing their security. Guaranteeing it! What more could they ask for? And they all said they were coming. In the end, every single one of them said they would come. So many of them lied to him. They lied to their pastor, to their shepherd—and lying to me is like lying to Christ, the pastor thought.

Ellis' absence was the worst. He'd been deacon for only two months. Pastor Sears had been unsure about his appointment, but the other deacon, the faithful Deacon Linden, had vouched for him. Ellis had not even needed convincing. He swore up and down he and his wife would be there. Pastor Sears had believed him. Lies! the Pastor thought vengefully. He knew that, when this was all over, when the authorities had caught the evil behind this terrible tragedy, he himself would make sure that Ellis did not remain a deacon for long.

"I know that recent events have us all nervous," the Pastor was saying. "But it is only through our faith in our Lord and Savior Jesus Christ that we will find our salvation. Brothers and sisters I do not fear death. I have been prepared for the Rapture since I was born again. It is coming. Mark me now, it is upon us. Remember the words of our great Prophet, Ellen Smith, when she said..." Pastor Sears went on automatic pilot, repeating the profound teachings of his faith's great leader. He looked at the rest of the group present. The Otterly's were always good and faithful people. The Corcoran family was perhaps the finest young family in his church, always leading the way. He smiled when he saw young Mr. Sunbury and his wife and child. Mrs. Sunbury had pleaded with her husband not to go; he had confided as much to the Pastor last night over the phone. But the Pastor had reminded him of his obligation in keeping the Lord's Day holy, that the wrath of God and the Army of Christ were for all of those who were truly unfaithful. He had told young Mr. Sunbury to assert himself, that the man must be the master over his wife in order to ensure a happy, fulfilling marriage. The fact that they had come swelled the Pastor's heart with joy; truly, they were saved.

"My friends," he continued, "I ask you to take a moment and look around this room. We have with us four brave individuals here to guard over us and protect our rights to worship. It is a dark time, brothers and sisters. I fear that the anti-Christ will soon be upon us. His messenger is at hand. But think on this, brothers and sisters; has this messenger harmed us? Has he crossed the threshold of this church? I tell you no, no, one hundred times no, my friends! The faithful have been spared, as they always will be. God has protected us, and He has provided for us in the guise of these men and this woman who watch over us now. We ask for God's love and protection to watch over them, and pray they have all been saved and called to God's love and guidance. For only those who have been called will be saved on Judgment Day." Richards threw a quick glance at Murney and gave her a sly smile. He knew that as an avowed atheist she hated listening to this guy more than the rest of them put together. He chuckled softly to himself. Seeing her face almost made standing here falling asleep on his feet and being bored by Pastor Yakkety-Yak worth it. Almost.

"SO a bunch of circus freaks are the ones doing all this?" Abe asked incredulously from the backseat. "What, are they pissed because people kept throwing popcorn at them?"

"This is not funny, Abe," Rabinowitz said maternally.

"Do you hear me laughing?" Abe replied. The truth was, they could both hear the anxiety in his voice, mainly because they could hear that same anxiety in their own voices. "Okay," Abe continued, "so now we know where these guys came from. The question still is, what are we going to do about it?"

"*We* aren't going to do a damned thing about it," Cal said. "*You* are going back to police headquarters under the oh-so-watchful eyes of Officer Davison. And I'll tell him that if he lets you give him the slip again he'll be working a desk for the next ten years. Velvet and I are going back to Eden Hollow. Alone."

"Cal!" They both cried in unison, though for entirely different reasons. Cal could tell that Rabinowitz was concerned about their heading back to the church by themselves. "Relax," he said to her quietly, "we're just going to do a little reconnaissance. Once Mr. Coffin decided to be helpful instead of being a royal pain in the ass, he drew us a useful map of the hollow and the surrounding area. We're going to head down to the other side of the creek and get a good look at exactly how many of those things are out there. Once we get a bead on their number we'll hotfoot it back to town and report what we know to the FBI."

"But what about me?" Abe piped up. "This is my truck, after all."

"When you take us back to the station house we'll swap vehicles with you."

"But you might need me out there. What if those things spot you?"

Cal shook his head ruefully. "As formidable as you were with a baseball bat and a plasma television to threaten, I don't think this is a good place for an unarmed civilian and potential target to go."

"Then give me arms!" Abe said, immediately adding, "you know what I mean."

"Have you even shot a weapon before?" Cal asked critically.

"I was the Pennsylvania State Junior Rifle Champion two years running," Abe said proudly.

"Really?" Cal said, impressed.

"I know I can help you out there," Abe said. "And besides, I'm more safe with you than anywhere else. It's not like Officer Davison did such a good job keeping an eye on me anyway."

Cal looked at Rabinowitz. She gave him a small nod of assent. "Okay, fine," Cal relented. "We still need to head to the station house to gear up. And you're staying in the car. The entire time."

RICHARDS woke with a start. He'd heard a noise. He strained his ears. Nothing. He took a deep breath, inhale, exhale. He'd only been out for a second. Literally asleep on his feet. He hoped he was getting overtime for all this.

He watched as the pastor's sermon grew more intense. His arms flailed wildly and his voice pitched in tenor and tone. Damn, Richards thought to himself, doesn't he ever shut up? I mean, seriously, what does it take to get this guy to stop blabbing?

He found out a second later when a man's body was hurled through the window located directly behind him and landed with an unceremonious *thump!* directly in front of the pastor's pulpit.

"HOW does that priest guy figure into all this anyway?" Abe was asking. Cal sighed. He should have trusted his first instinct and taken the young man back to the station house. Or he could simply drop him off here, miles from anything.

Rabinowitz was trying to answer his questions. "We don't know. We can't say for sure he fits into this at all. Right now, he's just a person of interest. That's all."

"Yeah, when they say that on TV it means the guy is guilty as sin." Abe laughed at his own joke, but quickly grew quiet as they approached the river. They were now directly opposite Eden Hollow. A small grove of poplars, blanketed by larger, fuller fir trees, blocked the river from their view, but Elmer Coffin's directions had brought them right to the spot. They were here.

Without a word Cal and Rabinowitz stepped out of the truck. Abe clambered over the seat and slid behind the steering wheel. Each carrying a pair of binoculars, the two officers carefully made their way through the trees and down the bank. They hid behind a couple of large fir trees, ideal coverage for staking out the other side of the bank. The creek was maybe thirty feet wide here, and no more than ten feet deep, running lazily downstream. At present they were about forty-five feet from the opposite bank. Cal trained his binoculars over the water. He found the crumbling walls of the church in the distance and trailed his way down to the river's edge. There was a good-size clearing. Eden Hollow.

Cal looked for any sign of recent inhabitance. He could see nothing—no campfire, no trash, not even any signed of disturbed leaves. There was, however, a large fallen oak, it's roots massive and gnarled, blocking his view of part of the clearing. It seemed that there was a sharp rise at that point. Several people could easily be concealed behind the rise. Cal lowered his binoculars. He thought about moving his position, but decided it was too risky at present. He knew they had been there. He knew they would be there. The question was, where the fuck were they now?

THE first thought that ran through Pastor Sears' mind was a glimmer of satisfaction at recognizing that the man who came flying through the window was none other than Deacon Ellis, who apparently made it to services after all. The second thought, right on the tail of the first, was a blinding wave of dread when he realized that he was going to die.

"Dear Lord, protect me!" he cried as the three doors of the church burst open simultaneously. Men in long dark robes were suddenly everywhere. Panic gripped the church. The Pastor could see the FBI agents pulling out their guns. But they were too slow. The men in black were upon them. They carried wicked-looking knives, but they did not use them on the officers. Rather, they seemed to grab at them. One of them had the woman agent around her neck, as if choking her, and her eyes grew wide, and she gasped for air before slumping to the ground. One of the agents had managed to pull out his firearm. Shoot them all! the pastor heard his mind scream. The agent leveled the weapon and fired twice into the chest of the figure coming towards him. The gun made a terrible echo, but the man did not stop, or even slow down at all. He grabbed the agent by his face—by his face!—and though the long arm of the black robe hid the man's hand, when he pulled his arm away, Pastor Sears saw streams of blood pouring out from where the agent's sleepy eyes had once been.

His faithful had remained frozen in their seats this entire time, as if believing that the agents, or God, or someone, would save them. But no one did, and the dark men turned their attention to them. Some of the faithful ran—or rather, tried to, but they were struck down. Pastor Sears closed his eyes to the din, closed his eyes to the screams and pleas for mercy, closed his eyes to the prayers and the thumping of bodies and the soft crunch of a baby's skull and even to the gentle babbling sound of blood leaking out of small holes. He closed his eyes, welded them shut, not opening them again until he heard—until he heard nothing, peace, a stillness that filled his soul with even more dread than the awful, terrible cries and sounds of the faithful being slaughtered only moments before.

He opened his eyes.

They were dead, all of them, every faithful member of his flock who had kept the Lord's Day holy, each of them dead, their eyes wide open and filled with unremitting terror. They looked empty, each of them, as if this was the Rapture, the moment they had been waiting for, but it was false, wrong, a great disillusionment.

Only he was alive. Him and the dark men.

They surrounded him, a dozen at least, a ceremonial circle of sharp knives and black, lidless eyes. Yes, he saw them now. Their robes had been torn in the massacre, their hoods pulled back, their faces revealed, and their arms…their arms…yes, Pastor Sears saw them, and knew them, knew what they were—"Demons!" he cried. "I curse you in the name of Jesus Christ. You shall not touch His holy vessel here on earth. You shall not cut down the truth and the way. You shall not impugn this holy place with your black souls. You shall not! You shall not!"

Oh, but they shall.

The first knife caught him in the side, piercing his kidney; the second in his chest, collapsing his lung; the third in his thigh, severing the femoral artery; the fourth his gut; the fifth his genitals; and the sixth his neck, altering his final furious shouts of rage and agony into pitiful, blood-soaked gurgles. Pastor Sears quickly lost track after that, not realizing that the seventh blade had pierced his heart, the eighth his back, and the ninth, and final blow, had sent his head reeling across the church, straight in amongst the bodies of his congregation, the shepherd finally joining his flock in the eternal rest of the faithful.

CAL'S left foot was falling asleep. He could feel the familiar pins and needles sensation starting in his toes. Damn, he thought. They'd already been there an hour and had seen no signs of anything except squirrels and rabbits. Maybe this was all a wild goose chase, he thought. With everything that had been happening, all the deaths, all the killings, and Ramirez…well, it's no wonder he was believing all this talk of snake men and ancient Biblical cults. Standing there, in the shade of a fir tree, his left leg giving in further to that numbing sensation of falling asleep, things seemed clearer, less fantastic, more—more normal.

Maybe that guy did have on some Kevlar body armor. Why not cover the head as well? Or maybe it was simply adrenalin. He'd probably dropped dead seconds after they left. Or maybe…maybe he wasn't a guy at all. Maybe it was a robot, Cal reasoned. Could they make robots like that now? He wasn't sure. He'd seen them in the movies, but he didn't think they could do that in real life. Not yet, anyway. Well, maybe they could. It made more sense than the alternative.

Damn! The leg was totally asleep now. Cal did his best to flex it without making any noise. He looked over at Rabinowitz. She was still poised behind the tree, eyes searching the far bank of the creek, ready for action at a moment's notice. She certainly didn't look like her leg was falling asleep. Cal sighed. He watched the sunlight as it gently reflected off of Rabinowitz's strawberry-blond hair. God, she was beautiful. Long legs, gorgeous hair…and she was right. She definitely had an ass that simply would not quit.

Whoa! Cal's mind yelled. Slow down! This is not exactly the time or the place. Still, it was always easy to be distracted on a stakeout. The long hours and lack of action made it easy for the mind to wander. And Cal did enjoy letting his mind wander all over Rabinowitz. She was definitely his kind of woman. Smart, funny, aggressive. Looked good dressed up like this morning, or dressed down for field work, like now. And definitely looked good with a gun. He smiled. It wasn't exactly a standard female accessory, but somehow, it did something for him. How hot had it been when she turned her gun on that old guy this morning? Very Angie Dickinson. Cal watched as Rabinowitz pulled her pistol of its holster right now. His smile turned into a dopey grin. It did look good on her. Especially now, the sun glinting off her hair and that gun barrel as she frantically waved it at him…

Waved it at him? Cal snapped out of his reverie and trained his binoculars across the riverbank. There they were! One, two, five, six…six of them total…walking hurriedly down the path from the church, walking quickly towards the bank of the creek…walking straight into the creek? What the fuck? Cal was puzzled by this. Where the hell could they be going? Why the hell would they want to wade cross the creek? Where could they be heading?

With a start, Cal suddenly realized they were heading straight for them.

ABE was bored. An hour ago he'd been extremely nervous; forty-five minutes ago, rather tense; and fifteen minutes ago slightly anxious. But now, sitting in the driver's seat of the car as it slowly heated up, Abe was mostly bored, and more than a little bit sleepy. He'd like to have the radio on and the air conditioner up full blast, but Cal had instructed him to turn the engine off and be as silent as possible. Abe sighed. He'd like to fall asleep, but he knew he had to be ready to leave at a moment's notice. Still, his eyelids felt so heavy, and he had barely slept two hours the night before, and it was stifling in here, and he was so tired...

Abe was so tired that he never noticed the figures in black robes sneaking up behind him.

CAL didn't bother maintaining his silence any longer. "Run!" he shouted to Rabinowitz. With a quick movement he turned around and began bounding up the steep slope back to the jeep. He slipped, but managed to pull himself back up in time to hear Rabinowitz scream, "Look!"

Three more figures in black were coming down the hill towards them.

RABINOWITZ had seen Cal stumble, and made a move towards helping him up the slope when she saw them. She had shouted a warning to Cal before pulling out her gun. She wasn't sure it would do any good, but she didn't know what other choice she had. She pointed her gun at the figure closest to her, pulled the trigger, and prayed.

BLAM! *BLAM!* Abe was startled into alertness by the sound of shots. "Shit," he said, instantly turning the key in the ignition. He expected to hear the engine roar to life, but only heard a nimble *click* and a whining *whirr* from his truck. "Come on, come on," he said, pumping the gas pedal and turning the ignition over again and again.

"Fuck, fuck, fuck, fuck, fuck!" he yelled, slamming his hand hard against the steering wheel. *Now what do I do?* he thought. A second later Abe was distracted by a blur of dark movement as a cold gray fist pounded into the driver's side window of his truck.

"JESUS Christ," Agent Nguyen swore to Dan, surveying the bloody slaughter of the Seventh Day Adventists before him. "I told those mother fuckers not to...god damn it, get me a fucking phone, now! I am going to cancel all the fucking church services in this town tomorrow, and I do not give a fuck what any of these asshole priests say! Move it!"

Dan slowly took in the devastation before him. He couldn't believe...he had never seen...something like this was incomprehensible to him. He had to get out of here. Now. He staggered outside. He went to his car. He was looking for his keys, fumbling in his pocket. Dan felt his stomach lurch suddenly, and for the first time in his career as a cop he was sick, throwing up his lunch all over the side of his car. When he was done, he found his keys, opened the door, sat heavily inside the driver's side seat, and slammed the door behind him. And then Dan did something else he had never done in his twenty-two years as a cop.

Dan Moore began to pray.

God help us. Help us all.

OUT of the corner of her eye Rabinowitz saw that Cal was shooting at the ground in front of one of their pursuers. She realized why a second later when loosened dirt and pounding blasts caused the figure in black to lose his footing and fly pell mell down to the bottom of the hill. It was a good strategy, but the second figure was too close and was on Cal before he could even get one round off. "Cal!" Rabinowitz shouted. Her own pursuer was too close to fire at his feet, so she shot him twice in the chest. He barely paused. Rabinowitz aimed for his knee. He stumbled when the shot struck home. Rabinowitz sprinted to her right as fast as she could, backtracking to put more distance between her and the guy in black. All she had to do was get around him and she could make her way up the hill and to the truck. She backpedaled a little more, took aim at the guy's other knee, but missed this shot. The ground was more level here, so she took off down the riverbank, the man in black lumbering behind her, while six other figures slowly made their way across the water. Shit! Rabinowitz's mind screamed as she saw the bank suddenly sheer up in front of her. She couldn't go forward. She whirled around. The figure chasing her was closing in. The water, and the advancing figures, were at her back.

She was trapped.

Rabinowitz checked her gun and gritted her teeth. She would have to make every shot count. Not that it would matter much in the end.

QUICK as a flash Abe flicked on the automatic locks. Panicking, he scrambled out of the driver's seat and into the back of the SUV. Nothing would deter the figure in black. His fist kept pounding and pounding the glass. Abe knew it was a matter of mere seconds before the window shattered. He needed to get out of the truck. He slid across the back seat to the opposite side door. He fumbled with the locks for a second before he noticed them. Two more figures in black.

He was surrounded.

Abe didn't know what to do. So he screamed.

CAL had managed to send his first attacker flying, but the second one had caught up too fast. He turned his gun on him point blank but the figure was suddenly on top of him, pushing Cal to the ground. One cold hand grabbed the wrist of Cal's gun hand. Smacking the hand on the rocks below, he forced Cal to surrender his weapon. Cal kneed his assailant in the abdomen, but the guy seemed to barely feel it. Shifting his weight, Cal could feel his legs pinned underneath him. The guy's grip was iron. Cal could barely move. The black shadow of the cowl stared coldly at him, the left hand of his attacker still withdrawn into the robe. Cal figured it must be holding a knife. He needed to contain that hand as well. With his own free hand he reached into the sleeve of the robe to grab at his attacker's wrist. If he could contain the guy's arms, maybe he could twist his body out from underneath him. It was the best plan he could come up with.

Only when Cal reached up his attacker's sleeve, he didn't find an arm up there at all.

RABINOWITZ placed her back up against the rock face. She faced her assailant eye to eye. He was close, but he approached her warily, still limping a bit. Maybe she couldn't kill him, but she could hurt him. Right now, that seemed good enough to her. She'd wait until he was really tight—a few feet away—before blasting his balls off. See how much he liked that.

But the figure stopped advancing. He stayed ten feet from her, patient. Rabinowitz's own breath was coming in ragged gasps and spurts, panting hard from running up the hill. But her attacker wasn't breathing hard at all. In fact, he didn't appear to be breathing, period. He just sat there, waiting. What the fuck for? Rabinowitz thought.

The sloshing sound of water meeting fabric answered her question. He was waiting for his friends. They were less than ten feet from shore. Once they arrived, well…Rabinowitz knew then that all hell would break loose.

IT was a snake. A fucking snake! Cal grabbed the snake up the guy's sleeve. Jesus Christ! he thought. They fucking carried the snakes in their sleeves! Cal was relieved to realize that he had the snake by its neck. He could feel it writhing and undulating against his grip, the tongue flickering back and forth against his wrist, but those fangs, those huge fangs that Cal knew this snake must have, couldn't reach him. Not quite.

He suddenly realized that he had a weapon in his hands. If he could pull the snake free from the sleeve, he could turn it on his attacker. Cal thought with grim satisfaction of how much he'd enjoy seeing the snake biting into the face of the thing on top of him. With a massive tug Cal pulled at the snake. It stretched, but seemed rooted in place. Cal pulled harder. The figure on top of Cal was struggling with him, as if pulling back. The harder Cal pulled, the more the figure struggled. Cal didn't understand. Why couldn't he wrench the snake free from the man's arm?

Then Cal realized with sickening dread: *the snake was the man's arm.*

SEVEN black figures surrounded Rabinowitz. She could see them now. Their faces, their arms, their evil. This was it. She knew she was going to die. Her mind tried to form a coherent thought, to make peace, to say good-bye, but nothing could pierce the shrieking going on inside her head. She was going to die.

One of the snake men fell.

It went down so quietly that the others did not notice it at first, but Rabinowitz did. It stunned her, silencing the shriek of her mind. Then another fell, and another. They were still closing in on her. Eight feet away. One more fell. Five feet. Only two remained. Two feet. One fell, and one was upon her.

Then Rabinowitz felt nothing: no pain, no fear, no panic, only the desire to sleep, to fall, to close her eyes and never open them again.

CAL struggled with the thing on top of him. His revulsion and horror were matched only by his one intense, incessant thought: *Do not die. Do not die. Do not die.*

Then, without warning, the thing suddenly stopped struggling. It slumped on top of Cal. For a moment he was too stunned to do anything. Then, with a quick movement, he thrust it off of him and scrambled to his feet.

A man was standing in profile before him. He was a dark man, with dark hair and flashing black eyes, but he was a man. He was dressed all in black, but these were not robes, just simple black trousers and shirts. He was a handsome man, around Cal's age, trim, and in good shape. In his hands he held some sort of weapon, a gun, but like no gun Cal had ever seen before. He was yelling at two other men, dressed just like him, who had scrambled down the slope towards Rabinowitz. She was lying in a heap on the side of the river, but she looked okay. Cal could see she was still breathing, anyway. All around them the black-robed men lay inert, crumpled all along the leaf-strewn riverbank. And there was someone else, too, someone moving on Cal's right. He turned to see who it was.

Abe.

He was okay. They were all okay. Well, they were alive, anyway. "But…how?" Cal asked. He turned towards Abe. The young man held the same weapon in his hands that the other men did. Cal saw two of the men pick up Rabinowitz and carefully but quickly begin to carry her up the slope. "Abe?" Cal asked, looking at him for an explanation.

The young man shrugged, his face still dazed, but his expression happy. "They saved us," he said plaintively, making his own way up the steep slope.

"Who?" Cal asked, turning to face the first man he saw. The man was speaking. "Come quickly my friend. They are only unconscious, and will rouse themselves in a minute or two. We must go now." He spoke with the trace of a continental accent. Gesturing their need for haste, the handsome man reached out his hand to help Cal up the slope.

"Who—who are you?" Cal asked again. The man turned to face him, and Cal finally saw the square of white cloth around his neck, placed securely in his collar.

The handsome man gave Cal a small, formal nod. "Father Antonio Padua, at your service."

FATHER Padua! Cal's mind began to race at the sound of that name. This was the guy they'd been looking for, the one they wanted to talk to, the one they thought might be behind it all…and here he was, saving them from those things! Then he must be helping them, Cal's mind ran. He must be a good guy…right? So we can trust him.

Right?

They had little time to think. Cal could see several of the snake-men already stirring. Father Padua was still urging Cal to move quickly up the slope, and the sight of their enemies rousing themselves was all the encouragement Cal needed. Abe was already up the slope, and Rabinowitz had been carried by the other two men and was out of sight. Cal followed Father Padua up the steep hill as fast as he could go. "What do you have up there?" he said between deep gulps of fresh air. "A car? A truck? A bulldozer might be good."

"We have a vehicle waiting. Quickly, my friend," was the priest's response. Cal noted with some small measure of disgust that the priest was hardly breathing deeply and resolved to work out more in the future—that is, if they survived the night.

Running after the priest, Cal rounded a corner and saw the two men gently loading Rabinowitz into the backseat of a red mini-van. "You've got to be kidding me," he said, climbing into the backseat of the van behind Father Padua while one of other men—probably priests as well, Cal reasoned—got behind the wheel. "A mini-van? You guys drive around in a mini-van?" It was an absurd question, but it was the only coherent thought Cal could wrap his mind around right now. The priest shrugged in response. "It was the largest vehicle the rental company had," he said matter-of-factly. Suddenly remembering the snake-men, Cal turned to look behind him. He was shocked to see the black peaks of their hoods as they were struggling up the hill. They looked weary and sluggish, but Cal still felt alarmed. He grabbed Father Padua's arm and said, "Shouldn't we get out of here?" Turning to the man behind the wheel, Cal heard Father Padua bark an order in some foreign language. In response, the man turned over the ignition and drove away as quickly as possible, the snake-men stumbling after the mini-van as best as they could, but quickly being outpaced. Cal couldn't believe it. They'd made it. He was so happy at the thought that he stuck his tongue out at the snake-men as the dark figures receded into the distance.

Cal turned to look at the men who had saved them. The driver had dark smooth hair and shimmery, copper-colored skin. His flashing eyes peered intently at the road as he drove swiftly away from the river and back towards town. His companion, who sat in the passenger seat beside him, was also dark, African, Cal thought, a wiry but handsome man. He had turned to look at Rabinowitz, his face filled with concern and he chafed her wrist and spoke to her softly, probably praying, Cal thought. "Is she going to be okay?" Cal asked Father Padua. The priest nodded. "She will be fine," he said, his voice soothing and gentle. "She will sleep for several hours, but she will wake up with no ill affects."

"Why did you shoot her?" Cal pressed.

"We did not shoot her," Father Padua replied.

"Then who did?"

"I did," an ashamed voice spoke up. Abe was sitting next to Rabinowitz, holding her head in his lap. He was still sweating profusely from his exertions, though he looked like he had already wiped a bucket of sweat on his sleeves. He refused to meet Cal's eyes when the police officer glared at him. "You did?" Cal asked. "But I thought you were the Pennsylvania State Junior Marksman champion, or some shit like that. Two years running, you said."

Abe squirmed under Cal's gaze. "Okay, I lied," he said. "I'm sorry. I just wanted to help. I knew you wouldn't bring me unless you thought I could help out there."

"Instead, you almost got killed," Cal said.

"But he is fine," Father Padua intervened. He turned a gently smiling countenance towards both men. "You are all fine."

"Yeah," Cal said, his mind suddenly reeling with questions. "We are, thanks to you. Now don't get me wrong, because I'm grateful as hell for your rescue, but how did you know where to find us anyway? And who are you guys? And what are those things out there? And what the fuck is going on here?"

The priest's gentle smile never wavered. It was almost a bit creepy, Cal thought, to see him looking so placid and calm at a time like this. "And what makes you think I can answer all those questions?" he said, almost teasingly.

Cal studied the priest carefully. The man had a voice like velvet—smooth and dark. He had a benign face and an easy, affable manner. And yeah, there was no denying it—the man was handsome, classically Italian in his features and charm. So of course it was easy for Cal to not like him. "Call me crazy, Father," Cal replied, "but a bunch of priests driving around like a group of crazy soccer moms with dart guns—I don't think you're out on a spiritual retreat, if you know what I mean."

The priest's smile never wavered, never changed. He placed a hand on Cal's arm to reassure him. "All will be answered in time, my friend," he replied. "For now, simply be assured that you are safe here with us."

"But—"

"In time," the priest repeated, his big brown eyes boring right into Cal. "All in due time."

DAN sighed. He checked his watch. It was four o'clock. He took a deep breath. Didn't matter what time it was anyway, he thought. I can't go home.

He wanted to. He wanted to go home and crawl into bed without even peeling his clothes off, with Cheryl on one side of him, and Ned, their chocolate Labrador retriever, on the other. He wanted to drift off and forget any of this had ever happened. Forget that he was the sheriff, forget that he was supposed to be protecting the people in this town, forget that he'd buried one of his men this morning, and most of all forget the sight of all those bloody, broken bodies piled one on top of the other in the center of that church today. Dan had seen some shit in his day—fuck, he'd seen some *shit* in the past week—but he'd never seen anything like that. A tumbled, twisted pile of human wreckage, all thrown randomly together like a bunch of loose socks in some messy kid's dresser drawer. The sight of all those—people, those poor people—even now Dan could barely stomach it.

Dan sighed again. He didn't know where Nguyen was, or what he was doing. It was obvious to Dan that there was nothing he could do, nothing that was going to stop these guys. As far as Dan was concerned, there was no point in doing anything anymore. The bad guys had won. They were unstoppable. If they could do stuff like that, like what he had seen today…

He sighed for a third time. He was fighting back tears, but was too numb to even know why. He only knew one thing: he really, really wanted to go home.

CAL woke up quickly, as if startled by a loud noise, but the room was largely silent, save for the hushed tones of whispered conversation and the gentle breathing of someone sleeping next to him. Rabinowitz.

Cal turned to look at the woman sleeping beside him. It had been so long since he'd shared this simple experience, since he'd known the simple pleasure of actually sleeping with another human being in the same bed. It was an intimate gesture, even if it had been brought about by sheer exhaustion rather than any desire for closeness. Cal gently brushed a few stray strands of hair out of Rabinowitz's face. He could see why the name Velvet fit her so well. Here, peacefully asleep, there was such a softness to her features, a creamy ease in the little smile she was wearing right now as she slept. Perhaps she was dreaming, and if the look on her face was any indication, her dreams were peaceful, sound, and good. Cal smiled, gently. She deserved dreams like that.

Part of him wanted to embrace her, to pull her body into his, though he knew he had no right to do so. It had just been so long, so long since he'd shared any intimacy with anyone. So long since he'd been anything but the closed-off, alcoholic asshole cop with any other human being. But with her, with Velvet, he felt different, more calm, more able to open up. Cal laughed, in spite of himself. Here he was pushing forty and he was still acting like a bratty teenage kid in so many ways. He smiled. For a moment, just a moment, forgetting all about murder and massacre and snake-men and evil, Cal wondered if he would ever grow up, wondered if he would ever be happy, wondered what Rabinowitz would do right now if he kissed her, just once, and lightly, his lips just brushing deftly up against hers, a feather touch, nothing more, just one, soft, intimate kiss.

And then he remembered where they were. And why they were here.

Cal stirred, feeling suddenly restless and disturbed. They were in a small suite in a hotel in the middle of town. He could see the three priests huddled together in a corner. He wasn't sure what they were doing at first; the one he had spoke with, Father Padua, was holding a cup over the other two, who were on their knees in front of him, praying. *Holy crap*, Cal thought, suddenly realizing that Father Padua had a chalice in his hands. *They're saying Mass.* Cal watched as the two men drank from the chalice in turn. He caught a glimpse of the dark red liquid inside the cup. *Wine*, he thought as the acrid smell of alcohol suddenly hit him. He shook his head gently. With everything he'd been through the last two days, Cal couldn't even remember the last time he thought about booze. Guess something good came out of this after all, he thought, though the sudden and strong smell of the wine tugged at a craving deep within. Cal pushed it aside, doing his best to ignore it.

He continued surveying the suite. Abe was asleep on the second bed in the room, gently snoring as he wrapped his hands and legs around the gaggle of pillows that surrounded him. It was almost absurd, the peace that the two of them reflected, that Cal himself must have radiated only moments before, when he knew those things were out there, carving up people, and surely looking for the three of them right now.

He had been surprised when the priest behind the wheel of the mini-van had directed it to this simple hotel in the middle of town. "The Holiday Inn?" he'd said at the time. "We're fighting for our lives and you're holing us up in the Holiday Inn?" He wasn't sure what he'd been expecting. He'd half-thought that Catholic priests might have access to some sort of stronghold, a secret bunker located underneath the sprawling Catholic church on Clark Street. But Father Padua had assured him they were perfectly safe, in that same gentle and insistent tone he'd been using all along.

Upon entering the room the two other priests gently placed Rabinowitz on the bed. Abe sat down on the second bed in the room, then, thinking perhaps the better of it, lay down on his side, his body exhausted, but his eyes intent, darting across the room from one man to the other, perhaps wondering what was to happen next. Cal felt a million questions tripping over themselves to get off his tongue, the heaviness in his own eyes betraying his exhaustion. The handsome Italian priest saw this. "Sleep now, my friend," Father Padua said. "You certainly have need of some rest. Sleep, and we will talk when you wake."

Cal had tried to protest. "Someone should stay up, to watch over Velvet, and Abe…"

"And so I shall," Padua replied. He lay Cal down next to Rabinowitz. "We shall keep vigilant watch, I assure you. And remember, my friend, God is watching you. God is watching over us all. Remember that." And Cal, strained by lack of sleep, felt himself drifting off so easily, the priest's words ringing over and over in his head: *God is watching you. God is watching us all.*

Now, wide awake, Cal's mind was again reeling with questions. He got up quietly from the bed, walked over to the trio of priests, and asked his first one:

"Got anything to eat around here?"

Thirty minutes later the five men were rapidly devouring a large onion-and-pepper pizza. The smell and the noise even managed to rouse Rabinowitz, who quickly snatched two pieces for herself. "Oh man," she said, folding the slice of pizza and scarfing as much of it into her mouth as she could, "this is the best pizza I ever had." She quickly chewed and swallowed, taking another huge bite. "Mmmm!" she said. "I'm sure this is just your average delivery pie, but to me, this is the best thing I have ever tasted. Of course that's probably because I never thought I was going to have pizza again—or anything else, for that matter. So does someone want to explain to me why we're still alive, how we ended up here, and who are all the guys dressed like priests anyway?"

"Yeah," Cal said, popping one last piece of crust into his mouth. "I definitely think now is the time for some answers."

"Only," Abe added, taking the last piece of pizza for himself, "I think we need to order another pie first. I don't know about you guys, but I'm definitely still hungry. And maybe something with meat this time?"

Father Padua smiled indulgently at them all. "Of course, my friends," he said. "It is time that I tell you everything I know. After all, we are combatants together, warriors of God ready to die for our cause, good, Catholic soldiers, are we not?" Cal, Abe, and Rabinowitz looked at each other in stony silence, each of them paused in mid-chew. "Uhh, is that a pre-requisite for all this?" Cal asked cautiously.

Father Padua's smile lessened only a little. "Well, you are all good Christian men, are you not?"

Rabinowitz's answer was sharp and to the point. "I'm a woman," she replied, "and Jewish."

"Well, I'm gay," Abe popped up. All eyes turned to look at him, as if his response made little sense. "What?" he said. "That answers the question just as much as being Jewish does."

"And what of you, my friend?" Father Padua said, turning his eyes towards Cal. Cal felt himself wilting under the priest's benevolent gaze as it rapidly became stern. "Me?" Cal asked. "I don't know what I am, to be honest. I'm not Jewish—and I'm definitely not gay. Definitely not gay. I was born a Catholic, I guess. We never went to church as a kid, except, of course, for weddings and—and funerals..." he added, his voice trailing off.

Father Padua took a deep breath, holding the air in for a long while before letting it all out. "I see," he said. "And yet, is it of any consequence? I saw with my own eyes your willingness to give your lives for this glorious cause. I believe you have been sent by He-Who-Knows-All-Things to help us in our divine mission. Yes, I will give you the answers you seek. I will tell you what I know."

"And order another pizza," Abe interjected. All eyes turned on him again. "What?" he asked again defensively. "Look, I may get stabbed, and I may get poisoned, but I'll be damned if I'm going to die of starvation before any of that other shit happens!"

Father Padua smiled again, that same indulgent smirk. "Yes, my friend, we will order another pizza," he said.

"FIRST of all, you must understand this, for it is very important: there is true evil in this world, evil that dwells not only in the hearts of men, but in creatures that are not quite human. I know you will believe me when I tell you this, because you have seen them for yourself."

"Yes, but what are they then?" Rabinowitz asked. "And what do they want?"

"And why don't bullets kill them?" Cal added.

"They cannot be killed by bullets or through any other means known to us," Father Padua replied gravely. "They are impervious to all our weapons. They are, as you say, immortal." Cal's eyes opened wide when he heard this. Even having seen it himself, even having shot those motherfuckers right between the eyes, he'd still never even considered the idea that they were immortal beings. "As to your other questions," Father Padua continued, "well, perhaps it is best if we start at the beginning."

"As you know, my name is Father Antonio Padua. As you may have guessed, I am an Italian from birth, born in the small provincial city of Abruzzi. I was orphaned as a boy and was cared for by a reverent order of Basilian fathers, who clothed me and educated me, before I entered into the priesthood myself at the soonest possible age. My companions here are Father Katanga and Father Deep, who would tell you similar stories if their English was as passable as my own. But my main point in introducing us in this manner is to demonstrate our devotion to the church and our early indoctrination into its ways.

"While still a young priest in Abruzzi I was sent on pilgrimage to Rome, where I visited with a learned Cardinal attached to the Vatican there. Many of the specifics of that visit are not relevant to this conversation, and nor, frankly, would I be permitted to reveal the secrets I was told during my time there. I can only say that it was in Rome, as a young man, that I first learned of an organization within the church called the Order of the Nazarenes."

"Nazarenes?" Cal interrupted. "Abe, weren't those the people you told us about, those early Christians who were killed off by the Essenes?"

Abe was nodding eagerly. "Yes," he said. "But I thought the term Nazarene was long lost to common church practice. Father Padua, what connection do you have to the Nazarenes?"

Father Padua was taken aback by Abe's question. "Forgive my hesitation," he said. "It appears that you know more about our current situation than I had surmised."

"Not as much as we'd like to," Cal said. "But please, continue your story."

Father Padua gave Cal a small nod. "Yes, well, as I was saying, it was there, in Rome, that I first learned of the Order of the Nazarenes. To answer your question, my young friend, the term as used is merely an homage to the sacrifices of the earliest believers, and is not directly connected to those people swallowed up by history millennia ago.

"There is much I cannot tell you about the Order of the Nazarenes. I can say this: it is a small order, small but dedicated, whose sole mission in this world is to seek out the threat of evil that comes from the inhuman inhabitants of this realm. That is our sacred duty, and while many of our brothers have died for the cause, we know it to be a high calling, one that very few within the church are ever approached for or indeed even aware of."

"Wait a second, hold on," Rabinowitz interrupted. "I know I'm still a little groggy from getting shot by that dart gun and all, but are you saying that you guys basically go around fighting the devil all the time? Or is it just a bunch of guys in black doing exorcisms on autistic kids and stuff."

Father Padua let loose a small laugh. "We do perform exorcisms when necessary, though that ritual is more common to other members of the church. But to answer your more serious question, we are prepared to fight the devil, yes, and his brethren on earth."

"Brethren? Like what kind of brethren?"

"Demons, fallen angels, the inhuman enemies of God and the church."

"Wow," Rabinowitz said, her voice barely a whisper. "Seriously? You go around fighting demons all day?"

Father Padua's face still radiated that indulgent, wiser-than-thou smile. It was almost a smirk, really. Cal was really starting to hate that smile. "Of course not. Such demonic activity is really rather rare in this realm. Perhaps once or twice a generation our Order is called into service. But we are ever vigilant and ever ready. The enemies of God and mankind are very, very real—as you have all seen."

"Okay, so what is going on here?" Abe asked. "Are those things demons or what? And how are these snake guys connected to the Essenes?"

"Again, my young friend, you impress me with your knowledge," Father Padua replied. "But you are wrong in one aspect of your question. These 'snake guys' as you call them are not connected to the Essenes. They *are* the Essenes."

"What?" Cal exploded, incredulous. Rabinowitz looked just as stunned as he did.

But not Abe. "Of course," he said, understanding dawning over his face. "Gaius Constans. 'They became snakes.' He meant what he said literally. The Essenes became snakes—or snake-men anyway."

Father Padua nodded in agreement with Abe. "Now I understand the source of your knowledge," he said. "Yes, what Gaius Constans has to say about the Essenes is very much true."

"My friends, let me tell you the happenings of two thousand years ago that have brought about the tragic events of the last few days. What am I about to tell you is unknown to all but a very few members of the church. It is information that the earliest church fathers felt should be kept out of the hands of the believers. But now I find it necessary to take you into my confidence and tell you of those fateful events of so many years ago. I only ask that the information I share with you today remain between us, though, of course, I ask this only as a courtesy. I cannot force you to comply with my desire in this area, and nor do I wish to do so. You may share the knowledge of what you learn here with others, though, I hasten to add, without any direct proofs of what I will say to you today, most people will think you quite insane." And with this he smiled, that same, indulgent, smirking smile. Cal was trying hard to listen, but something about that smile, that handsome face, made him just want to pound the good Father's teeth in.

"Let me begin by asking you a question, my friends: why is it that none of the Gospels of our Lord Jesus Christ contain any evidence of what transpired in the middle years of his life? We hear all the relevant details of His glorious birth and of His heroic mission to save us all in the last years of His life, but save for one brief incident where Jesus routs the moneychangers in the temple of the Lord, we hear nothing of Him as a youth."

"That's not entirely true," Abe said, speaking up. "There are texts—the Apocrypha—that do talk about Christ's childhood years."

"Yes, but these texts, while instructive in an allegorical way, are not accepted as canonical authority by the church. Most of them were written in the centuries after Christ's death and resurrection. No, my friend, what I ask you is, why do none of the four authors of the accepted Gospels—Matthew, Mark, Luke, or John—why do none of them detail the intervening years of Christ's life?"

"Presumably because he had not met them yet," Rabinowitz said with a shrug. Cal tried to look Rabinowitz in the eye, to gauge her take on all this, but she seemed too intent on what Father Padua was saying to catch his glance. Cal shook his head. Frankly, if the priest didn't get to some kind of point sooner rather than later, Cal was likely to fall back asleep right here.

Father Padua turned to Rabinowitz. "A very intelligent answer, my friend, but then how do they provide details of our Lord's birth? Surely this was before they had met Him as well. Of course, it is because He told them. And if He told them the details of His birth, it seems a curious omission that He did not tell them the details of His life as well."

"Okay," Cal said, trying to move the priest along, "so why don't the Gospel writers talk about Christ's teenage years then?"

Father Padua smiled at Cal. Keep it up, priest-boy, Cal thought menacingly. Keep it up and one of these days I will knock that smile right off your face. "Ahh, but they did," the priest was saying. "At least, the Gospel of Mark, the earliest of the four, told the story of our Lord's intervening years on Earth. And what a curious story it told.

"After the incident in the temple, Mary, the Mother of God, grew concerned for her son's welfare and education, as any mother might. If her son was to be the Messiah, then it seemed best to her that He receive proper religious training. So the Mother of God, in her infinite wisdom, sent her only begotten child to live amongst a devout religious community, a Jewish sect renowned for knowledge of the Torah and their peaceful, devoted lives. She hoped that, while there, her son would receive guidance about His role in saving this world and opening the gates to the next."

"Holy shit," Abe swore, then, quickly apologizing, he added, "sorry, I didn't mean to blaspheme like that, but you're talking about the Essenes, aren't you? Mary sent Christ to live with the Essenes."

"For a time, yes," Father Padua replied. "She thought that He might be able to learn from their respected elders. However, as was always the case with our Lord, it was He who taught them, and despite our Lord's age they exalted Him into their highest circle of knowledge and reverence."

"He became the Teacher of Righteousness," Abe continued. "Just like Gaius Constans says, the Teacher that came from outside the community. Holy sh—I mean, holy poop! You mean Aucter was right all along?"

"Ahh, you refer to the theories of the English theologian," Father Padua said. "My friends, I see I have underestimated your knowledge of what is going on here. Truly, I am in awe of what you have uncovered."

"Well, there's still a lot that we don't know," Cal said impatiently. "Like, who are those guys and what do they want? And how do we stop them? Important stuff like that."

"Of course, my friend, and we will get to those questions soon," Father Padua said. "But to continue my narrative, Jesus came to live with the Essenes. He quickly became their spiritual leader. It was with them that He began His evangelical mission. Though our Lord found the Essenes skeptical of His preaching at first, soon, they hailed Him as their Teacher.

"But what went wrong?" Abe said. "I mean, from what Gaius Constans says, something went terribly wrong."

"Human nature," Father Padua pronounced mysteriously. "Free will. These are of course our greatest gifts from our Lord, but they are also our most terrible burdens as well. As our Lord preached to the Essenes about everlasting life, a strange transformation overcame them. They began to believe, not in life after death, but in life everlasting on Earth. They began to lust for it. And our Lord made man, still too young and too naïve to understand the true nature of human beings, He did not see the corruption of their souls until it was too late to stop them. Nonetheless, our Lord felt that it was His duty to try."

"So let me see if I have this straight," Cal interrupted. "Rather than seeing this whole 'everlasting life' as a metaphor, the Essenes believed they would actually live forever?"

The remark had its desired affect—Father Padua's smile disappeared. He turned a rather stern face towards Cal. "It is not a metaphor, my friend," he replied, his voice tight but controlled. "When you die, you ascend into heaven where God will receive your immortal soul."

"If I believe," Cal needled. "If I deserve it."

"Yes," Father Padua said, his tone of voice never wavering for a moment. "If you are a good man, your soul will rise after your death, and the joys of heaven will be yours. But this is exactly what the Essenes could not fathom. Their hearts lusted for eternal life now. They could not wait for our Lord's resurrection and rebirth."

"So what happened?" Cal asked. Now he was the one smiling. "I mean, clearly, they somehow managed to get eternal life. Isn't that why we can't kill them?"

"Yeah," Abe said, sputtering for the words, "you said that earlier—that they're the Essenes. But how can that be? How can they be immortal?"

"Treachery," was Father Padua's response. "Deceit."

He continued. "This is how it happened, my friends. Once their hearts became inflamed with the desire for immortal life, the twelve men of the Council of Elders devised a cunning plan to trick our Lord into giving them what they most desired. They presented to Him a document, a scroll, hammered onto metal, a delicate and precious object. They said the object contained our Lord's most important teachings, and they wished Him to inscribe His name to the document. They said that they would then take that document with them when they spread the holy word of our Lord, when they preached His teachings all across the land."

"But they were lying," Rabinowitz said softly.

Father Padua nodded. "Indeed. For what the scroll contained was not the greatest teachings of our Lord, but rather heresy, reckless perversions of His word. To put it simply, my friends, writ upon that scroll was a promise for everlasting life—not after death, but now, here one earth. And our Lord—in his trust and faith in his first followers—He ascribed His name to it."

"The Gold Scroll," Abe whispered, so softly that no one else could hear him. "A promise of immortal life. Amazing."

Cal gave off a short, barking laugh. "I don't believe this," he said. "I don't believe this at all. Are you trying to tell me that we're here— that all this shit is happening—because God neglected to read the bottom line in a contract? You've got to be kidding me."

"It is no joke, my friend," Father Padua replied. "Once the scroll was inscribed with the name of our Lord, the promise was sealed. A startling transformation overcame the Elders who had conspired against Christ. Immortality was theirs."

"Wait a second," Cal interrupted. "I thought God was infallible. How could he get fooled like that?"

"You must remember that God was on Earth in the guise of a man. He was as mortal and as fallible as you or I."

"So what happened?" Rabinowitz asked. Cal could tell by the look on her face that she was buying every word that was coming out of the guy's mouth. Cal snorted. He sure as hell didn't believe it all.

Father Padua continued his story. "Once He discovered He had been deceived, Jesus fell into deep grieving. Through prayer, He asked His father for guidance and wisdom in knowing what to do. But the Lord of Heaven was angry at the deception of the Essenian elders. He set his wrath upon them, casting them to the earth and turning them into snakes—the very same punishment that befell the serpent in the Garden of Eve. They would have immortal life, but would have to spend it crawling on their bellies. Thus our Lord was avenged, and His only son left the Essenes, destined to live out the rest of His life in fulfilling the covenant His father had made with mankind. All this Christ told to Mark, who duly wrote it as part of his gospel."

"So why isn't it there anymore?" Abe asked.

"Because the early church fathers worked to excise all references to the Essenes from the gospels. Why this was done, I cannot say. Perhaps they did not wish the first followers to become confused over the question of everlasting life after death."

"But that seems rather risky," Abe said. "A fragment of the early gospel could theoretically appear at any time. I'm surprised they didn't find anything like that amongst the Dead Sea Scrolls. Even the tiniest fragment could make a big change in how we perceive the gospels."

"We are of course aware of this possibility, my learned young friend," Father Padua said with another of his indulgent smiles. "And we are ever-vigilant to ensure that this does not happen."

"But how could the church prevent—oh, duh!" Abe said, smacking his hand on his forehead. "How stupid I've been. All the guys who lead these types of digs tend to be priests, right? I bet there's some kind of directive to look out for any of this lost gospel and make sure it doesn't make it to the light of day. That probably explains why some of the Dead Sea Scroll fragments have been suppressed for fifty years, right?" Father Padua's same smile answered all of Abe's questions.

"We're all missing the really important question here," Cal challenged. "How did these 'immortal snakes' become 'immortal snakemen'? And you still haven't told us what they're doing now, with all these killings. What are they trying to accomplish?"

Father Padua keenly scanned his watch. "I will you tell you, but I must speak in haste, if we are to begin preparations for tomorrow. Exactly how the Essenes became what they are is unknown, but I can say this—it is clear, from what they intend to do, the Fallen One himself is behind their transformation."

"The Fallen One?" Cal asked. "You mean the devil?"

"Yes, my friend. I am afraid that there is great evil at work here."

"But how could the devil undo something God himself had commanded?" Rabinowitz asked. Cal smiled at her question. Maybe she was finally not buying this guy's story hook, line, and sinker.

"The Fallen One has great power," Father Padua warned. "Do not underestimate his abilities. To preserve the Essenes as he has, the Fallen One had to pour all of his power into them. It taxed him so much that he has not been able to appear on this realm ever since.

But this was his design all along—for he created them with one specific purpose in mind."

"What?" Abe asked softly. Cal could hear a tinge of fear creeping
into his voice. He could tell that he believed everything Padua was
saying, even if Cal did not. If only he knew what Rabinowitz was
thinking…

"To bring about his own dark resurrection," Father Padua intoned.

The priest's words hung in the air ominously, remaining unchallenged. Cal let the stillness hang for a moment, silently urging Abe or
Rabinowitz to challenge what Father Padua had just said. But both of
their faces looked frozen in a combination of awe and fear. He knew
that if anyone was going to speak, it was going to be him.

"I don't get it," he said. "What exactly are we talking about here?"

Father Padua bore his dark flashing eyes right into Cal's pale blue
orbs. "The return of Satan here on earth," he said quietly but intently.
"The rise of the anti-Christ."

DAN stood up from his chair and paced around his tiny office a bit.
He was worried. He hadn't heard from Cal or Rabinowitz all day, and
was starting to think maybe something had happened to them, like
something had happened to Ramirez.

"Fuck!" Dan swore softly to himself. Why'd he bring Cal into
this? Why'd he force him to come back? Because he'd believed in Cal.
Because he thought Cal was the man to get it done. And because he
had no idea what he was getting him in to. Now, though, Cal was
probably dead, dead like Ramirez, his body cut to shreds, or worse,
two small holes in his neck…

Stop it! Dan's mind screamed. He had to stop thinking like this.
But this thinking, this incessant, awful thinking, was all he could do.
There wasn't anything else he could accomplish. Nothing he could
do to stop the killings, nothing he could do to help anyone at all,
nothing he could do to make that awful anxiety go away.

Well, almost nothing.

Dan sat down heavily in his chair. He quietly, stealthily pulled
open the bottom left drawer of his desk. He lifted up some stray files

he'd casually thrown in there a few days ago. He reached down to pick up what he had left in the drawer.

A small knock interrupted his actions.

Quick as thought Dan slammed the drawer shut with a heavy bang and went immediately erect. "Come in!" he said, trying to quash the guilt he felt etched all across his face.

It was Garcia, one of his own officers. "Still no word on Detective Evans, Sheriff," she said calmly. She knew this would not come as good news.

"He hasn't checked in?" Garcia shook her head. "What about Rabinowitz? Any word on her current location?" Garcia shook her head again. Dan pounded his fist on his desk. "What about that graduate student whose been helping them out? What was his name? He had a funny name."

"Abe Ruth, sir."

"Yeah, that's right. Isn't Davison supposed to be watching him? Maybe he knows where they went."

"Davison's here, sir. In the station house."

"What?" Dan exploded. "Get him in here, now!"

Garcia opened the door of Dan's office and stuck her head out, shouting at someone to get Davison. Seconds later Officer Davison poked his head into the office. "You wanted to see me, Sheriff?" he asked.

"Get your ass in here!" Dan yelled. Davison moved all the way into the tiny office and gently closed the door behind him, hoping that his obvious care would make Dan a little less angry. It didn't. "Didn't Cal assign you to watch that Ruth kid?" the sheriff demanded. "If you're here, where is he?"

Davison shrugged. "I don't know, sir. He went off with Detective Evans and Agent Rabinowitz."

"He went off with Cal and Velvet?" Davison nodded. "When?"

"This morning, sheriff. After the funeral. Detective Evans said I was relieved from watching him, sir. Was that okay?"

Dan sighed, the wind already out of his sails. "Yeah, go. I'm sure Agent Nguyen can find some use for you." He watched as Davison timidly scurried out of his office.

Nguyen. He could hear the FBI man now, screaming at the few officers left in the station house. Dan shook his head. He knew it was futile. He knew they were all dead. Cal and Velvet and that other guy, too, probably all dead, just like Ramirez, just like those four agents from this morning, just like Dan would be at this rate.

Dan went back to his drawer, opening it again, his eyes glued to his office door the whole time. He slipped the files aside and pulled out the flask he had hid there. It was ironic. How many times had he screamed at Cal for drinking on the job, how many times had he busted Cal's ass for being drunk when on duty. And here he was, doing the very same thing. Yeah, well fuck all that, Dan thought as he unscrewed the cap, tipped his head back and took a healthy belt from the shiny flask. Bourbon. Warm, harsh, good for what ails ya. Dan held up the flask in a mock salute. "Here's to you, Cal," he said, taking another hit. Maybe if he drank enough he could stop seeing all those dead bodies. Maybe he could stop worrying about Cal and Velvet lying dead in some ditch somewhere. Maybe he could stop caring about all those people dying out there. Maybe he could stop worrying about it and let someone else have that job.

Maybe, Dan thought. But I doubt it.

"HOLY shit," Abe said quietly. There was no need to apologize for his words this time; they all felt like saying the same thing.

Cal was uncomfortable. He didn't believe what the priest was telling him; on some level, he *couldn't* believe what the priest was saying. "The anti-Christ?" he said, his voice quaking more than he intended. "Do you expect us to believe that?"

"Whether you believe in it or not, Detective, it is true," Father Padua said. "The Fallen One preserved the Essenes in their current form for the exact purpose of bringing about his rise. How he did this no one can say. But the proof of it you have seen with your own eyes. And now the time has come. The Essenes have risen up. And their intent can only be but one thing: to begin the reign on earth of the anti-Christ himself, to return Satan to this realm.

"Listen, my friends, and understand this. He has spent the last two thousand years storing up his power. He has been preparing for this. His followers have paved the way. They have the ceremony in hand. They will attempt his resurrection. His ascension. All that we have seen tells us this."

"When?" Abe asked, his voice a hushed, reverent whisper. "When will they do it?"

"Tomorrow," the priest replied gravely. "On Sunday. On the Lord's Day."

"But—how?" Abe sputtered.

"Because it has been so decreed. Think of it, my friends. Sunday is the day of worship, the day of rest. But it is also the day of belief and the day of power. Think of these killings that have gripped this community. What is their ultimate purpose? To simply kill the religious leaders? No. They have a darker purpose than that.

"They wish to drive out the faithful, my friends. They wish to create an atmosphere of fear so great and intense that no one—that no Christian—will go to worship tomorrow. That no man or woman of God will dare to celebrate the mass. Catholic, Protestant—in the end, it does not matter. All services are intended to honor the same God. And when people come together to honor Him, the Fallen One cannot rise. It is the only thing that will stop him."

"So that's why they've been killing the clergy in town," Rabinowitz said. "To prevent any masses from being held tomorrow."

"Yes," Father Padua said, nodding. "If they succeed in driving the faithful from this town, they will have created the perfect area in order to perform their dark ceremony."

"Then we have to make sure that doesn't happen," Rabinowitz cried.

"It is too late," Father Padua said sadly. "The faithful have fled before the sickle. It was announced earlier—all masses to be held tomorrow have been cancelled. There will be no church services in town on Sunday."

"Except for one," Abe said, his meaning perfectly clear to all.

"Yes," Father Padua replied. "And unless we can stop it, tomorrow will be the last Sunday any of us will see."

"OH, come on!" Cal exploded. "The last Sunday any of us will see? You've got to be kidding me. Are you trying to tell me the world will end tomorrow unless we stop this ceremony from happening?"

"The world as we know it, yes," Father Padua evenly replied. "Unless we act, the reign of the anti-Christ will commence. We are the only ones who can prevent that from happening."

"And how do you propose we do that? We can't kill them, for Christ's sake. What are we supposed to do?"

"Cal," Rabinowitz said quietly.

"No, Velvet, I want to hear this, I want to hear what the big plan is. I am assuming you *do* have a plan, don't you?"

Father Padua leaned closer to all three of them. "We must prevent the ceremony from ever taking place. We must get the Gold Scroll."

"You mean the scroll that gave the Essenes immortality in the first pace?" Abe asked.

"Yes. Upon their transformation into the Fallen One's acolytes, the Essenes, in the ultimate act of blasphemy, transcribed the details of their black ritual onto their pact with Christ. Without it, they cannot complete the ritual. Here is what we must do, my friends. They cannot begin the ritual until sundown has commenced. We must steal into their enclave just prior to that and obtain the scroll. Once we have it, we run. Their window of opportunity to complete the ritual will be gone once midnight has passed. The ceremony will remain incomplete."

"And then what?" Cal asked sarcastically.

"And then we destroy the scroll, once and for all," the priest intoned.

"Oh, come on!" Cal said, standing up. "Three priests, two cops, and a graduate student against a dozen immortal snake-men? Doesn't seem like good odds to me!"

Father Padua stood up to face Cal. "Do not underestimate our strength, my friend. We have been training for this moment all of our lives. We are strong in body and in faith. Our very order was created for the exact purpose of defeating these evil beings. We have succeeded once; we will succeed again."

"They've already tried this?" Cal asked. "When?"

"Of course!" Abe answered, not waiting for Father Padua to speak up. "Gaius Constans speaks of it, only he doesn't know it. When the Essenes started going around and killing the Nazarenes, they weren't just killing them for heresy, they were killing them to set up the perfect conditions for the ritual!"

"Yes," Father Padua confirmed. "Members of my order managed to stop them by stealing the scroll, frustrating their plans to raise the Fallen One. They even left in its place nonsensical scrolls made out of copper, a sort-of joke, if you will, on the ancient Essenes."

"So what happened?" Cal asked. "How come you still don't have the scroll?"

"The Romans," Father Padua answered. "The contingent of men from my order who first stole the scroll were stopped by Romans. They were executed and their goods confiscated. For centuries the scroll has been lost to history. But as long as they did not have it, all was safe."

"But now they have it," Rabinowitz said. She sounded fearful.

"Yes," Father Padua replied. "They have it, and they are preparing to use it." He turned so that he could address the entire room. "Now all is explained, my friends. I hope you understand the gravity of our mission. We stand together as the final warriors of this realm. Between salvation and oblivion there exists only us. But this is our sacred duty. You have only been drawn in through the circumstances of your jobs and the nobility of your faith. If you wish to leave, no one will stop you. If you wish to stay, and fight, and work to stem back the rising tide of evil, then we will gladly accept your assistance. The decision is yours."

Abe stood up. "How can we help?" he said.

Rabinowitz was soon beside him. "Just tell us what to do," she added.

All eyes in the room turned towards Cal. "And you, my friend?" the priest asked him.

It had been a few days since Cal had been to a meeting—though it felt like months—but this is what he felt like when it was his turn to share, all eyes on him, expectant, asking him to rip out his chest and pour his heart out just one more time. It went against every feeling his gut had to share then, but he did so because he knew it was good for him, part of his recovery, part of the healing process.

But now his gut could only tell him one thing, over and over: *something is definitely wrong here.*

"Why here?" Cal asked. "Why Chambersburg?"

Father Padua shrugged. "Why anywhere, indeed, my friend? One place is as good as another."

Cal was shaking his head. "No. None of this makes any sense. Something's not adding up here."

The priest was moving slowly towards him. He wasn't smiling now, and somehow that lack of smile was much creepier that the sickening, holier-than-thou smile had ever been. "What is not adding up, my friend? I have told you everything we know."

I'm not so sure about that, Cal thought. Aloud, he said, "What about the message? The one they left at the crime scene?"

"It was intended to scare off the local believers. It has done its task."

"'He does not belong to you!' It sounds like something more is going on there." The priest was closer to Cal now, almost touching him. Cal could feel himself getting angrier and more panicked by the minute. *Something is definitely wrong here.* "It doesn't make sense!" he shouted, more forcefully than he intended. The priest was touching him now, his hands gentle and reassuring on Cal's arms. Cal almost wanted to weep, but he choked back his emotions. His gut was speaking: *something is definitely wrong here.*

"It is not a question of sense, my friend," the priest said, softly, intimately, in his ear. "It is a question of faith."

"No!" Cal didn't know why he felt the way he did, but he did know one thing: he had to get out of there. Now. He pushed Father Padua away from him and stormed towards the door. "Cal!" Rabinowitz shouted as he stomped out the door and into the hotel corridor. "Let him go," Cal heard the priest's voice say. He sounded colder now, perhaps angry. "He does not have the faith." It was almost a challenge, but Cal had no desire to turn back.

He barreled down the hall towards the elevators. He pushed the button; it lit up, and Cal waited. And waited. He pushed the button again, and then again, five times rapidly. "Come on," he seethed. Finally the doors opened. Cal walked inside and hit the "L" button. He didn't know exactly where he was going. He couldn't even remember where he had parked his car. He checked his pocket for his phone. Not there. Was it upstairs still? Or had he lost it when fighting that snake-man? Either way it was long gone. Great. And to top it all off, those things might be out there somewhere, looking for them. Cal didn't care. He only knew that he had to get away from it all. Clear his head.

Get a drink, a little voice deep inside him said.

The elevators doors opened on a bright but empty lobby. Cal sighed. He had no idea what time it was. He looked outside—it was dark. He strode quickly through the lobby and hit the door hard on his way out.

The front door led immediately to a small, poorly-lit parking area. Cal paused. He wasn't sure where to go from here. He should probably go back in, find a phone, call the station. Dan was probably frantic wondering where they were. But something kept Cal from going back in. He wanted out; he wanted away from this place. Looking around, Cal saw a restaurant across the street from the hotel, still brightly lit up for the night. He could call from there. He started walking.

He thought he heard someone else walking, too.

He heard an echo, to be exact, at least that's what he thought, an echo of his own footsteps. But the echo seemed off his timing, faster in pace than his own steps. Cal stopped and looked around. He listened. He saw and heard nothing. He started walking again. There it was! The same sound, the same insistent *tap tap tap* of hurried steps. He started to walk faster. The sounds also increased. Cal whirled around, but he could see no one. But he could feel them, feel them out there, in the dark, in the night. He stopped, readying himself for the attack. They were out there. He could hear them, hear their steps; he could feel them. His head whipped madly from side to side. They were out there. Somewhere. They were coming straight for him. He couldn't see them. But they were there. There! On his left, someone, some*thing* coming. Cal turned, bracing himself for the onslaught…

Rabinowitz.

"Jesus, Velvet!" Cal exploded in obvious relief. "You scared me half to death."

Rabinowitz gave Cal a meaningful look. "We need you, Cal," she said. "Please, stay."

Cal opened his mouth, but no words came out. He didn't want to disappoint her by saying "no," so he said nothing at all. "Cal," she said again. She placed her hand on his arm. They were close. Really close. Cal could smell her. She smelled like sweat, new leather, and green apple shampoo. Cal's heart leaped—it was not a bad combo at all. "I'm sorry," Cal said. "I don't know what it is. Something—something just doesn't add up." He wanted to kiss her. More than anything he wanted to kiss her, to melt in her arms and pretend, if only for a minute, that none of this was happening. But he didn't. "My gut just keeps telling me that something is wrong," he finally said. He turned to go.

"Cal?" Her voice was quiet, but insistent. "I think we're doing the right thing," she finally said.

He turned towards her, placed his hands on her hips and pulled her in close. "Velvet, why don't you come with me. We can go upstairs, get Abe, and figure this out between us. I don't trust that guy. He's too—too smooth, too assured. Something about him rings false. I—I can't say exactly what it is." He was almost holding her now. Their eyes were locked together. If he moved closer, perhaps just an inch, he thought they'd kiss. He wanted to kiss her so badly. More than anything, more than getting away from here, more than being safe, more than having a drink, he wanted to feel her lips, push them against his, and taste her, know her and understand her. One more inch and he thought it would happen. But for all his resolve, all his desire, that last inch might well have been a mile. Cal didn't budge. Finally, Rabinowitz did.

She pulled away.

"I'm a cop," she said. "Cal, I have to do something. Father Padua has a plan. I don't know if it's the right thing to do. I do know we could all die trying. But Cal, if there's even the smallest chance that what he says is true, then I have to do something. I have to help out. I—I hope you understand."

"I do." Cal placed one hand gently on her cheek, and she moved to accept his touch. She cradled his hand in hers for a moment, and then, gently, she dropped it between them. He let her go. "I just hope you understand what I have to do."

"And what is that, exactly, my friend?" a voice said from the dark. Father Padua stepped out of a shadow and into the light of the parking lot. "I am sorry to interrupt you, but Agent Rabinowitz, we are making preparations for tomorrow. There is much to do."

"Of course." She took two steps away from Cal. He felt her slipping away. He wanted to grab her, to do something to bring her to him. But instead he let her go, watching as she walked back towards the front entrance of the hotel. "I am sorry," Father Padua was saying to Cal, "that my story upset you so."

Cal leveled his gaze at that of the priest. Neither was smiling. "I'll be fine," he said.

"And what are you going to do now, my friend?" the priest asked. Cal shrugged, noncommittally. The priest gave him a small nod before stepping away and following Rabinowitz back into the hotel.

Cal hadn't answered Father Padua out of any sense of defiance or opposition. The truth was, he didn't know what he was going to do. At least, he hadn't know a few seconds ago. But now he did. Now he knew exactly what he was going to do.

"I've heard your story," he whispered to the receding figure of the priest. "Maybe now it's time I hear the other side. But there's something else I need to do first. And I can't do it alone."

DAN'S mind was reeling. It was partly exhaustion, partly the Jack Daniels. He had no idea what time it was. He thought briefly about going home, but instead took another slug of liquor.

He heard a gentle knock and saw someone twist the knob on his door.

There was no time to hide the flask back in his desk. Quick as a flash Dan slipped it into his pocket. Then he looked up to see who was coming in uninvited.

It was Cal.

Dan felt his body flood with relief. He felt his eyes get instantly wet. "You son of a bitch..." he said, faltering.

Cal suppressed a smile. "Nice to see you, too, Dan" he said.

"Where the fuck have you been?" Dan demanded. He hoped Cal couldn't smell the alcohol on his breath.

Cal sat down heavily in the chair opposite Dan's. "You wouldn't believe me if I told you," he said.

"Is everything okay?" Dan asked.

"Yeah." This time Cal did smile, a lopsided grin. "Right as rain. You?"

"Couldn't be better," Dan quipped, trying to sound light. He paused, then continued. "Seriously, Cal, where have you been? We've been trying to reach you every way known to mankind."

"I lost my phone," Cal replied. He leaned forward. "Dan, I know who's doing all this. And I know where they are."

Dan tried to stand up, but felt a wave of dizziness overcome him. He sat back down as deftly as he could. "Let's go," he said, trying to cover the fact that the room was spinning out of control. "Let's go get the motherfuckers."

"It's not that simple," Cal said. "But if you're interested, I have a plan."

"Cal, we've got to get going, they're going to be killing again, who knows how many this time."

"They're not, Dan. At least I'm pretty sure they're not."

"How do you know that?"

"Do you want to hear my plan or not?"

Dan leaned back in his chair. This was good; it gave his head time to clear up. "I'm all ears," he said.

FATHER Padua followed Rabinowitz back up into the room. Fathers Deep and Katanga were sitting with Abe at the small table in the suite, looking at a crudely drawn map. "Come," he said grandly, sweeping Rabinowitz in front of him and into a chair. "Let us make preparations for tomorrow. Your presence will greatly assist us in our plans to contain the Essenian threat."

Rabinowitz sat down and exchanged a cautious glance with Abe. "Okay," she said. "Let's hear your plan."

"Yeah," Abe echoed. "I just hope it's a good one. I'd definitely like this to not be my last night on earth," he added, trying to sound light but coming off more scared than anything else.

"Relax, my young friend," Father Padua replied. "I have faith that our plan will succeed, and when it does, we will ensure the future of every inhabitant on the earth."

"And if we fail?" Abe asked nervously.

Father Padua paused, searching for the right words. "Have faith, my friend," he finally said. "Have faith."

THE LAST SUNDAY

"**VELVET?** Velvet? Velveeeet."

"Mmm."

"Are you awake?"

"I am now."

"Oh, sorry. Really? You were sleeping? How can you sleep at a time like this?"

"Ambien."

"Oh. You have any more?"

"Sorry."

"That's okay. I don't think I could sleep even if I took a hundred pills. I'm too nervous. Frankly, I don't know how you can sleep with only taking just one."

"What time is it?"

"Two a.m."

"That's how I can sleep. Because it's two in the morning."

"Oh. Right. Sorry. Go back to sleep."

Rabinowitz felt herself drifting off again.

"It's just that I don't see how any of us can sleep. But the priests are sleeping. I mean I think so. I can hear someone snoring. I wonder which one of them snores."

"Abe—"

"Do you think it's Father Padua who snores? That's okay. I wouldn't kick him out of bed for it. He is totally hot."

"Abe—"

"I mean, I know this is totally gross and inappropriate, but if I was like sixteen or seventeen I would so want to be his altar boy, if you know what I mean."

"Abe!"

"Oh, sorry, I know, that's totally wrong to say. It's just that—it's my stomach. I can't sleep with my stomach like this."

"There are still a few slices of pizza left in the box."

"Oh, it's not that. I'm not hungry. I'm *nervous*. My stomach's all knots. You know."

Rabinowitz paused, sighed, and rolled on to her back, her arm thrown over her forehead. "Yeah. I know."

"I mean, I've never done anything like this before."

"Sure you did, Abe. You did it yesterday."

"Yeah, but I mean this is important. Like life-or-death important. Like end of the world important. I don't know if I can do this."

"You will. You've got guts. I've seen them. When the time comes, you'll be prepared."

"You think it's a good plan? I've been running the plan over and over in my head, wondering if it's a good plan."

"And?"

"I don't know. I can't think of any other plan, so I guess it must be good. Don't you think?"

"It's simple: we run in there, dart guns blazing, grab the scroll and get the hell out of there. Simple as pie." Yeah. Right.

"I still think I should be the one driving the getaway van."

Rabinowitz did not totally disagree with this. "I know, but Father Katanga needs to do that. It has to be one of the Order, in case—"

"In case something goes wrong."

"Nothing is going to go wrong."

"Yeah, I know, but like, what if the scroll isn't there yet? Or what if we just can't run into wherever they'll be? What if we have to walk? Or what if they have guard dogs or something?"

"I don't think they need dogs, Abe."

"You know what I mean, Velvet."

"Father Padua and the others have done the necessary recon. There's one entrance. It'll be tight but we can do it."

"But what about—"

"Abe. We can do it."

"Yeah, I guess. I mean, it's not like we have a choice, do we?"

Rabinowitz sighed. She was wide awake now. "No. No, we don't."

"But what if—I mean, what happens if—what do we do if they get one of us?"

"We discussed that, Abe. You already know the answer to that."

"Yeah, but—I wouldn't want to leave you behind, Velvet. I mean, if I could, I'd try to get you free."

Rabinowitz smiled softly to herself. That was nice of him to say, but she knew he meant it the other way. "Don't worry, Abe, I'll keep my eye on you in there. You'll be fine." If only she could be sure. If only she believed any of them would be fine.

"What are you going to do tomorrow?" he suddenly asked.

"Huh?"

"Tomorrow. I mean, we aren't going to go anywhere until sunset, right? So what are you going to do?"

"Oh. I don't know. I hadn't thought about it."

"It could be important, you know. I mean, it could be the last time—"

"Abe!"

"I'm just saying it *could* be. I mean, what are you supposed to do in a situation like this? Eat a really good meal? Pig out on chocolate?"

"How about getting laid?" Rabinowitz suggested lightly, playing along.

Abe considered this. "Naah. Too much work. Besides, I'd have to take my shirt off." Surprised by this, Rabinowitz started to giggle. She was relieved to hear Abe was giggling as well. "I hate doing that in front of people I don't know."

Still giggling, Rabinowitz suggested, "How about the mall? We could max out our credit cards. We may not have to pay them off after tomorrow if the world ends."

"Naah," Abe laughed. "The mall in Chambersburg sucks."

"What? Don't you have any good stores?"

"Not a one."

"No Banana Republic?"

"Nope."

"Really?" Rabinowitz was surprised. "What about a Lord and Taylor's?"

"Don't have it."

"Well, how about a Border's Bookstore?"

Abe snorted. "In Chambersburg? Definitely not."

"Victoria's Secret?"

Abe laughed. "How would I know if there was a Victoria's Secret in the mall? I don't exactly shop there."

"I don't know, you could always get something nice for—" Rabinowitz was about to say "your girlfriend," but then remembered that was wrong, so instead she said, "your mom."

Abe laughed loud at this. "Yeah, I can see that. Here you go mom, here's a lovely peek-a-boo bra and panty set for Mother's Day."

Now Rabinowitz was laughing out loud. "Well, at least you have to have a Gap."

"Oh yeah, of course we have a Gap."

"Good old Gap. You can always find a Gap."

"Welcome to the Gap. Can I sell you some crap?" Abe said in his best Valley-girl voice. Loud laughter ensued from the both of them.

"Shh! Shh!" Rabinowitz said between fits of barely-restrained giggling. "We're going to wake up the priests!" She listened as the chuckling died down between them. That felt good, she thought. She couldn't remember the last time she had laughed like that. She let out one last laugh, sighed, and smiled.

They grew silent.

"I wish Cal was here," Abe said suddenly. "I know it sounds stupid, but somehow, that'd make me feel better."

"Me, too," Rabinowitz whispered, so soft that Abe could not hear her.

MAYBE we should call him," Abe said to Rabinowitz. They were eating scrambled eggs and wheat toast for breakfast.

"Who?" Rabinowitz replied, though she already knew who Abe was talking about.

"Cal," he said. "Let's call him."

Rabinowitz shook her head. "I've already tried," she said. "He's not answering his cell."

"It's probably dead," Abe said. The two exchanged a significant look. Rabinowitz knew they were both thinking the same thing: that Cal himself may be dead somewhere.

"Do you think he's right?" Abe asked suddenly. "Do you think they're holding something back from us?" He had lowered his voice, as the three priests were in prayer on the other side of the suite.

Rabinowitz shrugged. She usually trusted her detective instincts, but this time her instincts were telling her nothing. Maybe she was just too tired. "I don't know," she finally said. "You know more about all this stuff than I do. Do you think they're on the level?"

Abe considered her question. "Several scholars have always wondered why the Gospel of Mark is so short and disjointed," he said. "If it had been heavily edited, well, that could explain a lot." He thought about Rabinowitz's question some more. "I guess everything Father Padua said made sense," he finally declared. "But in the end I just don't know enough to say for sure."

That's definitely what was bothering Cal, Rabinowitz mused. He's always used to being sure, at least on something like this; but with everything that had been going on, and everything that had happened to him over the last couple of years, his confidence had been totally shattered. Maybe he would never be able to be sure about being a cop again, she wondered. Maybe that was why he left. Maybe.

Lost in her thoughts, Rabinowitz did not realize that Abe was still speaking. "I'm sorry, what did you say?" she said.

"I said, do you think we're doing the right thing?" Abe repeated. "I mean, are we really going to be saving the world tonight?"

Rabinowitz paused. To be honest, she wasn't sure at all. "Yeah, I really do think so," she lied, hoping that her answer made Abe feel better. She sighed. Nothing would make her feel better until this whole thing was over. She checked her watch. Twelve hours until sunset.

"I still can't believe half of what you told me," Dan said to Cal. They were in the basement of the station house. It smelled damp and musty, but looked clean to Cal. "Of course, if even a quarter of it is true, it's still pretty fucked up."

"Yeah, well, now you know what's going on," Cal said as Dan fumbled with a set of keys on front of a locked metal door. Cal had never been down in the basement before; he wondered what was kept here. "You're willing to help me?"

"I'll do what I can," Dan replied stoically.

"So what are we doing down here?" Cal asked.

In response, Dan finally managed to unlock the door and swung it open wide. With a loud click he dramatically flicked on the overhead light. Bright fluorescent light filled the room.

"Holy shit!" Cal said, surveying the contents of the room. It was filled with weapons. "Damn, this certainly isn't police-issue, that's for sure. Machine guns? Grenades? A flamethrower? Dan, where did you get this stuff?"

"Remember that militia we busted back, what, five, six years ago? You heard about that. A few of their more interesting toys might have found their way down here. Along with other items of note that have come our way over the years."

Cal grinned. "That has to be the most illegal thing I ever heard a small-town sheriff doing," he said.

Dan grunted. "Hardly. Now why don't you look around and pick out something useful, okay?"

Cal still had a grin on his face. "I don't know where to start," he said.

Dan grunted as he picked up the flamethrower, testing its heft and aim. "Pick something good for snake-hunting, I guess," he said.

THEY were driving in the mini-van towards the church. No one spoke; Rabinowitz half-expected Father Padua and his cohorts to pray the entire way there, but they sat silent as well, steely determination covering their faces. They looked ready. Rabinowitz sighed. She hoped she would be, too.

She went over the plan in her head once again. Katanga would wait in the van, ready to drive off when they recovered the scroll or to seek some kind of help in case they failed. Deep, Padua, Abe and Rabinowitz would circle around to the back of the church. Best guess was that the Gold Scroll would be kept in the basement, since the main floor of the church was so exposed. There was one staircase leading down to the basement. Padua would go first, followed by Deep and Abe. Rabinowitz would bring up the rear. Each of them carried one of the air-loaded dart assault weapons. Rabinowitz stared at the gun in her hand. It was surprisingly light. She'd been pretty good practicing with it earlier today, but at the close range they would be in, missing wasn't an option.

The basement had three rooms: the main room the staircase fed in to; a small coal storage room located behind the stairs; and a narrow but deep storage room on the other side of the main room. The plan was simple; to go in guns blazing, grab the scroll, and hightail it out of there. Whoever made it back to the mini-van took off with Father Katanga. Whoever didn't, well…

Once they were in the van the plan was just to drive like hell. Once the clock struck midnight, find a way to destroy the scroll. That was it. If they managed to do that, the good guys would have won.

It was a good plan, Rabinowitz thought. Solid. She looked over at Abe. He looked nervous, but she felt she could count on him when the shit hit the fan. She hoped so, anyway. She didn't want to lose him.

Maybe it was good Cal wasn't here, she thought. Cal didn't like someone else being in command. This way, he was out of harm's way. He would stay safe.

Rabinowitz sighed. She wished she was out of harm's way, too.

THEY parked the van only a few hundred yards from the church. Once they drew closer, Father Katanga would back it up to make a faster getaway. Padua, Deep, Abe, and Rabinowitz stood outside of the van together. Padua grabbed both Abe and Rabinowitz's hands, while Deep did the same. Padua began to pray. "Bless us, oh Father, your warriors in our hour of battle. Give us the strength, courage, and wisdom to serve you and avert evil on this holiest of days. Amen." The others mumbled "Amen" in reply, and, after a brief pause, Rabinowitz did as well: "Amen."

They stole quickly along the side of the road, hunched low and moving as quietly as possible. The sun was just now setting, and the shadows on the road played tricks with Rabinowitz's mind. Everywhere she turned she thought she saw snake-men leering at her from the side of the road. Get over it! she said to herself. It's only in your head.

They were approaching the church. Padua motioned them to stop. Rabinowitz craned her neck to look. There, in front of the building, was a lone sentry. He hadn't bothered to conceal himself in a robe anymore; only a simple tunic covered his gray, scaly flesh. He was shaped like a man, and for the most part looked like one, except for his skin and face, and, of course, his left arm. Rabinowitz could see that while the sentry stood perfectly still its hand moved freely about, independently, as if on its own, the serpent's tongue flicking in and out to taste the night air and its black, beady, lidless eyes constantly surveying the terrain around it.

Padua aimed, fired, and hit the sentry with a dart right in his neck. The sentry wavered for a second, then fell silently to the earth. The group paused, wondering if another of the snake-men would come to his aid. When none did, they moved ahead cautiously. Padua led their way into the church. Rabinowitz brought up the rear, taking one last fearful glance behind her before entering the building. The shadows seemed to dance in the rising light of the moon, tricks of wind and gently wafting water from the nearby river. Rabinowitz closed her eyes, closed them tight, and then opened them again; everything seemed still. She crept into the church with the others.

Perhaps, if she had stayed a second longer, she may have seen the sentry rise, as perfectly as if he had never fallen, and she may have also seen those shadows, those dancing, still shadows, slowly converge upon the entrance of the church.

THE inside of the church was a complete wreck. A large tree limb had crashed through the ceiling decades before, leaving a gaping hole in its wake. The floor also had a few wide holes in the center of the room; Padua moved his group far from them, to avoid anyone falling in. The large chamber was covered with dirt and dust, and the signs of animal life were everywhere: squirrel nests, mice droppings, large cobwebs that stretched halfway across the ceiling. Rabinowitz walked through one and disgustedly wiped it off her face.

The place appeared deserted. Padua silently signaled the group to follow him to the stairwell. This is it, Rabinowitz thought to herself as they approached the steps. They paused to listen, but heard nothing. Padua placed his foot on the first step. It groaned loudly with his weight. He grimaced, paused, and then, mustering up his courage, began the descent into the cellar.

Deep followed him, then Abe, and finally Rabinowitz. She hugged
the wall to make as little noise as possible. The cellar was dark. Padua
clicked on his flashlight, and the rest of the group followed suit. Four
beams of light swept through the cellar in a desperate search of life.
They found no one, no sign of anyone at all. Rabinowitz wondered if
perhaps the priests were wrong, and that the ceremony was not going
to be held here at all, or if perhaps the snake-men had moved, when
suddenly, on a table in the center of the room, she saw it.

The Gold Scroll.

Padua saw it at the same time Rabinowitz did. Both froze their
lights onto the scroll. Even in the dim haze of their flashlights the
scroll reflected a brilliant light back at them. Rabinowitz was amazed
at how beautiful it was. It had been unraveled, as if in preparation for
the ceremony, and stood proud and elegant against a wooden rise, a
thin but powerful sheet of hammered magnificence. The ends still
curled. In the dim glow created by her flashlight Rabinowitz could
see faint etching scratched into the surface of the sheet. It was
breathtaking. She had never seen anything like it.

By now all four of them were staring at it, their lights and their
eyes transfixed by the impressive scroll. Rabinowitz heard Padua
mutter something to Deep, and the priest nodded, hesitantly moving
forward, towards the scroll. One step. Two, and, no sign of the
snake-men. Three, four. Deep was halfway there now. He had only a
few more steps to go when the group heard a noise. They paused,
holding their collective breaths. The noise was so slight as to be almost imperceptible, a gentle rustle, almost moist sounding. Rabinowitz strained to listen to the sound over the pounding of her heart.
What was it? she asked herself.

Suddenly they heard a different sound, a steady *thump thump thump*
coming from the stairwell. Frantically the group swung their lights in
that direction. It sounded like someone coming down the stairs, only
the sound was too light, not heavy enough to be a person. Their
lights revealed no one on the stairs. Maybe something had fallen
down the stairs. Rabinowitz shined her light at the foot of the steps.
There was something there, something dark and round. Rabinowitz
took a step forward and shined her light directly on it.

It was a head. Father Katanga's head.

Rabinowitz stifled a scream. Beside her, she could hear Abe whimper in the dark. She didn't know what to do. She was about to run when she heard Father Padua scream, "Get the scroll!"

But before any of them could act, light flooded the old church basement.

Rabinowitz blinked rapidly, adjusting to the brightness. She could now see lights tucked away into the basement beams. She didn't need to ask where the electricity came from—a steady humming sound told her the lights were powered by a generator nearby. And she didn't need to ask who had turned them on—they were surrounded by them right now.

Ten—no, make that eleven snake-men filled the room, their left arms writhing wildly, their right hands each holding a long, curved knife. Rabinowitz wasn't sure where they had come from, and right now she didn't really care. She frantically checked the exit. Blocked. Without thinking, she raised her gun and fired at the snake-men blocking her path to the door. *Thwap! Thwap! Thwap!*

They were all direct hits. But rather than falling, as the sentry had fallen, the snake-men stood their ground, as if they didn't feel the potent tranquilizer in the dart at all. The others were firing now as well, but none of the snake-men were affected. Rabinowitz aimed for one of the arms of the snake-men, hitting the head of the snake itself right between the eyes. The arm recoiled, hissed loudly, but still remained unaffected, writhing and coiling around itself as it had before, as if only waiting for the opportunity to bite someone.

Father Deep was the first one to react. He made a mad dash towards the scroll. He only got two feet, however, before one of the snake-men stepped forward. It thrust its knife far into Deep's belly. Father Deep stopped cold, his face freezing in a mix of a surprise and pain. With a savage gesture the snake-man lifted its arm up, violently slicing the knife through Deep's upper body. Rabinowitz saw the knife emerge at the base of the neck and watched in horror as Deep's left and right sides fell apart, sagging to opposite sides of his hips before his entire body tumbled unceremoniously onto the floor.

Rabinowitz screamed now. There didn't seem to be anything else to do. Abe was frozen beside her, his eyes completely transfixed on Father Deep's twisted remains. Father Padua stared at the snake-men in cold, helpless fury. Slowly the other snake-men advanced on the group. They circled around them. Rabinowitz felt helpless. "Fuck!"

she screamed, throwing her gun at the closest snake-man. It bounced harmlessly off its chest. There was nothing they could do now. They were going to die—and the rest of the world was going to die along with them.

"Hey, assholes!" a voice suddenly shouted from above. All eyes turned towards the sound. A large form came crashing through one of the holes in the ceiling, landing right next to the scroll. It was Cal! Rabinowitz's heart did a double-take when she saw him. She could see that he had a duffel bag slung over his shoulder and a tank of some kind strapped to his back. A fuel line running from the tank to a device in Cal's hands told her what it was. "I'm not sure what any of you snake-things understand about modern technology," he was saying. "But this here is a flamethrower. Now, while it may not be hot enough to melt gold, I'm sure I can erase some of those fancy marks I see all over that sheet." This caused a stir amongst the snake-men. "Yeah, I can see you don't like that idea one bit. Now, my friends and I are going to walk on out of here sweet as you please. If you're all a bunch of good little boys and girls, I'll even leave your little trinket here unharmed."

"Forget about us!" Father Padua screamed. "Destroy the scroll! Now!"

"Sorry, padre, but I'm in charge now," Cal said. "But before I go, I was hoping I could get the answer to one, simple question. Abe? Abe, are you still with us, buddy?" Rabinowitz looked over at Abe. He still looked frozen with fear. "Hey, Abe, buddy man, come on, perk up now, I need to know something and I think you might be able to tell me. What's parousia? Hey, Abe can you hear me, man? What's parousia? Velvet? Padre? Either of you two know?"

Father Padua shook his head. "Why is it so important, Cal?" Rabinowitz asked.

For an answer, Cal patted the duffel bag at his side. "See, this morning I had the most interesting conversation with one of your friends here." With that Cal tipped the bag over and dumped its contents out onto the floor. It contained the head of one of the snake-men. "See, I figured that you all may be immortal or impervious or whatever, but I had a hunch that you still wouldn't like to be caught blindsided by a machete right across the neck. So I met this guy out in the woods and gave it a try. Seems I was right about that. I tied his body to a tree so we could have a nice conversation undisturbed. Unfortunately, Velvet, these guys don't like to talk that much. He only said one word, over and over and over. Parousia. I figure if that's the only word he knows, it must be pretty damn important. So I'm just wondering what it means."

"Perhaps I can tell you," a voice boomed from the stairwell. Rabinowitz whirled to see who it was. She saw a man's legs appear on the steps, watched as the came sprightly down them. She could see the flesh of his hands, tan, healthy flesh—definitely human flesh. And then she saw his face, a face she had seen before, though never so animated or alert, and certainly never so alive—

"Professor Grund!" she gasped. The old man smiled at her. "Ahh, my dear, how nice to see you again. It was so good of you to visit an old man in the nursing home. Rarely did I ever have such pretty company. Of course, you visited me as well, Father Padua. I'm afraid I wasn't very forthcoming with either of you, I know. And Detective, how resourceful of you. This certainly is a very interesting situation we find ourselves in. But ahh, listen to me go on when there is a question on the table, and such an important question, too. Perhaps I can answer it for you, hmm, Detective? After all, I am considered an authority in Biblical languages, though it is rumored that my memory it not quite what it used to be."

By now Grund had walked easily amongst them, surveying the scene casually. The snake-men all parted before him reverently. For a moment, the rest of group was too stunned to speak. "I don't believe it," Cal finally whispered. "You're one of them. You're an Essene."

Grund gave Cal a wolf-like smile. "Yes. Or, to be more precise, I *am* the Essenes."

Cal shook his head. "I don't get it," he said.

"Don't you understand?" Father Padua hissed. "He is their leader. He is their Teacher of Righteousness."

Grund smiled wickedly at the handsome priest. "That is precisely what I am," he said. "And it is too bad you did not figure it out sooner. But your suspicions were pulled in other directions, were they not? All those questions you asked about my old student, Beatrice Miller. Surely you suspected her and not me. And why would you suspect me? I was a doddering old man, barely capable of coherent speech or thought. It made for an excellent cover." He chuckled low in his throat. "I was able to coordinate these unfortunate but so necessary killings without any suspicion being attached to my knowledge of the Essenes. After all, I'm just a harmless old man, aren't I?" He stood in front of Rabinowitz now, gently caressing her cheek with his dry, leathery skin. His eyes bore right into hers. "You have no idea how old a man I truly am," he said to them all.

"You're not a man," Padua hissed in reply. Rabinowitz thought he might move to attack Grund, but instead he merely stood his ground, staring at the professor with rage in his eyes.

"No. No, I suppose I'm not," he said. "Certainly our Heavenly Father took care of that, didn't He, when He cast us out of paradise and turned us into lowly animals?"

"You were never in paradise!" Father Padua spat. "And He is not your Father. You do not deserve to speak His name!"

"That is where you are wrong, my friend," Grund intoned coolly. "He is more my father than He is any of yours. I was the first to worship the divinity of His only son. Do not forget that."

"And you abused that worship!" Padua screamed. "You perverted it to your own evil ends. You did not worship Him. You are not worthy of Him!"

For answer Grund raised his hand and struck Father Padua a blow across the face. Padua collapsed on the floor, but rose quickly to his knees, holding his chin in his hands. "You forget yourself, priest," Grund spoke, his eyes inches from Father Padua's. "It is not wise to cross me," he added. "But," he continued, straightening himself, "it seems to me that there still is a question on the floor. One that deserves an answer. Perhaps our young student here has recovered enough to answer the question." Abe moved his eyes, finally, to peer at Grund, but he said nothing. "Then again," Grund added, "perhaps he does not know. It is, after all, an obscure term nowadays, and though my former student was well-schooled, it was likely something I neglected to teach her."

"Then why did you kill her?" Abe suddenly asked, feeling the fire in his voice.

"Because it fit my plan," Grund replied smoothly. "And because I could not take the risk of her revealing too much. Had I known how well you were taught, my young scholar, I might have taken the time to have you eliminated as well. Oh, do not fret," he added, attempting to sound consoling, "she will get her reward soon. We all will."

"Hey, over here," Cal said to Grund. "Yeah, look at the guy with the flamethrower pointed at your precious scroll. The one who actually asked the question. If you ever want to stop blabbering away, maybe we can work out something here. See, my friends and I, we'd like to leave, and I bet you don't need your scroll getting a little charbroiled, if you know what I mean."

"But we have not yet answered your question, Detective," Grund said. Rabinowitz could clearly see that the professor was enjoying all this. "Perhaps, though, your friend Father Padua can answer it for you. Hmm, Father? How about it?"

"I do not know this term," the priest replied tersely.

Grund's smile was wicked. "I believe that bearing false witness is a serious offense, *Father*," he added sarcastically. "I know full well that you know what the term means." The only answer from Padua was a stony silence. "Very well, then" Grund shrugged. "To answer your question, Detective, the word *parousia* refers to the second coming."

"Second coming?" Cal asked puzzled. "Of the devil? Isn't that what you're trying to do, to raise the devil?"

Now it was Grund's turn to look confused. "Where did you get that idea?" He turned to Padua. "Have you been telling more lies, Priest?"

Padua refused to meet Grund's gaze. "Do not listen to him. He is evil."

"You *have* been lying to them," Grund said. "My, my, I must say I did not expect this behavior at all. Trying to raise the devil? Detective, I am a Christian. I worship the same God as you. I have no interest in the devil, I assure you."

"No interest in the devil, huh? A Christian? You have a funny way of showing that."

Grund's eyes narrowed. "Heretics, every one. Nonetheless I grieved for all of their deaths. But it was necessary, I assure you."

"Necessary for what?" Rabinowitz challenged.

"For parousia, my dear. For the second coming."

"Of the devil?" Cal pressed.

"No," Grund replied. "Of Christ."

Grund's answer stunned the group into silence. "You better explain yourself fast, Grund," Cal said, jiggling his flamethrower in the direction of the scroll. "Or I'm going to have myself a barbecue, understand?"

"There is no need for such rash behavior. I am a Christian, Detective. I was among the first Christians, as a matter of fact. Jesus of

Nazareth came first to our village and preached first to us. *To us.* We were His chosen ones. To us He promised His gift of eternal life."

"The eternal life of the soul!" Father Padua screamed. "Not of the body, corruptor!"

"You have no right to speak to me!" Grund screamed back. "I worship Him in the manner He truly intended. You Catholics with your masses and traditions are false Christians—heretics! You have no right to speak to me!"

"Then speak to me," Cal said. "And get to the point, fast. My trigger finger is getting itchy."

"He promised us eternal life. That was His gift. His promise! Was it wrong to write it down, to ensure He kept His word? We meant no deception; it was our understanding of His words."

"It was your greed, your arrogance!" Padua shouted. Grund glared at the priest.

"So what happened?" Rabinowitz asked.

Grund's visage clouded over darkly. "He grew angry at our deception. Deception! It was what He had promised us! So God cast us out of His kingdom, and cursed our eternal life with the form of His divine punishment. There we were, Christians no longer, barely conscious of thought or reason, wanting only to crawl in the dirt and mud on our bellies, the lowest being in His eyes."

"And then the other one came. The Fallen One. He rescued us. He promised to use his magics to turn us back into human beings. But he was not strong enough. Only I came out fully formed. I was their Teacher, their leader when the Christ had left us. I came out as I was. But my brethren, my fellow elders—they would remain forever marked with the signs of His displeasure."

"But why?" Rabinowitz shouted. "Why would the devil turn you back into human beings?"

"Because he had been cast out, too!" Grund roared. "He knew our pain. He had felt it as well. He only wished to help us."

"That is not the reason why!" Father Padua screamed. "It is parousia! The Evil One wishes to commence the parousia! He only brought you back to fulfill your second deception. You are his disciples, the servants of Satan, children of the Evil One!"

"You lie!" Grund shouted. "He only wished to preserve us, to help us. He understood the pain of being cast out, of losing the grace of God!"

"What is the second deception?" Cal asked, his voice tight and angry. "What is the priest talking about, Grund?"

"Parousia," Grund said. "The second coming. His return. We can make it happen. We can make Him come back! Christ himself will be reborn on Earth."

"How?" Rabinowitz asked.

"There," Grund said, pointing towards the scroll. "Even before He came to us we knew that someday He would leave. But He told us He would return. He promised to return! He said that when His kingdom was closest to failing, when a holy day would pass and no mass be sung in the town, when no one would go to worship at His house, then that would be the day He would return. So we devised a ceremony, and a sacrifice—a great and terrible sacrifice—since such joy, such bliss cannot come without great sacrifice."

"So all these clergymen being killed—all those people—were murdered so you could bring about the second coming of Christ?" Rabinowitz whispered incredulously.

Cal was more blunt. "I don't think Christ would take kindly to your killing all His followers," he said.

"It was unfortunate, but necessary," Grund said. "Their deaths will save the world. Think of it, my friends. All of you, think of it! He will return. He will be among us! No more war. No more poverty. No more disease or death. Peace and joy will reign over the earth for a thousand years! A thousand! That was His pledge. That is our vision. Why must you struggle with this?" Grund took a step towards Cal. "Think of it, Detective. Would you deny the world a chance for peace? An end to hunger and strife? Or perhaps there is someone you have lost whom you would like to see again? He will make it all happen. That was His pledge. That is what we were created to do. To bring about the parousia."

Rabinowitz could see uncertainty etched across Cal's face. "Is it true?" Cal shouted. "Father, tell me, is what he says true?"

Father Padua paused, then nodded. "Yes, my son. It is true."

"Then why the hell are we fighting this?" Cal roared.

"Because of what happens next. You cannot force our Lord to come before His time. It will bring about the Tribulation."

"Tribulation?" Cal asked, confused. "Is that bad? It doesn't sound bad."

"That's the anti-Christ," Abe interjected softly.

"Yes," Padua continued. "Yes. Listen, Detective Evans, listen to me closely. What this man—this thing—says is true. He can force our Lord to walk amongst us again. But that is not how it is supposed to happen. The Scriptures are clear on this. First comes the Tribulation, the time of the anti-Christ. Then the parousia, when Christ will come to rescue the earth from the clutches of evil. If the Essenes are allowed to force the parousia to happen before it is time, when the Tribulation occurs, there will be no one to stop the Evil One. He will reign unchallenged on the earth. That is why he helped the Essenes all those years ago. Not because he sympathized with them—but to advance his own evil scheme."

"That will be a thousand years from now!" Grund thundered. "And do you really think He will allow that? Our Lord will intervene! Our Lord will save us." Grund turned again towards Cal. "Think of it, Detective. Paradise on earth. Eden restored. All our dreams made flesh. To be reunited with the dead. Peace and prosperity. Would you deny the earth its only chance at true joy?"

Rabinowitz could see the struggle going on in Cal's mind. She knew he was thinking of Dani. She wanted to help him, to reach out to him, but she didn't know what to say. She saw him looking at her, staring into her eyes, seeking some kind of guidance. She had none to give.

Cal wavered again, then, with a guttural cry of "Nooooooo!" she saw him turn the flamethrower towards the scroll and unleash its flame.

The scroll was instantly immersed in bright blue flame. The stale air of the basement became hot and stifling. Cal burned the scroll for a full two minutes at the highest possible setting, until the flamethrower tank itself gave out, spent of fuel, while the rest of them watched, helpless to intervene.

When he was finished, the Gold Scroll glowed red. But then, suddenly, it cooled, returning to its original brilliant sheen. Rabinowitz looked at the scroll. She could see no damage done at all.

They had failed.

And now they were going to die.

"You fool," Grund said. He took two steps towards Cal and swept the flamethrower from his hands. With another mighty blow he knocked Cal to the floor. "Did you really think you could damage such a sacred object? Our birthright was taken from us millennia ago when foolish members of the church feared our power and stole our sacred scroll. Do you not think they tried to destroy it? They could not do so. Instead it remained hidden by Roman hands for two thousand years. But I found it. I have searched through the centuries and at last it has come home. I will not be denied. None of us will be denied! We will be reunited with Him." Grund walked amongst them now, ranting all the while. "I offered you salvation. I offered you the chance to see the design of His glory. I offered you a glimpse into the truth path to righteousness. You have denied our offer and our vision. As such, we shall show you no mercy." As he spoke, Grund rolled up his sleeves, exposing his bare arms. "For the Lord shall descend from heaven with a shout!" he chanted, raising his arms over his head. "A sacrifice, my brethren! It is time! A sacrifice for the return of paradise!"

As Grund spoke the Essenes came forward to crowd around him. The others watched transfixed as Grund raised his arms up to his sides, outstretched in a crucifix-like pose. As each of the Essenes crowded around Grund, Cal half-crawled, half-scrambled his way over to Rabinowitz's side. "I think we're about to be sacrificed," he said. "I know," she replied, not knowing what else to say. "I'm sorry I couldn't save us," he said. In the midst of all her terror and dread, Rabinowitz found Cal a brave smile. "For what it's worth, I'm glad you're here," she said truthfully. Cal found a smile to return. "Thanks, I think," he replied. The two watched in horrified awe as the snake men began to circle their leader. Rabinowitz watched as the hungry mouths of their left arms snapped forward, hungry snakes out to kill. She saw one clasp itself onto Grund's arm and bury its fangs into him. The man winced but did nothing to shake the snake's mouth off of his arm. One by one, the other snakes did the same, pumping and pouring their venom into him. "Come, my brethren!" Grund thundered. "Give me your poison. Pour your lifeblood into me. Yes! My will be done this evening, my brethren, and He will be restored to us! He will walk again amongst us!" By now the last of the Essenes' snake-arms had sunk its teeth into Grund. Rabinowitz watched in amazement as Grund's arms began to swell and change color, getting darker, purple and brown. They seemed to be thickening, even, to be changing. "It has begun!" Grund roared. "Look!" Cal whispered. Rabinowitz watched as the snake-men fell down in front of their Teacher, seemingly dead. "Cal," she said, "I don't think we're the sacrifice." Cal could only nod in response. They were both too terrified to wonder what was going to happen next.

Suddenly Rabinowitz heard the sound of a rushing, gale-force wind, though she felt no breeze. At the same moment, Grund began to chant in an unfamiliar language. "Epsil ehn parousia," she heard him hiss. She watched as his body continued to change. His arms thickened and deepened in color. Soon they were too heavy to hold up and fell to Grund's side. Rabinowitz watched as they seemed to meld into his side, to fuse into him. Grund continued chant all throughout his transformation. "Epsil ehn parousia. Epsil ehn parousia!" Rabinowitz saw him grow taller, watched as his face begin to misshape, to pulse and seethe in metamorphosis. "Aghhhhhisssss!" she heard him scream, his howl transforming from a guttural cry of pain into an enraged hiss. In utter amazement she saw the man before her melt away and transform into a snake, a living, breathing, terrifying fifty-foot monster.

"It was the last gift of the Fallen One!" the snake hissed. "To ensure that our will be done! The great sacrifice must take place!" Rabinowitz was amazed that the creature could speak. Despite its altered appearance, though, she could still recognize Grund from the desperate insanity in the creature's lidless eyes.

"Stop! Evil creature, stop! I command thee!" Father Padua strode bravely forward, his crucifix held before him. "In the name of God the Father, I condemn thee to hell!"

"Your faith won't help you now, heretic!" the snake-Grund hissed.

"Back, foul fiend!" Padua said, stepping ever forward. "In the name of the Father, I command you. In the name of the Son, I command you. In the name of the Holy Spirit, I—ieeee!" Father Padua screamed as the giant snake bent down and took him in his mouth. Rabinowitz grimaced when she saw the snake's enlarged, dripping fangs pierce the priest's chest and groin. "Ieeee!" Padua screamed, writhing in agony, impaled on the fangs of the snake. Rabinowitz could only watch as Grund raised the priest up in his mouth, unhinged his jaw, and swallowed the still screaming man whole in one swift gulp.

"Oh my God!" Abe said. Cal swallowed hard. Rabinowitz found herself blinking back tears. Suddenly Cal realized they were no longer being watched. "Let's go!" he said, pointing towards the stairs. But

Grund saw them. "Stay!" he hissed, and with a devastating flick of his tail he crushed the staircase. Now they were trapped. "Witness!" he continued. "The ultimate sacrifice!"

"Hey, asshole!" a voice shouted from above. Grund looked up and saw a spout of flame shoot down at him. He screeched as his snake face and head lit on fire. Rabinowitz looked up. "Dan!" she yelled. She saw the sheriff working a flamethrower almost identical to Cal's, sending showers of white-hot flames towards Grund. The snake writhed in agony and pain, but did not look defeated. "Heretic!" he hissed, smashing into the basement ceiling with all his might. The floor above cracked and split, sending Dan tumbling hard onto the basement floor. "Dan!" Cal shouted as he tried to reach his stricken friend. Grund's tail blocked his path. "Fools!" he screeched. "Heretics! You barely delay the inevitable. I will finish the ceremony. I will prepare the ultimate sacrifice!" And with this the still-flaming head of the Grund-snake reached behind itself and bit hard and deep into its own flank. "Cal!" Rabinowitz said, realizing what it was doing. "He's the sacrifice! Grund is the sacrifice!" The snake writhed in agony as it pumped its own deadly venom into its body. Finally, it released its fangs. "Now He will walk amongst us again! My dying gasp will be the shout that calls the Lord down from the heavens!"

"What do we do, Cal?" Abe asked. The three were backed into a corner of the basement, trying to avoid the writhing snake. "I don't know!" Cal replied. "But whatever we do, don't let that snake die!" Suddenly Cal saw someone moving behind the snake, circling around it. Dan! "Don't worry!" he shouted above the roar of the snake and the sound of rushing wind. "I'll nail it!" Rabinowitz saw that he held a grenade in his hand. "No!" she and Cal shouted simultaneously. Cal launched himself at Dan, knocking the grenade aside a second before he flung it at Grund. The grenade skittered across the floor and landed in a corner. "Take cover!" Cal shouted as he and Dan hit the deck. *BOOM!* The grenade exploded, crumbling the corner foundation of the church and sending half of the first floor into the basement. The church filled with dust and dirt, choking Rabinowitz and the others. Coughing, she shouted through the haze. "Cal!" she called, hoping he was still alive. "Velvet!" he responded, coming through the dust, dragging an injured Dan behind him.

The snake still writhed in the center of the basement floor, its body now covered with dust and debris. "Soon!" it intoned. "Soon

He will walk amongst us again!" Rabinowitz turned to Cal. "What do we do? How do we stop it?" Cal shrugged. He had no answer for her.

"Mass!" Abe suddenly said.

"What?" Rabinowitz responded. "What are you talking about?"

"What time is it?" he asked her.

"What do you mean? What does that have to do with anything?"

"Is it after midnight yet? Tell me that!"

Rabinowitz checked her watch. "No. Why?"

"Then we have time."

"Abe, what are you talking about?" Cal asked mystified.

"Mass!" he said. "A Catholic mass. Both Father Padua and that snake guy said that the ceremony could only be fulfilled on a day when no mass would be held. That's why they killed all those people in the first place. But if we hold a mass right here and now, then the ceremony won't work!"

Cal's eyes opened wide in excitement. "It's worth a shot," he said. "We've got at least until that thing dies over there. But how can we do it? None of us are priests."

"It doesn't matter," Abe replied. "At least, I hope it doesn't matter. All that matters is faith. And the act itself. And what is the defining act of a Catholic mass?" Rabinowitz and Cal both shook their heads. "Transubstantiation!" The two police agents still looked confused. "The body and blood of Christ! The host and the wine! I figure if we do that it should be enough. There's only one problem," he said. "We don't have anything to act as the host and the blood."

"Wait!" Rabinowitz said, reaching into her pocket. She pulled out a packet of saltines. "I kept these from the soup I had at lunch. This should work as the body."

"Great," Abe said. "What about the wine?"

The group looked frantically around the room. Glancing down at Dan, Cal saw the silver flask sticking out of his coat pocket. He picked up. "Here!" he said, shaking it to make sure there was something in it. "This should work!"

"Great!" Abe said, taking both the crackers and the flask and handing them to Cal. "Me?" he said, astounded. "Why should I do it?"

"You were raised a Catholic," Abe said. "I don't know how the ceremony should go."

"I only went to weddings and funerals," he said, thrusting the packet into Rabinowitz's hands. She thrust them straight back. "No way," she said. "Jewish, remember?"

Cal sighed. "But—but I don't think I have any faith," he said plaintively.

Abe shrugged. "You'd better find some—fast!" he said, noting the deathly sounds overtaking the Grund snake. "I don't think we have much longer!"

"Velvet," Cal faltered turning to look at her. Even now, even in the midst of all this dirt and grime and evil, there was something so radiant about her. "I—I can't do it."

"Yes, you can," she said, taking his hand into hers. "Think of something that inspires you. Think of God, or Dani, or anything Cal. Just do it!"

Cal took a deep breath. "Okay, here goes," he said. He opened the packet of crackers. "Uhh, this is my body, so eat it up and when you do, think of me being holy and stuff. Umm, okay, now we all eat the crackers." They each took a piece and swallowed it quickly. "Amen," Cal said. "Amen," Abe and Rabinowitz replied.

"What are you doing?" the Grund snake hissed. It tried to lash at them, but the debris that had fallen on it before was pinning it down. "No!" it shouted, wriggling to set itself free before the ceremony was complete.

Cal opened the flask. Even amongst all this dust and debris he could smell the bourbon inside. "This is my blood, so when you drink it, think of me and be holy," he mumbled. I can't do this, he thought. Not alcohol. Please, God. He looked at Rabinowitz. Did she know what he was thinking? "Hurry up!" Abe shouted, noticing that Grund was almost free.

Cal brought the flask to his mouth. He could smell the overpowering aroma of alcohol. He knew once he drank it that familiar flushed taste, that spicy heat that followed the liquor down his throat and into his gullet would wash over him. It would have him in its clutches all over again. But he also knew he had no choice. He put the flask to his lips.

He drank.

It tasted...it tasted...frankly, it tasted like water. Dan must have finished the bourbon and filled the flask with water, Cal thought. But there was no time to analyze it. He passed the flask to Rabinowitz, who took a quick sip, and then to Abe, who choked as the liquid passed his lips. "Whoa!" he said. "Amen," Cal intoned, and the other two echoed him: "Amen!"

"Noooo!" Grund yelled, finally freeing himself from the debris. He advanced towards them. "How does it end?" Rabinowitz yelled. "The mass? How does it end?!" Cal searched his memory. A familiar phrase popped into his head. "The mass is ended; go in peace," he said. "Thanks be to God." As if understanding their role, Rabinowitz and Abe echoed Cal: "Thanks be to God!" Defiant, Cal turned to face Grund. Throwing the flask at him, he shouted, as loud as he could, "THANKS BE TO GOD!"

There was a sudden tumult and a sound like a great shout being sucked down a person's throat. And then there was nothing but silence: dead, calm, blissful silence.

Rabinowitz looked around the basement. Nothing had changed. Everything looked the same. But she knew, somehow she knew. "You did it!" she said to Cal, excited. "We did it!" he replied, half-laughing, half-crying in relief, throwing his arms around her in jubilation.

There was only one problem. Grund.

"What have you done!?" he shouted, raising himself up as high as he could. The poison wracked his system, but he still inspired dread. "What have you done?! Heretics! We could have had paradise on earth. He would have walked amongst us! But you have ruined it! And now I am dying, and will never know His grace again!" Grund drew himself up, rearing his fangs at them and flicking his tongue wildly. "I may die," he hissed, "but I will kill you all first. I will crush your bones between my jaws. I will suck every drop of blood from your bodies. I will—"

"Hey, asshole," a voice interrupted from above. "Suck this!" Rabinowitz looked up in time to see a flush of smoke and hear the whistle of something being fired right at Grund's head. "Duck!" Cal cried, throwing himself on the two of them as they hit the deck. Rabinowitz saw out of the corner of her eye a missile strike the snake's open mouth and slide down its gullet. For one split second, the snake seemed impervious to the blow. But then Rabinowitz heard a tremendous *boom!* and saw the snake explode from the inside. She covered her eyes, but could feel the warm shower of blood and snake flesh raining against them. When she uncovered her face, all she saw was a twisted headless body lying where Grund had once been.

It was over.

It was all over.

They were still alive.

Rabinowitz looked up to see who had saved them. "Agent Nguyen!" she cried. "What are you doing here?" She turned towards Cal, who was grinning. "Always have back-up," he said.

"Hey," Nguyen called down, "are you okay?" Cal was kneeling by Dan as he spoke, who slowly stirred. "Anyone get the license plate of that snake?" he lamely joked. Dan looked around. "I take it the fact that we're all alive means that the good guys won in the end," he said. Cal nodded and helped Dan gingerly to his feet. "Good," Dan said. "Now how about getting me to a hospital?"

"Nguyen!" Cal called up. "How about getting us out of here, huh?"

Nguyen flashed them an "okay" sign. "I already called for back-up, an ambulance, and a really big ladder," he said. "Until then, just sit tight." As an afterthought, he added, "Hey, what about my line as I blew that thing sky high. Pretty good one, huh?"

"It's been done before," Abe replied with a lopsided grin.

"...AND that's how Nguyen managed to be at the right place, at the right time, wielding a rocket launcher," Cal said to Rabinowitz and Abe with a lopsided grin.

Rabinowitz smiled. "And you were against bringing in the Feds," she quipped.

Cal returned her smile. "I guess even the FBI is good for something."

It had been almost two hours since their ordeal in the church basement. Cal, Rabinowitz, Dan and Abe were now free from the cellar, having climbed out on a fire department ladder almost an hour ago. Largely against his will, Dan had been sent to the hospital for a quick once over.

The scene was one of controlled chaos. Nguyen was efficiently ordering local fire and police officers and his own agents to cordon off the area. No one was allowed to actually go in the basement.

Even if they did, Cal doubted few of them would ever come close to figuring out what had really gone on down there. He still didn't quite believe it himself.

Nguyen was approaching them now. "I don't have to tell you that you all did good work in there," he said. "But for the record, and on behalf of the entire U.S. government, thanks."

Cal pointed his head in the direction of the fallen down structure. "What are you going to do about that place?" he said.

"We're going to knock it all flat," Nguyen replied. "Tonight, as a matter of fact. Got a couple of dozers coming. Section it all off like it's a hazardous dump. Post the land as do not trespass. Then fill it all in with concrete. Hopefully, in time, people will forget what happened here."

"What about the scroll?" Rabinowitz asked.

Nguyen shrugged. "I can't think of a better place to leave it. Can you?"

"And the 'Clergy Killer'?" Cal asked, half-seriously.

"Dead. That's the official report, anyway. Name being withheld until we can make something up. And don't worry, all due credit will go to one certain local police detective and one certain ATF agent."

"And a local graduate student as well," Rabinowitz added. Nguyen nodded his assent.

"Hey, don't forget to give some credit to yourself, as well," Cal said. "You really came through, Nguyen." He stuck his hand out for Nguyen to shake. The agent accepted it proudly. "It was an honor to work with you, Detective Evans," he said, smiling broadly. "But let's not make a habit out of it, shall we?"

"No problem," Cal replied before Nguyen stalked off to supervise the destruction of the church itself.

"You're awful quiet," Rabinowitz said to Abe. "You doing okay?"

"Yeah," he replied slowly. "At least, I am for now. I still can't believe we're actually alive."

Cal nodded ruefully. "I know what you mean," he said.

"I think, after the adrenalin of all this wears off, I'm going to have some serious PTSD."

"PTSD?" Cal quizzed.

"Post-traumatic stress disorder," Abe replied. "I'm going to need some serious therapy."

Rabinowitz laughed. "Well, after this, facing your dissertation committee will feel like a breeze," she said.

"Are you kidding?" Abe replied. "You have no idea who's on my committee. I'd rather face ten giant snakes than my dissertation committee."

"Hey, careful what you wish for," Cal said. "You just might get it."

"Yeah, well right now I'm wishing for a big cup of coffee and a good night's sleep," he said, eyeing some styrofoam cups being passed out by one of the paramedics. "You think they have any donuts over there?" he added, wandering off to find out.

Cal turned to Rabinowitz. They were alone now. "Velvet," he started, "I—" He stopped when he felt a lump form in his throat and tears well up in his eyes. Damn, why now, he thought, after everything, after all this, why do I do this now?

Rabinowitz just smiled at him. She took his hand in hers and pressed it to her heart. "You did it Cal," she said softly. "You saved us all."

"Did I?" Cal asked, his voice more bitter than he intended it to sound. "I threw away a chance at paradise, Velvet. The world could have had everything it desires. Was that really my decision to make?" He cast his eyes towards the ground to hide them from her.

Rabinowitz gently placed her forefinger under Cal's chin and tucked his head so that their eyes met. She smiled softly at him. "You did what you had to do," she said.

"But did I do the right thing?" he pleaded. "Does the world have to suffer for the decision I made?"

For answer Rabinowitz leaned forward slightly. She placed her lips directly onto Cal's. For a moment she held them there, their lips caressing lightly, then, finally, she pushed them in closer, so that now they were kissing, finally kissing, a long, slow, languorous, meaningful kiss. When they slipped apart, Rabinowitz spoke. "I think the world is pretty okay as it is," she whispered. Cal slid his arms around her body and held her tight, her curves pressed up against him, and moved to kiss her more deeply, but a teasing finger between their lips blocked him. "Just so you know," Rabinowitz said, "this isn't one of those horror-type movies where the hero saves the day, gets the girl, and then dumps her before the sequel. If you kiss me now, Caldwell Evans, you better be prepared to be kissing me for a long time to

come." Cal's smile grew wide at her words, and his only answer to
her was another long, lingering smooch.

Finally, they broke apart. "You've got a little lipstick on you,"
Rabinowitz said, smiling shyly and pointing at Cal's lip. Cal reached
into his pocket for a napkin. As he pulled it out, a small plastic coin
fell to the ground. "What's this?" Rabinowitz said, bending to pick it
up. She handed it to Cal.

"That's my one-day chip," he said. "Well, good thing Dan didn't
have any alcohol in that flask after all, or I'd have to give this back."

"What do you mean?" Rabinowitz asked.

"The flask," he said. "Smelled like bourbon, but it tasted like water. Dan must have emptied the flask at some point and filled it up
with plain water. I'm glad, too. Even one sip of liquor and I'd have to
give this baby back. No matter how end-of-the-world the circumstances might be."

"Cal, what are you talking about?" Rabinowitz said. "That flask
contained pure Kentucky bourbon."

"Velvet, I know what bourbon tastes like. Believe me. It contained
water."

"Bourbon."

"Water."

"Bourbon."

Cal sighed, then laughed. "Are the next fifty years going to be like
this?" he chided, faking exasperation.

Rabinowitz snuggled up against him. "I hope so," she said, as he
put his arm around her and they both began to walk away from the
church.

THE NEXT SUNDAY

THE church was razed immediately, the land filled in with dirt and sand and finally concrete. Signs were posted, warning of a possible toxic hazard. People stayed away. The whisper through town was that the land was cursed; no one had much reason to go there anyway.

Sure, a few curious onlookers decided it might be interesting to drive by slowly, as if hoping to catch a glimpse of whatever dangerous event had occurred. Rumors ran rampant through the town. But for the most part, people remained uninterested in the area, and, by the next Sunday, the faithful were back in their churches. The television had trumpeted the death of the Clergy Killer, and peace finally descended on the small town. Time passed. Fears ebbed. Things returned to normal.

And the land of the Essene church lay dormant.

Even now, to look at it, one would never know what had happened there, the holy cosmic battle that had been waged. Even now, to look at it, one would never know that this plot of land was any different than any other plot of land.

Unless, of course, one happened to notice one very peculiar thing. There were no animals on this land. There were no squirrels, no rabbits, no mice nor birds nor even insects, nothing that crawled or hopped or scampered or flew across this land. No, only the most observant eye would realize that only one animal species lived in and around this cursed plot of land.

Snakes.

The land was crawling with snakes.

ABOUT THE AUTHOR

MICHAEL G. CORNELIUS is the author of the award-winning novel *Creating Man* (Vineyard Press, 2001: Finalist, Lambda Literary Prize, Nominee, Independent Press Award and American Library Association Award,) and is co-author of the popular *Susan Slutt, Girl Sleuth* detective parody series. He has also published short fiction in numerous journals, magazines, and anthologies, including *Velvet Mafia*, *The Egg Box*, *Futures Mystery Anthology Magazine*, *The Spillway Review*, and *Encore*, as well as in anthologies from Alyson Press, StarPress Books, and others. Currently chair of the Department of English and Mass Communications at Wilson College in Chambersburg, PA, Michael received his Ph.D. from the University of Rhode Island.

Michael is also a Pennsylvania state Humanities Council scholar in the field of Horror Cinema, and in his spare time, Michael enjoys reading, golf, football, tennis, and anything to do with the BBC-America television show "Bargain Hunt."

He can be reached at mcor7215@postoffice.uri.edu. Visit his website here: www.michaelgcornelius.com.

ALSO AVAILABLE FROM
BREAKNECK BOOKS

COMING IN 2007 FROM BREAKNECK BOOKS

By Eric Fogle
"This will definitely be one of my top ten reads of the year and I would recommend that this book makes everyone's 'To Read' list…" – Fantasybookspot.com.

www.breakneckbooks.com/fog.html

THE LAST KNIGHT

By Jeremy Robinson
"A new dark continent of terror. Trespass at your own risk." – James Rollins, bestselling author of Black order and The Judas Strain

www.breakneckbooks.com/antarktos.html

By Craig Alexander
"…an action packed race against time and terrorists. Absolutely riveting." – Jeremy Robinson, bestselling author of The Didymus Contingency and Raising the Past.

www.breakneckbooks.com/nineveh.html

BREAKNECK BOOKS
PUBLISHING COMPANY

Printed in the United States
77663LV00004B/50